THE MEDIATOR

Michael Carrion

Published by NoName Publishing

Copyright © 2024 by Michael Carrion

The moral right of the author has been asserted.

ALL RIGHTS RESERVED

This is a work of fiction. Names, characters, places, and incidents either are the product of the author's imagination or are used fictitiously, and any resemblance to actual persons, living or dead, businesses, organizations, companies, events, or locales is entirely coincidental.

The text of this edition is unabridged.

Carrion, Michael
The Mediator / by Michael Carrion

1

OCTOBER 3, 2020

My lawn is a beautiful shade of unwavering deep green. I sit alone on my back porch and look upon it with pride.

It is a far cry from the lawns of my youth – the varying shades of yellow and brown and multiple greens, the ugly mix of grass and weeds and weeds and more weeds. I remember playing among those patchy brown splotches of dirt and the utter absence of life where vegetation refused to grow.

This is better. This is beautiful.

It's a war of sorts, maintaining a healthy lawn. Invasive species of endless weeds are always just below the surface waiting for their chance to rise up. They are aided in their efforts by subterranean insects, always searching for new ground to conquer, feeding off the roots of healthy grass.

It is a battle that never ends.

Over the years, a series of renovations have slowly shaped my home into a beautiful oasis. The kitchen is my wife's favorite transformation. The master bathroom is a close second. That bathroom alone took our contractor a full twelve weeks to accomplish, but the final product was quite exquisite. When guests are given the tour, they never fail to 'ooh' and 'ahh'.

But for me, this porch is the crowning achievement. A gable roof with dark wood architectural framing extends from the home to provide an additional 500 square feet of outdoor living space. To my right is the amazing piece of granite we chose to complement the over-sized stainless steel grill. I sit at a custom-made walnut dining table that comfortably seats six. It is the perfect place for intimate get-togethers, where our guests can enjoy the comforts of the outdoors. Where we can feel the cool breeze tracing over our skin and hear it rustling through the trees. Where we are protected from the sun and any rains that may come.

I see movement out of the corner of my eye. An insect has crawled out from the grass and onto the concrete. Its movements are strange, herky-jerky. It thrusts forward an inch then stops abruptly. It stands still, but not perfectly still. It wavers back and forth ever so slightly, like a drunk struggling to maintain balance. It looks... I don't know, confused maybe.

Again, he moves forward, but stumbles to one side. An attempt to regain his footing fails and he rolls over onto his back. His legs kick frantically, but he goes nowhere, bicycling helplessly into the air.

I watch as the desperate wheeling of his legs begins to slow to a stop. He lies there motionless for so long that I wonder if he has passed on from this world. As if to answer that question, his legs kick yet again. Slow this time. Very slow. The motions are no longer fluid, like an old-time ticking clock with the battery nearly drained of juice. Suddenly, all six legs flail in a disorganized violent wretch. It's over quickly and now only one leg is moving. It's the front right leg. The closest thing you would call to an arm, I suppose. It stretches slow and deliberate, reaching out in my direction. The arm grows longer and straighter until it seems to be pointing directly at me.

He seems to be reaching out for help. More likely, he is merely identifying his killer. I watch him for a long time. Minutes. I don't know how many. I watch, but he never moves again.

On the table in front of me is a half-used bottle. I purchased it for just under thirteen dollars at my local hardware store. It's quite ingenious really. You screw it to the end of a garden hose and simply water your lawn. The process took all of ten minutes.

My eyes go to the label... *kills over 250 different species.*

I have a hard time wrapping my head around that number. For all the different people on this earth – the different colors, the different cultures, the different genders and languages and customs… it all amounts to just one species.

Just one.

250 different species.

I take a deep breath and smell the chemical laden air. My eyes take in the lush green grass of my back yard. It looks peaceful. There is no sign of the mass suffering and death that is taking place beneath the blades. I can't see them writhing in pain, nor can I hear their screams. Would it matter if I could? Millions of tiny little screams… would that change anything?

I wonder how many different lives exist in just one square foot of my lawn? How many families? Mothers? Fathers? Sisters? Brothers? New born babies?

Whatever the case, they are gone now.

And my lawn is a beautiful shade of unwavering deep green.

The king-sized, gel-cooled, mattress is adjusted perfectly to my desired firmness. I feel the welcoming touch of high thread-count Egyptian cotton. The ceiling fan gently circulates the air kept at a consistent 70 degrees. Blackout curtains defend my space from any offending light. It is the perfect recipe for a good night's sleep.

And yet I am awake.

I stare up into the ceiling that I know to be white, but in this darkness it is merely a void.

A loud incessant buzzing overtakes the silence.

Across the room, as far away as I could get it, stand three glowing red numbers, floating in the emptiness. 4:00. Years ago, I grew immune to my phone's attempts to wake me. Tardiness became a problem, leading me to purchase the old-time digital clock with its obnoxious, impossible to ignore, buzz.

That worked for a while.

Over time I developed a love/hate relationship with the snooze button. For my wife it was all hate. Eventually my sleeping mind trained my fingers to skip the temporary solution and perform the more complicated task of actually turning the alarm off.

Extreme tardiness became an issue.

And so I moved the alarm to the far corner of the room, forcing myself to rise to the occasion.

My wife groans and, once again, I rise.

I shut off the alarm and feel my way through the darkness. I slide the barn door aside, allowing me entry into the master bathroom.

Taking a seat on the bench of our beautiful stone shower, I allow the hot water to pummel my stiff muscles into submission. I leave the exhaust fan off, prompting the steam to envelope me in its warmth.

I reach out, grasping the lever. I turn it ever so slightly to the left. The stinging heat burns my skin. Again, ever so slightly to the left. The scalding water rushes down. I watch as my white skin grows red.

With one quick twist, I turn the lever full-stop in the other direction. A sharp inhale fills my lungs as the shock of cold water seizes my muscles. A shriek that only I can hear fills every recess of my mind. I force myself to endure. To feel. It is my favorite moment of every day. That moment when I feel.

Standing on the vanity is a little orange pill bottle. I ingest a single pill as I have every day for seven years.

Wiping the fog from the mirror, I stare at the reflection before me. I don't know this man, but I know I don't like him. The swirling steam reasserts itself and he slowly disappears.

I stand beside my wife's half of the bed. I can't see her, but I can hear her breathing. I stare down at the space where I know she must be. I feel my fingers pushing rhythmically into my palm, like the squeezing of an invisible stress ball. Slowly, my eyes begin to adjust. Her form becomes clear.

Her body is contorted into a pose of restless sleep. She's always posing, even while she dreams. Her arms are thrown out strangely, each joint held at an unnatural but somehow artful angle. Her hair is mussed, several locks laying wildly across her face. Her chest rises and falls. Her spaghetti-strap top has ridden up, a sheen of perspiration covering her midriff. Her panties have twisted up a bit, providing a shadowy peek into the flesh that lies beneath. She grew hot in the night, kicking the sheets down around her ankles, revealing the curves of her well-honed legs.

To the untrained eye, she is really quite beautiful. Her chest heaves with a sudden intake of air. She stirs a bit and settles into a new pose. No less strange, no less artful.

I watch her breathe. A few strands of loose hair stretch across her lips. I watch them rise up with each exhale, then slowly float back down.

I walk softly down the hall, passing the two bedroom doors where my kids lie sleeping. Opposite those doors is a long unbroken wall full of framed pictures. Each picture tells a snippet of the life of a happy family. I know they are there, but the hall is dark, and I can't see them.

I find the remote for the living room TV and turn it on. Politics again. It's not news if it's not politics. And it's not politics if it's not news. I am treated to the latest outrage. The latest topic that we can all disagree on. But we won't agree to disagree… we'd much rather fight.

I turn the TV off and find my entertainment elsewhere.

As the coffee drips, I stand before the microwave, watching my bacon and egg biscuit spin around in lazy circles. I watch as electromagnetic radiation penetrates deep into the sugars and the waters and the fats that make up my breakfast. From the outside it appears uneventful, my food taking leisurely laps around the space. But a closer look, closer than my eye can see, would show those components vibrating at a cellular level. Molecules are being torn apart and forcefully deformed. I wait for the internal violence to reveal itself. It's just a matter of time.

The cheese begins to bubble. The bacon spits and pops.

The two car garage is inhabited by my wife's over-sized SUV on one side and my Mercedes S-class on the other. It is a beautiful car that helps me to effortlessly spread the word of my status and success.

I see my reflection in the driver's side window as I grab the handle. I stop and look at him once more. I hardly recognize him. I do not know this man, but I know I don't like him.

I open the door and he goes away.

I take a seat behind the steering wheel and push the start button, bringing the engine to life.

I reach up and press a button, prompting the overhead door to release me into the world.

But nothing happens.

I push the button again. Still nothing. I reach up and pull the garage door remote off the visor. I crack open the battery compartment to find a powdery white substance hemorrhaging from the end of a battery.

"Goddamnit," I say, tossing the remote aside.

The leaky battery needs replaced. The leads probably need cleaning. It's a simple solution. I think about the spare batteries that reside in a drawer just inside the kitchen. I think about the tiny cleaning brush that hangs on the wall in this very garage. I think about the song that is playing on the car's radio.

I like this song and so I listen.

A metal shelving unit sits in front of my car, filled with the leftovers from all of our various home improvements. There are multiple cans of paint. I see cabinet hardware and wall tiles and wood flooring. A couple rolls of designer wallpaper sit atop a collection of granite samples. My view of these objects is becoming slightly distorted as fumes begin to rise from the hood.

I reach out, press a button, and the window glides downward. I recline my seat, close my eyes, and listen to the music.

Three songs come and go from the airwaves. I'm feeling light headed. But I am not afraid.

I am not afraid of death.

If I am not afraid of that, why should I fear anything? Why should I fear the judgment of the people I know?... The people I barely know?... The people I don't know at all? Why should I build my life around garnering your acceptance? Why should I strive for your envy?

I am willing to be nothing. Nothing at all.

I am free.

I find myself longing for the lawns of my youth. I long to play among the yellows and browns and multiple greens, where the weeds grow freely and the insects survive my existence.

What could life be for a man who is truly free?

Spare batteries sit in a drawer just inside the kitchen.

I raise my head and my mind swirls. Suddenly a pounding drum of sheer pain attacks me. An incessant pulsing pressure threatens to blow open my skull. I press my palms into my temples and wrap my fingers around my head, attempting to hold my skull together. It feels as if my brain is growing beyond the limits of the bones that contain it.

I claw at the door handle and manage to prop the door open. I step out and raise up, clinging to what little balance I can manage. I let the world stop spinning and take my first step toward a new reality.

2

I must be acting strangely, because the clerk at the 7-11 is looking at me like I'm crazy. I pay him for a bottle of ibuprofen, a pack of full-flavor cigarettes, and a lighter.

In the parking lot, I sit on the hood of my car, down a few pills, and light my first cigarette in over a decade. It tastes like shit, but I smoke it anyway. With each inhale the pounding in my head grows stronger.

Feel it.

I make it to the building where I work, but not quite to my office. I feel sick and I'm forced to stop in the restroom.

A disheveled co-worker is at the mirror, preparing for another day. His name is Paul and he stands in boxers and a wife-beater, shaving his face.

I stumble past him and make a beeline to the nearest toilet stall. I kneel before the porcelain and wait for the coming storm. It comes on schedule.

The bulk of the storm has passed and I hear Paul's voice from outside my stall.

"Sounds like somebody had a good time last night."

"Not really," I tell him, spitting into the bowl.

I give it a flush and wait for a possible second act.

"Well then what? You get knocked up? Are you a miracle of science? That would be amazing."

I take the time to remember I'm free. A truly free man doesn't need to lie about anything.

"Carbon monoxide poisoning," I say.

"Carbon monoxide?"

"An aborted suicide attempt."

"Aborted? You know that's frowned upon in this state. From what I hear it might be illegal soon."

I laugh and the pounding in my head grows. I spit once more into the toilet.

I say, "I can assure you that the abortion of a suicide attempt is and will remain lawful. Even in Oklahoma."

"Ehhhh, the way I understand it, all abortions will be illegal, except in the case of rape. Is that what happened? You weren't raped were you?"

"Fraid not."

I give the toilet another flush for good measure and struggle back to my feet.

I exit the stall and shuffle to the sink. Paul is putting the finishing touches on his shave.

He says, "You know we're not even allowed to say 'committed suicide' anymore?"

"I've heard," I say, splashing my face with water. "Not sure I understand that one."

"I think it's to protect people like you. The ones who fell short, ya know?"

I see Paul's tube of toothpaste on the vanity. I point at it, asking a wordless question. He shrugs, so I place a bit of paste on my finger and begin to scrub my mouth clean.

"Explain," I say.

"Well, being committed to a task is a positive thing, right? You say someone committed suicide, you're basically giving their corpse a pat on the back. Which I'm fine with, they had a goal and they accomplished it. Good for them."

"Right."

"And then there's you. You *tried* to kill yourself. Unsuccessfully. It's like the ultimate in failure, right? You can't even do that properly. It just confirms how worthless you were already feeling.

And why did you fail? Because you weren't committed enough. Translation – *You half-assed it. You can do better.* Further Translation – *If at first you don't succeed...*"

I say, "So the word 'committed' sends the wrong message?"

"Exactly. At least that's what 'they' think."

"They being?"

"The people who say we can't use that word anymore."

"I take it you don't agree."

"I think if someone wants to die, who am I to question their goals? And if they suck at accomplishing those goals, maybe a little encouragement is a good thing."

"I see where you're going and, believe me, I appreciate your efforts. But I don't need the encouragement. I'm not gonna try try again."

"No? Why not?"

"Because I don't feel like I failed. I feel like shit, but I don't feel like a failure."

"Do tell."

"I realized something. The only reason I wanted to die was because I saw no value in living. The only reason I saw no value in my life was because I was afraid to truly live it. I'm not afraid anymore."

After nine years of schooling, I entered the professional world as a baby lawyer, cutting my teeth at a corporate litigation firm. By all accounts, it was a good job, but something was missing. Several years into a promising career, I dramatically shifted gears.

I felt a calling to public service, and so a Public Defender I became. I defended the poor, the down trodden, the nearly always guilty. Everyday, I expended my time and my sweat attempting to help my clients escape a fate they so richly deserved. Some of my biggest wins felt like my biggest losses, setting a monster free to create more victims.

It quickly became a grind. I often fantasized about opening my own firm, or plying my craft for a charity I supported, or maybe taking a step back to write the Great American Novel. After five years at the public defender's office, I again shifted gears.

But I didn't steer into my hopes. I didn't accelerate into my dreams. I drove straight to where the money flows.

Wentworth Strategies has been my home away from home for more than six years now. It was an easy transition, considering the fact that my wife's maiden name is Wentworth. Her father, my boss, was more than happy to practice a little nepotism by proxy.

I became a financial analyst, a stock picker. Every day I stare at these same nine monitors, studying the news tickers, the ever-evolving charts, the earnings reports, and, worst of all, social media.

Over the years I have earned my way into a sizable, but windowless, office. Each morning I miss the sunrise as I scour for the modern day equivalent of gold.

In the early days, my prospecting was only for the benefit of the company and our clients. But feeling empty and needing something to fill that void, I too decided to play the game.

I started my account with five thousand dollars. To this day, I've never added to it, nor have I taken anything away. It just sits there waiting for something enticing to come along, something too good to pass up. Each year I take a few bites at the apple.

By January of 2019, I had built my account up to just over twenty-eight thousand dollars. On Friday, January 25th, around 10:40am, I heard a whisper of a dam break at a mine in Brazil. It belonged to the Vale Mining Company, ticker symbol – VALE. It wasn't a company I'd analyzed, but I decided to take a risk. I bought ten thousand dollars in put options, which is basically a high risk / high reward way to bet against a stock.

By the end of the day, I was up four thousand dollars. I let the bet stand over the weekend and by Monday morning I was up sixty thousand.

Meanwhile, in Brazil, 270 people had lost their lives. To this day, eleven of them have yet to be found. And the sixty grand in profits did little to fill my void. Perhaps it even added to it.

It'd be nearly a year before I made another bet.

I hear a knock at my open door. Long ago, management requested that office doors remain open, an attempt to foster collaboration among coworkers. As a result, I set up my office so that I'm nearly always facing away from the door. This saves me from the constant look-ins and the forced return of smiles as people pass by. I've also found that it discourages people from stopping in, a nice little bonus.

But it doesn't always work, hence the knock.

I turn in my seat to find Ted and Larry standing in my doorway, their face-masks uselessly dangling from one ear. Larry looks like your average weasel. If I were a filmmaker and casting the role of used car salesman, I'd give Larry a call. That would be the only reason I would ever call him. Ted is a large and intimidating figure. He dresses like a cowboy with a buckle to match. Rare is the conversation where he doesn't make some mention of his college football career.

"The Wax Man!" Larry says.

"Larry. Ted," I say.

They accept that as an invitation and enter my space. Larry takes a seat, while Ted props an ass cheek on the edge of my desk.

"We were looking at Peloton." Larry says. "Looks like you put it at Sell."

"I did."

"Why?" Ted asks, dismayed.

I look at the piece of paper Ted is holding in his hand.

"Seems to me you've already read the report."

"We were thinking maybe you'd lost your marbles," Larry says.

"The higher-ups see this," Ted waves my report. "They're gonna think so too."

"Thought maybe we should save you from yourself," Larry adds.

I say, "Let me guess. You just bought heavy?"

"Of course we did," Larry says. "It's a winner."

"Could be a game-changer."

"Okay," I say. "Well I appreciate you guys looking out for me."

Larry eyes me for a bit before speaking again.

"You should update your recommendation. It's not gonna look good when the dust settles."

"I totally agree," I say.

Ted says, "We like having you around. Don't wanna mess that up."

"Of course."

Thankfully, Larry rises from his seat. They start to make their way out the door, but I'm not that lucky. Larry turns back.

"Oh, you know, it's been awhile since we got a referral from you."

I say nothing.

"Growing the fund is a team sport," Ted says. "We went to the Cotton bowl my senior year, but we never would've won a single game if we didn't work together."

I smile and nod... because I'm an asshole.

"Great," Larry says. "We'll talk soon."

They turn to go and I'm happy for it.

This isn't the first time we've had a conversation like this. Each time, I just go along to get along. Through sheer force of habitual cowardice, I did it again.

But I am no longer a coward. I am afraid of nothing.

"But..." I say.

They stop and turn, surprised.

"...There are the moral and ethical issues that I'm trying to get my head around."

"What are you talking about?" Ted asks.

"Well, you operate an actively managed fund. But the only thing you ever *manage* to do is make your clients far less than the S & P."

"Hold on now," Larry protests.

"You manage to charge a higher fee. You even manage to increase their tax liability."

"Our clients make money," Ted says.

"Less money, but sure. The truth is, the only people I've ever sent you are people I absolutely hate."

"What the fuck is your problem?" Ted growls.

"Have I not made that clear? My mistake, let me be more forthright. My problem is you. You're a thief. Telling people they've put their money in the right hands, then buying shit you should be selling. Are you trying to lose?"

"Screw this guy!" Ted says. "All high and mighty. Ethics? Morals? You know what I heard about you?"

"I do not. Can we keep it that way?"

"I heard you made millions off the Coronavirus."

"Right," Larry says, "And not for the company either. For yourself."

"I don't make money for the company. I'm an analyst. What they do with my reports is up to them."

"Is it true? Mister Ethics. Are you a profiteer?"

"That is what I've been trained to do. So yeah, twelve grand in Novavax options. It was a good bet, due to their flu vaccine. I was only gonna do a grand, until I heard about this mysterious virus in Wuhan…"

"Ethics my ass," Larry says.

"I got out in August, which was way too early, actually. Still, I did the math and at the time I cashed out, I made just over eleven dollars for every body that dropped."

"You prick," Ted shouts. "My mother was one of those bodies."

"You ever go to her grave?"

His eyes flash.

"Cause if you do, thank her for the Whopper and fries."

Now, maybe I'm stupid, but the attack surprises me. The former defensive end tackles me straight out of my chair. The upended chair careens awkwardly across the room as my body tumbles to the floor. His substantial weight is on top of me and he's swinging wildly. I throw an arm around the back of his head and bury my face into his neck and shoulder. I hold tight, keeping us so close that it's hard for him to land a meaningful blow. Still, the back of my head and my ears are being battered endlessly. I keep slamming my skull into the side of his jaw, just hoping that maybe it hurts on the other end. There is no evidence to show he even feels it.

My other arm is wrapped around his body, gripping onto his back, holding him close. I risk losing hold of him and begin throwing blind punches into the area where I think his kidney or liver or some other internal organ might be.

My head is throbbing. If not for the adrenaline, the pain would be unbearable.

Suddenly, Ted is scrambling and bucking like a wild animal. Even more wild than before. It feels like panic. I hold tight. Just one good punch taken from a man his size would leave me dazed and helpless. I can't let him create that distance. I stop punching and pull my hands to each other. I interlock my fingers and squeeze tightly onto him.

I hear wheezing, asthmatic breaths, right beside my ear. This is definitely panic. I let go and push him off.

Ted scrambles away, crawling across the floor. He makes it to the far wall and turns over to face upward. He appears to be hyperventilating, unable to catch a meaningful breath.

Larry comes to his aid.

"Breathe, buddy, breathe."

I notice that my office is far from empty now.

A couple more coworkers rush to Ted's aid, while four others stand just inside my doorway with eyes wide. Another half-dozen or so stand in the hall, popping their heads this way and that, trying to sneak a peek inside.

Ted clutches his chest near the left shoulder.

"He's having a heart attack!" Larry yells. "Somebody call 911."

I pick myself up off the floor and dust myself off. I look at Ted and feel the urge to walk over and give him one stiff kick in the gut.

Instead, I push my way through the crowd and out into the hall. I walk in the general direction of the exit, listening to the confusion of the crowd.

"What happened?"

"Is everyone okay?"

"Did anyone call the cops?"

I hear the voice of my boss, Carl Wentworth.

"Mister Waxman. William!"

I keep walking and don't look back.

3

I have no idea where I am. I know it's a bar. I know it's the first place I saw after exiting the parking lot at work for the last time. I couldn't even tell you the name of the place.

I sit at the bar with a plate of nachos and a single beer in front of me. I've been here for hours, my aching mind drifting off in a million or so different directions.

The crowd is getting larger and louder.

"You need to drink more if you're gonna eat that."

I look to find Paul propping himself onto the stool beside me. He signals the bartender.

How did he find me? Or did I just happen upon his favorite spot?

"I don't disagree with you," I say.

"What?!"

"I don't disagree with you," I say, raising my voice to match the volume of Happy Hour.

The bartender arrives, "whatcha need?"

Paul says, "You tell me. You see that girl over there?"

He points at a beautiful young redhead across the bar.

The bartender looks.

Paul continues, "Within the hour, I'm gonna offer her my heart."

"You?" The bartender says. "That girl?"

"That's what I'm saying, Barkeep. You've got work to do. Write me a prescription. And here's the thing, and this is important, I wanna feel like I'm the one doing her a favor. Like really believe it."

The bartender chews on that.

"I got something for ya. You might not remember anything."

Paul knocks on the bar.

"That's perfect! Set me up. And one for my friend here too."

Paul turns his attention to me.

"What the hell got into you today? And why didn't you wait til I was in the vicinity? God, I would've loved to have seen that."

"Yeah, that was selfish of me. Sorry about that."

"You're forgiven. It was enough to see him carted away in an ambulance."

"They took him to the hospital?"

"Yeah, they did."

"He alright?"

Paul shrugs. He doesn't care.

I try to decide if I do… something tells me I should, but I feel nothing.

The bartender arrives with our drinks. One mixed drink each, plus an assortment of shots. Paul wastes no time.

"I think I might be done." I say, thinking out loud.

"Oh, you can stop thinking. You're definitely done. You were fired before you hit the door. But what do you care? You're on the Novavax gravy train."

"That's not what I'm talking about."

"So what are you talking about?" Paul asks before downing a shot.

"You know I've been on antidepressants for the last seven years?"

Paul does a double take and looks at me with a gaping mouth and exaggerated wide eyes.

"This is my shocked face," he says. "That's not exactly headline news, William. We're all on antidepressants."

"But I'm not depressed. I don't think I ever was."

Paul cocks his head a bit, unbelieving.

"You're not depressed?"

"What if I'm just... chronically unhappy?"

"Chronically unhappy? I do believe you've just stumbled onto the definition of depression."

"No. There's a difference."

"Ehhh, I'm not sure there is."

"Depression is a clinical condition. It's the unhealthy result of a chemical imbalance. Your life could be perfect. Be everything you want it to be, and you would still feel this way. But unhappiness, that's different. It's a healthy response to the fact that you're living wrong. Our brains are trying to tell us something."

"Maybe it's trying to say you need a different pill."

"No! No pill."

"No pill? Seems like a rash decision. Pills are good. I like pills."

"The pills are the problem. They're just an easy way to make the unhappiness semi-bearable. Just bearable enough that you never actually have to make the changes that need to be made."

Paul downs his mixed drink and drops down from his stool. He steps behind me, puts his hands on my shoulders and speaks into my ear.

"Here's what you do. Call your doctor. He'll put you on a nice new regiment. You'll be right as rain. I'm gonna go fall in love now."

Paul gives my shoulder a pat and walks away in pursuit of his dreams.

I watch him go and immediately discard his advice. Today I feel more alive than I have in many many years. For so long I have been on a single lane road with endless tolls but no turn-offs and no exits. Now the road before me has countless forks and all of them are open. The possibilities are endless.

Paul sits across from me at a booth. His dreams have been dashed. He looks at me sadly.

"You think my wife will take me back yet? It's been three weeks."

"I don't know. What'd you do?"

Paul doesn't answer and looks across the room. I follow his eyes to find his dashed dream. She's being courted by another man now.

"Look at her," Paul says. "Just moving on like nothing ever happened between us. I gave her my heart. Bought her three drinks."

My drunk mind loses track of his words. I find myself staring at my hands.

"You ever work with your hands?" I ask.

"I probably will tonight."

"I feel like I wanna build something. You know? Everything I own, somebody else made it."

"What are you gonna build?"

"I don't know. I wanna be inspired. You remember that feeling? To be inspired? Just get lost in an idea and follow it to its fruition."

Paul stares at me, but I don't think he sees me. His face is blank. He blinks very very slowly.

"I must be going now," he says.

"You can't be driving like this."

"I won't, I won't. I'll sleep in the car," he slurs. "I can't afford to keep paying for hotels anyway."

He struggles to rise from his seat and stumbles his way toward the exit.

I'm alone.

My eyes find a TV. The sound is muted, the closed-caption text popping up at the bottom of the screen. A sour faced CNN reporter is talking shit about Donald Trump and trying like hell to pass her opinion off as hard news. I look at her pinched faced scowl and the only word that comes to mind is "cunt".

I want to talk to… somebody… about… something. The subject of that something is up for grabs. I've got a lot of thoughts about a lot of things and I feel like I haven't spoken in years.

I grab my beer and stand up. The world doesn't move as quickly as I do, so I pause for a bit to let it catch up. I walk in the direction of the bar and hear the voice of Clarice. I don't know Clarice, but trans-she is loud and has been holding court at the bar for some time now. I picked up the name through unintentional eavesdropping. When I first laid eyes on Clarice, I was exiting the men's room, while trans-she was headed toward the ladies'.

"That boy didn't know who he was messing with," Clarice says. "I warned him, but he didn't believe it. I said, boy, cancellation is coming. It's coming!"

Clarice's gaggle of followers laugh.

"I swear to God, people done lost their minds. It's about respect. Show me respect. Respect who I am. I ain't never disrespected you, why people gotta come up in here and act like they in charge of who I am. My black ass ain't puttin' up with that shit. Got no right. No right! And they find out quick too. Hear me roar motherfucker! Hear me roar!"

More laughing from Clarice's audience.

"Excuse me!" I say. "Excuse me."

Clarice looks at me. Everybody looks at me.

"I got a question for ya, if you don't mind."

I cut through the crowd and steal a spot at the bar.

"What you wanna know?" Clarice says.

"This is a serious question that I've been contemplating for some time."

"Alright then. Spill it."

"Say you got a white guy..."

"Oh, I got a white guy. Hell, I got several white guys."

The laughter comes again, on schedule. Clarice is loving it. It's really making trans-her day. I wait for it to die down.

I say, "Now this person... could be a girl, could be whatever, but for the purposes of this conversation, let's make him a dude."

"Alright. I'm with ya."

"This guy feels completely disconnected from his community. He's got no interest in the culture, the customs, the conversations, the everything that comes with being white. But he's got black friends. He's exposed to them, their families, their world... and he loves it.

Strangely, he feels absolutely connected and at home in that culture. Now, first of all, is that offensive?"

"Hell no. I get that shit. Black culture is amazing."

"Right! I feel the same way. Perfect," I say. "But, he feels so strongly, he starts watching black movies. Listening to black music. Dressing according to black fashion. Speaking in a black cadence. Using black dialect."

"You talking about cultural appropriation?"

"Maybe, you tell me."

"Mmm hmm. That shit is problematic," Clarice says.

Clarice's followers all nod in agreement.

"You see, that's what I've heard, but why? I mean you should know better than anyone. You were born a man, physically. But you're not a man, are you? Your heart and soul and being are fully entrenched in womanhood, right?"

Clarice looks at me warily, but sort of nods.

"Is it so far fetched that a white person might find their heart and soul and very being in blackness?"

"Man, that's different."

"How so?"

"You can't change your skin."

"Not yet. A hundred years ago, you couldn't get a sex change. Was gender identity not valid a hundred years ago?"

Clarice abruptly stands up.

"Boy, gender identity ain't dependent on no goddamn sex change. You about to piss me off. I can't do this shit!"

Clarice dramatically throws her hands up and turns to walk away.

"I'm trying to understand. I mean the fundamental differences between man and woman are much more pronounced than black and white."

Clarice turns back.

"You know what? Fine. If that's where his home is. Where his heart is. If he's living his truth… I got no problem with it."

"Okay. Good. I'm glad to hear it. That means you're not a hypocrite. Great."

"People need room to exist," Clarice says. "To be themselves."

"I totally agree. But I am wondering if there's a line. That's what I'm trying to figure out. I mean, what if this guy... we'll call him a biological white... What if he starts wearing make-up to look more black?"

"You talking about black-face now? What the fuck!"

"No, not that shit from the old movies. I'm talking about realistic, professional makeup to darken the skin."

"Boy, you about to make me lose it."

"And what if this person starts demanding that the rest of the world accept him as black? Not sorta black, or black adjacent, but actually black. Just as black as the next guy. Like allowed to use the United Negro College Fund type black. What if this person managed to create a world where even black people had no choice but to refer to him as black or be branded a bigot? What do we think about that?"

Clarice stares at me, speechless.

I continue, "I guess that would be okay, because obviously this biological white person knows everything there is to know about what it means to be black. Just like you know everything there is to know about what it means to be a woman."

Clarice takes an aggressive step toward me. I don't flinch. I'm quite certain I'm about to receive a fist or at least a stern talking to. Whatever it is, the new me has decided to let it happen.

But neither happens. Clarice silently turns and walks away.

I yell after trans-her.

"I mean blackness in America can't be that nuanced, right? It's been decades since any real oppression. At this point, why shouldn't Whitey be allowed to determine what blackness is all about?"

Clarice walks on, disappearing into a crowd.

I look to the several audience members that remain. Their faces say it all. I am a terrible human being, unworthy of their boundless liberal sympathies. Most of them are women. Women who I'm certain feel the oppression of the overwhelming patriarchy. Who complain about it every chance they get. But by all means, men should be allowed to determine what constitutes womanhood.

How could I or any man possibly determine that? I didn't grow up a little girl. I didn't watch the boys grow stronger and faster and leave me in the dust. I didn't, one fateful day, bleed from my special place, and continue to do so every 28 days for the next forty years. I don't know the PMS. I don't know the cramps. I never felt the boys leering at me when my breasts started to grow without my permission. I never had to worry about an accidental pregnancy and all that might entail. I never felt my biological clock.

Why?

Because that and a million other things are not a part of my reality and never could be. I know absolutely shit about what it means to be a woman. And neither does Clarice.

I start to say these things, but stop short. What's the point? Somewhere deep down, they know it.

Instead, I signal for another beer. There's a new bartender, a tattooed girl who looks to be in her late thirties. She manages to be simultaneously tough and sexy.

Around the corner of the bar sits one of Clarice's aforementioned audience members.

"You are such an asshole!" she says.

"Just living my truth," I respond.

The bartender arrives and sets my beer down.

"On the house," she says.

She gives me a little smirk and walks away. I watch her go.

"Now that's a woman," I say.

Clarice's audience member stomps off in a huff. But of course there's another.

"Don't you wanna be on the right side of history?" she says.

"The right side of history? Is that where you think you are?"

"Uhh, yeah. We're talking about people. Inclusion. It's pretty cut and dry."

"Tell that to your female athletes who lost opportunities to men. Better yet, tell that to the rape victims who don't get to feel safe taking a piss."

A guy shows up to defend the girl's honor. Probably her boyfriend. They look like a proper fit. He's very hipster with skinny jeans, an ironic mustache, and his hair in a bun.

"Is there a problem here?" he says.

"You mean other than your general appearance?" I ask.

Suddenly, I feel strong hands gripping my shoulders from behind. My body is ripped backwards off the stool and sent hurtling down.

The back of my head bounces violently off the unforgiving floor. My vision dims and I see stars. Through the stars, I see Clarice lording over me and feel the rapid-fire kicks into my ribs and abdomen.

The hipster arrives, joining in on the fun, stomping with delight. I see a fist growing larger and larger until I see nothing at all.

4

I wake to find myself lying flat on my back on a booth bench, knees bent at the bench seat's edge, feet resting on the floor. The bench is covered in the same cracked black vinyl as before, so I'm guessing I haven't left the bar. I think it's been a while since anyone has scraped the gum from the underside of the table.

The noises of nightlife are gone, replaced by the sounds of cleaning.

I raise my head and feel the expected ache. I swallow the pain and pull my body up into a seated position. The barroom looks completely different. The moody atmosphere is gone, chased away by the flip of a light switch. Across the room, chairs have been stacked onto tables and a waitress is vacuuming the floor.

"You're alive," a voice says.

I look over. Across the table from me sits a portly man, dressed in a business suit. He is clearly inebriated.

"That girl gave you quite the beating."

"Yeah, well, she hit like a dude."

The man laughs drunkenly.

A waitress arrives at the table. She removes a couple empty bottles and gives the table a quick wipe. She ignores my presence.

"Beer?" I say.

"We're closed," she responds, and immediately walks away. She yells at someone distant, "Lita! Your charity case is conscious!"

"I think that's you," the man across the booth says. "You're the charity case. I'm Gary."

Gary reaches across the table to offer me a handshake.

I accept it, "William."

"Nice to meet you, William."

"Who is Lita?"

Gary just smiles. He produces a flask from his inside jacket pocket and takes a swig.

"What do you do, William?"

He offers me the flask and I take it.

"I talk too much, apparently. Less than twenty-four hours ago I was sitting in my car, just sitting there, trying to figure out how long it had been since I actually said something. You know, something of consequence."

"What did you decide?"

"I didn't. I couldn't even remember the last time I'd actually spoken my mind. A decade? Maybe. I don't know. Just coasting through, not rocking any boats."

"You look like you rocked some boats today."

"I capsized the damn boat. Now I'm unemployed and everything hurts."

I close my eyes and massage my temples. I feel a tap on my elbow.

"Hey, hey," Gary says.

I open my eyes. Gary has leaned in close across the table. He grips my wrist, not with aggression, but with care.

"Good for you, man. Good for you! You're alive. Back from the dead, yeah? Hell, I'm jealous."

I can't help but smile. Gary returns to a seated position.

"What do you do, Gary?"

"They say the sign of a good negotiation is everybody walks away unhappy. That's what I do. I'm the guy that makes everybody unhappy."

"Really?"

Gary digs a business card from his wallet.

"I am a professional Mediator in all matters of legal consequence. So… when this new found voice of yours results in a contentious divorce, this is the number to call."

I look over the business card with interest. Gary Trindall.

"Mediator, huh? Does that mean you're a lawy-"

I look up to witness Gary slow-motion falling asleep.

Alone again.

The TV's are still on and this particular TV is set to Fox News. I look toward the entrance and realize that from the perspective of an entering customer, all the TV's on the right are tuned to Fox News. All the TV's on the left are split between CNN and MSNBC. Funny.

The smug face of Tucker Carlson is talking about something, but from this distance I can't read the words. Looking at him, the c-word reenters my mind.

The screen cuts to a clip of Joe Biden followed by another and another and another. It's clearly a 'worst of' video... A vast collection of flubs, misspeaks, and lost-the-thread moments of which I'm sure there were plenty to choose from. The man is clearly not fit to be president. His only saving grace is that he's not Donald Trump. In just less than a month, we might actually elect a man to run this country, that isn't even fit to run a household. The funniest part is that he may actually be a vast improvement.

The tattooed bartender arrives at the table.

"I'm locking up. You ready to get this show on the road?"

"Uhh."

"Look at me," she says, bending down to get eye to eye. She holds up a finger in front of my face and moves it to one side and then the other. She gives a little shake of the head.

"You'll have to ride with me."

She gestures to Gary.

"Here, help me with this guy."

We proceed to half escort and half carry Mister Trindall to the exit. He helps at first, but the further we go, the heavier he gets.

We make it out the door and lean him against a wall. I press my weight into his body, pinning it in place, while the bartender, who I've decided is probably Lita, locks the front door.

She comes back and addresses Gary with a sharp slap across the face.

"Hey! Gary! Look at me. Look. Look! There you are. I am not your mother. I am not going to carry you all the way to the car. I'm not gonna do it. You are going to walk. I'll be right beside you, but you're gonna walk. Okay!"

She slaps him again.

"You hear me? Do you hear me?!"

Gary begins sobbing, while I just hold him there.

"Oh my God," Lita says. "I can't do this. You little baby! One foot in front of the other. Let's go!"

"I'm sorry Lita. I'm so sorry!"

"Yeah, yeah."

"You're so good to me."

Lita takes one of his arms and drapes it over her shoulders. I do the same and we begin the trek toward the car.

It's a struggle to insert his limp body into the backseat, but we finally shove him in.

"If you throw up in my car, I swear to God, I will strip you naked, take your wallet and your watch and sell your car to the nearest chop shop. Don't you do it Gary."

Lita goes around to the driver's side. She looks at me and says, "You coming?"

I slide into the passenger seat, while she gets behind the wheel.

"Guess he does this a lot?" I ask.

"Ya think? He's a complete mess. You hear me Gary? You're a ridiculous mess."

"I'm sorry Lita," he slurs. "I really am."

Lita leans toward me and puts a hand on my leg. It's such a simple, nothing touch, but it radiates through me, instantly activating long dead senses.

"He's actually really sweet," she whispers. "Great tipper."

And just like that, her hand is gone. She uses it to start the engine. As she drives, she uses it to steer the vehicle. We halt at a stoplight and I just stare at her hand, resting uselessly against the steering wheel. I imagine her taking this opportunity to again touch my leg. I long for it.

The light turns green.

Lita pulls the car into a motel parking lot. She parks in front of the lobby doors.

"Grab his wallet for me, would ya? Left breast pocket."

She gets out while I do as she asks. She reaches in through the open window and I hand her the wallet. Lita marches through the lobby doors. Before they close behind her, I hear her say, "Guess who's back?" in a sing-song voice.

I watch her through the glass doors. She really is something to look at. I put a hand on my thigh and imagine it is hers. My senses are alive. She looks good from behind. I watch her closely. My hand moves lightly over the surface of my pants. An involuntary shutter runs through me.

It all feels so foreign. It's been years since I last felt the touch of real sexuality. My infrequent forays into my wife's body should hardly count. They'd be better described as regularly required maintenance, often joyless and sometimes unsuccessful. It's as if that piece of myself has atrophied over time due to lack of nourishment, withering away into nothing. Even my self-love sessions in the shower are mostly a chore, half-hard and uninspired.

I watch Lita as she returns. I want to see her face overtaken by pleasure, feel her skin as the goosebumps form, know her taste as I ravage her body. I want to devour her.

She motions for me to roll down the window. I do. She leans over, resting her forearms against the door. She's close and her position allows me a nice view into her cleavage.

"Room 301," she says. "It's right over here. Let's unload this piece of shit."

She removes some bills from Gary's wallet. She stuffs a few of them into her bra. She holds a couple twenties out to me.

"For the assist," she says.

"I don't want that."

"You're gonna earn it, so take it. We still got two flights of stairs to contend with."

She's convincing, so I take the money.

36

We practically have to carry him up the stairs. He pretends to help, but I don't think it'd be much different if he were dead.

We throw Gary onto the bed. Lita hands me his phone, while she adjusts his body for sleeping.

"Look in contacts and find Sarah. Text her – *Drummond Motel, Room 301, Lita.* I have a deal with his wife. After the activities of this spring, she said, 'Never again. NEVER AGAIN!' So now I get paid to find him shelter and put him to bed. Like a baby. Like an itty bitty baby."

Lita pinches the grown man's baby cheeks. I have a bit of an issue with the way she's treating him. She's quickly becoming less attractive. Then again, maybe he deserves it. If you drink yourself into worthlessness, maybe you deserve what you get.

She turns and looks at me.

"You ready to get out of here?"

I look at her once more. Her attractiveness has been fully restored.

"Sure," I say, extending a hand forward for a shake. "I'm William, by the way."

The morning light manages to squeeze through and around the curtains. I look over and see Lita lying on her side, facing away from me. She's sleeping soundly, an eye-mask helping her to reject the daylight.

I find my pants on the floor and dig my phone out of the pocket. Along with my phone, I find Gary's business card. I have 8 missed calls, 3 new voicemails, and 18 unread text messages.

I call up the website for Gary's business, Trindall Mediation Services. I study it for several minutes.

I toss my phone back onto my pile of clothes and head to the bathroom.

I always need to pee in the morning, but it's been a while since I've woken to an erection. I'm forced to dial back my memories to an earlier time when such things were common. It took me several of my teenage years to develop the best technique for proper erectile targeting of a toilet bowl. Thankfully, it's a little like riding a bike and I manage to not make a mess.

I return to the bedroom. I see the form of Lita's body, shrouded by the blanket. Under that blanket lies skin so soft and smooth that it feels unnatural. It feels so much different from my wife's. Warm, welcoming, wonderful.

I slide under the blanket and huddle into her warmth. I run my fingers lightly over the surface of her skin, stirring her senses. Her sleeping body awakens.

We are alive.

I lock the knob on Lita's front door and shut it behind me. Lita lives less than a mile from the bar, so I decide to walk.

It's a nice day. We're just coming out of an excruciatingly hot summer, so strangely, even 68 degrees feels a little chilly.

My thoughts go to all those missed calls and the woman that made them. I've never been a cheater before. I've always believed it to be the cruel act of a selfish person. Then again, so is marrying someone you don't love. My wife doesn't love me and, truth be told, I don't believe she ever did.

They say that there are plenty of fish in the sea… But what if you don't like fishing? Over time, I have come to the conclusion that that was my wife's problem. I wasn't the fish she was hunting for, but she was oh so tired of fishing. I'm certain she considered throwing me back. Ultimately, It was her skills in the kitchen that convinced her otherwise. She thought, *'With the proper prepping… the right amount of marinating… and a hefty dose of seasoning… this fish will be exactly what I'm looking for'.*

I am a Settle Fish. And I am not alone. We are a plentiful fish, scattered liberally throughout the world. The species can often be identified through its sad eyes, its general air of desperation, and in a pinch, its pharmaceutical history.

I find myself wondering if Settle Fish should be excused of the judgment that comes with infidelity. Perhaps Settle Fish, as a species, should be free to do as they will.

By the time I reach my car, there is zero doubt that my actions were not only justified, but righteous.

I am a Settle Fish, my conscience is clear.

I drive to the Drummond Motel and climb the steps up to Room 301. I start with a light knock and progress from there. Eventually I'm banging on the door and yelling.

"Gary! Hey Gary! Wake up!"

The door finally jerks open. Gary stands hunched before me. Disheveled is an understatement. He looks like he's been to war.

"Wha? What is this?" Gary says.

"Gary! There you are. I'm here to take you to breakfast."

He rubs his red eyes.

"I'm not hungry."

"Then I'll buy you a coffee."

"No thank you. I just need to sleep."

He tries to close the door, but I plant a foot inside to block it.

"You've been asleep for years Gary. It's time to wake up."

He looks at me but doesn't say a word.

"Tell me I'm wrong."

5

We find a diner less than a mile away from Gary's motel. I order a pitcher of coffee for the table. The coffee is bad, but we drink it anyway.

We sit at a booth along a large row of windows with a view of the parking lot. We talk while shoveling over-cooked eggs and under-cooked hash browns down our throats.

I like the man. I get a good feeling about him, despite his tendency to drink himself into oblivion.

I spend the better part of our meal pitching him on an idea that hit me like a lightning bolt just last night. Or at least, so I thought. Some of the details of the idea are so perfectly formed they must have been percolating in my unconscious mind for months, maybe years.

"Why the hell are you talking to me about this?" he asks.

"This is how you make a living, is it not?"

"I get that, but all you've ever seen is me at my worst. And the truth of it is, that's me at my normal."

"Every night?"

"Not every night, but more often than not."

"Why is that, Gary? Why do you do that?"

"I don't know. I just… feel. I can't say how other people feel things, but if they feel things the same way I feel things… then I can't figure out how this world hasn't fallen apart already."

He puts a finger to his forehead

"If what goes on up here is normal, if this is what we all go through, then I gotta give you all a round of applause. I don't know how you do it."

Gary points to a random couple eating breakfast.

"How are those people not teetering on the edge of annihilation?"

"Maybe they are."

He shrugs, "Maybe they are, but I don't think so. I think I'm different. Sometimes I hate myself for not having an excuse. I grew up in a good family. No one ever abused me. I have no trauma. But I'm different. I've always been different. I'm like hardwired for depression."

"Help me understand. Give me an example."

Gary takes a sip of coffee and nods his head.

"Sure. My dad was a hunter. He used to fill up our freezer with enough venison to feed us for a year. The next year, not sure how old I was but I was just a kid, he asked me if I wanted to join him on his hunting trip. He didn't force me. He just asked and I said 'yes'.

"The first day, he showed me how to break down the gun, oil it, clean it, put it back together. Later, we had target practice and I got to feel all that power in my hands, like an extension of myself."

Gary takes a sip of coffee, remembering.

"The next day, I had this nearly mature fawn in my sights. She was breathtaking. Her spots were long gone and she was sitting right on the edge of adulthood. Her whole life in front of her. I could feel my pulse pounding. I steadied my breathing. In and out. In, out. I felt myself relax, looking at this beautiful girl through the scope. She was right there... right there with me. It was cold, so I actually see her breathing and I realized that her breaths and mine were perfectly synced. And the heartbeat I was hearing... that wasn't just mine, it was ours. We were connected. I felt something so pure, so beautiful. Truthfully, and I mean this, to this day it's the greatest moment I've ever experienced. My Dad beside me. And this beautiful girl. Nothing could've made it better.

"And then I hear him whisper, 'take the shot son'. And so I did. On the walk over to her, silent tears were gushing from my eyes. I knew in that moment that I had just killed a part of myself. Maybe the best part. When we got there, I looked down into those blank eyes and felt my Dad's arm wrap around me. He gave my shoulder a squeeze and said, 'Good job, son'.

"I hated myself for what I'd done. I hated myself even more for being happy. Because I was. I was happy.

"Eventually we strung her up. We drained her of her blood. Skinned her. Butchered her until she was gone. All that was left was this meat... this horrible thing that I had done. And every day I would ingest that thing. Taking it into me. Making it a part of me. Breakfast sausage in the morning. Chili at night."

He takes another sip of his coffee. I watch him and he looks down, avoiding eye contact. But I can see the moisture in those eyes.

I say, "I thought you said you never suffered any trauma."

He looks at me, but says nothing.

"It's your Dad. Of course you craved his love. Of course you wanted him to be proud of you. But killing something you find beautiful in order to achieve that? That's bound to leave a mark. It's not strange that you would feel conflicted."

"I still see that fawn to this day. Nearly every day of my life. You don't think that's strange? She's barely a fawn anymore. Something more like a monster. People who say monsters don't exist, never made one. That's how they come about, you know, we create them through our own actions. They come in all shapes and sizes. Some hold no shape at all. They are merely a memory, an intangible void floating around like mist minus the water. They have no weight, no force of will. They are nothingness. Yet in your mind... they rule."

I look at Gary and shake my head.

"I think the world is full of people seeing fawns. Fawns that would have long since died, regardless of whether or not you killed them."

Gary scoffs.

"You've made a choice, Gary. You've decided to keep your problems, to hold them close, to nurture them. But never have you decided to reckon with them. Of course they're still with you. You're the only thing keeping them alive."

"Because I was the only thing that killed that fawn."

"And then you ate it. Perfectly natural behavior. Look at me, I'm eating a pig, as we speak. Do I feel sad about it? Sure, there's a little sadness there. It does make me sad. But it also makes me strong. It also allows me to live another day. Do you hate lions for eating Wildebeests? It's what they need to carry on. It's also the natural order of things. How can you hate a lion for simply doing what it has to do?"

"But we aren't lions. We don't need to kill."

"Sure we do. You're eating right now."

"I'm eating a pancake."

"Which was made from wheat. A living thing that we grew and then slaughtered in an effort to collect its fruit for the sole purpose of making you that pancake."

"Are you seriously comparing wheat to…"

"Yes. Yes I am. It's easy to empathize with animals, because they're close cousins. They have eyes and ears and noses, and so we see them with our hearts and not just our minds. Plants don't get that same love. But is there really a difference between hanging a twelve point buck's head on your wall and displaying a dozen roses in a vase? Because they're just so damn beautiful as they slowly rot away."

Gary grimaces.

I say, "We don't know what we don't know. Do these things think? Do they have emotions? Do they have a brain and we just can't see it, because we don't know what we're looking for? You know there are plants out there who release toxins when they hear a caterpillar eating their leaves?"

"Yeah, I don't think they hear it. They may feel it. They don't hear it."

"Wrong. They absolutely hear it. A group of scientists ran an experiment where they recorded the sound of that caterpillar eating those leaves. And then later, sans caterpillar, they played the sound to that plant, and guess what happened?"

"The plant released the toxin."

"Yes it did. We look at that plant and we don't see a thing with ears, but they can hear. What else do they got that we can't see? Complex thought processes? Emotions? We haven't even figured ourselves out. What exactly do you think you know about these lifeforms that are so very different in so many ways?"

Gary looks down at his pancake and drops his fork. It clatters on the table before coming to rest.

"Well now I can't even eat this," he says.

"Living things eat living things. It's natural. It's even required. You don't have a choice. You throwing down your fork at the thought of eating a pancake is the opposite of what I'm trying to tell you."

"That's my whole point. This is how my mind works. I can't help it."

"It's not that you can't help it. It's that you don't. When something is broken, it remains broken until you fix it. There's nothing strange about that. You are not special. This is not a tragic, romantic story about how you feel more deeply than every other human. This is a tragic story of you feeling pain, but refusing to face it. And then fetishizing your emotional turmoil."

"I am not fetishizin-"

"Open your eyes, Gary. Look around. You are not special. Hell, you're not even depressed. You're just chronically unhappy."

"I'm not sure you understand the definition of depres-"

"You're depressed, okay. Fine. But you're not clinically depressed."

"I think my doctor would disagree with you. In fact, I'm certain he does."

"That's because your doctor doesn't work exclusively for you. He also works for the pharmaceutical companies. He has to balance your needs with their needs. If you were a pie chart, you'd be like forty percent his client, and sixty percent his product. He's selling you to them. And you are very valuable, because you're a walking subscription. You are constant revenue. That's what you are.

You're a number on a spreadsheet. Their goal is not to fix you. Why would they want to lose all that revenue to a healthy mind?"

Gary sighs, "It's too early in the morning for this conversation."

"It's too late in your life for this conversation. We're getting old, Gary. We don't have any more time to waste. Let me ask you this… Do you like your job?"

"I have a great job."

"So did I, but it made me want to kill somebody. Nobody in particular, just somebody. And when I couldn't convince myself to become a murderer, that somebody became me."

"You're suicidal?"

"Not at this minute, but I'm proud to say it's an option."

"You're proud?"

"Look, when the opportunity presented itself, I wasn't opposed to it. That's the truth. But then I started to think. Like really think. What could I accomplish if I'm not afraid of death? If I don't fear that, of all things, what's holding me back? The prospect of making a fool of myself? If I just can't live with some public display of stupidity, I suppose there's an easy way to handle that. Because I'm not afraid of death."

"You've found freedom… in being suicidal?"

"And you could too," I tell him.

"One slight problem, I am afraid of death."

"That's why I'm here. To tell you that your life will be drastically improved if you behave as if you aren't."

"That may be true, I don't know. But what if it all goes horribly wrong? What if everything you've been talking about goes to shit and we lose everything and everyone we ever cared about. You apparently have a solution for a problem like that. I'm just screwed."

"That's why I'm suggesting a partnership. We make up for each other's weaknesses. If it comes to that, I'm not opposed to a little murder-suicide… if that makes it easier."

"It does not," Gary states emphatically. "It absolutely does not. I'm afraid of death! Why would I agree to be murdered?"

"You don't have to agree. We can just... have an understanding."

"That's not a solution I'm comfortable with."

"It's cool. I get it. We don't even need to talk about it anymore."

"You understand that we *don't* have an understanding, right?"

"Sure. I see where we're going. I think we can move on."

I smile and Gary rubs his aching head.

"Why am I having this conversation?"

"Because you know, deep down, with the life you're living... death would be a fucking miracle."

Gary is clearly bothered by this statement. He looks at me for a long while.

"I've got a meeting," he says and begins gathering his things. "Thank you for breakfast. I'd be lying if I said it was nice to meet you or that I hope to see you again."

Gary rises from his seat and walks away. I watch him go.

He stops and just stands there for a moment. He turns and approaches, meeting my eyes.

"I'm afraid that was unclear. It was not nice to meet you and I hope I never see you again."

Again, Gary leaves me. This time he makes it out the door.

My booth is a window seat, which gives me a great view to witness Gary's disappointment when he realizes that he has no transportation. He curses and digs his phone from his pocket.

I rise from my seat and exit the diner to find Gary leaning against a column.

I say, "Nothing worse than making a dramatic exit, then realizing you don't have your car."

Gary wordlessly shows his annoyance.

"Cancel your Uber. I'll take you to it."

"They're just five minutes out," Gary says.

"The ride will take five minutes. Either way, I'm gonna talk to you for the entirety of the interim."

Gary sighs, "I feel like there's something very wrong with you."

"There's something very wrong with all of us. Like, one problem I have... I have 12 million dollars burning a hole in my pocket. And all I want you to do is help me spend it. I don't know why that makes me an asshole, but whatever. I accept the position of asshole in this partnership."

"What exactly are you suggesting?"

"I'm suggesting we buckle down and change the whole world."

"With 12 million dollars? That's a lot of money if you're looking to buy a small business. Change the world, not so much."

"It's enough to get started. Tell me my vision doesn't sound like a miracle waiting to happen? I spent twenty minutes giving you a vision of the future. Did it not speak to you?"

"Look," Gary says. "There's something that you apparently don't know, but absolutely should."

"What is that?"

"Political third parties are a joke."

"If that's true we'll spread laughter throughout the land. This country could use it."

"I'm not kidding, William. Look at the last hundred years. Third Parties simply don't work. It's a stupid idea."

"Okay, let's look at the last hundred years. In the last century, name a time when this country has been more divided."

Gary thinks about that, but says nothing.

"The answer is... maybe the sixties? That was a pretty tumultuous time. But it's hard to say. Look at this world we've built ourselves. My gut tells me that the real answer is never more than now. Next question, in the last century, when has the average person been more empowered to get their own message out? Answer – Never more than now."

I see a slight nod from Gary.

"When polled, what percentage of voters identify themselves as independents? How many Gary?"

"Last I knew, low 40's"

"Never more than now. That's more than identify as Democrats. More than as Republican. And... In the last hundred years, there's never been a third party that didn't have an opinion. There's never been a third party that didn't have a platform. Just like the Donkeys and the Elephants, they all say the same shit - 'This is how the country should be'. Gary, I'm telling you, the American people are hungry for something. But it ain't another goddamn opinion that isn't their own. That's why third parties fail. The people are hungry for a voice. And the Mediator Party just wants to serve the food."

"The Mediator Party? You call it the Mediator Party?"

"You inspired me. You're my muse," I tell him.

"A Party without a platform?"

"We seek the proper solution to best reflect the collective will of the people. That's it. That's the platform."

"Let me make sure I get this right. You're suggesting we start a third party?"

"Yes."

"The Mediator Party?"

"Correct."

"And if they get elected-"

"When they get elected," I correct.

"Sure, *when* they get elected, they'll collect the *vast* and *varied* opinions of the *entire* populace on *every* issue?"

"Right."

"And they'll use that information to craft legislation that ultimately makes everybody unhappy."

"Exactly! I'm not sure I'd frame it quite like that. We might want to work on the messaging a bit, but yes, that's it."

"How are we collecting this data? How are we determining the collective will of the people?" Gary asks.

"That's something we have to figure out. But we live in the age of technology, I can't imagine that's a hurdle we can't overcome. And if we can't, I'll buy a gun."

I say it with a shrug, but Gary doesn't seem to appreciate my attempt at humor. He starts to complain, but ultimately brushes it off.

"Okay," he says. "Why me?"

"Because I'm a good judge of character. And because you need it. You need a mission, Gary. That's all you need. Once you get heated up, all that depression will just burn away. You are never more alive than when you have an obsession!"

A car pulls up. Gary's Uber.

Gary sighs and thinks for a moment.

He says, "It's a lovely sentiment. It really is. I wish you luck."

Gary turns away from me. He enters the car and my muse rolls away.

I watch the car go until it disappears from view. I walk back inside and reclaim my seat. My half eaten cinnamon roll sits there, but I'm no longer hungry. I resist the urge to throw it across the restaurant and instead shove it away from me.

'Stupid', he called it.

It strikes me that the value of an idea must be graded on a circular scale. Why else would stupidity and brilliance so often be confused for one another? If you wish to be brilliant, you must risk being stupid.

I flag the waitress down and talk her out of a pen.

Words begin to flow out of me, through the pen, and onto a napkin.

I write.

And I write.

And I write.

6

APRIL 22, 2021

I was just a few weeks into the writing of my book when Oklahoma's penchant for unpredictable ever-changing weather threw me a major curveball. As the old saying goes, 'if you don't like the weather... wait.' That said, it rarely freezes in October. When it does, it's generally for just a moment in the night. Never does it freeze all day, every day, for three straight days before the leaves even fall. And never does it rain for the entirety of those same three days.

Never say never.

On October 26th, temperatures dipped just below 32 degrees and stayed there. The rain came down wet, soaking power lines and trees before quickly turning to ice. For three straight days the freezing rain coated our cars and our streets and our homes.

Trees became crystalline sculptures, a half inch thick sheet of ice coating every branch, every limb, and every leaf that had yet to fall.

Hundreds of thousands of Oklahomans would lose power. I was one of them. Every day, for six days, I would sit in the candlelight, furiously jotting my thoughts into a spiral notebook. The wind would howl and a deafening crack would inform me of yet another branch giving in to the weight of it all. This was always followed by the thunderous sound of a literal ton of ice and wood crashing down to the earth.

November became the season of chainsaws. Every day I would listen as homeowners cleaned up the mess and piled it high on the curb. Through it all, I wrote.

No one was prepared for such wide spread damage, least of all the waste collectors. Come Christmas time, several of my neighbors decorated their giant piles of dead trees with Christmas lights. Why the hell not? Apparently it was there to stay.

It was late January before my street was finally cleared of the debris. I was heavy into proof-reading my book as I watched them haul it away.

It's April now.

Nearby, there is an invisible line that separates Oklahoma City from Bethany. Normally, it's hard to tell when you've left one place and entered the other, but I can tell it today. While OKC has finally cleared the deck, Bethany has barely even made a dent.

Driving through the City of Bethany, I can't help but laugh. We are six months removed from the carnage, and yet in front of nearly every house sits a six foot tall, thirty foot long reminder.

The city must be broke. The infrastructure is far from ideal. Much is in disrepair. The water systems are falling apart. Waste removal has yet to instill a single recycling program of any kind. They can't attract businesses. There's not even a single Starbucks.

I pull into the driveway belonging to Joel Smith. He is a recent acquaintance who spoke to me of Bethany's long slow descent into blight. He wants to fix it. He thinks maybe he should run for City Council. And I think maybe I should help.

We spend several hours fleshing out a plan for Joel's future. It's a productive meeting and I feel good about his prospects. As evening nears, I take my leave, pointing the Mercedes in the direction of OKC proper.

It's early evening and a small crowd has gathered at Full Circle Bookstore. I begin counting heads but manage to lose count despite the small number. I estimate the group at about thirty souls. The size of your average classroom.

Today, I will be their teacher.

The event at hand is the launch of my first book, *A Love/Hate Letter to America.* Truth be told, I self-published the book two months ago on Valentine's day, but Post-Covid, the bookstore has only now reopened itself to public events.

A young woman by the name of Lyndsie introduces me. I approach a small podium and open my book to the last chapter. I look at the words I've written and I speak.

"Dear America," I say.

I look up from the page and stare into the crowd. I make eye contact with several, letting them know that I am speaking directly to them.

"The one thing I know to be true is this: The only thing worse than a Republican is a Democrat."

A chair screeches loudly. I look to see a young man angrily rise from his seat and wordlessly stomp away.

"Or did I get that backwards? I suppose it depends on the day."

A couple people chuckle, but mostly it's crickets.

"My name is William Waxman and I do not have a voice. Many would say that is my own fault. That I have chosen to be voiceless. 'Those who don't vote, can't complain about the results,' someone once told me. I understand the sentiment, however I can no longer agree with the conclusion. Is making a choice between two bad options what it means to have a voice?"

I look up toward the audience, pleading with them to provide me with an answer. I let them ponder the question a moment longer.

"I have grown tired of serving my purpose and never being represented. I have lost the desire to scream into the void. If that's what having a voice is, I think I'll pass."

I look down at my words and slowly close the book. I don't need it. I know these words. They are my words.

"You see, I am what you might call a reasonable man. I understand the arguments on the left. I also comprehend the reasoning of the right. I know that they are each somewhat correct and they are both absolutely wrong. There is a reason the political pendulum continually swings from one side to the other and back again. It is because the real answer lies in between.

"Moderation may not be sexy, but it is the only reason this country hasn't suffered one of two horrible fates. A far left society is not something I ever want to even think about. A far right society would be a truly ugly place to live. Luckily, the inefficient moderation that is achieved through the constant back and forth from Democrat to Republican has, as of yet, saved us from either fate.

"There will always be the idiots on the far left and the morons of the far right."

"Fuck you prick!" A pretty young woman with purple hair blurts out. She rises from her seat and noisily escapes down the aisle.

I gesture to her as she leaves.

"Their vote is assured no matter the cost. It is the reasonable people that keep this country from descending into one chaos or another. It has fallen on us to keep the pendulum swinging. But, sadly, within this process *we* are never truly represented. Why do *we* have to choose between the mass burning of fossil fuels on one side or allowing men to displace women within the sporting world on the other? Why are there only two ridiculous options for us to consider?"

The purple-haired girl never makes it out the door. She stands in the distance, leaning against the end of a bookcase full of mystery novels. She stares at me as I speak.

"The answer to that question is the Two-Party System. It is a system that was created at a time when there were no computers. Nor were there telephones or telegraphs or even The Pony Express. There really was no viable way to determine the collective will of an entire country. The response was to hold the votes and accumulate the brightest minds of the two most prevalent opposing viewpoints. We left it to them to debate their way to the legislation that would form the future of our country. It made perfect sense at the time.

"Times have changed. We live in a world of great technological advancement. A world of inter-connectivity. We now have the means to collect the data. We have the ability to plumb that data for all of its worth, sorting it into categories and sub-categories to our heart's content. Entire multi-billion dollar companies exist for no other reason than to analyze data. So why must we continue to elect officials who so poorly represent us? Why must we rely on the divisive platforms of politicians who can't seem to agree on much of anything? Why must we be so inefficient? So unproductive? We must... because the game is rigged.

"The Democratic Party and the Republican Party are powerful organizations. While technically they fall under the category of 'non-profits', the money still flows. Salaries, even exorbitant ones, are not considered profit. Nor are consulting fees or influence peddling or stock tips or backroom deals or kick-backs that never see the light of day. Make no mistake, the two parties are big business. They may oppose each other, but they also feed each other. They are two sides of the same corrupt coin. Their elected members have used that power to create laws to ensure that their system remains the only viable choice. It is an exquisitely built system that makes it nearly impossible for any outsiders to break through. Like any good business, the Two-Party System has created a framework to ensure its own survival, even in the face of its consistent failure to adequately serve its customers, The People.

"I believe that the time has come to challenge that system. At a time when presidential supporters are storming the capital, we must stand up. At a time when Free Speech is in question, we must stand up and be heard. At a time when the divide between the two parties has grown to the point of absurdity, we must challenge the system.

"I am proposing a third party. I call it the Mediator Party. It is not an official organization, and even if it were, it would have exactly one member. Currently, it is merely an idea in my mind. That said, it is an idea worth sharing. I imagine a collection of reasonable people. A Party without a platform, save for one simple statement: 'To serve the collective will of the people'. That is the sum total of this Party's advocacy.

"The Mediator Party will seek to create a world where voters not only select their representatives, but also make their voice heard on any and all subject matters in which they have an opinion. At no cost to the taxpayers, the Mediator Party will spearhead the creation of a detailed, in-depth, survey that can be filled out in a myriad of ways by any and all voters.

"For those who wish to get down to the nitty-gritty of all policy considerations, voters will have the opportunity to fill out the long form in full. For others, there is the short form, which uses statistical analysis to fill out the long form on your behalf. And then there are those who may choose to simply vote the same as a trusted individual or organization. If a person wants to vote the same as the Republican Party, they can do so with the click of a button. If they want to 'Vote Like Bernie Sanders', they can, so long as Bernie submits his votes to be public. And of course that voter could always go back and change a few answers, choosing to vote mostly like Bernie, but not completely. Others still, may leave the bulk of the survey blank, only voting on the categories that matter to them. Just how involved anyone wants to be is, of course, up to the individual.

"All this data would then find its way onto the amazing computers that have so changed our lives. Analytic programs will sort through the vast opinions of the American people creating an expansive database that would be published and available to all.

"How do Americans feel about gun control?" The general numbers as well as subheadings would quickly populate the screen. *How about just the state of Kansas? Or maybe the city of Birmingham?* It's all there, ready to be discovered.

"Whether the legislation being written is city, state, or federal, this is the place to find the data that tells exactly how the full constituency feels about that particular subject. For the Mediator Party, these aren't just numbers, they are marching orders. Orders to write legislation that best reflects the collective will of the people. Orders to serve not just the political majority, but the people as a whole. To seek out the compromise. To find the midpoint of public opinion. And every vote counts the same. Whether you're Bill Gates or a homeless woman on a library computer, your vote tallies no different than any other. This is a true Representative Republic. This is what it means to have a voice.

"To the money men, the corporations, the special interest groups… take your problems to the people. If your organization wishes to sway legislation, you can do so by convincing the people to vote accordingly. Beyond your effect on the voting public, the Mediator Party has no further interest in your participation in the legislative process.

"To the squeaky wheels, the radicals, the agitators… let your voice be heard by the people. But understand, the Mediator Party is not listening. Your vote and the votes of the people you reach are all we can hear.

"Now is the time. Let us bring the wild swings of the pendulum to an end. Let us give the people their voice. And let us actually listen."

I look to my audience and place a hand upon my chest.

"Sincerely, one American," I say. I stretch an open palm out before me, calling to my audience.

"Is there a second?" I ask.

"I'll second that!" A young man raises his hand from the back row.

"I'm in," a middle-aged woman says.

I'd like to say that I can reliably move an audience to stand up and join the fight, but it helps to have friends. Both of my vocal audience members are plants. I may have lied that I was the only member of The Party. There are a few now, fighting the good fight.

It works, and several people begin to raise their hands. A couple more even open their mouths.

"Sounds good to me."

"That'd be nice," a voice says wistfully, clearly skeptical of its chances of success.

I say, "If you desire to have a voice, raise your hand."

I step out from the podium and hand out a single sheet of paper to each raised hand. On that paper are the exact words I just spoke in very small print. At the bottom of the page, they are invited to write their name and contact information.

I attempt to hand a form to a middle-aged man with his hand raised, but am intercepted. The interceptor is a well-built man with a bit of a gut. He has a full beard covering half of his reddened face. Atop his head sits a baseball cap, wrap-around sunglasses perched upon the bill. The cap isn't red, but it might as well be. He looks like a Proud Boy or some parallel retardation.

He snatches up the piece of paper, wads it into a ball, and dramatically spikes it to the ground.

I look him up and down.

"Moron on the right, I presume?"

"You ain't shit!" the man spits.

"You're right. I am not shit. I think you might have that market cornered."

Confusion washes over the man's features.

I explain, "That was me saying that while I am not shit, you absolutely are. Does that make sense?"

"Boy, I will pound you into the damn ground!"

"Please do. That could make national news. Probably do wonders for my book sales. You know what, maybe you should buy a copy and then beat me to death with it. That'll definitely get people talking."

The man looks around and sees multiple spectators have taken out their phones. Smile!

"This is bullshit! You stupid pussies with your stupid phones!" The man yells, frustrated. He looks back at me.

I watch as his violent desire grows. I give him a little smile.

He says, "YOU AIN'T SHIT, MOTHERFUCKER!"

"Thank you. But we've already established that."

"YOU CAN GO TO HELL!"

"Okay," I say.

The man storms off in a bluster, making sure to knock over a pyramid of stacked copies of my book. I have half a mind to ask the phone holders "Did you get all that?", but I don't. From the looks of it, there are at least four different angles of the encounter. I'm sure they got it. I'll be sure to collect those videos and see if I can use them to create an opportunity.

My MAGA friend violently makes his exit, but not without a few last words of wisdom, "Pissant liberal pedophiles!"

The stranger next to me laughs.

I say, "From one liberal pedophile to another, I think that went pretty well."

He shakes his head and looks at me.

"Some people," he says. "What do you think goes through a man like that's head? When he's alone with his thoughts, what's going on in there?"

"Shit. I got no clue. I tell you what, why don't you hit me over the head with a hammer a few times and if I manage to survive, ask me again."

The excitement fades and several of my audience members have managed to escape the building. That said, a surprising number have chosen to stick around, purchase a copy, and stand in line for an autograph.

Officially, the event ends at 8 o'clock, but many have failed to leave. They hang around and ask questions. Some appear to be excited by the prospect of a third party. Others are clearly cynical. They challenge my plan and its viability with questions intended to bring down my house of cards. But my house is strong and each challenge is met with confidence.

A man says, "But wouldn't the reform you're suggesting require a constitutional amendment?"

"It would not. We are not talking about a government run survey, or even a mandate for representatives to vote accordingly. The survey would be paid for and operated by the Mediator Party. That said, participation would be open to all citizens, not just Party members. Elected members of the Mediator Party would then use those results as their guiding light, seeking to create and/or support legislation that falls within the boundaries of the survey's findings."

"To serve the collective will, as you said," A woman states.

"Correct."

She says, "But what does that mean? Collective will? Doesn't that ultimately just serve the majority?"

"Not at all. This is about tempering that tendency to serve the majority. The intent is to find the relative midpoint on public opinion. Now, that midpoint would, of course, move based on the severity of popular opinion. Hence, if a survey result shows a 55% to 45% liberal lean on a particular policy, then according to the Mediator Party any law on that particular policy should have a slightly liberal bias, but only slight. However, if the result was 70% to 30%, then the law would require a much stronger liberal bias, but still never forgetting that other 30 percent. I referred to the Mediator Party as a 'Party without a platform', but it would be more accurate to say that the survey actually works to determine The Party's platform. And that platform will adjust with the results of each new survey."

Another woman steps forward and says, "The people are ill-informed though. Half of them are operating on fake news. These are people driven by personal passions inconsistent with the facts. Don't you think it's dangerous to put those people in charge?"

"*Driven by personal passions inconsistent with the facts.* Correct me if I'm wrong, but I believe that particular virus has long since infected both Houses of Congress."

The woman considers that and tilts her head in concession.

I say, "The difference is, the members of Congress are fully vested in instilling one version or another of crazy. This either results in a stalemate or a law that is out of whack with the actual populace. On the other hand, the Mediator Party is fully vested in finding the midpoint of all that crazy, seeking a moderate solution that leaves no voice out in the cold."

"But she's not wrong," an older man speaks up. "The people have a tendency to be ill-informed, uninformed, and everything in between. Our Congress is at least informed."

"Well that's a double-edged sword isn't it? You hold the people accountable for being uninformed, while giving them no say in policy concerns. Why would people educate themselves on matters that we've given them no ability to affect?"

"They can affect them. They have a vote."

"Do they?" I ask.

"Yes, they do."

"They have a vote on the one or two things that matter most to them. After that, they have no say at all. We exist within a system that doesn't allow us to have any diversity of opinion. You are not allowed to be both pro-life and pro-environment. You are not allowed to be in favor of gun-control and also against raising taxes on the rich. A person can certainly be all those things, but they damn sure won't find a representative. All they can do is decide which parts of themselves to ignore. And so, yeah, you stay uneducated, because 'what's the point?'. The Mediator Party is an attempt to allow people to be fully themselves, while knowing that their stated opinion will actually play a part in what happens. Understand this, simply asking the question, 'What do you think about this?', will likely lead a good number of people to educate themselves on that topic. This knowledge will then get shared with family and friends and so on and so forth. We need to give people a reason to be informed, before judging them for being uninformed."

The purple-haired girl who called me a prick is still loitering around the outskirts. She watches, but never says a word.

Finally, she enters the fray.

"What about Social Democracy?" she asks.

I look at her, "What about it?"

"Well look at the Nordic countries. It's clearly the ideal. If we move to your system, we'll never achieve it."

"Clearly?"

"What?"

"I'm taking issue with the word 'clearly'. Why is it so clearly the ideal?"

"Have you seen the World Happiness Report?"

"Okay, so you want to be like Finland?"

"Of course."

"So what's the first step? Get rid of all the black people?"

She is taken aback.

I say, "To be fair, Finland is nearly one percent black, so we won't have to get rid of all of them. Just the vast majority. Ninety... ninety-five percent."

"That is not what I was saying."

"Sure."

The woman considers my point.

"You're saying it's apples and oranges," she says.

"I'm saying it's apples and... couch cushions. Not even remotely the same thing."

"They're not that far off."

"Really. You're suggesting that racial differences in America is a minor problem? A little addendum that's hardly worth considering?"

"No, I'm not saying that," she says.

"That troubling history that is prevalent here and not so much there couldn't possibly be a major factor in the happiness differential?"

"Maybe it does play a part," she says, frustrated.

"Maybe?"

"But that doesn't mean that Social Democracy isn't a good thing. I think it's a very good thing."

"Are you a student?" I ask.

"Yes," she says, managing to seem offended by the question.

"Where?"

"OU."

"And where are you from?"

"I'm from here."

"Okay. So, you're paying about 12,000 dollars a year on tuition. If you were from out of state it would be three times that. Would you like to guess who's paying the difference?"

I look around the room.

I say, "Raise your hand if you pay taxes in the state of Oklahoma."

I raise my hand. So does every onlooker.

"Did you go to public school?"

"I did," she says.

"Twelve years of free schooling. Who do you think paid for that?"

I raise my hand. Unprompted, so does everyone else.

"Ever visit a public library? We bought you that right."

She shakes her head in a lazy attempt to invalidate my point.

I continue, "You know what SoonerCare is? That provides medical care for low income families. We also have state-run homeless shelters. State run elder care. Food stamps. Monetary aid. State mandated unemployment compensation. Worker's comp. Our government even regulates for-profit businesses like OG&E, limiting how much they can charge. Why? In the interest of the public welfare, that's why. And this is all just Oklahoma. You wanna go federal, we can talk about Social Security, Medicare, Medicaid, Minimum wage, Disaster relief... Do you want me to go on? The question isn't 'Can we achieve Social Democracy?'... We already have it. The question is, 'How much of it do we want?'. Which, in my estimation, is a question best left to the people. It's also a question the Mediator Party will be sure to ask."

"So, we could become like the Nordic states?"

"If the populace wills it, sure. If the votes say we need more social welfare, then the Mediator Party will do its best to make it so. Next time around, if the voters say it's gone too far, we will then pull it back."

"See. That's the problem."

"The People will have the reins. If that's a problem, if you don't like that, it's because you are an aspiring Autocrat. Which is all the Republicans and Democrats have become... aspiring Autocracies."

"You think my Party is an aspiring Autocracy?"

"Don't take my word for it. They're proving it daily. You've got only half the Senate, plus the tie breaker. Last month you managed to pass 1.9 trillion, that's *trillion*, in Covid Relief without a single Republican vote. No attempt to negotiate or take their views into account. None of that. Because you didn't have to. And you're about to do it again on a so-called infrastructure bill for a few *trillion* more. The only problem you got is that one guy on your own team might have an issue with it."

"I hate Joe Manchin!" she says.

"Maybe you should hate the Democrats. For not practicing Democracy in good faith. For completely ignoring half our representatives."

"The Republicans would do the same if they could!" She argues.

"Yeah, they would. That's my whole point. Hate them both! Hate everybody that thinks they know what's best. Which is just another way of saying 'Hate everybody'. Because we all seem to think that, don't we? But we're all wrong!"

I turn away from the young lady and begin addressing the entire store. A couple people appear to be recording me. Customers who had nothing to do with my book reading have taken notice and I engage them too.

"We need to work together or it's all gonna fall apart. People think, 'No, that can't happen. Not here', but I'm telling you it can. Did you think Trump could ever really happen? Cause he did. That man was our President. Did you think an entire summer of riots in every major city could happen? It did. Did you think CHAZ or CHOP or whatever they called themselves could happen? Who here thought that Abolishing the Police would ever become a valid political argument? Somehow it did. How about January 6th? Anybody see that coming? It happened. Tell me you don't see the cracks forming. Right now, this minute, we are structurally unsound. Our government, our country, is faltering and it has been for a while now. Somebody has to do something. I know you don't want that somebody to be you. I don't either. I'd rather just live my life. But goddamnit, if the people of this country don't stand up, we are going to lose something very precious. And make no mistake, The People is us. It's me. And it's you."

I return my gaze to the purple-haired girl.

"It's you," I say again.

On the coffee table sit the remains of the Mediator Party sign up forms. I pick one up and place it on a hard cover book. I take it to the purple-haired girl, presenting it to her with one hand and offering a pen with the other.

"Do this with me."

She looks at what I'm offering her for a long moment. Finally, she steps forward, and accepts the challenge.

Four hours have passed and I find myself at a bar. The alcohol is beginning to make its presence known, humming through my blood and into my brain.

I sit at a booth with my most trusted members of the Mediator Party, my planted audience members, who seconded my call for change. Sitting next to me is April. She is my age, somewhere in the realm of forty. Something about her company is quite enjoyable. She's all rough edges, wearing jeans, a simple t-shirt, and short spiky hair cut like a boy.

I'm quite certain if she were growing up today, someone would try to convince her that she was non-binary. I like to think her younger self would laugh in that person's face.

She is often loud and brash and funny as hell.

Across from April is Lonnie. He's two years removed from college and still carries the 'Bro' culture from his years in the fraternity. You can hear it in his laugh and you can see it in the way he chugs his drinks. Upon meeting him, it was clear that he was lost in this adult world. He needed something and so I gave it to him. To keep him, I will need to foster his endless need for camaraderie. Any work I give him will need to be a team sport, full of love and laughter.

Next to Lonnie and across from me is the girl with the purple hair. Her name is Scarlet. The very first mind that I ever changed. She may well have been the first to ever read my book. She found it on Amazon while researching an assignment on political systems. She finished it in less than a day. Come the next morning, I had an email in my inbox.

She is four months early to the bar scene, but in our company no one bothered to card her. She quietly nurses her beer. I watch her, captivated by every little nuance. She does that to me. I don't know why. I don't just see her or hear her, I experience her.

She's not even old enough to drink. Which makes me twice her age.

April says, "Oh man, I am still jazzed from that. That was amazing!"

"Yeah it was," Lonnie adds. "We got thirty-two signatures! I even got a few employees."

"Nice!" I say, and high-five Lonnie across the table.

"You were killin' it, dude," Lonnie says. "Had 'em eating out of the palm of your hand!"

"I'm telling ya, there's something about watching someone get converted right before your eyes. Something powerful about it." I look at Scarlet. "But it wouldn't have worked if you hadn't sold it."

"That was easy. All I had to do was remember who I was before I read that damn book."

"Damn book? Why's it gotta be a 'damn' book?"

"I don't know," she says. "I kinda liked being an autocrat. You took that from me."

"My apologies."

"I forgive you. For now."

She gives me a little smile and it fills me with so many things that I don't know what to do with.

I say, "I forgot to tell you guys, I got an email this morning. Could be an asshole yankin' my chain, but something about it seemed legit. I don't know. Could mean real money. Take us to the next level."

"You mean we might actually get paid?" April asks

"Love it! Show me that green!" Lonnie says.

April and Lonnie high-five.

"Alright, let's not get crazy now," I say. "Volunteer work is so much more rewarding."

"To hell with that!" April says, downing a shot. "Show me that green!"

April and Lonnie laugh while completing yet another high-five. They try to include Scarlet, but she's off in another world.

April looks at Scarlet. "What's wrong with you? You're never this quiet."

Scarlet looks up from the beer she's staring at. She doesn't look sad or bothered. Serene, I would say.

"I don't know. I guess I'm just reveling in this feeling."

"What feeling?" April asks.

"You don't feel it?" Scarlet asks. She looks at me, "You don't feel it?"

"I cannot confirm nor deny," I say. "At least until you say more words."

"It's like electricity or something. I don't know, it feels like I'm connected to something. Something bigger than me. Bigger than all of us. This is real. We're actually doing this. And it's gonna work, I can feel it. We're gonna change the world."

"Yeah we are!" Lonnie says.

"I like the sound of that," I say.

April says, "I do too, but we need to slow our roll. Remember the plan. Stay focused. It's all about the state."

"Party pooper," Lonnie says.

"Am I wrong?" April says, looking to me.

"You're right. We gotta stay on target." I say.

"I know," Scarlet says. "I'm just having a moment."

I continue, "We have less than nineteen months until the midterms. Nineteen months to set the stage. The clock is ticking. We take the state. One of the reddest states in the union. That's proof of concept. After that, there won't be any stopping us. We take the whole country!"

"Hell yeah," Lonnie says.

We each raise our drinks and clink glasses.

7

OCTOBER 13, 2023
30 MONTHS LATER

Just like it sounds, Debbie's Disco Diner has been around for quite some time. It opened in '74, to be exact, just a few years before I took my first breath.

A framed photograph near the entrance shows the owner, her arms thrown triumphantly into the air. She stands in front of the building with colorful balloons and a banner reading GRAND OPENING hanging overhead. She is flanked on both sides by her staff of smiling waitresses dressed in matching uniforms of colorful bell-bottomed jumpsuits.

As I make my way to my regular table, I see the owner through the kitchen service window. Her triumphant posture and toothy smile have been lost to the rigors of time. The corners of her lips appear to be permanently turned downward. Even as she speaks, the frown is clearly evident. It's as if her skin reformed around her most consistent emotional display.

My waitress gives me a nod as she delivers drinks to an older couple across the way. The disco jumpsuits are nowhere to be seen, replaced by simple jeans and whatever T-shirt the waitress pulled from her closet that morning.

"Usual?" she asks, hustling back toward the kitchen.

She doesn't bother to stop or even look at me.

"Yep," I respond.

A formerly fantastic array of disco colors are painted in large geometric shapes along the walls. The presumably once bright and vibrant yellows and purples and reds and blues have clearly faded and dulled over the years. A mirrored disco ball hangs unceremoniously from the ceiling. Its thousands of little mirrored surfaces have lost their reflective luster due to a layer of visible dust clinging to the surface.

Autographed pictures of John Travolta, The Bee Gees, Donna Summer and various other disco icons are scattered about the place. Their images are frozen in time, no hint of the wrinkles they currently hold or the coffins some now inhabit. The lively tunes that I imagine once emanated from the speakers have long ago been displaced by a selection of soft rock muzak.

It's the kind of place you go when you've decided you don't much like people and you prefer your servers to feel the same.

Each morning I come here, eat my simple breakfast, sip my subpar coffee, and revel in this wasteland of unfulfilled promise. This is who I've become in the aftermath of the first Tuesday after the first Monday of November, better known as Election Day

"You excited?!" Morgan asks. He arrives as he always does, suddenly and without my permission.

As per usual, he takes a seat across from me despite the lack of invitation.

I say, "To see you? Always. After all, it's such a rare occurrence... you accosting me every morning."

Morgan is a tall, skinny man who always seems just a bit too chipper. A bit too talkative. A bit too ever-present. He's wearing the same thing he always does – Khaki pants and a polo shirt with the insignia MT CONSTRUCTION sewn into the left breast pocket.

"Come on, you know what I'm talking about," he assures me.

I just look at him.

"You don't remember? Are you kidding? Today's the day I change your life forever."

"That's not necessarily a good thing. The easiest way to change someone's life is to do something really bad. You're not armed, are you?"

"No."

"Then please tell me what we're talking about."

"My God. You really don't remember."

"But I am listening."

"Today's the day!"

"Yes, you've said that. Today's the day."

"Not the day. The date! Today's the date. You agreed to let me set you up on a date."

"I sarcastically agreed."

Morgan frowns, "That's not how I remember it."

"Morgan, I was clearly employing sarcasm. It was very clear."

"Mmm?"

"Let me see if I can remember what I said. Oh yeah, 'Sure, you can set me up on a blind date and maybe afterwards you can chop off my fingers one by one'. Does that sound familiar?"

"It does. I have to apologize, I haven't scheduled the second part, but the date is set my friend. Tonight, nine o'clock, at *Bromeo's*. Remember, her name is Melody and she'll be the girl with the yellow bow in her hair."

"Why don't you just show me her picture? Then I'll know her when I see her."

"Because that's not the way this works, William. You've got to see her for the first time. Her beauty washes over you. And you'll remember that moment for the rest of your life. Don't forget who you're talking to. I am an expert at this."

"So you've said."

"No less than three marriages have taken place due to my exceptional skills."

"No less than three? That sounds like three. I mean, if it were more, you'd say a higher number, right?"

"I'm leaving room for more love to grow."

"Okay, so we can agree that the number, currently, is three. How many divorces?"

"What?"

"Of those three, how many divorces?" I ask.

"Look, I find love connections. It's what I do. I don't know how I do it, I just-"

"How many divorces?"

"It's a different skill-set, William. I'm not a marriage counselor. I can't be expected to maintain healthy relationships."

"I've already had one divorce. I don't need another."

"I saw you the day you got divorced. That's the happiest you've ever looked."

"Let me get this straight. Are you suggesting that I should get married, live miserably for… years probably, so that I can eventually find happiness through divorce?"

"I'm just spit-balling here."

The waitress arrives with my coffee and food.

"Thank you," I say. "I'm starving. I could eat my weight in pancakes."

"Anything else?" the waitress asks.

"No. This… is perfect."

I catch a glimpse of movement near the entrance. I look to find three men entering. Two bulky and tough looking men in suits are accompanying a much smaller, much frailer, looking man.

The smaller man immediately surveys his surroundings. He's looking for something. The man's name is Simon and that something is me.

I return my attention to Morgan.

"Uhh… I'm gonna need you to find another place to be."

"Huh?" Morgan says.

"I appear to have a visitor."

"So you want me to…"

"Yes, Morgan, I want you to… fuck off."

"Well that doesn't seem like the nicest way-"

"I don't have the energy for this. If I promise to show up for your stupid date, will you just go?"

"Sure. I can do that."

"Thank you," I say.

Yet he just sits there, motionless.

"What are you doing?"

"I'm waiting," Morgan says, expectantly.

I just look at him.

Morgan says, "You said, *'if* I promise to show-' "

"I promise to show up for the stupid date. Happy?"

"Well you said 'if' the first time. It's not like you actually made a promise."

"But I've made it now. Okay? I get it. You can go."

Morgan shakes his head and slides out of the booth.

He grumbles, "Seems like that was a lot harder than it had to be."

Morgan finally walks away. He eyes Simon as they pass. Simon's bodyguards eye him. Morgan quickly looks away and finds himself another table.

Simon approaches my table and we meet eyes.

"You're a hard man to find."

I shrug, "I've never had any trouble."

Without me offering, Simon helps himself to the seat across from me. The man always seems a little bit tipsy or high or in some way less than sober. I don't know if it's alcohol or pills or just the strange effects of being one of the richest men in all the world. Whatever it is, he has a tendency toward the dramatic.

"Would you like to know where I just was?" Simon asks.

"I prefer to mind my own business."

"I was at the offices of the Mediator Party."

"Oh yeah? How they doing over there?"

"I would think you should have that information. You are, after all, the leader of the Mediator Party. Imagine my surprise when I find out you haven't stepped foot in the building in over eleven months."

"I left the building in good hands."

"To my understanding you didn't even make an appearance in February."

"February?"

"Four elections. Oklahoma City Council."

"Right, right."

"All of which you lost."

"I'm focusing my attentions on other Party matters."

"From what I hear, you're building a house. Forgive me, but that doesn't sound like a Party matter. Sounds like a personal matter."

"First of all, I am not building a house. The house already exists. I'm simply renovating it."

"That hardly changes the thrust of my argument."

"Are we in an argument?"

"Yes. We are."

Simon levels his gaze upon me. There is no mistaking his disapproval.

"Okay, look, I understand you're upset."

"Wait," Simon throws a finger up. "I don't think I like it in here."

Simon looks around, judging the place.

I say, "I guess you could always buy it. Change it to your liking."

"I could, couldn't I? Ehh, I don't really care to own property in this state. Truth be told, you're the only reason I visit."

"I'm flattered."

"Why don't we step outside. Let's have a smoke."

I light a cigarette as we turn the corner into the alley beside the restaurant. One of the bodyguards produces a cigar and takes great care in cutting off the tip. I try to imagine how much that cigar must cost, but honestly I don't have a clue. The bodyguard produces an expensive lighter and proceeds to hold the tip of the cigar over the flame, but not actually touching the flame. Apparently we are going to rely on extremely hot air to eventually do the job. He twists the cigar between his fingers, seeking out the perfect burn.

It is taking a very long time.

Simon seems enthralled with the process, watching astutely and ignoring me completely.

From time to time, the bodyguard waves the cigar around with a flourish of his hand, before again returning it to just above the flame. This process repeats itself over and over.

And over again.

I'm half way through my cigarette when the bodyguard finally hands over the perfectly rendered cigar to an eager Simon. Simon blows softly on the burning end, gives his own little hand flourish, and stuffs it into his mouth. He intakes the smoke and lets it waft out.

"Mmm. Nice work, Thomas."

The bodyguard gives an appreciative nod.

Simon turns to look at me.

"So, you were saying that you understood how upset I am."

"I didn't say 'how'. I know you're upset. I wouldn't presume to know how upset."

"Would you like to guess?"

"I'm upset too, Simon. Working with my hands is therapeutic. It helps me think. And me thinking is what we need right now. It's what you need. It's what The Party needs. You saw the debacle that was election night. You should see the need for me to put my thinking cap on."

Simon's demeanor softens. He looks at me like a proud father.

"Election night. You know what I saw? I saw the first glimpses of success. I saw an upstart political party secure three victories in its first ever election."

"Out of sixty-eight campaigns."

"We put someone in the State House. You know how long it took the Libertarians to elect someone to state level legis-"

"Seven years, I know. I also know what the Libertarians do for a living. They lose, Simon. They throw a damn party when they get two percent of the presidential vote. Which, by the way, has happened exactly once. One time, in fifty years. You might take a pause before emulating the Libertarian Party, cause we don't have that kind of time. This country will be a wasteland in fifty years."

"And you're thinking," Simon points out.

"In 1919, Adolf Hitler became the fifty-fifth member of the German Workers' Party… in its political infancy. Fifteen years later, he was the Fuhrer. The unquestioned leader of the country."

"So that's who we want to emulate? Adolf Hitler?"

"Not the man," I say. "The timeline. It just shows what's possible."

"I'm at a loss for words, William. I don't know how to respond to your admiration of Adolf Hitler. Maybe thinking is the wrong move for you."

"Not just thinking. I'm studying the landscape. I'm reading. I'm planning."

"What are you reading? Mein Kampf?"

"The Art of War, actually. I have to start thinking like a general."

"A general?"

"Seek to fight, only after victory is assured. A proper plan can bring victory before a single shot is fired. Proper planning is the only way forward."

"Eleven months?"

"It's a complex battlefield. There are so many fronts. So many campaigns to consider. Not just political campaigns, campaigns to put a real dent in the Two-Party System. It's not a minor undertaking. It's a war, Simon. It really is."

"And war requires money," Simon says. "Am I right thinking that?"

"Absolutely. Funding is a major consideration."

"And where do you get this funding?"

"Well, currently we have a number of avenu-"

Simon cuts me off. He dramatically raises his hand up and feverishly points down at his own head, while dancing a sort of jig.

"AND WHERE DO YOU GET THIS FUNDING?!"

"You're referring to yourself."

"Ahh, you caught that. Good man. What is it going to do to all of your planning when this funding suddenly goes the way of the Dodo bird?"

"You don't want to do that."

"I increasingly do. Sadly, you and your stupid mouth have made me a believer in things I previously accepted were out of my control. I don't like things being out of my control. It feels good to think I might actually have the power to fix... this. I don't want to go back to accepting my impotence. But I'm at a crossroads, William. I can't watch myself go broke, while you think."

"I know how much money you have. Forbes told me how much money you have. The amount you're pledging will never put you in the poor house."

"But I'm not getting any richer! That's what people like me do. They get richer. But not me. Not since I met you."

Simon comes toward me, while producing a folded up piece of paper from his pocket. He presses it into my chest.

"What is this?" I ask.

"That is a list of engagements you will happily be attending."

Simon walks off toward the parking lot. I follow while reading the list.

"Membership drives. Fundraising. Podcasts?"

"Each and every one," Simon tells me.

"The timing is wrong."

"Take the loss, William. I will allow you to think, but you're gonna have to learn to chew gum and gaze your navel at the same time."

"Some of the greatest victories come unopposed. Now is the time to position ourselves. To rack up quiet victories, not beat our chests. Our enemies practically don't even know we exist."

Simon stops and turns to face me.

"They know you exist. You've won elections for God's sake. You've written books on the matter."

"Books that nobody reads but intellectual blow-hards."

"I've read them," Simon protests. "Am I an intellectual blow hard?"

"Yes, Simon. You are not of the public sphere. Podcasts are a different beast. *These* podcasts in particular. You're talking about announcing ourselves on a national stage. It's the wrong time."

"A great general adjusts to the contours of the battlefield," he says. "Sun Tzu eat your heart out!"

Simon steps forward and wraps his arms around me. He holds me close for several seconds, gives me a final awkward squeeze, then pulls back. He lovingly grasps my shoulders and smiles at me.

"It was good to lay eyes on you, William. You're one of my favorite people. Now get your ass to work!"

Simon steps toward his limo, a bodyguard hustling to open the door.

"My eggs are cold!" I yell at him.

He throws a dismissive wave over his shoulder without looking back. I watch as they file into the limo and drive away. I imagine they are headed directly to Wiley Post Airport and an awaiting private jet.

I look at the list in my hand.

"Shit."

Morgan sticks his head out of the restaurant.

"Was that Simon Petit? Were you just hugging Simon Petit? I'm never buying your breakfast again."

"You never bought my breakfast before."

I head back into the restaurant, where my cold eggs await.

"And now I never will," Morgan says.

"You know, Morgan, I just realized that I don't know you outside of this restaurant. I could completely remove you from my life by simply finding another place to eat."

8

I roll the window down and let the night air swirl around me as I travel down the neon lit road. I am surrounded by life. The lights draw them in like moths every night. A whole society at play right outside the confines of my truck. I can hear their loud music, their incessant chatter, their braying laughs… All of it running together like a poorly conducted orchestra.

Since Election Day last year, I have all but removed myself from society. The bulk of my social circle consists of waiters and waitresses, grocery store clerks, and whoever happens to be working the register at my local hardware store. And Morgan. With few exceptions, these are the extent of my human interactions. Even these are rare, as I make use of the self-check option whenever possible.

Tonight will be different. Tonight, I, William Waxman, have a date, if you can call it that. En route to that very date now, I can't help but feel a tightness in my chest. I try to ignore it, but it's there. I light up a cigarette and try to calm my nerves.

I rev the engine as I pass a coasting sports car with the top down. The girl in the passenger seat yells something I don't understand, rises up in her seat, and lifts her top. The young girl unveils her recently sprouted sexuality while releasing the primal scream of youth. A throng of liquored-up onlookers return her call from the open-air section of one of the many bars that line the road. Crowne Boulevard is full of these types, slowing traffic, *Cruisin' the Crowne*, as they say. Six lanes of traffic, three in each direction, separated by a median with regularly scheduled cutouts, make it easy to simply drive around in drunken circles…

The cops don't seem to mind. As long as the city gets their cut, I guess. Between general sales tax and the various tariffs imposed on liquor and marijuana and whatever-the-hell-else, I can only imagine the endless dollars filling the coffers of our various minders.

I don't get the opportunity to witness the girl's breasts. All I see is her bare back as I speed past. I see a trace of thong partially obscuring a single tattoo just above her ass crack, a common placement that has earned its own special nickname – *The Tramp Stamp*. When I first started hearing that term, I expected the numbers of women choosing to bare it would dwindle. A couple of decades later, I have been proven wrong, women lining up at tattoo parlors across the nation, eager to be branded a tramp.

As I pass the bare-chested girl, I pump the accelerator once more. I check the side-view to witness the self-proclaimed tramp break out into a sudden convulsive coughing fit. Her fit is no doubt fueled by the toxic fumes spewed from the tail pipe of my ancient truck. I laugh a little, but beneath that laughter sits a twinge of guilt.

I strongly believe in balance... in all things. By my own standards, I should be seeking to counteract any imbalance that I find. One only need open their eyes to see – we are an ecosystem out of balance.

Not long after Election Day, this led me to a dealership specializing in Electric Vehicles. I liked what I found there, whizzing along quietly on a test drive. I marveled at the engineering that could lead to such an experience. It was clearly a powerful machine, and yet they had somehow channeled all that power into a calm and serene experience. It was impressive.

On that same test drive, I saw an old 1980's Ford F-150 parked in the lot of a grocery store. A phone number was written out in white shoe polish across the windshield. 4 SALE - $800 obo.

Perhaps if the light hadn't been red I would have cruised by without a second thought. Perhaps then I could have made that salesman's day. Perhaps then I could have become a proper steward of Mother Earth. But the light was red, so perhaps it was fate.

The salesman was sitting in the passenger seat, blathering on about this and that. I couldn't hear a word. I just stared at that beat up relic, transfixed. The dented body. The faded blue paint. The gas guzzling engine that I knew resided under the hood. I couldn't take my eyes off of it.

"Green light," the salesman had to tell me.

Back at the dealership, I told the man I had to think about it. I walked away and quickly dialed the number, which I had memorized without even trying. The voice on the other end said he could meet me in twenty minutes.

The voice belonged to a plump old man with white hair and a sun-dried face.

"Looks like you already got a set of wheels," the man said with an admiring whistle.

He was referring to the 2020 Mercedes S-Class. A car that spoke to my status. That garnered me envy. That left me empty.

I told him, "It's a lease and I'm ready to take it back."

"Hold on now. I thought maybe you needed a side vehicle. You're trying to replace *that*... with *this*?"

I nodded.

"I'm afraid you're gonna be disappointed," he said, handing me the keys, "But what the hell, let's go for a ride."

"I'd rather go by myself, if you don't mind."

The man looked wary.

"Tell you what," I said. "Why don't you go for a ride of your own?"

I held out my fob and offered it to him, dangling it like a forbidden treat.

A big smile formed, his wrinkles shifting like ripples on a pond.

"You for real?"

"I'll meet you back here in exactly fifteen minutes," I said.

I slid inside the cab of the pickup and for a moment searched for the button to start the engine. But, of course, there was no button. I shook my head and stabbed the key into place. I expected it to cough and whirr as I turned the ignition, but instead it roared to life. I shifted into drive and could actually feel the primitive transmission drop into gear. The entire truck seemed to shake and rattle and vibrate on some long lost frequency. It felt like a caged animal, dying to break free.

The truck crawled forward, louder and louder, as I eased on the pressure. I found my way to the main street and put my foot down hard.

I could see the toxic fumes rising from the hood. I could even taste it on my tongue. The growl of the engine filled my ears. The power of it reverberated through my entire being. It all seemed to resonate so clearly, as if this beast and I had become one animal. I felt in tune. In tune with this beast. In tune with myself. In tune with the world, viewed through a dirty cracked windshield.

But more than anything, it was the smell. This was the smell of unbridled power. It was the smell of destruction. The smell of a warming planet. The smell of setting fire to your own home and sitting down on the couch to watch it fucking burn.

It was intoxicating.

Roaring down that street, I looked around at the world that we'd created. I looked at the men. I looked at the women. I looked at the either-ors and the neither-nors. I looked at the buildings we chose to erect and the signs of all the things we liked to buy and sell. I looked at everything. Every ad. Every product. Every church steeple. Every piece of trash that littered the ground. And I knew, without question... this smell... was the smell that we deserved.

A few minutes later I was handing over eight hundred dollars. I didn't bother to negotiate.

It's eleven months later and I still love that smell. I push in the truck's built-in lighter, wait for it to pop, and light myself a cigarette. I take a deep drag and hold it in. I let the tar settle into my lungs before blowing out what remains.

The bar scene slips into my rear view and traffic lightens up a bit. I see the sign for my destination – *Bromeo's*.

I wonder if that's someone's name or if it's an amalgamation of 'Bro' and 'Romeo'. I'm hoping it's not some kind of theme restaurant. Or if it is, not an obnoxious one.

I pull into the lot and find it about half full. Easy parking. I finish my smoke and toss it out the window.

Walking toward the front entrance, I see a family of large people entering the place. When I say large, I really mean fat. Not quite obese, just generally bigger than they ought to be. Your basic American family. One of them, a guy in his fifties, is holding the door for the rest of them. The last one, a boy who might be twelve, waddles through.

I'm still a good 20 feet away and yet the man continues to hold the door. He looks at me, expectant.

I stop.

He makes a gesture with his hand, waving me inside, as if maybe I'm confused by the whole situation. Which, I guess, maybe I am. I am confused as to why he's still standing there. I'm confused as to why he has the urge to help someone who obviously doesn't need it. Does he actually think that what he's doing is helpful? Does it make him feel better about whatever sins he commits behind closed doors? Does it help him to convince himself that he's a decent person? Or maybe he just enjoys that little slice of power, knowing that his actions will prompt me to speed up my gait and hustle to accept his supposed kindness. Is it control? Is that what he's after?

"No, you go ahead," I tell him. "I'm kind of a wiz at opening doors. I don't mean to brag, but it's always just come easy to me."

The man looks at me strangely.

"You too, it seems," I say. "Very impressive. You have nothing more to prove."

The man grimaces, shakes his head, and goes inside.

I manage to walk the next twenty feet and open the door without incident. Entering the restaurant, I see the aforementioned family discussing their needs with the hostess. I take a moment to look around and realize that I've been here before.

This was *Julio's*. A Mexican restaurant that I remember enjoying back in my early twenties. The decor is different, but otherwise it looks the same. There's a dining area on the left, another dining area on the right, and a large rectangular bar in the middle. I always sat on the right. It was the smoking section, back before the world passed judgment.

My eyes go to the bar. There are several patrons in small groups scattered around it. At the far end, sits a woman wearing a yellow bow in her hair. She sits alone, staring down at her phone. She raises the phone, screws up her face, and snaps a picture of herself.

The face she makes appears to be a comical representation of anticipation, fear, and anxiety.

She looks at the screen, frowns, and does the whole routine over again. Apparently satisfied this time, she types something in and, I assume, sends her image out into the ether.

I have never in my life taken a selfie. Not one. I'm very proud of this fact. That said, I have co-starred in a few. My former wife would periodically require me to make an appearance next to her… kissing her cheek or snuggling in close with happy eyes and a beaming smile. When I say "Co-Star", you can take that literally.

It was a show.

And I was acting.

Since the divorce, I have taken a solemn vow never to act again.

The woman with the yellow bow takes a drink and continues to stare at her phone. She smiles to herself. She must have gotten a 'Like' or a 'thumbs up' or whatever else people are striving for these days. I study her. Most people would describe her as attractive or pretty. A few might even say beautiful.

I consider my next move. Who is this person? What does she need?

Every person, each and every one, has constructed a canvas on which to paint themselves. They are not a blank canvas, as the work has already begun. But many of them, in fact, most of them, are unhappy with the art that is themselves. The portrait they have created is lacking. Something's missing. It feels wrong, shallow, lacking the depths to which they aspire. With few exceptions, the paintings fail to make use of their full canvas. They are but a few strokes around the center and a small collection of specks in the corner.

The trick is to see the picture they are attempting to conceive. To truly see it. Not just what it is, but what it wants to be. To study their painting is to learn them completely. Who they are, but more importantly, who they want to be. To see the boundaries of their canvas is to know where you can safely lead them, to understand who they are willing to become. To take their hand and guide their brush is to become their Teacher, their Hero, their Love. And, with some canvases... their God.

So... How can I become her God?

"Hello there. Are you meeting somebody?"

I look to find the petite little blond hostess. She has a nice smile on full display.

"...Or maybe a table for one?" she says. "Or of course you can always help yourself to a seat at the bar."

I steal another glance at the girl with the bow in her hair.

"You know," I say. "I think I might be leaning toward Taco Bell."

"You can't do that," the hostess says. "Our unbelievable shrimp Brochette is on special today. It's world famous!"

"Really? World famous?"

The hostess nods enthusiastically.

"So if I were to take a trip to France, they'd be talking about the shrimp that you serve right here?"

"Probably," she says earnestly. "It's really good."

"And how would they describe it?"

"Well... they would tell you that it's a beautiful jumbo shrimp, stuffed with spicy jalapeno and foamed cream cheese, wrapped in smokey bacon, and smothered in a tangy barbecue sauce. Though they would probably say it in French. I took Spanish."

She shrugs cutely.

My stomach calls out to me. I enjoy trying new food concoctions and the shrimp sounds... well, at the very least, interesting.

I say, "I need a table as far from the bar as you can possibly get it."

I'm happy to say that the Jumbo Shrimp Brochette is absolutely fantastic. I wasn't sure how that combination of ingredients would meld together, but I'll be damned if it isn't the best thing I've eaten in a long time. I was skeptical about the "world famous" bit, but now I'm thinking-

"What the hell?!" a voice says.

The voice is nearby. Very near. Despite the exclamatory nature of the words, they are delivered in a hushed tone. Like an irate librarian might sound.

The voice says, "What is this? You piece of shit! You're eating?"

I look to see the woman with the yellow bow standing beside my booth. She is the irate librarian. Suddenly, my shrimp-high is gone.

"Shit," I say.

I look over my shoulder and see the entrance to the restrooms behind me.

"The restrooms," I say aloud. "Son of a bitch."

I look at the woman with the yellow bow.... Melody.

"That was a tactical error on my part," I tell her.

"You left me sitting at the bar," Melody says. "You just let me sit there? I've been waiting for twenty minutes."

Normally, I might feel bad for my clear breach in etiquette, but this situation is anything but normal. Though this is the first time I've seen her in person, I've known Melody's face for some time now... ever since Morgan first made mention of her. She is a spy, intent on infiltrating the Mediator Party at the highest possible level. I know this to be true, because Morgan is a spy, though not a very good one. I long ago sniffed out his clumsy attempts to infiltrate my world.

I've constructed a number of possible outcomes to the events of this evening. My preference is to turn Melody away from her current master. To do this, I will need to pierce the veil of Melody the Spy, reach in and grab hold of Melody the Person.

I say, "Look, I understand your anger and I don't mean to minimize it, but here's what I don't understand... this was supposed to be a blind date. Completely blind. The only thing either of us was suppose to know was that you would be wearing a yellow bow."

"And…"

"And how did you know it was me?"

"Does that really matter right now?"

"It absolutely does," I tell her. "I never would've stayed to eat if I knew you could identify me. I'm not an asshole. I was seduced by that little blond girl, but I could've resisted. And if I had known, I would have. I would have fought through it."

"You would've fought through it?" she parrots.

"Yes. I would've left."

"You would've left? You would've stood me up, that's what you're saying. And somehow that makes you *not* an asshole. What world do you live in?"

I look back over my shoulder.

"I cannot believe I didn't think of the restrooms. Such an oversight."

I look at Melody. She stands there, fuming. I'm almost certain it's not an act. As planned, I believe I'm getting under her skin.

I say, "How did you know it was me?"

She goes spastic, snatching her phone from her purse and fumbling with it.

"When you were late, I asked Morgan to send me your picture."

She shoves the phone screen in front of my face. Sure enough, it's me playing Co-Star in another selfie. True to my vow, I didn't act in this one, clearly annoyed. The selfie's Star is Morgan.

"Happy?" Melody asks. "Can we get back to why you stood me up? Because I would really love to know."

"I really don't think you would," I tell her.

She looks at me with predictably murderous eyes, but there are other things to see in those eyes. Things that are deeper and harder to define.

Her anger is real, no question. Well, I guess there are a few questions… Is Melody the Person angry that I had the gall to stand her up? Or is Melody the Spy angry that I've made her job difficult? Or is it both? It's hard to know exactly what I'm reading in those eyes. Either way, regardless of her own duplicity, I'm certain Melody the Person is feeling a little insecure right about now.

I say, "I gotta be honest with you, I don't believe it's my place to tell a woman what she does or doesn't want, but as to why I stood you up... I don't think you want to know."

She says, "Well, thank you for your honesty. Now let me be honest with you. I don't really give a shit what you think!"

She emphasizes her point by sitting down firmly in the seat across from me. She stares at me, wild-eyed.

"Tell me. What was it? Am I not pretty enough? Is that it?"

I shrug, "How would I know?"

"You would know though, wouldn't you? I mean, you showed up, didn't you? You're here, aren't you?"

"That's true. I am here."

"And you looked at the bar. You found the girl with the yellow freakin' bow. You looked at her. And then... What? Not pretty enough?"

"Again, how would I know?"

"Jesus Christ! Am I having a stroke? What is wrong with you?"

"You're confused. Let me explain."

"That would be great."

"Let's imagine that me and you are sitting here having a conversation."

"Does that require imagination?" she asks.

"I wasn't finished. You've asked me to speak, yes? Is that what you want?"

"By all means..." She gestures that the floor is mine.

"As I was saying, we are sitting here having a conversation. And suddenly... you disappear."

"I'm sure you'd like that," she mumbles under her breath.

"And I don't mean disappear like you go off to some other dimension or cease to exist. I mean, you're still here, just not visible."

"Am I hiding?"

"No. You're not hiding. You've... you know... disappeared. You're... not visible."

"You mean IN-visible?"

"Yes!" I say. "Yes, exactly. You suddenly turn invisible. Now, here's the problem... If that were to actually happen, I'm not sure that I would even notice."

Melody's eyes flick toward me.

I'm definitely striking a nerve, pushing at the edge of her canvas.

"What the hell does that mean? I'm what?... Insignificant?"

"Maybe," I say. "But that's not what I'm getting at. You see, *you* are invisible. But just you. Just the things that are organically you."

She nods, "So my clothes are still visible?"

"Yes," I say. "Your clothes are absolutely still visible, because although you're wearing them, they are not you. Hence, your clothes are still here. And... So is your face. And your lips. And your eyebrows. And definitely those eyelashes. I hesitate to say *your* eyelashes. Though, technically I guess they are, because presumably you paid for them. Also, if I'm not mistaken, a good portion of *your* hair."

I pause for a moment, gauging her reaction. I look into her eyes and find them empty. *Keep going*, I tell myself. *Dig deeper.*

"You understand, right? You are invisible, but nothing has really changed. Everything I'm looking at, it's all still here."

She says nothing. Stone silent.

"Correct me if I'm wrong, but it looks like on top of all that, you're also wearing what I think they call... is it contouring make-up? Is that right? I think that's right.

"As hard as I try, Melody, I can't get my head around that. I mean, really, how much does someone have to hate themselves, to buy a product that promises to... at least to the eye... change the very shape of your face? Not only am I going to cover literally every facet of everything, but what I really need now is something that tricks people into thinking that my skull is formed differently than it actually is. We're talking some deep, deep issues here."

I feel like I've said enough. I stop and wait for her to speak. Still, she says nothing. I grab a shrimp and take a bite, attempting to patiently await her response.

I chew.

I swallow.

Still nothing.

She's not really even looking at me, staring off behind me. I realize that maybe she actually did need the restroom.

"Do you need to go pee or something?"

She takes a deep breath and shifts her eyes to me.

I say, "Okay, I get it, I'm an asshole, right? You're sitting here thinking that this is about me looking at you and deciding that you're not pretty enough. But what if that's not what this is? What if this is about *you* looking at *you* and deciding that the best course of action is to spend your money, your time, and your energy creating this elaborate disguise? Does that sound like someone you'd want to date?

"See, I'm not even sure that I'm guilty of standing you up. As far as I'm concerned neither one of us showed up to this damn thing. I was told I was going on a date with Melody. But where the hell is Melody, you know? I don't even know what she looks like, but I know I don't see her."

Again, I await her response. Her silence is unnerving. Again, I turn to Shrimp Brochette for comfort.

"You really gotta try these shrimp. These things are amazing! You need a drink? I'll get you a drink."

I raise my hand to flag down a waiter. Suddenly and without a word, Melody is out of her seat. She rushes away, toward the exit.

Melody is gone, not that she was ever really here.

There were always many possible outcomes to this so-called date. Her leaving was, of course, high up on the list. I wonder what Morgan's next move will be? This is the closest he's gotten to cultivating a relationship outside of breakfast. Perhaps he'll bring a fresh-faced version of Melody to the diner in the morning.

I have to admit, the prospect makes me smile. I was looking forward to exploring her canvas further.

A few moments and one shrimp later, the waiter arrives.

I say, "Can I get a box for this?"

9

I exit the restaurant, tomorrow's breakfast in hand. I turn down the walk and see the yellow bow.

Interesting. Perhaps the night isn't quite over.

She's leaning against a handicap parking sign, facing away from me toward the parking lot. I have no choice but to pass near her on my way to the truck. I can only assume this is intentional. She still has a job to do.

I hear a sniffle as I grow near. I can see over her shoulder. She's on her phone, a ride-sharing app on the screen. I hear another sniffle and she wipes her nose.

I say, "Well, here's the good news…"

Her body tenses at the sound of my voice. Is she acting? Is it real? It's hard to tell. I prop myself against the neighboring handicap parking sign.

"…They say the key to any healthy relationship is honesty."

She turns, red face and watery eyes.

"Are you kidding me?! Please leave me alone."

"Waiting for an Uber?" I ask. "I could give you a ride."

"Are you dense? I don't want to be anywhere near you. I certainly don't want to get into a car with you."

Melody stomps away. If she's acting, she's very good.

I say, "I know it's scary, but I would like to see you."

Strangely, I mean it. I so badly want to see the real Melody.

Melody stops. She turns and looks at me, studying me.

"My God. You are dense."

"Maybe," I say. "That's very possible."

I push myself off the handicap sign and take a couple steps in her direction. She takes a couple steps back.

"But for whatever reason, I want to see you. Not all this you got going on... *you*. Just you. That's what I want to see."

She appears lost somewhere between anger and confusion.

I walk slowly toward her, closing the distance between us.

"When's the last time someone really looked at you? No walls, no artifice, no bullshit standing between you and them. They looked at you and they saw... you. That's what I want. I want to see you, Melody. So I'm asking you a simple question. Do you want to be seen?"

Melody sits quietly in my passenger seat, the wind lifting her hair into crazy whirling circles. On a stretch of straight road, I find the opportunity to watch her for a moment. She appears to be in shock, like the victim of a violent crime.

Which Melody am I looking at? I truly believed I'd be able to tell. I'm quite good at reading people, exploring their canvas, and making them mine. It is a talent, I suppose, I had all along, lying dormant beneath the surface. I always seem to know exactly what is true... what is a lie... how to break them down... and build them back anew.

But in this moment, I simply can't tell.

I pull into a 24 hour drug store and find a nearly empty lot. I park it between the lines and turn to the zombie beside me.

"You want to come in?"

She doesn't look at me.

"I'll wait," she says softly.

"I'll leave the radio on for ya."

She says nothing.

An entire wall, stretching from one end of the store all the way to the other is completely devoted to an array of colorful cosmetic products.

I study the wall, walking the length of it, but find nothing there I want.

I turn around and find additional shelving units filled with foundations and lipsticks and eyeliners. I walk the length of the shelves, but again don't find what I'm looking for.

I turn the corner and enter the next aisle. The sheer volume and variety of products is leaving me slightly dizzy.

I find myself thinking about all the hours of labor devoted to simply affording the right to wear all this shit. I think about the countless hours spent applying it to one's face. I think about the women who refuse to even leave the house without first 'putting their face on'. I think about the permanent lip tattoos and injections and anti-aging creams. I think I want to kill myself again.

Finally, I find a display of products that are devoted to the removal of every other product. I study the individual boxes, reading the directions in an effort to learn the process. Several minutes later, I've collected a number of things that I think will do the job.

I approach the cash register and with each step the smell grows stronger. It is the pungent odor of homelessness. I revert to my COVID-19 social distancing protocols. The man at the register looks to be in his fifties, though I wouldn't be surprised if the streets have added a couple decades to his true age. I'm not sure if he's muttering to himself or making an honest attempt to communicate with the cashier.

The man is plastered. He obviously doesn't need the 'Forty' he's attempting to purchase with the pocketful of coins he's dumped all over the counter.

The cashier is a young woman with large breasts. I can tell that much, but any further features are a mystery to me. My eyes find nothing but the long fingernails that demand to be seen. 'Long' is definitely an understatement. The bright yellow talons extend no less than two inches from the ends of her fingers.

I watch as those awkward fingernails struggle to separate and count out the change that is littered across the counter. I listen to the sliding and clicking and clacking of metal and acrylic. It's excruciating. The drunk tries to help and it only gets worse, both participants failing to function any better than small children. I search for the comic value that I know must be there.

But I don't find it. These days it is getting harder and harder to find it.

Meanwhile, the cashier is having a conversation with another woman who appears to be taking inventory of the products they like to keep out of reach of customers.

"So do you like him?" the other woman asks. "Or is he just another dud?"

"Undetermined," Fingernails says. "But he's hot."

"Well that's something."

"Mmm hmm. Far from perfect... but..."

"But... he's hot!"

They snicker.

"Let's just say he's got potential," Fingernails says. "A few tweaks here and there..."

"Oh no. Don't even. You can't change a man. You best keep looking."

Finally, the transaction is complete and the drunk staggers off into the night.

Fingernails looks at me and I set my products onto the counter. She begins ringing them up, struggling to handle each item. She truly can't do anything easily. Such is the cost of beauty some might say.

I look to the woman who is keeping inventory. Her name tag says Kim.

"You know you're wrong about that," I say.

"I'm sorry?" Kim says.

"You can't change a man. That's not true," I tell her. "Now I'm not saying it's easy. It's a big undertaking and it has its difficulties, but if he loves ya... it can be done."

The two women give each other little secret smirks.

Kim says, "You really believe that?"

"Absolutely. You can change what he eats. What he watches on TV. The company he keeps. The way he dresses. Even the way he talks. And if you're really good, you can get him to drop whatever stupid dreams he may have. Get him to do the things he always promised himself he'd never do, like a soulless job with nice fat paychecks. I mean how else are you gonna afford that dream house, right? With four big bedrooms, the spacious master bath, and the kitchen that is just to die for. The trick is, you gotta be patient. If you take your time, do it right, he may not even know it's happening."

"It's twenty-three thirty-eight," Fingernails says.

I keep talking while reaching for my wallet.

"But there is one problem with that. You see, one day he might find himself staring into the mirror wondering who the hell that is looking back at him. And the longer he thinks about it, the more he'll remember. He'll think of all those little things, barely even noticeable at the time. The constant suggestions. The disapproving glances. The passive aggressive comments. The million or so little nudges.

"He'll remember a clear pattern that played out over many years and countless subject matters. How, at first he resisted, then he compromised, and eventually he acquiesced. He'll remember how it happened over and over and over until finally he stood in front of a mirror staring into the eyes of a stranger. And then maybe one night, while you're sleeping, he'll find himself standing over you. The blanket pushed down below your thighs. A sheen of perspiration coating the skin of your half naked body. Your chest rising and falling as he imagines his hands wrapping around your throat."

The women are staring at me, speechless.

I smile.

"But maybe you shouldn't worry about all that," I say. "Chances are he won't actually do it. More likely he'll just run to the store and buy his first pack of cigarettes in ten years. How much did you say it was?"

"Umm, Twenty-three Thirty-eight," Fingernails says.

I pull the credit card from my wallet. I look at the card and see my name spelled out on its surface. I look at the two women. Kim is staring at me, mouth open. Fingernails is uncomfortably studying her namesake. I look past them, to the wall, where a security camera studies me, unblinking.

"You know what, I think I'll pay cash."

The automatic doors release me to the parking lot. I look to the spot where I parked and find nothing but an empty space. I gaze across the lot and see my truck idling near the exit. I see her silhouette on the driver's side. There is no traffic to stop her from completing her escape. And yet the truck just sits there grumbling.

Am I witnessing a battle between Melody the Person and Melody the Spy? The Person is scared and so badly wants to escape. But the Spy won't let her.

Or...

Perhaps Melody the Spy has been eradicated.

All that is left is the raw emotions of an actual human being. A part of her wants to escape, but that is not her true desire. Perhaps, despite her fears, Melody wants what I'm offering her. She wants to be seen.

Whatever the case, it doesn't look like she's going anywhere.

I light a cigarette and start walking.

I open the passenger door and pull myself into the seat. Her head is bowed, resting against the steering wheel.

I say, "So, where do you want to go?"

"I don't know," she says.

I nod my head. She's nervous and second guessing the events that brought her here.

I ask her the only question I can think to ask. A question I sometimes ask myself.

"Do you want to wake up tomorrow the same person you were today?"

I see the slightest of twitches as my words meet her ears. So slight I wonder if maybe I imagined it. She sits there quietly, unresponsive. The question just sort of lingers in the air, mingling with the toxic fumes from the idling engine.

She inhales deeply, her body coming back to life. She raises her head and turns to look at me. Her watery eyes stare into mine. I think she's about to say something, but nothing comes out. This is the real Melody, I am sure of it. She simply looks at me, unblinking, like the security camera. It feels as if she's staring into my soul and inspecting what she finds. I look back at her, trying like hell not to hide.

I want her to see me too. At least part of me.

Melody guides my truck down the road.

Other than some sporadic directions, we never say a word. Strangely, the silence is not an uncomfortable one. It feels calm and inviting. For some reason, I believe it is the same for her.

"Take a right here," I tell her.

We coast down the street until we reach the home with the "SOLD" sign in the front yard. I tell her to pull into the driveway.

I exit the truck and walk toward the front door.

I have done very little work in the last eleven months. By 'work' I mean received pay for labor performed. That said, in that time I have performed more physical labor than the last 20 years added together.

And it all went to the same place – this house.

I step up onto the porch and turn back to see Melody still sitting behind the wheel of my truck. The engine is running. It's not too late to turn back. She continually chooses to move forward, but only after waging an internal battle with herself.

The keys to the house are on the same ring that holds the truck key. So I simply wait and watch as the battle unfolds.

They say that a man's biggest fear is to be the victim of a woman's ridicule.

Embarrassed... humiliated... emasculated...

While a woman's biggest fear is to be the victim of a man's violence.

Beaten... raped... murdered...

I wonder if that's what she's thinking about. Is she imagining me beating her?... Raping her?... Killing her?... Are there visions of violence dancing through her head?

I wonder what she sees. Am I overpowering her? Is she trying to fight back? Trying to scream?

But my hands are too strong. The weight of my body too heavy.

Can she feel my hands gripping her neck? Can she feel the air cut off from her lungs?

Can she hear the silence of her own screams? The rip of her dress? The grunts of her attacker?

I see these things. I wonder if she sees them too. I believe she does.

She sees my potential.

And yet she moves forward.

The sound of the idling truck dies off as Melody shuts down the engine. The door swings open and she steps out. She walks to me and hands over the keys.

I unlock the door and hold it open for her.

She hesitates for just a moment and steps inside.

"Oh my God," she says. "This is amazing."

I study her face and body, searching for the lie. I see no deception. She seems honestly moved by my work.

I shut the front door and lock it.

Her eyes wash over the space, taking it all in. The open floor plan. The dark stained woodwork. The meticulously tiled fireplace. The polished concrete counter tops, embedded with bits of green glass.

"The wood floors are beautiful," she says. "I love the way it feels. It's like a piece of art."

She begins studying the individual details. I too, take it all in. I feel a sense of pride well up in me. There's something beautiful about committing your time and sweat to the act of creating something with your own hands.

"You must've spent a fortune," she says. "I think you overbuilt. How much did you sell it for?"

As always, it all comes back to money. That thing that drives us. That thing that rips the passion right out of our souls.

"That's not why I did it," I tell her.

She looks at me, but says nothing.

"Come on," I say, leading her down the hall.

She follows.

I lead her to the bathroom door and gesture for her to enter. She hesitates, but does as I ask. She looks around at the luxurious bathroom that I built.

"Oh man! I would kill for a shower like that."

I set the drug store bag down and empty its contents onto the vanity.

Melody is facing away, marveling at the shower. I take her by the arms and turn her to face the mirror. Her body tenses at my touch, but she doesn't fight me.

"Don't move," I tell her.

Her eye's leave her reflection and study her surroundings.

She says, "I love the paint color you ch-"

"Stop talking," I say.

She stiffens. Her angry eyes meet mine in the mirror.

"If you have real words, you can use them," I tell her. "But that's not what you were doing. You're trying to distract yourself from this moment. Don't. Just be here."

I slip the shrug off of her shoulders, dropping it to the floor. Goose bumps cover her exposed arms.

She takes a deep breath and her stiff body slowly softens.

Standing behind her, I remove the yellow bow and set it aside. I run my fingers through her hair and then begin massaging her skull. I glance to the mirror to see her. She attempts to hide her discomfort, but it's clearly on display.

I see her fear. Fear of embarrassment. Fear of being judged. Fear of my intentions. Fear of me, plain and simple.

My fingertips find what they are looking for. I can feel the base of the many hair extensions clipped into place. I snap a clip loose and carefully remove a bit of her facade. I set it aside and move to the next.

I watch her reflection, drawn to the ever-evolving mix of emotions that pass through her. Her eyes are welling up. Her breathing has grown shallow. She sees me watching her and quickly looks down.

I remove the last lock of false hair from Melody's head. Her full-bodied mane has disappeared in a matter of minutes, leaving only the thin limp hair she deems unworthy.

I run my fingers up through her hair and massage her scalp.

I whisper in her ear.

"I prefer this."

She doesn't believe me.

I turn her around to face me. We are a mere inches apart. I can feel the heat of her body radiating in my direction.

I place my hands on her hips. She winces but doesn't stop me. I lift her up and set her down on the vanity. We stare at each other for a moment, searching, but it's no good. She's still hiding.

I reach up, my hand moving near her eyes. She winces and pulls back with a sudden jolt. In this moment she appears to be a trapped animal, desperate to escape. I don't let her. I move in closer.

"Shh. Shhh. Close your eyes," I say.

She doesn't want to.

"You're okay. Just close your eyes."

A tear forms in the corner of one eye. Her features suddenly contort into an 'ugly cry', but just as quickly it is gone. She's a fighter, refusing to breakdown.

Melody takes a deep breath, drops her defensive posture, and closes her eyes.

I slip my hand behind her and cradle her head. She is trembling. I hold her steady, carefully, gently peeling the false lashes from one eye and then the other.

I move to the supplies I purchased, grabbing a pad and applying eye make-up remover. She closes her eyes again without me having to ask. She has fully submitted to the process. I press the pad into place and allow the chemicals to do their work.

I remove the pad, tossing it aside on the counter. I find myself drawn to the discarded pad. It looks like a miniature abstract painting. I see several shades of eye shadow melding seamlessly into one another with an artist's touch. The cloudy mix is broken by the curve of eye liner offset by bold flecks of mascara. For reasons I can't explain, it's all strangely beautiful.

I prepare another pad and begin the process on the other eye.

Next, I purge the gunk from her face with a solution of make-up remover.

I massage soap into her skin and rinse it clean with a wash cloth.

Melody opens her eyes and looks at me. She looks different, free of all the impurities coating her skin. I see the true shape of her face. I see the freckles I would have never known existed.

I see her imperfections.

I see her.

"There she is."

Again I take her by the hips. This time she doesn't shy away. I lower her down from her seat on the vanity. She stands before me, lip trembling, as I reach up to touch her face. I turn her to face the mirror, inching forward to press my body against her backside.

Retrieving the yellow bow, I place it back where it began. For the longest time we both study her in the mirror.

"I would've shown up for her," I whisper.

I wrap my arms around her waist and she melts into me. I slide my hands under the hem of her top. Her skin is hot.

We lie side by side staring up at the ceiling. Our naked torsos are separated by the slightest of spaces, while our legs have managed to tangle and weave together.

There's nothing like the senseless love that blooms when two souls fit together in the dark.

"This is crazy," she says between ragged breaths. "I've never done this before."

I too am having trouble catching my breath.

"What's that?" I ask.

"A one night stand."

"Is that what this is?"

She says, "Well this is how they happen, right?"

"I guess it is. But I don't think it qualifies as a one night stand if it continues onward."

"No?"

"No," I tell her. "I suppose the odds are against us though."

"Why?"

"Well, in a vacuum, the chances of two people agreeing on a positive outcome is twenty five percent."

"Wait, wouldn't it be fifty-fifty? It's either yes or no."

"No..." I say, pointing to myself... "Plus no" I say pointing to her... "Equals no. Yes (me), plus no (her), equals no. No (me), plus yes (her)..."

"Equals no," she says.

The fourth option sort of lingers there, floating around unspoken.

Melody says, "Perhaps we should make it a two-night stand. Gather more data."

I think about that.

"Yes," I say.

"Yes," she says.

10

It's three in the morning and I'm shirtless, cooking up a bit of breakfast.

Melody sits on a bar stool, bottomless in my kitchen. Other than her panties, she wears nothing but the white button-up she stole from my closet. Her elbows rest on the counter, her hands weaved together to prop up her chin.

If I were a painter, I imagine I might feel the need to grab my brushes and a canvas.

I steal a glance between cracking eggs and she gives me a hazy little smile. Her eyes are glassy and tired. The events of the evening have disrupted her sleep schedule, but it seems, like me, she doesn't want it to end.

"Alright. I'm telling you, these are amazing."

I pull the reheated shrimp brochettes from the pan and place a couple on a plate for Melody.

"Ugh. Those things are giving me flashbacks to everything you said at the restaurant. That shit was damaging. Like really. I think you broke me a little."

"A man once told me a story about how some people become stronger at the broken places. I suggest you do that."

"Really? And who told you this?"

"I believe his name was Ernest."

"Right. And he told you this personally?"

"I think he told a lot of people that story, but I was one of them."

She shakes her head.

"You are such an asshole."

As per usual, my attempt at frying eggs has failed and quickly become a scramble. Proper scrambled eggs need cheese, so I rush to the fridge, grab a block and pull the grater from the utensil drawer. I hurriedly grate the cheddar straight into the pan, then use the spatula to mix, mix, mix.

The breakfast sausage is browning nicely. Almost done.

Shit, I forgot the toast. I grab a couple slices of bread and drop them in the toaster.

Returning to the eggs, I add a little salt and pepper.

Melody laughs.

"What so funny?" I ask.

"You're like a chicken with its head cut off. You look like you're cooking for a hundred people."

"Or... just one very important person."

"Aww," she smiles sweetly.

"And I suppose you could have some too," I say.

"Seriously? Did my dad just show up?"

"What?" I say. "It wasn't that bad. It was kinda funny."

"It was exactly that bad. And it wasn't funny at all. Now I feel like I have to be on the look out for puns and unsolicited lessons on all the things you've learned while watching the history channel."

The toast pops up just as I'm scraping the eggs onto a couple of plates.

I say, "Did you know that from the time you finish dinner till the time you wake up, you've probably gone about twelve full hours without eating. You've essentially been fasting. Which is why they call the first meal of the day breakfast. Or... break fast."

Melody buries her face into her hands.

"Oh no," she says, shaking her head. "This is why you get to know someone before you sleep with them."

I place Melody's plate in front of her.

"Dig in. I think you'll find it egg-cellent."

"Okay, are you messing with me or is this a true representation of your sense of humor? I'm sorry, I just have to know."

I smile.

103

"I'm serious, William. Give it to me straight. I have to know."

I lean in close.

"What do you think?"

She looks at me, studying.

"I think you're messing with me."

I give her a little smirk.

"Eat your food. Wait, don't forget this."

I spoon out some red tomatillo salsa onto her eggs.

"This stuff will change your life."

Melody takes a bite.

"Mmm. Oh wow. That is good. No wait, it's egggg-cellent. Damn, maybe a few puns aren't so bad if they come with food like this."

We eat in silence for several moments. It feels nice. It has been a long while since I've shared intimate space with a woman and actually felt at ease. Alive, but not on edge. At peace in the moment. Truthfully, it's a bit magical.

Sadly, I'm afraid it will end soon.

"So," she says. "Besides non-profit home restoration and making killer scrambled eggs, what exactly do you do, William?"

"Don't judge me, but… I run a political party."

"Really?" she says, judgmentally.

"It's true, I know. You don't have to say it. I'm despicable. But not really, because my Party is going to fix all of it."

"Republican?"

"No."

"Democrat?"

"No."

"See, you say 'I run a political party'. I hear 'bullshit artist'."

"And that wouldn't have been the case if I had said 'yes' to either of the previous questions?"

Melody tilts her head in concession.

"Those two parties are on their way out. They've outlived their usefulness."

"How so?"

"They don't serve the people. Consider this scenario – You got a progressive Democrat. You got a conservative Republican. We hold a vote. Fifty-two percent vote for the Democrat. Forty-eight for the Republican. So what happens? The Democrat takes office and spends the entirety of their term trying to enact highly progressive ideals. All the while justifying it by saying, 'the people have spoken'."

"Well they did, didn't they?"

"Sure they did. But what did the people actually say?"

"They said the Democrat won."

"This person's job is to serve their constituency. Their entire constituency, not just the one's that voted for them. Proper representation of the people would require this politician to push for moderately progressive ideals. Moderate legislation, with a slightly progressive lean. That's what the people said. You can't just forget the forty-eight percent who went conservative. They lost the vote, but that shouldn't make their opinion meaningless."

"Well that's just not how it works."

"Can you look at the political system as it exists today and say 'It works' at all?"

Melody raises her eyebrows and tilts her head, but says nothing.

"So maybe the way it currently works, is wrong. Maybe ignoring the portions of your constituency that didn't vote for you is a problem. Maybe we shouldn't make it the status quo to alienate large swaths of the population."

"Well, when you put it like that…"

"And so the Mediator Party is born."

"Mediator Party?"

"That's right."

"Sounds like a boring party," she says. Suddenly she's very animated, thrusting a fist into the air, "Woo hooo! Conflict resolution! Yeah! Negotiation bitches!"

"It's not that kind of party."

"That's probably for the best."

"Democratic Mediation. What we do is right there in the name. We find the compromise that best represents the collective will of the people. Imagine, every other year, a new political survey comes out, packed with all the questions that a person might have an opinion on. It's just sitting online, waiting for you and every other citizen to fill it out. You have an entire year to do so, at your leisure. Plenty of time to research, should you be so inclined. You can do it all at once. Bit by bit, when you get a free moment. Here and there, when you get bored… Or maybe you just answer that one question that really sticks in your craw. It's all up to you. And when you're done, when that next session of Congress is called into order, you'll know that you are represented. From there, the Mediator's job is simple… Enact what the people want. That's it. No wiggle room. No activism. No bullshit. Just do as you're told."

"That actually sounds reasonable," she says.

"We're talking about a system that removes activism from the halls of congress. Big Tech, Big Oil, Big Guns, Big Lobbies with Big Opinions… all of them lose all that power they've been stealing from the people of this country. No more out-sized influence. No more pandering to your base. Just legislators representing their citizens, each and every one."

I move closer. Her hands are folded in front of her on the bar. I rest my hands softly upon hers.

I ask, "Does that sound like a bad thing?"

"No," she says. "It actually sounds like a breath of fresh air."

My hands lovingly grip tighter onto hers.

"So then why are you fighting against it?"

"What?"

"Why are you here, Melody? Which of my enemies do I have to thank for such a wonderful evening?"

I watch her closely. If a picture is worth a thousand words, that is exactly what she gives me. I've never seen anyone so still, so unmoving. I try to read those thousand words, but they appear as some illegible chicken scratch, like a doctor's handwriting or a language I don't understand.

Melody breaks eye contact, looking down. She takes an audible breath and slowly exhales. As the air empties her lungs, her eyes rise up to meet mine. Her lips are curled into a slight smile.

"Is this a joke?" she asks. "Another facet of your sense of humor?"

I lean in.

"What do you think?"

Her smile vanishes from sight.

"I think you're paranoid."

"No you don't."

"You're scaring me, William."

"Wow. That might actually be true. A nice change of pace."

"Look, William, I don't kn-"

"Wait. Before you say anything, there's something you need to hear. From this point on, I will treat you fairly and kindly so long as you are honest with me. Even if I don't like what I hear. If you're honest, you're safe. Now, what were you saying?"

I can see the calculations taking place in the depths of Melody's mind. She studies me. Her gaze subtly drifts toward the front door. If she hadn't noticed before, I'm sure she's seeing it now – The deadbolt requires a key to be operated, not just on the outside, but the inside as well. It's a fairly normal practice when exterior doors have windows in them, for fear of a broken window providing easy entry. But my door is window-free, so clearly my double-sided lock has little to do with keeping people out.

She hasn't seen the backdoor, so she'll have to assume it has received the same treatment. A mad dash for an exit simply won't work. Her choices have narrowed – Words or Violence. And in the category of words… Truth or Lies.

"Goddamnit," she says. Her body takes on the posture of defeat.

I release her hands and take a step back, half expecting her to reverse course and delve into violence. Within her reach is a fork, a butter knife, a ceramic plate, and a half empty glass of orange juice.

"Go sit on the couch," I tell her.

She steps off her bar stool.

"Can I do something about my clothes?" she asks.

"You can take some off if you like."

She sighs, and shakes her head before making her way to the couch. She plops down like a frustrated teenager then grabs a throw pillow to modestly cover her thighs.

I open a kitchen drawer and remove one of several pre-rolled joints. I also remove a lighter and ashtray.

I enter the living room and set the ashtray on the coffee table before taking a seat next to Melody. She seems surprised that I chose that seat. She scoots away, managing our distance. She turns her body to face me, retreating until her back is up against the far arm of the couch. Her legs are tucked in tight and her body hunched. The pillow serves as a sort of shield.

I mirror her positioning, resting my back against the opposite arm of the couch. But I don't mirror the language of her body. I am open and at ease.

"So, Melody," I say, "I find myself wondering… Hired Gun or True Believer?"

I lean forward and offer her the joint. Again she seems surprised. She hesitates.

"Take it if you want it."

I just stare at her until she tentatively takes the joint from my fingers.

I say, "I don't think you noticed the double-sided lock until things got tense. Which leads me to think that you're probably not a Hired Gun. You're a Believer. Yeah?"

Melody is hesitant to answer, but ultimately does.

"I guess so," she says.

"A strong believer. We've got that in common."

I smile at her. She returns a forced smile, just a bit.

I say, "Willing to lay in a strange man's bed, type believer. So, what is it you believe in so strongly? Who exactly do you work for?"

"You remember those highly progressive ideals you were talking about?"

"Democrats?"

She gives a sarcastic little thumbs up accompanied by a tongue click.

"The Party?" I ask.

"Not exactly. I work for a Political Action Committee."

"Ahh. A Political Action Committee who takes large donations from 501c's, I bet."

She chuckles, "Gotta love dark money!"

"What is your mission, exactly?"

Melody thinks for several moments before responding.

"First, determine if you are still active. The office on Allen Street is still functioning, but you don't seem to be involved anymore."

"I know this one. I can help you with that. I needed a break. So after election season, I took one. But I am going back. Very soon, in fact. So, you've got that information, now what do you do?"

"Use my feminine wiles to infiltrate the organization."

In a showy way, Melody removes the pillow from her lap to indicate her 'feminine wiles'. She drops the pillow on the floor and leaves it there.

Her body is open now, no longer hiding. An interesting change in tactics. I find myself studying her bare legs and following them to their ultimate destination. My eyes rise further to meet with hers. There's something there, something new, something I haven't seen before.

I say, "I'm supposed to be taken with you?"

"Mmm. That's the plan."

Her bare foot pushes forward, making contact with mine.

"And you're supposed to be taken with me," I say. "Hook, line and sinker, you fall for all my nonsense and allow me to lead you into a world of political intrigue."

"Something like that."

"So are you?" I say, my foot sliding forward, gently gliding against her calf.

She squints at me.

"Am I what?"

"Taken with me?"

She thoughtfully considers the question as my foot continues onward, tracing lightly against her inner thigh.

"You? Maybe," she says. "All your nonsense? I don't know."

I say, "Ahhh, but you can't dismiss it, can you?"

My foot advances further until there is nowhere left to go. I press into a wall of flesh covered by a thin piece of fabric.

I watch Melody's face as her lips part and her eyes widen, then narrow. Her body begins to unfurl and then suddenly contract in what appears to be an involuntary spasm. Her breath releases in short rhythmic bursts.

She manages to speak between the bursts.

"It's worth… further… consideration."

11

I lie naked across the couch, my head resting against the arm cushion. Melody lays atop me, her cheek resting upon my chest. I can feel her index finger tapping against my ribs, in time with the beat of my heart.

It's quiet.

I reach out and grab the remote off the coffee table.

"How about some music," I say.

"Mmm," she responds.

I activate the YouTube app on the TV and type in '90's Music'.

Glycerine, by Bush emanates from the speakers.

"I love this song," she says.

I've spent my life avoiding the quiet. When it's quiet I can hear him.

I suspect we all have that person inside of us we've been forced to lock away. Those thoughts that can never be shared. That voice that is best ignored.

When I was just a child, I gave him a name – The Wax Man.

Buried deep in the cavernous recesses of my mind, The Wax Man lives in a cell that I built for him long ago. As hard as I tried, I was never able to fully soundproof his prison. To this day, his faint distant voice often penetrates the cell door.

Over the decades, I've developed a number of ways to drown him out. Music helps. Playing stupid games on my phone. The ever present noise of trash TV. The white noise of a box fan set to high when I lay down to sleep. Anything to distract me from his words.

Lately, I hear him much more clearly. Is he speaking louder? Or am I straining to hear?

"How did you know?" Melody asks in a sleepy voice.

It takes me a moment to understand her question. *How did I know?... that she was a spy?*

"I've known Morgan wasn't what he said he was for some time now. He tried too hard. Always offering to help me fix up my house. Always trying to bring up politics. Always probing for a way in."

"So when he tried to fix you up on a date…"

"Just another way in."

"And yet… you said 'yes'."

"I tried to say 'no'. Many times. He was persistent."

Melody pushes her forearms into my chest, propping her self up a bit. She looks down on me. Her breasts dangle, making the slightest of contact with my skin.

"My eyes are up here," she says with a smile.

"Sorry," I say, shifting focus.

"You know what I think?" she asks.

"What?"

"I think I succeeded."

"Do you now?"

"I think you are taken with me."

I stare into her eyes, lost in their depths.

"Unfortunately," I say sadly. "I think you might be right."

Her eyes crinkle, a little confused by the dreadful tone of my voice.

She doesn't know what I know. She has no idea that another man has entered our most intimate of moments. He slipped in through the backdoor, hidden by the thrum of a grunge guitar and Gavin Rothsdale's haunted voice. She has no clue that he stands directly over her, just behind the couch. She doesn't see the industrial sized zip-tie that he holds in his hand. Unfurled, it would be four feet long, but it's already been looped, creating a noose large enough to easily slip over her head. The man holds it by its tail and moves ever closer.

Her eyes cross in confusion as a strip of white plastic passes before them. It's already too late. The zip-tie slips under her chin. With sudden violent force, the man punches down between her shoulder blades, pinning her to me. Within that same effort, he pulls ferociously on the tail of the zip-tie.

I hear the excruciating zip of the noose locking into place. The man immediately releases his hold on her and steps away.

Suddenly, Melody is off the couch, staggering around aimlessly. She claws desperately at her throat. The tie has been zipped so tight that her neck looks a bit like an hourglass.

The speed at which her face grows red is surprising. Her maniacal eyes look accusingly to the man who did this to her. His name is Redfield, a trusted member of the Mediator Party. He watches her dispassionately.

Melody can't even begin to breathe. Blood begins to seep from the scratches she continues to uselessly gouge into her own skin.

She turns to me, eyes pleading for help.

I sit on the couch and watch her sadly. A piece of me wants to go to her. To rescue her from this horrible moment. But instead I do nothing. It's too late. Her story has already been written. I wrote it weeks ago.

Her horror stricken face suddenly goes blank and her limp body collapses to the floor.

Redfield approaches Melody's unconscious body. He kneels down and uses a padded strap to bind her hands behind her back. He lifts her head and places another large zip-tie around her neck. He carefully tightens it – loose enough that it won't choke her, but tight enough that it can't be taken off over her head. Redfield produces a pair of wire cutters and uses them to snip the original zip-tie free. He has no choice but to dig into her skin to accomplish this. He does so without hesitation.

Melody wakes with a sudden intake of breath. Her oxygen deprived brain starts right back up into that same moment of panic.

Her body jerks around violently, but Redfield's knee in her back will let her go nowhere.

"Calm down," Redfield says. "You're okay. Calm down."

His voice is kind, soothing even. Her body stills.

Redfield grabs a handful of Melody's hair and directs her head. On the floor, directly in her eye-line, is the discarded zip-tie. Redfield touches it with a gloved hand.

"Do you see this, Melody? Do you see it?"

"Yes," Melody says.

"Good. Very good."

Redfield collects the discarded zip-tie, places it in a baggie and stuffs it into his pocket.

Redfield tugs lightly at its replacement around her neck.

"Do you feel this?"

"Yes."

"I have no desire to hurt you, Melody. There is a plan in place and it does not require that I damage you or cause you pain. Do you understand?"

Melody begins sobbing.

"You'll need to stop crying, so that you can answer my question," Redfield says.

Melody is lost in her tears.

"You'll need to stop now."

Redfield tightens her noose, one click.

Melody whimpers into silence.

"Do you understand?"

"Yes. Yes."

"Good," he says.

Redfield shifts the tail of the zip-tie into her vision.

"This is your leash. You go where your leash takes you. Do that and everything will be fine."

Redfield gives her a reassuring nod.

"Starting now."

Redfield rises, pulling on the tail as he does. Melody frantically attempts to get on her feet. She struggles, but manages, without the use of her bound hands.

"Turn around," Redfield tells her.

She turns to see a woman wearing a yellow bow in her hair. In fact, the woman is wearing everything that Melody once wore. The same clothes. The same make-up. Even the same extensions in her hair. For all intents and purposes, Melody is confronted by the woman she was only a few hours ago.

Melody looks at her, takes a tragic breath, and again begins to cry.

The woman's name is Sarah, a trusted member of the Mediator Party. She holds in her hands a pair of disposable coveralls and a pair of shoes. Sarah takes a step forward, sets the shoes down, then holds the coveralls open near the floor.

"Step into these for me," Sarah says.

Redfield gives the leash a tug and Melody does as she's told. Sarah pulls the coveralls up to Melody's waist, over her bound hands, and fully into place. She zips it shut, the sleeves remaining empty.

"That's better," Sarah says.

She retrieves the simple slip-on shoes and holds one open.

"Right foot please. Perfect. Left. Great."

Sarah rises up and is face to face with Melody. She has in her hand Melody's phone.

"What is the code for your phone?"

"Uh, um..."

Redfield gives Melody's leash the slightest of tugs.

"Two three eight one."

Sarah tries the code.

"Perfect! And... oh, there's the Uber app. That's all I need. Thank you!"

Sarah sits on the arm of the couch and orders an Uber.

"Eight minutes," Sarah announces.

Redfield gives the leash another tug and leads Melody away toward the backdoor.

"Hey," I say.

Redfield stops and turns. Melody turns with him.

I look at her, mournful.

"I did enjoy seeing you."

All emotion drains from Melody's face. All of it.

It brings to mind the horrid sight of an open casket funeral. My Mother's features were the same as they ever were. The same nose, same chin, the same distance between his eyes. With those eyes closed, she should've looked as if she were merely sleeping. But she didn't look that way at all. She was nothing but an empty shell.

That is how Melody appears in this moment. Utterly empty.

Redfield gives her leash a pull and Melody's empty shell turns away from me. I listen as their footsteps carry them across the house and out the back door.

Sarah takes the seat next to me. She looks me over and for the first time I remember I'm still naked.

"Hello Sarah," I say.

"Hey boss," she says with a suggestive eyebrow raise.

I modestly grab the nearby throw pillow and place it in my lap. Sarah throws me a comical pouty face, unfazed by the macabre details of the moment.

She sees my distress and her demeanor changes.

"You liked her," she says.

I nod slightly, but say nothing.

She leans into me and rests her head on my shoulder.

"We do what we have to do," she says. "I'm sorry it hurts."

I take her hand and we sit there silently for several moments.

Sarah says, "I was surprised to hear the music. I really thought you were gonna call it off. Try to turn her. Make a double agent out of her."

"That was my hope. Something about her last personality shift. I'd never be able to trust her."

"Yeah," Sarah says with a nod. "Bitches be crazy."

Sarah's conversion to the cause was fairly straight forward. Some people need a little excitement in their lives. And some people so badly wish to make a difference in this world, fighting for what's right. Sarah was both these things.

Unfortunately for her, despite what some might tell you, she was born at the wrong time to fight for women's equality. She was a little late to be a gay right's activist. And the Abolitionist movement was long ago decided.

This country is full of people like Sarah, searching for a great injustice to rectify. Some end up fighting for a woman's right to kill her unborn child (even when it was her own actions that put it there). Some fight to feed and house the homeless (even as they refuse to be productive members of society). Some shake a stick for the environment (while providing little in the way of actual solutions).

Sarah found herself unable to fully commit to any of these options. She wasn't moved by the battle against micro-aggressions, or vaccines, or border wars, or PC culture, or capitalism, or any other supposed wrong that was really just a list of pros and cons. She needed something real. Something irrefutable. A truly Great Fight.

All I had to do was convince her that *my fight* was this generation's Great Fight. Lucky for me, it is.

Sarah has been pivotal to this operation. It was her who allowed me a look inside Morgan's home. She went on two dates with the man. The first ended exactly as we hoped it would, with him taking her back to his place. Unfortunately, he successfully blocked her view of the alarm pad as he punched in the code.

And so a second date was scheduled. This time she made sure to get him too drunk to be security-conscious. It worked like a charm. Even better, he was too drunk to perform, saving her from a second defiling.

Historically, whether I arrived for breakfast at eight or nine, Morgan never failed to be there. And so, two months ago, at eight in the morning, we used a lock pick to enter the man's home. We found his spare key hanging on the wall. We saw the posters of Che Guevara and Chairman Mao. We saw the coffee table book of famous photographs in history. We saw the room in the back, dedicated to the intensive study of yours truly.

The tone of a text message breaks through the silence.

Sarah checks Melody's phone.

She says, "Text from Morgan. '*Where the hell are you!*' "

I look as she types a response – *Leaving now!*

She checks the Uber app. "Car will be here in three."

In three minutes Sarah will exit out the front door and meet Melody's Uber. It will be caught on the surveillance cameras of my paranoid neighbor across the street.

On the ride to Morgan's house, FauxMelody will receive another text –

MORGAN – What the hell are you doing? Are you still with him?!
MELODY – Exactly what you asked me to do!
MORGAN – I asked you to worm ur way into his heart. Not his pants! No one loves a slut!

Upon reading the text, Sarah will say out loud, "Asshole! Sorry. It's nothing. My boyfriend is a jerk."

This may or may not lead to further interactions with the driver. Either way, the driver will likely remember what she said.

The man controlling Morgan's phone and sending Morgan's texts is Diego Marin, a trusted member of the Mediator Party. Currently, Morgan is being held hostage within his own home. Under the threat of violence, Morgan has been drinking for several hours now, one forced shot at a time. I suspect that Morgan is beyond drunk at this point. The kind of drunk that can lead a man to make bad decisions.

"Uber's here," Sarah announces.

She gives me a peck on the cheek and hurries out the door.

I sit alone, naked on the couch.

By now, the real Melody's journey is well under way. The house behind mine is owned by another trusted member of The Party. Melody will have already been marched through an opening in the back fence, which, according to plan, will have immediately been closed.

She will have been led to the garage and loaded into a minivan. The trip will take approximately eight minutes. At which point, the driver of the minivan will drop off Melody and Redfield at a discreet entrance to the concrete drainage ditch that weaves like an artery through the bowels of Morgan's neighborhood.

Built to accommodate Oklahoma's violent thunderstorms, the sunken concrete ditch is ten feet wide with seven foot tall walls. On either side of those walls stand an additional six feet of wooden privacy fence, a requirement of this particular neighborhood's Home Owner's Association.

I check the time. They should be starting that journey now. Depending on their speed, the walk through the ditch should take no more than fourteen minutes. The only fear is the possible presence of juvenile delinquents, evidenced by the sporadic graffiti decorating the otherwise gray walls. To solve this problem, Redfield has a spotter walking two minutes ahead.

I imagine Melody walking that path. I try to conceive what she might be thinking, what she might be feeling.

Upon reaching their destination, a panel of fencing will be displaced and a ladder will be quietly lowered. The ladder will lead to the backyard of Morgan Turnbull.

Before entering the sliding glass door, Redfield will slip paper booties over both his and Melody's shoes. They will step onto a floor covered in clear plastic.

They will likely see Morgan sitting at the dining room table. They might also see Diego, gun in hand, suggesting he take one last drink.

If things go according to plan, Sarah will have beaten them there. She will have changed into a pair of coveralls and put on a hair net. She will carry Melody's outfit back to its original owner.

Melody's wrists will be released from their bindings and she will once again be made to change clothes.

Sarah will methodically snap each hair extension back into place on Melody's head. Once complete, Sarah will tighten Melody's leash, cutting off oxygen to her brain.

I wonder if Melody will again claw desperately at her neck. Will she fight til the last drop? Or will she accept her fate? Will she use her final thoughts to curse God? Or will she beg for his forgiveness?

After Melody loses consciousness, make-up will be applied to her face.

If Diego has done his job properly, Morgan will have passed out by now. He will be placed on the floor, his back leaning against a wall. Melody will be laid before him, her head resting in his lap.

Redfield will place the original zip-tie and the wire cutters onto the table, evidence of torturous abuse.

Redfield and Sarah will collect Melody's discarded coveralls as well as the plastic sheeting from the floor. They will exit, leaving Diego to finish the job.

Diego will lock the sliding glass door behind them, and then proceed to make a mess of the place. The kind of mess you'd expect from a domestic squabble.

Shortly after, he will retrieve a gas can from the garage. The gas will be poured directly over Morgan's head, splashing and dripping down onto the lady in his lap. Dropping the gas can to the floor, Diego will toss a lit Zippo into Morgan's lap, before exiting through the side door of the garage. Using a spare key we long ago made, Diego will lock the door behind him before escaping into the night.

With the smoke detectors connected to the alarm system, the fire department should be there quickly. Though the two souls inside will be lost, the house will be saved. The police will no doubt find the room dedicated to the obsessive surveillance of one William Waxman. They may also take note of the coffee table book with a Buddhist Monk in flames on the cover.

I have imagined this sequence of events many times, but this time is different. This time my imaginings are being brought to life. It's a strange feeling.

I look at the time. Melody should be entering Morgan's house right about now. She has a few minutes of life left to cling to.

I sit alone in the quiet of my living room, counting the seconds as they pass. I see a small splotch of blood on the hardwood floors. I retrieve some bleach from the kitchen and scrub it clean.

12

OCTOBER 16, 2023
386 DAYS UNTIL ELECTION

Michelle Lee is already waiting for me as I pull up to the address. Other than some peeling paint, the house appears to be in decent condition.

"Thanks for meeting me," Michelle says, leading me onto the porch. "The house has been in probate for months, but we're finally free to sell it."

"This was your father's house?"

"Yeah."

"I'm sorry for your loss."

Michelle shrugs, "It's been agreed that we can accept an as-is offer of one-sixty."

"One-sixty? Seems low for this neighborhood."

"You'll see why," she says, opening the front door.

The walls are absolutely covered in an endless collage of pornographic graffiti, offset by copious amounts of trash covering the floor.

"It appears we have a house guest," Michelle says, an edge to her voice. "If you buy it, that'll be your problem to deal with."

"Understood."

In the den, much of the hardwood floors have been violently dug up and used as firewood.

Michelle says, "Whatever you do, don't read that wall. Unless, of course, you wanna stab your eyes out."

I ignore her advice and take a moment to read the sad story of Michelle's uninvited house guest.

I say, "I brought paperwork for a quitclaim deed. We can fill it out and file it today. I can put a cashier's check in your hand by lunch time."

The Home Depot is fairly busy for a Monday. As always, I pick the shopping cart that has a wonky wheel. It keeps trying to make me veer to the left.

With regular corrections every three or four steps, I conquer another of life's challenges.

Pushing my cart down an aisle, I come to a stop, impeded by another cart left sitting in my path.

I speak loudly, "It is completely predictable that another person might choose to travel down this aisle."

The woman I'm talking to is engrossed in the study of the various products that captivate her interest. She turns and looks at me, confused.

"When you stop, it's customary, or at least it used to be, to park your cart on one side of the aisle or the other. Certainly not smack dab in the middle."

She looks at me and then at the cart that stands in my way. Her confusion disappears. It is replaced by something else – fear. How could someone be so mean as to point out her carelessly selfish behavior in such a straight forward and honest way?

The terrified woman quickly retrieves her cart and moves it without a word of apology.

"Thank you, so much," I say, returning to the task at hand.

Shopping done, I get in line. After several minutes, It's finally my turn.

"Hello," I say, and offer a smile.

The tattooed clerk says nothing in reply, just a generally dissatisfied look on his face.

He scans all the little items before coming to a four foot long piece of angle iron. It has no barcode for scanning, which is normal for this particular item. It just requires a few punches of buttons on the computer. Apparently, the young man either doesn't know this or doesn't like it. He looks at me, bothered, his nose ring twitching from the flaring of nostrils.

"What is this?" He barks.

I'm not sure what I've done to deserve the harsh delivery, so I decide to be less than helpful.

"I'd say it's a piece of metal," I tell him with a shrug. "I don't know its formal name. We're not that close."

His dissatisfaction morphs into extreme annoyance.

I say, "If only there was someone who worked here."

The clerk sighs and searches for the item on his computer.

I say, "You ever wonder if you're in the wrong line of work? I feel like customer service may be outside the bounds of your skill-set."

He sneers, but refuses to look at me.

"Perhaps a stocker may be more appropriate. As in stocking products on the shelves, not stalking clients through the store. I'm guessing that would be against company policy. Though, full disclosure, I haven't read the company policy. You may be in luck."

"Total is fifty-eight forty-two," he says. "And this is angle iron, by the way."

His words are not particularly shitty, but his tone definitely is.

"Thank you for the education," I say. "You know what I like with my education? A smile."

The man's eyes flash over to me. A little staring contest ensues. I can tell he's used to winning these kinds of battles, but I stay strong.

He says, "I ain't about to smile for you on demand."

"No? Come on. Just a little one."

I wait patiently for my smile.

The clerk attempts to wait me out, testing my resolve. I give him a smile of my own.

I hold my intentionally creepy grin and just wait.

"Kiss my ass!" he says. "To hell with this place!"

The clerk rips off his orange apron and throws it to the floor. We are right by the exit, so he doesn't have far to go. I watch as he marches off into the daylight, cursing.

I look behind me to the waiting customers.

"I think this lane may be closed."

One of the people in line moans.

Another says, "You're an asshole."

They all sadly and angrily relocate to another register.

I call out to them, "I am not the asshole here! I know it doesn't feel like it, but I just improved this ecosystem."

"Dickhead," another shopper says.

"In small but far-reaching ways, this moment will reverberate throughout society... for years to come."

Nobody seems to appreciate the service I've just performed on behalf of all of them.

A wide-eyed employee approaches.

"What just happened?"

"Looks like you're down one employee. I'm all rang up, but I haven't paid yet."

"Uhhh, it's not my register. I can't touch it."

"That's okay. Perhaps you could call a manager. I'll wait."

These are the consequences of my behavior. I now have to wait. It would've been so much easier to just let that man treat me like shit. The transaction would be complete and I'd probably be stepping into my truck at this very moment.

But he would've learned nothing.

I like to imagine a world where we are all generally kind to each other. A world where we respect each other. Where we routinely pull our carts to the side. We never double park. We never cut the line. We never do the things we know are wrong simply because we can.

We can, because we know we'll almost certainly get away with it. We know our victims will shrink from confrontation. We know that those victims are unwilling to endure the hassles that come from standing up. Standing up almost always comes at a cost.

Sometimes that cost is nothing more than an anxious feeling in the pit of our gut. Sometimes it's fear. Fear of confrontation. Fear of reprisal. Sometimes it's actual reprisal. Sometimes, like now, it's merely inconvenience.

Whatever it is, I will gladly pay the cost. But it is a lonely road.

What if we were all willing to pay that cost? What if we were a team? What if instead of speeding up when someone tailgates us, we emphatically showed them our brake lights? What if we didn't sit and stew about it when someone talks during the movie, but instead we called them out, one and all?

What if the wheel that works got rewarded, while the squeaky one got relegated to the junkyard? What if our flaky friends stopped being counted as friends at all?

What if being a selfish prick didn't pay dividends? What if that behavior got corrected at every turn?

Perhaps then we wouldn't be living in a nation of narcissists. A nation where even the good people, seeing the assholes get their way time after time, have learned to lean into their selfish impulses.

It's only human. We adapt to the environment in which we live. And boy have we adapted.

The manager arrives and I pay him with three twenties.

I step out of the store with a bag of goods and a piece of angle iron. I wait for a car to pass and hustle across the drive. In the main lot, I notice what looks to be a brand new heavy-duty pick up truck. It's clearly somebody's pride and joy. I can tell by the way it's parked crooked across the line of two premium parking spaces.

I look around and notice that foot traffic is light. In the midst of the hustle and bustle, I'm suddenly alone. I cut across in between the vehicles, passing by the truck's passenger side. A quick jab of the angle iron and the passenger window shatters into a million pieces.

I keep walking as if nothing has happened. A man I hadn't noticed eyes me as I veer down the next lane. I give him a nod as we pass.

"You have a good day sir," I tell him.

He says nothing in return, but I can tell that he secretly approves of my actions. I don't believe the witness will be talking. I'm almost certainly on camera, though at this angle, I suspect the act was obscured. I'll be the most likely suspect, but no hard proof. Either way, having paid cash, they don't know my name.

I make a mental note to do my shopping elsewhere for a while. That's unfortunate, but such is the cost I've agreed to pay.

I smile, knowing that I've made the world a slightly better place.

It's a little after noon by the time I reach my newly acquired home. I test my new keys and they stick a little, but work well enough. Stepping inside, I find the place empty. My squatter is currently elsewhere, which is just what I was hoping.

I take a few measurements and prep the space for later. It doesn't take long.

I return to my current home, which I spent much of the weekend packing. I tend not to collect too much stuff, so it's progressing fairly quickly.

I consider getting back to it, but instead step out into the garage. While the sun is still shining, I might as well make use of it. The garage lighting is poor, so I open the overhead door and daylight floods my workspace.

Using some spare wood, my newly acquired angle iron, and a collection of screws, I begin to build something much less than elegant. To be honest, it looks quite stupid, but on the plus side, I think it'll work for its intended purpose.

It's nearing time for school to let out, so I lock up the house and hop in the truck.

The worst court loss of my life happened in family court. My wife was quite bitter about my filing for divorce and so she acted accordingly.

She accused me of stealing the 12 million dollars that she never knew existed. She only found out about it because she had someone comb through my finances.

Technically, I didn't steal it. Three months before I filed for divorce, I donated it to charity. She failed to see the distinction.

It was a newly created organization and she accused me of being the originator of said charity. Technically my name was nowhere near any of the paperwork.

She claimed that I was clearly heavily involved with the charity, to which I admitted that I would never donate 12 million dollars to an organization I didn't ardently support. Of course I would also donate my time.

She claimed I never discussed the money with her, which I admitted was true. I said that I didn't believe it was ever really our money. It was blood money. I never expected the horrible pandemic of 2020, and I couldn't fathom the idea of profiting from it.

It's fair to say the Judge hated me. He never believed a word I said, but technically there wasn't much he could do about it. Except, of course, take her side on every other issue. I tried to explain the plight of the Settle Fish, but he didn't seem to care.

Ultimately, my now ex-wife was granted full custody of our two children. I am allowed one unsupervised visit every other week.

And so I join the giant convoy of helicopter moms that snakes through the parking lot and continues for two blocks out into the street. Every day at this time, traffic is stunted for the sake of our helpless children who couldn't possibly be expected to ride a bus or, I don't know, use their legs.

Lindsey and Robby are two years apart, but for now they're at the same school. While I wait, I snoop on my daughter's social media accounts, created against my objections. I look at the pictures. Half of them are selfies. In nearly all of them she makes that ridiculous fish-faced, blue-steel, model pose. Every single picture, even the candid ones, she's always angled slightly to the right. Eleven years old and she's already decided she has a 'good side'. Her mother probably told her so.

Robby arrives and jumps into the passenger seat.

"Hey Dad."

"Hey buddy, where's your sister?"

"She's getting a ride with a friend. Mom said it was okay."

"Did she?"

I forcefully expel myself from the gridlock and point the truck toward Incredible Pizza.

We chow down at the buffet, but food just doesn't taste very good when you're angry.

"Hey Robby, why didn't your sister come?"

"I'm not suppose to talk about her with you."

"I'm her Dad. It's okay to talk to me."

"I'm not suppose to."

It's punishment. Her mother has turned her against me. I am the enemy. I can't imagine all the things that woman has said about me. I tore our family apart. I stole from them. I only see them once every two weeks, because that's how little I care.

I try to shake off the funk and enjoy the little time I have with my son. We finish our pizza and I suggest we check out the bumper cars or the Go-Karts or the mini-bowling. He tells me that he'd rather play arcades.

A nine year old boy would rather stare at yet another video screen than drive a Go-Kart. These children are doomed. I should've stayed married. Maybe then they'd stand a chance. I failed them in their early years, sleepwalking through life. Now that I'm awake, I'm still failing them due to lack of access.

I watch Robby play video games for an hour and stew about the whole thing.

I have to get him home by seven, so back to the truck we go. I wait for Robby to put his seat belt on and pull out onto the road.

"Hey Dad?"

"What's up Rob?"

"What Would Jesus Do if he found twenty dollars at school?"

"Hmm. Well isn't the better question, 'What Would You Do? What would Robby Do'?"

He says, "But I'm suppose to try to live like Christ."

"Well let me ask you something. Does Jesus know who that twenty dollars belonged to?"

"Jesus knows everything."

"Right, but you don't. So how can you live like Jesus if you don't know what Jesus knows?"

Robby furrows his brow, pondering.

"Tell you what, for the purposes of this conversation, let's just assume that Jesus only knows what you know. Okay?"

"Okay."

"So... Does Jesus know whose money that is?"

"Not reeeally."

"But..."

"But I found it by Mrs. Klein's desk."

"Where exactly?"

"On the floor."

"So does Jesus think that money is Mrs. Klein's?"

"Yeah," he says sheepishly.

"Okay. The original question, What Would Jesus Do? My guess is Jesus would do whatever served him best. Does Jesus need the twenty dollars? What exactly would it buy him? A twenty dollar bill gets him exactly twenty dollars worth of stuff. No more, no less. But is there a way to make that twenty bucks worth more than its face value? What if he gave it back? That could prove to be valuable. Maybe even more valuable. It buys him goodwill. It buys him trust. It even buys him a good reputation. Might it lead Mrs. Klein to show Jesus some preferential treatment in the future? Maybe she grades him a little less harshly. Maybe when she gives out treats or whatever, Jesus gets a little extra. So knowing all that, what do you think Jesus would do?"

"Give it back?"

"That's right. I think that's exactly what he would do. But here's the thing about Jesus, Robby, and this is the most important part... Jesus's goals and your goals are not the same. His goal was to be the Messiah. His goal was to gain followers. His goal was to convince people that he was the epitome of good. Your goal, I hope, is to actually be good. Those are two very different things. Do you understand what I'm saying?"

Robby takes a breath and exhales deeply, "I don't know."

"The point is, it's about doing what's right for the right reasons. And you can't rely on other people to tell you what that is. You certainly can't rely on someone's brilliant idea on how to sell a few million wristbands. That's not where the truth is."

I reach over and place the palm of my hand over his heart.

"You search here…"

I move my hand and place a finger against his temple.

"And you search here. And if you're honest with yourself, you'll know what is right. My hope is that you'll let that guide you."

Robby turns a pair of pitiful eyes my direction.

"So I should return it?" he asks, unsure.

"I think you should do what is right. In the end, you have to make the decision for yourself."

Robby starts to cry.

He says, "But I don't want to be like Jesus."

"No?"

"I don't want to give it back so I can get special treatment."

"But that's not why you'll be doing it."

"Still," he wails.

"Stop crying Robby. Use your head. Find a solution. You're on the right track. You wanna do the right thing, but you don't wanna get special credit for it. That's awesome and it's rare and it makes me proud. But that doesn't mean it's easy. Doing what's right is almost always hard. So suck it up and solve the problem. Any chance you can drop it on her desk or in her purse when she's not looking?"

"Maybe," Robby says, using his sleeves to dry his eyes.

We pull up to a red light.

"Okay. You remember that magic show we watched? It's all about misdirection."

I reach over and snap my fingers. With my other hand I appear to pull a coin from Robby's ear.

Robby looks at me, severely unimpressed. I must admit, I am not the best practitioner of magic.

The light turns green and again I drive.

"Do you not like Jesus?" he asks.

I sigh, and then shrug.

"I never met the guy. How about you? Do you like Jesus?"

"He's the son of God. Our savior. He died for our sins."

"And how do you know that?"

He blinks at me, "I have faith."

"Why do you have faith? Is it because your mother and your preacher and your Sunday School teacher have each and every one told you that it's what you need? That faith is what's required of a good Christian boy? Or did you find this faith all on your own? Did you read the Bible and know in your heart and soul that what you were reading was true? Is that what happened?"

I take my eyes off the road and steal a glance. He looks at me, perplexed.

I say, "Let's say for a second that God is real. Let's skip past that question and say that the God of Abraham, the God of the Old Testament, is absolutely, one hundred percent, the real deal. Now the question becomes, 'Was Jesus real? Was Jesus who he claimed to be?' "

Robby nods in the affirmative.

"How do you know?"

"Because he died for our sins."

"I've got news for ya, you nail a man to a cross and stick a spear in his side, he's gonna die. Son of God or not, that's going to be fatal."

"But only Jesus can come back from the dead. He was resurrected! He walked on water! He turned water into wine!"

"And that's proof?"

"It's in the Bible!"

"You know who else is in the Bible? The Devil."

Robby inhales sharply.

I continue, "He too is the son of God. And they call him Lucifer. You know what else they call him? The Great Deceiver. Not just any deceiver, The Great Deceiver! The King of Lies!"

"He's a bad guy."

"That's what they tell me. A very bad dude. But not really a dude... an angel. A very powerful angel. The kind of power it might take to say... walk on water... turn it into wine... rise from the dead."

"Nooo," Robby protests.

"You ever wonder why the Old and the New Testaments are at such odds with each other? How one is a God of Anger, while the other is a God of Love. How 'an eye for an eye' can become 'turn the other cheek'? It seems to me that Jesus Christ might be history's first major rebranding effort."

Robby stares at me, unblinking.

I say, "He's a shrewd angel. He is the snake, offering all of humanity an apple that tastes so much better than anything God ever gave us. He knows just how to capture an audience. Of course the masses will flock to a God who shows great compassion. A God who allows them their indulgences. A God who forgives our sins before we even commit them. Now that's the kind of God I can get on board with! An easy God. A God that requires little in the way of true goodness. A God that cares not what I've done or even what I will do, only that I accept Jesus into my heart. And all will be forgiven.

"You ever notice in church that there's at least two 'Praise Jesuses' for every 'Praise God'. Jesus is our hero. Unlike that old God, Jesus requires nothing of us. Only that we follow him. And where do we follow him? Straight to hell. Through one Great Deception, The Great Deceiver convinced billions to break the very first commandment. *Thou shalt hold no other Gods before me.*"

Robby takes a heavy breath.

"Is that true?" he asks. "Do you really believe that?"

I shake my head.

"I believe if we're going to latch ourselves to some fanciful world of almost certainly fictional beings... that story is as plausible as any other. And if we're gonna believe in The Great Deceiver, he should probably perform an act worthy of his title.

"But no, Robby, no I do not believe that Jesus was the devil. Nor was he the son of God. He was just a man."

Robby stares at me, a confused look on his face.

"Do you know what religion is, Robby? What it really is? Not to the masses who practice it, but to the architects who create it?"

Robby shakes his head.

"It's a societal framework. It's a means for creating a highly functional and morally sound community. But what happens, Robby, when the people begin to turn away from this God they were given? In effect, they are turning away from their moral framework. So what happens then?"

Robby shrugs.

"Well, things start to go very wrong. Society begins to break down. That's the world that Jesus grew up in. He saw morally corrupt behaviors becoming normal behaviors. When God no longer sets the rules, how do we agree on what is right, or what is wrong? How do we keep ourselves from falling down into a hellish existence? And so Jesus began to build a new framework, based on that existing structure. Is this making sense, Robby?"

"I think so."

"There's a lot of myth wrapped up in this, but Jesus – the man, not the myth – was just a guy trying to convince people to live good and honorable and productive lives. To some extent, he succeeded. It's two thousand years later and people are still striving to live within his framework. So no, I don't dislike Jesus. He saw a need for an intervention and he tried to save his society from itself? In that way, he was a great, great man.

"So let's fast forward to today. The fact is, Robby, Jesus's framework began to crumble long ago. Most so-called Christians have never actually read the Bible. They'll watch TV, movies, YouTube videos… Some of them even read books, but not that book. The Word of God, they call it. By their own belief system, the most important words ever written… and yet they won't read it. If they truly believed, don't you think they would read it? They should be so excited to read it!

"Truth is, the vast majority of Christians don't actually practice Christianity. They practice Religion Á La Carte. They pick and choose which teachings they adhere to and which ones must've been

133

a misprint, or a typo, or a flubbed translation, or 'he didn't really mean that'.

"According to the Bible, homosexuality was born of the devil. This is a teaching of God. Yet, most Christians, your mother included, believe that notion to be outdated. As if the Word of God is no different than a tile floor from the 1970s.

"And so, like everything else, we remodel it to our liking. Most churches out there that wouldn't dare give a sermon declaring homosexuality to be a sin. Let me say that in another way – Most churches wouldn't dare teach the Word of God. The Word of their Creator. The Word of an omnipotent being who knows all. That they won't teach.

"So... what does that tell us? It tells us that these institutions, these preachers, these church members, these lovers of the Word of God... are liars, not believers.

"How in the world can we be expected to exist in a world so full of lies? Where the majority of people still claim the lie, even while knowing, deep down, that it is, in fact, a lie? All in the name of a religion that declares lying to be a sin. This is quite the predicament we've created. That level of falsity has got to eat at a person's soul!

"So... What do we do? Well, we get really confused, that's what we do. Of course there's always the argument that the Bible was actually written by men, at the behest of God. But men are fallible, so it's sensible to say that some of those passages might be fallible too. Makes perfect sense. But how do we decide which passages are false? And who decides? That's a big decision, wouldn't you say? Because whoever decides that, in effect, becomes God. Think about that... who's more powerful, God or the person who decides when God is right... and when he's wrong? And if you've determined that you should decide for yourself, then you have also determined that you are, in fact, God. This is exactly what everyone does when they decide which church they want to attend. Picking the church that preaches most closely to what they've decided they believe.

"So... Where does that leave us? A society that has millions upon millions of little Gods running around. Well, it leaves us without a consistent moral code, that's for sure... even among

Christians. Religion Á La Carte doesn't exactly lend itself to a consensus. Jesus's framework, just like God's before him, has crumbled. We need a new framework, Robby. In a country with freedom of religion, that framework cannot be religiously based. Our moral standards should find their perch atop the laws we create. And those laws must be conceived within the melting pot of ideas that is this country, blending all those different flavors together into something that could never be called Christian or Muslim or Jewish or any other religion. Perhaps we could just call it America.

"As to the moral questions that aren't quite covered by law... The question of whether to follow the Golden Rule, or exist within the realm of finder's keepers... that's something you have to decide for yourself. If you want to lean on the teachings of Jesus to help you through that decision, that's perfectly fine. But understand, it will always be your interpretation of what you think Jesus would do. Ultimately, it always comes down to you. Who are you? Who do you want to be?

"That's what I want for you, Robby. I want you to listen to your mother. I want you to listen to me. But don't believe either one of us. I want you to listen to anyone you deem worthy of being heard, but don't believe them. And when you've heard all you need to hear, I want you to listen to yourself."

I pull the truck to the curb in front of the house that my ex-wife now calls home.

"Does that make sense, Robby?"

Robby nods, but says nothing. He looks at me, thoughtful.

"Mom says that Atheists are bad."

I nod, "I'm sure she does."

"Are you an Atheist?"

I think about that.

"These days, Atheism is practically a religion in itself. Just another tribe people use to define themselves."

Robby stares at me, unsure if I've answered his question.

"I'm a... Autocreationist," I tell him. "This world has taught me exactly what I can believe in. And I don't believe in anything I didn't myself create."

The words surprise me. Never have I thought those words, and yet they flow from my lips as if native to my very being. It scares me a bit.

"It's 6:59. You better go or you're gonna get me in trouble. Don't forget your backpack."

He opens the door and jumps out.

"Love you buddy."

"Love you too, Dad."

"I had fun. See you soon."

I watch him trudge up the steep walk to the front door. He starts to dig his keys out of his pocket, but the door swings open, saving him the trouble. His mom stands there, holding open the storm door. Robby walks in, disappearing from view. There's no reason to continue holding open the door, and yet his mother still stands there, scowling at me.

I give her a little wave. She sneers and shuts the door.

I drive away, thinking.

I don't believe in anything I didn't myself create.

I shake my head. This fucking world. The closer you look at it, the more cynical you get.

I reject that cynicism. That is not me. I still believe. I believe this world could be beautiful. Pull the right lever… Turn the right key… We could be beautiful. So very beautiful.

13

It's two in the morning as I drive through my new neighborhood. It's quiet. I kill the engine half a block from the house and let the truck coast the rest of the way.

I park it on the street out front and quietly exit the vehicle. Reflected in the moonlight, I can see the smoke rising from the chimney. My squatter is here, burning a fire to keep warm.

I retrieve the contraption I built earlier today from the bed of the truck. It's a bit bulky, so I throw it over my shoulder.

Walking around the side of the house, I open the gate and enter the backyard. I move toward the backdoor. It leads straight into the den, which is where the fireplace is located. The squatter will be right there on the other side of that door.

Slowly, and nearly silently, I slip the contraption into place. The contraption braces against the door frame, while encasing the knob, making it impossible to open the door from the inside.

I quietly back away, returning to the truck to grab a bag of tools from the bed.

Unlocking the front door is louder than I hoped. I have to jiggle it just right before the lock gives way. I open the door and look inside. I suspect the squatter may know I'm here now.

I hear and see nothing.

Among my bag of tools is a flashlight. I turn it on. All is calm. I step inside and shut the door making no attempt to maintain the silence.

Suddenly, I hear the sounds of scrambling coming from deeper in the house. Is that one person? Or multiples? Hopefully I'm not too terribly outnumbered.

I hear what sounds like someone tugging on the backdoor, but failing to open it.

I pull the screw gun from my tool bag and drive a three inch screw at a hard angle into the edge of the door, sinking it into the door frame. The door is now permanently locked to anyone who doesn't have a screw gun.

It sounds like just one person. I'm sure by now they've figured out that every window has also been screwed shut. There's no easy way out.

I aim my flashlight and ease my way forward. I enter the kitchen when suddenly a figure darts across the illumination and disappears down a hallway. I hear the intruder enter one of the bedrooms, followed by frantic, unsuccessful tugs at each window.

"If you're thinking about breaking a window, I have to warn you it's not as easy as they make it in the movies," I yell out. "It's not safety glass. It won't break into a million harmless little pieces. It's double pane and glued in tight. We're talking razor sharp shards. Most likely scenario is you'll cut yourself to bits. All I want is to have a conversation. After that, you'll be free to go."

I wait for a response, but all is quiet.

"Alright, well, I'm gonna wait by the fire. Come say 'hi' when you're ready."

I venture on toward the sounds of a crackling fire. Reaching the den, I shine a light onto the graffiti covered walls. For the third time, I stand in this room. For the third time, I study the story of my intruder.

It's an ugly story. Sadly, it's a story as old as time. I am surrounded by spray painted hints of sadness, anger, and betrayal. One wall in particular draws me in. Written in black magic marker, and covering the entirety of one wall, is a story I can't help but read once more. It is the tale of a father and a child. It's unclear if that child is a son or a daughter. What is clear is that this child has been broken.

There is something very special about my intruder. I am at once moved by the beauty of the telling and the horror of what is told. This is not the first time that my uninvited guest has brought a tear to my eye. I'm guessing it won't be the last.

I hear soft footsteps enter the room. I turn and shine my light onto a young girl with short hair. I can't tell how old, but I'm guessing early teens. She winces at the brightness of the light. I turn it off, the fire providing just enough illumination to get by.

"Hey there."

She doesn't reply.

"They still teach government in school?" I ask.

She just looks at me, wary of my existence.

"The three branches? You see, there's the legislative branch… They make the laws. Laws like trespassing, breaking and entering, vandalism, destruction of property."

To drive home my point, I gesture to the graffiti and kick at a broken piece of floorboard beneath my feet.

"And then there's the executive branch, They enforce the laws. What do you think happens if I call the police? How do you think that goes?"

She says, "Well you're a skeevy old man and I'm under-aged. How do *you* think that goes?"

I tilt my head and let her words sink in.

"I see where you're going."

"Kidnapping. False imprisonment," she says.

I put out a calming hand as a peaceful gesture.

"Alright, alright. You win."

She says, "We can compare apples to oranges if you want, but let's call it what it is… misdemeanors to felonies."

"Okay. I got ya. Round One goes to the juvenile delinquent."

She says, "I think it'd be best if you just unlock the door."

I notice the knife she's holding tightly in her hand.

"That's fine. I'll let you out, no problem. But let me just say one thing. Here's what I know… you tore up my house. All I want to do is fix it. And I could use an extra pair of hands. This place is days away from running water, heat, electricity, even an internet connection. Here's what else I know… You don't wanna go out in that cold and you damn sure don't wanna go back home."

"What do you know about my home?"

"Only what you told me."

I look to the writing on the wall.

"It's all right here in black and white. And orange. And purple."

I look at her. Her toughness is melting into vulnerability. These words were never meant to be for me. It was an intensely personal, therapeutic exercise that no one was ever meant to lay eyes on. At least not in her presence.

"I got a pretty good idea what happened to you in that place and I don't want you to go back there either. I'm offering you a different kind of place. I don't want… that. I just want the hands that broke it, to be the same hands that fix it. I want three hours a day. Three hours buys you a place to sleep."

She considers my offer. She seems intrigued.

"Will there be a washer and dryer?"

"You want a list of amenities?"

"I want more than a place to sleep. I want a home."

I hear a slight crack in her voice on the word 'home'.

"Sure," I say. "Sure, we can do that."

"And a meal. Three hours buys me a home and a meal."

Her eyes are beginning to water. I can just make it out in the flickering light of the fire.

"Deal. But I pick the meal. I won't be adhering to some menu you concoct."

"I eat what you eat. I don't want you feeding me Ramen while you chow down on pizza."

I nod.

"That's reasonable enough," I say. "I'm William, by the way. What's your name?"

"Astraea." she says. She pronounces it uh-stray-uh.

"Good to meet you, Astraea."

Astraea moves across the room and takes a seat on the hearth of the fireplace.

"You said there would be an internet connection?"

"I did."

"But I don't have a phone."

"Are you under the impression that I'm here to rectify all of life's problems? Let's be clear, that's what they call a false impression. The moment you try to take advantage of me will be the same moment I tell you to hit the bricks."

"You're not very nice are you?"

"Best I can tell, I'm the nicest person you know. I understand you're a sad girl, who's had a sad life, and you probably want someone to swoop you up and take care of you, but our relationship will not be based on pity."

"I'm not a girl," she says.

"I'm sorry?"

"I'm not a girl."

I look at her, confused.

"I'm non-binary."

"Oh. You're one of *them*."

"Don't be an asshole."

"Is that not your preferred pronoun?"

"Well not when you say it like that. Not when it's derogatory."

"So, I'm curious, if your doctor asks if you're male or female… you're gonna say neither?"

"That's a bullshit question."

"I'm just trying to understand what we're talking about here."

"Medically, I'm female. Socially, I'm non-binary."

"But you do understand what the definition of 'girl' is, right?"

"Here we go," she says with an eye-roll.

"A girl is a non-adult human female. Which is a pretty accurate description of what I'm looking at. Just like a woman is an adult human female. That's all these words were ever intended to be."

"But that's not how they're used."

"That's not an honest argument, Astraea. That is exactly how they're used. Though I concede, it may not be the only way they're used. Yes, a good number of people began assigning norms and expectations... and the stereotypical, society approved, ideal woman was born."

"Exactly. Don't you think that's a problem?"

"I actually do. I think it's a real problem. And it deserves a *real* solution."

"For instance," she says.

"Sometimes the simple solution is the best one. How about we just try being ourselves? You realize it's possible to reject stereotypes without rejecting biology, right?"

"Oh, come on. Gender is just a social construct."

"No, gender is real. The stereotypes, the expectations... that is socially constructed. That's what you should be fighting. You're fighting the wrong thing."

She looks at me, thinking about my words.

I say, "Tell me this, if we lived in a world where the majority of women stopped trying to live up to society's expectations of that word... they stopped allowing society to tell them who they should be... and it became the norm for women to just be themselves, whoever that may be... Would you still claim to be non-binary?"

"That is not a real world," she says.

"But if it was?" I say. "There would be no reason for any of this, would there?"

She says nothing, but I can see her mind working.

"Think of how much more powerful that is. For you to be exactly who you are. Look how you want to look. Behave how you want to behave. While understanding that you being a woman has nothing to do with any of that. Think of that mindset trickling through society. Where ultimately, you're just one example of what a woman can be. Every woman is exactly one example of what a woman can be. Masculine, feminine, the whole spectrum in between. Just you being you, moment to moment, day after day."

"That is not an honest argument, because that's not the society we're living in."

"You're right, it's not. You have to build it. Look around. You're already building a new society. You're just building the wrong one. Building on a shaky foundation is not the best of plans, Astraea. Which means you can't disregard verifiable facts. You can't ignore objective reality. You can't bypass the laws of nature. When you do that, even success results in failure. Eventually it all comes crumbling down."

Astraea shakes her head.

"You're just trying to confuse me."

"No, you're already confused. I'm trying to fix that. We want the same things, Astraea. We really do. I want a world where you can feel free to be exactly who you are. But I also want a world that actually accomplishes that goal. Can't you see that the path you're on doesn't actually fight against stereotypes? It does the opposite. It accepts them. It even reinforces them. It says, 'well this is what they say a woman should be, and that's not me, so I'm gonna claim to not be one. Does that make any sense at all?"

Astraea stares at the floor, unresponsive.

"The fight you're fighting and the fight you should be fighting... They are both revolutionary. But one of them is inherently negative. One of them requires that you make an 'other' of yourself. One of them requires that you tell a pretty blatant lie. One of them, in an interesting way, kind of suggests that being a woman is bad. Unless, of course, you're a man who wants to be a woman, and then it's beautiful. Make no mistake, you're throwing in with a group that requires you disavow a piece of yourself in order to meet their membership requirements. You are building a cage around yourself. And it's not even a cage of your own design. Someone else designed it. You didn't come up with gender-fluid, or non-binary, or they/them. These are someone else's ideas of who they think you should be. Sound familiar? Isn't that what you were rebelling against in the first place? You're conforming to their views on non-conformity. They've sold you a build-it-yourself prison cell, and you're just tinkering away. L... G... B, T, Q... It's all bullshit. The only letter that should matter when it comes to personal identity is U. And by U, I mean *you*. Who are you? Be that. The vastness

143

of what a human female can be has very few limits. Unless, of course, you keep building that cage they sold you."

I take a moment to drive a screw into the back door, locking it shut.

I return my attention to Astraea.

Dimly lit by the light of the dying fire, I can just make out that Astraea is silently crying. She's trying to fight it, but her sadness cannot be contained.

"I've made you cry, and I'm sorry for that. For what it's worth, my offer still stands. But I don't support the fight you're in, and I will not participate. If that's a problem, then you shouldn't be here when I get back. Before I go, I'm gonna change the locks on the front door. I'll leave a key by the door. I'll be back on Thursday. You've got a couple days to make up your mind."

I grab my tool bag and walk away.

I'm making short work of the locks. The dead-bolt is done and I'm halfway through the knob.

"You make it sound like it's easy," Astraea says from behind me.

I turn and look at her across the room. I keep working.

"I never said easy. Of course it's not easy. Being an individual is hard. If you want easy, stay on the path you're on. That's why you chose it, right?"

"What are you talking about? You think this path is easy?"

"Not easy, just easier. You chose it for the same reason inner-city kids join gangs. The same reason some people join cults. The same reason the church pews fill up every Sunday. The lonely road is hard. You want someone else to give you the answers. You wanna know someone's got your back. You wanna feel like you belong. Joining those people gives you that. And all you gotta do is sacrifice pieces of yourself."

I shrug.

"Hell, maybe it's worth it. Only you can answer that. But don't think for a second that you're any different than the girl who felt exactly like you, but decided to mold herself into society's version of what a woman is. You both gave up pieces of yourself. She just did it in a different way, because she sought acceptance from a different team. That's all it is. You sacrifice those pieces of yourself so that you can have a ready-made team. That's the bargain. They give you a community. And you give them one more soldier for their army. Symbiosis at its best. But be careful. Like any soldier, you are expendable."

"That is total bullshit. We are not an army."

"Really? Your team is not an army? Do they not instruct you to fight the good fight? Do they not teach that activism is an absolute necessity? Do they not train you how to respond in various situations? Do they not relentlessly fill your head with so-called facts? With passion for justice? With anger for the enemy?"

"We're being attacked. Of course we need to defend ourselves."

"Take a second and ask yourself why they didn't choose the path that I set out. The path of individualism. Maybe because individuals don't make the best soldiers. These people don't want individuals. They want you all thinking the same things. Moving the same direction. Doing what you're told. Afraid to step out of line for fear of being expelled. That's your team. Look Astraea, I understand. It's hard to find a team while staying true to yourself. Even if you do, it won't be a big team. Maybe a few members, at best. But you won't call them Crips, or Christians, or members of the Queer Community. You'll call them your family. Your chosen family. Your real team. You'll do anything for them. And them for you. These people are hard to find. And the minute you change yourself to fit the mold of your so-called Community, is the same minute you give up on finding your real team. Because only the real you can find your real team. The only team that truly matters."

I twist in the last screw and test the key. It works.

"Is there anything else? Because I'm done here."

Astraea looks at me for several moments before shaking her head.

I set a key on the floor.

"Your key if you want it. I'll see ya if I see ya."

I walk out, shutting and locking the door behind me.

It goes without saying, I will see her again. As much as that other group is offering her, they aren't offering her a home. When we are lost, we wish nothing more than to seek out home.

As she has already shown a penchant for following the leader, I suspect her conversion will be a fairly simple matter. In a world so full of confusion, our most valuable commodities are intangible and elusive. They come in the form of words like meaning, certainty, and purpose. These things are priceless. I will offer them to her and she will give herself to me.

14

I never listen to the radio anymore. There's too much to think about. Too many battles to plan. Too many variants to consider. I let my mind drift over the political landscape, trying to imagine my path to victory. I picture myself from my opponents' point of view, see me as they see me.

How would they deal with such a pest? How would they dispose of it?

An uninvited guest enters the fray inside my mind. She looks at me with dead eyes. She says nothing, just lingering there in the corner, watching me sadly. I focus my thoughts elsewhere, but her presence is no less felt.

My conscious mind beckons me back to the reality of my surroundings. I see the sign welcoming me to Denton, Texas. I check my speed, fully aware of the city's penchant for taxing travelers.

The drive to Dallas has been uneventful, at least I think so. Strange how a person can cruise down a highway at high speed, navigating one of the most dangerous machines ever conceived and have absolutely no memory of it.

Though I am back in the land of reality, she has followed me here. I feel her. A slow, sinking, gentle pull at my soul.

I should never have allowed myself to see her. Her mask rendered her powerless. It is Melody's true face that haunts me.

I arrive in Dallas with enough time to grab a bite to eat. I turn onto Lemmon. I stop in at Mia's and get absolutely lost in a plate of brisket tacos.

My hunger satisfied, I force myself back onto the road, driving toward the studio of a popular right-wing podcaster.

The studio is large and made up to resemble a man cave. I'm surrounded by wood and red brick and neon lights and the paraphernalia of American patriotism. I listen as the host spews his never ending complaints. It's clear that he loves the sound of his own voice.

Every third word or so, I can actually see flecks of spit ejected from the man's mouth. It's very distracting. He speaks with such angry force that I suppose it's unavoidable. The microphone's screen must be soaked by the end of every broadcast. I wonder how often they replace it.

He says, "We have hundreds of thousands of years of hard data, showing us that temperatures go up... and then they come down. It's a cycle that keeps repeating itself. It's normal!"

"We're in a warming stage," I say, nodding agreeably. "Have been for thousands of years."

"Exactly! It's all part of the pattern!"

It's amazing how these people manage to twist the facts into a partisan pretzel, willfully averting their eyes from anything that challenges them.

"And not just the temperatures," I add. "Sea level goes up... and down. CO_2 goes up... and down."

"Yes it does. YES IT DOES!"

"It's to be expected," I shrug.

"That's right."

I say, "Did you notice when you were looking at the data how the CO_2, throughout history... before we ever industrialized... before we ever built cars... it would go up and up and up and often get close to 300 parts per million, but not quite make it there, because then, of course... it would come back down. And then it would do it again. And again."

"It's a well established pattern, ladies and gentlemen!"

"Well it was. I mean if we're gonna make determinations based on that graph you got there, I suppose we should include that one little anomaly."

The man furrows his brow. He looks truly confused by my comment. Does he actually believe the words he's saying? Does he not see the anomaly?

I say, "In the early half of the nineteen hundreds, CO2 actually broke through that 300 mark. The mark that's never been crossed in all that cyclical data that you're leaning on, it got crossed. But, as expected, guess what happened next."

"Gee, let me think… It went down."

Where is this man's brain? Has he trained it to self-censor data that he doesn't want to see? Does he actually not see it?

I say, "No, actually. To this day, it just keeps going up. It's well over 400 now. And I can't for the life of me figure out why."

And with that, I throw down the gauntlet. I am not going to be his normal accommodating guest, echoing every ridiculous thought he spits into his microphone.

Three contentious subjects later, the man's face is as red as a beet.

I say, "I know, I know. You don't have to say it. Guns don't kill people… people with guns kill people. Or is it people with assault rifles kill people efficiently? I can't remember, how does it go?"

He says, "This is not a joke! Your willingness to limit my rights is astounding!"

"If that right is so important to you, shouldn't you be willing to sacrifice a single week of your life? It's nothing. All I'm proposing is a week long training course. One single week, and you are now free to purchase, possess, and use an assault rifle."

"What you're talking about isn't even an assault rifle!"

"Can we avoid the whole word games argument? You know exactly what I'm talking about. And they keep ending up in the wrong hands. We've got to do something about it. If the ardent defenders of the 2nd Amendment are unwilling to sacrifice a tiny portion of their time in order to keep that right, then maybe we need to start talking about a ban."

"That's just ridiculous. Look, here's the fact, mass shootings are a tiny portion of the murders that take place in this country. It's nothing!"

"So if you have a leaky kitchen faucet, you shouldn't fix it because your son takes really long showers?"

"I don't even know what that means."

"All I'm saying is, if you so badly want to go to a school and kill a bunch a kids, you should be willing to take a week-long course on how to do so safely."

"This is ridiculous," the man says, shaking his head.

"You know what I think is good? I'm glad you can't go to the store and buy C4. I'm glad you can't pick up an RPG on the way home from work. These things are a little too dangerous to be widely owned. And in this age of mental illness, maybe Assault Rifles are too. Maybe that's something we should consider."

"Age of mental illness..." he says mockingly.

"Well, let's face it, you gotta be a least a little bit off-your-rocker to spend your time listening to this show."

"Oh really?"

"Dude... really. That's not to say that I'm not impressed. This has got to be the best job in the world... assuming you're a sadist. I can't think of another realm of employment where your only job is to spread lies and half-truths in an effort to piss off the very customers that pay you. The madder you make them, the more happy they are with your product. It's somehow... beyond brilliant. They say do what you love, so... you know... congratulations!"

Freshly back in town, my stiff muscles long to exit the confines of my truck. Luckily, I'm nearing my destination.

My phone rings.

"Hello."

"What the hell was that?!" Simon says. "I thought you were suppose to be the voice of reason."

"Hey Simon. I guess you listened to the podcast?"

"I guess I did."

"In my defense, that podcast was not my idea. If memory serves, I believe it was yours."

"So I'm to blame?"

"We all make mistakes. I wouldn't judge yourself too harshly."

Simon says nothing, but I can sense his outrage.

I say, "Asking me to have a reasonable conversation with that man is like… asking a penguin to sunbathe. I don't know. I couldn't think of anything and I panicked, landing on a really bad analogy, I apologize, but I think you get my drift. He is not a reasonable man."

I wait for Simon's response, but hear nothing. I look at my phone and see that he has disconnected. How long ago did he hang up? Did he miss my poorly conceived analogy? I really preferred it when you could actually hear someone hang up on you. The crash of the handset into its cradle. The dial tone that followed. It was so much more meaningful, regardless of which side of the equation you were on.

I can see my destination on the right.

It was nothing more than a three story brick box when I purchased it. Red bricks piled thirty feet high with no sense of a purpose or personality. I often marvel at old brick work, but this was different, all craftsmanship and no artistry.

It was May 2021, and a collection of lost souls had managed to position themselves around me. Our conversations began to evolve from politics to more personal matters. I became a counselor of sorts, listening to a vast array of problems so different from my own and yet so familiar. I became a detective, seeking out and exposing the decisions that led them astray. I became a light, guiding them out of the darkness.

One of these lost souls was an architect by the name of Gabriel Travaldi. Throughout his career he had never designed anything he could look upon with pride. Sure, he had conceived of many a fantastical building, beautiful in both form and function, but they were merely plans on paper or ones and zeros on a computer. They were dreams never realized. He spoke of them as inventions that never found a prototype or screenplays that never made a movie. Ultimately, they were worthless.

He had grown weary of his daily grind, working for a corporate design firm, providing his architectural stamp of approval to designs he didn't conceive. The artist within had been so starved for so long, that Gabriel existed within a constant state of mourning, the best part of him slowly withering away.

I drove him to that pile of red bricks. He was unimpressed with my purchase.

"It's just a starting point," I told him. "It's a foundation on which to build a dream. You remember how to do that? Because that's what I need from you."

Gabriel wasn't happy with the site. He wasn't happy with my timeline. He wasn't happy with a lot of things.

I pressed him forward and eventually his mind began to shift. He began to see obstacles as opportunities for creativity. He began to see deadlines as challenges to be overcome. He began to work feverishly, the artist within roaring back to life. Gabriel created his original designs in only a few short weeks.

When the permits came through, twenty-eight of my lost souls volunteered their time. Some worked endlessly, while others gave what they could around their daily responsibilities. We labored days and nights and weekends, a mixture of sweat and laughter and companionship. Often, as the night grew old, we would lay down our tools and play a game of cards, or tell stories, or speak openly of the wounds we were trying so desperately to heal. Some nights the worksite became an impromptu night club with beer runs and mixed drinks and unexpected love.

On July 4th, Piper Halstead brought her husband and an outdoor grill. They cooked up burgers and hot dogs for all amid the music of banging hammers and squealing screw guns. The grill never left, each day becoming an excuse to add to our menu of grillable concoctions.

We were a collection of teachers and students, every one of us giving of ourselves and also taking from others. Each of us growing a bit each day, becoming something more, something better.

Throughout the summer, new faces began to trickle in, somehow drawn to the sense of hope that thrived within the fences of our construction site.

One day, a code enforcement official spent two hours inspecting our work. Eventually, he green-tagged it, permitting us to move forward. Still, he seemed a little concerned or confused by the state of our jobsite. Whatever was bothering him, he made no mention of it. He went on his way and I watched as he stepped outside the fence-line and entered his truck. But he didn't leave. He just sat there behind the wheel, watching the people work. He sat there for longer than I can say. So long, that I began to worry. Eventually, he put on his seatbelt and drove away.

My worry lingered and all I could do was hope that I wouldn't see the man again. Those hopes died just two days later, on a Saturday morning. No longer was he driving a city truck. He stepped out of his personal vehicle and marched onto our jobsite. Around his waist was a tool belt, the handle of a hammer banging against his thigh with each step.

"Thought you guys might want a little help," he said.

We did and so he stayed until nightfall. He would come back the next day and many more after that.

By the end of September, our 28 souls had expanded into 94. A party was held, commemorating the completion of a job well done. The event was bittersweet, each of us knowing that the greatest summer we'd ever spent had officially met its end.

The Daily Oklahoman did the first story. Two photo spreads in architectural magazines would soon follow. Gabriel Travaldi became a wanted man.

He works in California now, designing high-end homes and offices for the rich and famous. Every month he sends a check, tithing 10% to the Stasis Institute.

It has been eleven months since I have taken this drive. Approaching the property, I look upon it as if seeing it for the first time.

That pile of red bricks is unrecognizable.

153

The exterior is a mix of recycled glass and stone and timbers reaching five stories high. Wrap around balconies complement each floor culminating in a rooftop garden of vivid greens with splashes of purples and yellows and oranges and blues.

There is something in its shape that evokes thoughts and feelings that I can't quite grasp. It is at once a sculpture, a marvel, a monument, and a place where dreams come true.

I cross the bridge, driving over the stream that snakes in and around and through the building. I park the car and call Horace Teetum, who I know to be inside.

"Mister Waxman", he answers.

"Hey Horace. I'm about to come up. Do you know who's in the front lobby?"

"Umm, yeah. Della and Shandra are splitting duty."

"Last names?"

"Della Hooper. Shandra Lamb."

"Perfect. I'll be up in twenty or so."

I disconnect the call and log into a secure account on my phone. I pull up the relevant data on Mrs. Della Hooper. I look at her picture. I don't believe I've ever seen her before, so I study her face in an attempt to know her.

I click on a link, opening her file. She and her husband are members of the Mediator Party, funneled in through their involvement with The Stasis Institute. Their work with Stasis has been extensive, receiving Survey Sessions and Balance Sessions on all manner of subjects. From depression, to addiction, to relationship counseling, the Hooper Family has worked its way through a number of difficulties over the past 14 months. Their Advocate, John Prior, noted that Della and her husband were both making great strides on their path toward balance. We are now counseling their 12 year old daughter Penny on a number of self-worth issues. By nearly all accounts, their experience with Stasis has been a positive one.

Recently, both Della and her husband transferred their retirement and savings accounts to Stasis Financial Advisors. The current worth of these accounts is $109,376.32. My expected net profit on their deposits to the fund is 0.75% per year compounded. At its current value that equates to $820.32 and rising. Every two weeks another six hundred dollars is added straight from Della and her husband's paychecks.

I start all over again, beginning my research on Shandra Lamb.

A familiar smiling face greets me as I enter the expansive lobby.

"Della," I say, returning her smile.

"Mister Waxman! Welcome to the Stasis Institute! I can't believe I finally get to meet you."

Apparently, we've never met before. That makes this easier. I always intend to make a note in the file each time I meet someone. When did we meet?… What did we talk about?… That would make things a lot easier, but I always forget… so I struggle through.

I say, "I'm actually really glad to see you. I was just recently reviewing your progress in the program."

"Really? I didn't think you'd concern yourself with a peon like me."

I get close and lower my voice, privatizing the conversation.

"You're a valuable member, Della. Don't sell yourself short. Remind me, you're current focus is financial stability and weight management, correct?"

"Yeah," she says, regretfully. "Two areas where I struggle… as you can see."

"You've expressed some disappointment with the program."

She frowns, "I'm just not losing the weight. I've got 50 pounds that just won't go away."

"You've got a lot working against you. You're a child of the modern age. Look… I want you to do me a favor… it might seem weird but I want you to imagine yourself living thousands of years ago, in a time when your desires can be fulfilled through action and action alone. Go ahead and close your eyes. Really imagine it. If you want to go somewhere, you will do so by foot. Or you will capture an animal and spend many painstaking days and weeks training it to do your bidding. If you want water, you will take a bucket to the river, or maybe you'll dig a well. When you get hungry, you forage for food, or you grow it, or you kill it. Then you prepare that food with tools that you yourself crafted. Cook it on a fire that you had to build. Shelter? You had to build that too. Do you see it."

She nods, "Yeah."

"The you that you're imagining… I'm guessing she doesn't need a weight-loss program. That woman gets all the exercise she needs. And she respects the value of food, because she knows all the work it took to get it. This is the world that we were built to inhabit, Della, but it is not the world in which we live. An epidemic of obesity should surprise no one."

She says, "So… you want me to live like I'm in the Dark Ages?"

"No. I want you to think like you're in the Dark Ages. I want you to think about the value of food. Not how much it costs, but its intrinsic value. Dark Age Della would never put more on her plate than she needed, especially if she had a fridge to keep the leftovers from spoiling."

"I see what you're saying. Everything's too easy now. We've lost all perspective."

I nod, "I was looking at your financial reports. Your spending."

"Yeah?"

"Dark Age Della would never pay someone a hundred and twenty dollars every two weeks to clean her house. She'd be on her hands and knees, scrubbing that floor. You'd be surprised at how much balance can be achieved by simply cleaning up your own mess. Nor would she pay someone to do her grocery shopping for her, if she were lucky enough to have a grocery store. Nor would she buy her way into a freshly cut lawn, when she could very easily do it herself. I'm quite certain that Dark Age Della would love some of the perks of modern day life. Running water… Light on demand… An oven that heats up at the push of a button. You're living in paradise, Della, and you don't even know it. When you lose respect for those things, and then you start paying people to do every little task for you… that's when you become a glut. And that's as far from balance as you can possibly get."

Della sighs, "Wow. That's a lot of work you're talking about."

I say, "And all you get out of it is a healthier mind, a healthier body, and an extra ten grand in the bank every year."

Della squints her eyes at me and considers her response.

"Mommy! Look what I made!" a young girl says, jogging around the corner. She holds in her hands a painted canvas.

"Honey, no. Mommy's in the middle of a conversation."

"Oh, it's no problem. I've said my piece, Della. The next move is up to you." I cast my eyes to the young girl. "This must be Penny."

"Yes it is," Della says.

I say, "What do you got there, Penny? May I see?"

Penny looks at me, wary.

"Go ahead, girl," Della says. "Show the nice man your painting."

Penny turns the canvas around and I am hit with the force of a beautiful flower, its colorful vibrant petals splayed out to the world. The fantastic bloom takes center stage, filling the majority of the canvas. A study of the outskirts of the painting reveals something more. The grass that surrounds the flower appears dry, scorched, and faded. The stem of the flower is shriveled and collapsing under the weight of its bloom. Its leaves are wrinkled and wilting.

Della frowns and shakes her head, "Everything she does is so filled with sadness."

"We've all got some of that," I say and turn to look at Penny. "Only a select few can turn it into something beautiful. You ever sell a painting, Penny? Would you like to sell that one? How much?"

Penny shrugs, unsure.

"How about a hundred dollars?"

Penny's eyes go wide and she nods with excitement.

I complete the transaction as a familiar young woman walks onto the scene.

"Shandra!" I say.

She looks surprised that I know her name.

"Mister Waxman! It's an honor."

I offer my hand and she accepts it. She looks tired. Not the kind of tired that comes from a long day, but the kind that builds over months of worry and sleepless nights.

"The honor's all mine," I tell her. "How's Chris? Are the treatments working?"

Shandra looks at me strangely, surprised again.

"He's doing well. As well as can be expected, I guess, but we're hopeful."

"It's a hard road. I know you know that. But you were built to overcome obstacles. And so was your son. Ultimately, all we can do is fight. And from what I hear, you're doing that. We want to help you fight. Are we doing enough to support you?"

"Oh, the Institute has been amazing. I couldn't ask for more."

I study her and feel her frailty. She's barely hanging on.

"You couldn't? Or you're scared to? Are you afraid that our generosity has met its limits?"

"It's wrong to take more than you give."

"That's a true statement. But there's a time to give and there is a time to take. Understanding that balance is everything, and believe me, we know what time it is. Do you need help, Shandra?"

Shandra's eyes well up with tears. She steps forward, burying her face into my chest. She sobs. I wrap my arms around her. I feel her tears soaking through my shirt.

Shandra is only 32 years old. By all accounts, her son will be gone within the year. The support we give her now will pay dividends for decades to come. She's already a believer, but she will become a fanatic. She will support us and defend us through good times and bad. She will donate her money and volunteer her time. She will be a cog and a recruiter and a spreader of good news. She will be invaluable for the rest of her days.

I feel dirty, thinking this way. But that is the job I have made for myself. I collect people. They are investments. They are opportunities for growth. Each one that I cultivate has the potential for exponential gains. Through their labors, their relations, and their passions... the fortunes of an idea will grow.

I step onto the elevator and shoot a quick email to Shandra's advocate. Afterward, I jot a note into her file marking the details of our interaction. I've got to be better about that.

Next, I send a text to John Pryor, directing him to seek out ways to actively support Penny's artistic endeavors. She is a talented girl. Though her value in the present is likely nil, we must always be planting seeds. To focus solely on the present is to plan a demise.

The elevator car dings and the doors open onto the fourth floor. I activate the stopwatch app on my phone and immediately step out.

They are awaiting my arrival.

I find five people, off to the side, watching me closely. A sixth person stands before me at a small makeshift counter. He smiles at me.

"Hello sir," he says. "Are you here to register to have your voice heard?"

"I am. Is this going to take long?" I ask. "I'm on my lunch break."

"Shouldn't take long at all. I'll just need to see your driver's license or ID."

"Okay. Does my employee ID work? It has my picture on it."

"We can only accept state-issued IDs, sir."

I look over to our watchers and see them making notes.

"I guess we'll go with a driver's license," I say. I pull my license from my wallet and hand it over to the man.

"Is this address correct?"

"It is."

"Perfect," he says. "Now if you'll just place your right index finger on the reader here."

I raise my right hand, holding it at an odd angle.

"I don't have a right hand. Lost it in a tragic farming accident back in oh-two. Changed my life, I'll tell you that."

"I'm sorry to hear that sir, let me just make a quick adjustment."

He punches a couple buttons on his computer.

"Now, if you'll place your left index finger on the reader."

"Sure thing," I say and place my finger on the reader. I look toward the onlookers and say, "What if I didn't have a left hand either? Do we have methods for verification in the odd case of double amputees?"

A woman starts to say something.

I say, "Don't answer. Just know that an answer needs to exist."

The man waiting on me says, "Thank you, sir. We got it."

A printer spits out a paper. On that paper is a copy of my driver's license as well as general information on how to access and use the Mediator's voter survey website. The man hands me the paper and a little fingerprint reader.

"Here you are, sir. And this is your own personal fingerprint reader to verify that your vote is secure."

"Thank you. Are you planning to keep my driver's license?"

"Oh shoot. Sorry about that."

A couple onlookers groan.

The man hands me my license.

"Thank you for playing your part in our Democracy!"

I stop the timer on my phone. One minute and 58 seconds.

"Less than two minutes. What have you guys been finding?"

"On average, about a minute and twenty seconds per citizen."

"And what is this person called?" I ask, gesturing to the man who helped me.

Everyone looks confused.

"Clerk, receiver, sign-up specialist? What do we call them?"

"We hadn't really thought about that."

"Well let's do. Let's give them a name."

"We can do that," one of the on-lookers says.

"How many sign-up specialists can we house at each sign-up center?"

"We expect each sign-up specialist may require about fifty square feet. Not really, but that allows for waiting areas, a break room, things like that. So a thousand foot space could house twenty working simultaneously."

"Have you confirmed that this plan matches code? We cannot give our minders any reason to shut us down. Occupancy. Fire codes. We need all these things to be beyond reproach."

I get a few nods, accompanied by the continued jotting of notes.

"Have we looked into mobile sign ups? A tent in a parking lot? What are the logistics on something like that? What about the sign-up equivalent of a food truck?"

A man says, "We were thinking we might need a team to make direct visits to nursing homes."

"Great idea. What if we took it further? Can we get employers to let us schedule visits to the workplace? Office buildings? Warehouses? Factories? What about neighborhood sign-up drives?"

A young woman raises her hand, "I have a question."

"Are you a part of this team?"

She seems surprised by the question.

"Yes," she says.

"Then you don't need permission to ask a question."

"Oh. Okay. Umm. This might be stupid."

I say, "I don't know if you've noticed, but this is a stupid world. If it wasn't, we wouldn't be doing what we're doing right now. Consequently, the smartest people are the ones who aren't afraid to ask the stupid questions. What is it?"

"Well, I was looking at my grandma's fingers…"

"And…"

"They just look like a collection of wrinkles. Would a fingerprint reader even work on someone like that?"

I let my eyes pass over each individual.

"That's the kind of stupid question we all need to be asking. It may be that we need a number of alternative security options. Trying to find a one-size-fits-all solution may be inviting trouble. And for that matter, are fingerprints even necessary?"

The leader of the group, Horace, speaks up.

"From our polling there's a sizable group that would find anything less to be insecure. And the security of our votes is of the utmost importance."

I nod, thinking.

"Correct me if I'm wrong, but would these be the same people that would never in a million years agree to have their fingerprints stored in an online database?"

"I... don't know, but that sounds right."

"Right," I say. "Forget the fingerprint. I see too many problems. Here's what I want. I want to not buy fingerprint readers for the entire state of Oklahoma. I want two-factor verification. I want a PIN number in their head, plus a one-time password that gets sent to their phone every time they log on. If they're old or poor or for some other reason don't have a cell phone, we can provide them with alternate means."

"OTP tokens," says a man sitting off in a corner, drinking a cup of coffee.

"What is that?"

"It's a one-time password security key that generates a unique password every minute."

"And that password syncs with the main system?"

"That it does."

"Are we talking about a physical item?"

"Yeah. You can just keep it on your key chain."

The man dangles his keys, holding them by what looks a little like a key fob. A closer look shows a digital readout with six numbers displayed.

"Perfect. Let's do that," I say. "And you are?"

"This is Kevin Logan," Horace answers. "I asked him to sit in. He owns a small web-design and internet security firm."

"Stasis member?" I ask.

Horace nods, "Twelve months, I believe."

"Fourteen," Kevin corrects.

"How small?" I ask Kevin.

"I'm sorry?"

"Your firm."

"Uh, twenty-two, no, twenty-one employees. We just had to let someone go."

"Are you looking to expand?"

"Always," Kevin says. "How big a system are we talking about?"

162

"Up to 2.5 million users in the short term. Long term… a quarter of a billion."

Kevin's eyes grow large.

He says, "That's bigger than Facebook in all the U.S."

"Okay. So… what do you need from me to make that happen?"

15

It's moving day and I've agreed to a short break to rehydrate.

Astraea lays on the newly relocated couch, staring up at the ceiling.

"I don't know," she says. "Ya know, I just... I feel judged all the time."

"That's because you are judged all the time," I tell her.

I stand, forearms resting against the two-wheel dolly in front of me. I'm surrounded by furniture and boxes, but my truck in the driveway is still half full. I suspect another two trips to the old house will finish the job.

I look at my helper, lying on the newly relocated couch.

"I'm judging you right now," I tell her.

"That's what I'm talking about. I wanna be free from all that."

"I agreed to a water break. Not nap time. Let's go."

"Ughhh!" She grunts.

Astraea very slowly works her way into a seated position.

"You get what I'm saying though, right? That's all any of us really wants. To be free to be ourselves. To find unconditional love."

"Show me someone who wants unconditional love, and I'll show you someone who doesn't deserve it."

Astraea looks at me with the face of someone who just smelled something awful.

"So only the people who don't want it actually deserve it?"

"No. None of us actually deserve it," I tell her. "Answer me this, do you have a best friend?"

Astraea thinks on that, but seems unable to answer.

I try a different tact.

"Are there people at school you enjoy spending time with?"

"Yes," she says confidently.

"Are there other people who you avoid?"

"Uhh... yeah!"

"What do you think that is?"

She squints her eyes at me.

"It's judgment," I say. "Anytime you make a friend, that's a judgment. Anyone you choose to avoid, that's a judgment. Who you trust. Who you don't. Who you tell your secrets to. Who you want to kiss. Who you wouldn't touch with a ten foot pole. All judgments based on a person's character, their behavior, the way they make you feel. All of it."

"That's just so ugly."

"Sure. That's just life," I shrug. "Every single time you interact with someone, they are making judgments and so are you. And guess what, it's good. This is how you find your people. Judgment isn't always negative. Sometimes you are judged to be worthy. Make no mistake, you are absolutely free to be yourself. It only requires that you find the strength to do so, knowing you will be judged."

"I'm not sure I can do that."

"Do you believe that you're a worthwhile human being?"

"Yes," she says, with offense taken.

"Then you should want to be judged. You should welcome it. The only people who benefit from unconditional love are the people who are unworthy of that love."

"What does that even mean?"

"A lot of people think that the love between a father and daughter should be unconditional."

"What?! Why would you say that?"

"Do you love your dad?"

"Screw you!"

"It's just a question."

165

"I hate my dad!" She says with emphasis on every word.

"But I bet you loved him before he fucked you," I say.

Astraea's skin reddens.

I say, "So apparently your love was conditional. Don't violate me. Don't betray me. Don't treat me like trash. These are what you might call healthy conditions someone might have for anyone they choose to give their love to."

Astraea's angry eyes go soft. She looks down and studies the floor at her feet. A slight sniffle is followed by a wipe of her palm across her face.

Softly, she says, "What if I had said that I do love him?"

My breath catches and a slight crack forms on the surface of my heart. The sad truth of it leaves me momentarily unable to speak.

"Then that should be all the proof you need," I finally say. "That is not the kind of love you want."

She sits there, motionless.

I clap my hands.

"Okay. Time's a tickin'. Let's get back to work."

I head out to the truck, taking the dolly with me.

It's been two weeks since moving in and the renovations are slowly coming along.

All of the furniture in every room has been pushed to the center. We're finally getting around to repairing all the walls. Starting in the den, I patch each angry hole.

Astraea is on graffiti removal. A few days ago, we did a test to see if a painted on primer would cover the graffiti, but as expected, Astraea's story bled through loud and clear.

So now she follows behind me, applying a skim coat of joint compound over every inch of every wall.

I head to the next room and leave Astraea to bury her past in a thin coat of mud.

I approach the next gaping wound. Using a keyhole saw, I cut away the jagged results of an angry moment. I affix spare strips of plywood backing to the healthy remains. Using a freshly cut piece of wallboard, I fill the hole with something clean and unscathed by violence. I press joint compound into the creases before applying mesh tape to every seam.

The combination of all these efforts brings to mind the words of Hemingway – *Strong at the broken places*. Those words are forever tainted now, bringing forth the ghost that haunts me. I can't even listen to music without thinking of her name. She is my broken place and she seems to be growing stronger.

I find another hole and begin the process all over again.

I can hear Astraea moaning and groaning endlessly. I get the feeling her vocal gymnastics are for my benefit. She needs me to know just how miserable she is.

I yell out, "Clearly, you are not a fan of wall work. I get it. Message received!"

"But you're gonna make me keep doing it!" She returns.

"I can't make you do anything. You're free to sleep on the streets if that's what you'd prefer."

She responds with yet another dramatic groan.

I put my tools down and make the short walk to the den. I watch as she erases her horrific story so beautifully told.

"So what do you like?" I ask.

Her body jumps in fright and she nearly falls off the ladder.

"Jesus! You scared me."

"You live with somebody."

"I know that!"

"So… What do you like? What are you passionate about? What is something you could do all day and never complain?"

She doesn't answer.

"What about writing? You're pretty good at that."

"Pretty good. Gee thanks."

"You know what makes a person a better writer? Experiences. Doing things. The development of knowledge. Like it or not, what you're doing right now is making you a better writer."

"Oh thank you, thank you, thank you William! Thank you so so much!" She throws me a mock look of gratitude. "Screw writing. I want to be an engineer."

"Really?"

She looks at me, offended.

"Yes, really!"

I seem to have stirred a bit of feminism. My innocent expression of surprise was clearly the work of the patriarchy.

I say, "An engineer is a person who knows a lot of things about a lot of things. Everything you learn makes you a better engineer. You start combining all these different founts of knowledge, imagining how these different systems and products can interact with each other to solve new problems. I promise you by the time we finish this house, you will be a better engineer. You're welcome."

"Whatever."

The oven timer gives three pulsing beeps from the kitchen.

"Thank God!" Astraea says.

She hops down from the ladder and puts her tools on the floor. She walks past me out of the room.

"Taking a shower!" she says.

"Hey!"

She stops and turns to look at me.

"Remember the rules."

I point to her work area.

"The agreement was three hours," she says.

"The agreement was one meal. How many times a day am I feeding you?"

Astraea pouts.

"Clean your tools."

Astraea looks at me, a defiant visage growing across her features.

"I'm taking a shower!" she says.

She stomps off towards the bathroom. I hear the water turn on.

I take a deep breath and seek balance.

Stepping out into the garage, I open the electrical panel door. Having recently labeled each breaker, it only takes a second to locate the one marked HALL BATHROOM.

I flip the breaker into the off position.

I hear her muffled complaints.

"Hey! Oh come on! That's real mature!"

A short walk from the electrical panel brings me to the water heater. I reach up and turn the lever, shutting off the supply of hot water.

I listen. She screams. I smile.

16

NOVEMBER 6, 2023
365 DAYS UNTIL ELECTION

Every Saturday at exactly noon, the city's countless tornado sirens wail out their song of warning. Without fail, howling dogs join in the chorus. Several minutes pass before finally the silence returns. It is this phenomenon that gave birth to the name of OKC's newest weekly newspaper, *The Noon Siren*.

The Noon Siren is tucked into the turn of an L-shaped strip mall. Historically, this particular shopping center had never fared well in the art of commerce. For reasons unknown, it seemed to be a blackhole in the world. Every day thousands of cars would drive by, none of them seeking refuge in any of the strip mall's many available parking spaces. Over the decades, numerous entrepreneurs had leased out space within its confines. They came in the form of BBQ restaurants, Tattoo parlors, Boutique clothing stores, Donut shops, Diners, Art galleries, travel agents, etc. etc. None of them lasted long. Eventually, the mall would have more vacancies than functioning businesses. As time went on, the mall began to fall into disrepair and the owner had no interest in bringing his tiny little ghost town back to life. He tried to sell it for years. The property taxes alone were bleeding him dry.

Just short of two years have passed since the Stasis Institute purchased the property. On land value alone, it was a hell of a deal.

I pull my truck into the lot and find a space to park. The project is coming along quite nicely. All signs of blight have been erased through many hours of labor. The old boring facade has been reworked with an eye for architectural detail. Most importantly, the parking lot is nearly full. I take a moment to consider all the dreams this project has made possible.

On the corner sits a stand-alone convenience store and filling station. The owner is Kyle Tildon, one of the Stasis Institute's original members. Next door to that, you'll find Frankie's Garage. Frankie is a self-described gearhead, who always dreamed of owning his own shop. Stasis members are quick to support their own, which recently led him to expand his four bays into eight.

The strip mall houses The Noon Siren, The Fresh Taste Grocery, Claudia's Mexican Restaurant, The B&B (burgers & beer), Stasis Financial Services, Joanie's Wine House, The Fitness Team, Neil Smith Dentistry, Confier Insurance, and of course the offices of the Mediator Party.

Without exception, each business is owned and operated by a member of Stasis. On the other side of Tildon's sits another stand-alone building currently receiving a make-over. Once the regulatory filings are complete, we will have our own bank.

I dial my phone.

"What do you want this time?" Simon answers.

"I've got an amazing opportunity for you."

"I feel like I've heard this before."

"I found a publicly traded internet security firm. Their stock is currently residing in hell. They've got some problems, but a strong base of both employees and clientele. Ultimately they are an undervalued asset."

"Why are you telling me this?"

"Because I want you to buy them."

"You want me to own a business I have zero interest in?"

"I want you to own 51 percent of a business you have zero interest in."

Simon says nothing. I check to make sure he hasn't hung up on me again.

"We need it, Simon. We're about to roll out this Survey Sign-up plan, and it'd be a really good idea to pair that with an actual functioning website. We need the manpower and expertise to build a powerful and secure system. This thing has to be above reproach. I've got just the guy to run it. Plus I got another guy who has spent his whole life dreaming of orchestrating a hostile takeover. Come on Simon, let me get it for you."

Simon sighs.

"Are they profitable?"

"Not remotely, but we can work on that."

Simon sighs again.

"Send me your research, I'll look at it."

I step out of my truck and enter Stasis Financial Services.

Paul looks at me as I walk through the door.

He says, "Well I'll be damned. You're not dead."

"You miss me?"

"I wouldn't go that far. Glad you're not dead though."

I say, "It's not official yet, but I got a surprise for ya. Something you've always wanted."

"Your ex-wife."

"No. Much better than that."

I hand him a piece of paper.

"I need you to put together a plan to acquire controlling interest in this company."

Paul looks at me like a child on Christmas.

"Really! A hostile takeover!"

"You will have a budget."

"Of course. That's the fun part!" Paul says. "You've just made my day! Growing your fund is riveting and all, but it's not exactly... well, it's not riveting, I lied just now. The most exciting part of my day was reading about you online."

"Someone wrote about me?"

"Someone? Everyone. You don't know about this?"

"Know about what?"

"Apparently you're a murderer."

The news of a radical leftist strangling his girlfriend, dousing himself with gasoline, and lighting them both on fire had understandably earned a few headlines in the days after its discovery. In those days, there had been no mention of my date with the dead woman on that very night. Nor was there mention of the man's home-office full of various surveillance photos and copious notes pertaining to yours truly.

Last week, that changed. Someone tipped off the right wing media of Morgan Turnbull's official association with a Democratic Super PAC and his apparent mission to spy on the leader of the Mediator Party.

Fox News and several conservative podcasters wasted no time raising a stink over the behavior of the Democratic Party. They lambasted the poor hiring practices and loudly called out the morally and ethically reprehensible act of political spying. They described me as the leader of a rival political party, a small moderate organization of little note.

They managed to rarely speak my name or the name of my Party. No free publicity for me. They also managed to paint the Democrats as petty, scared, feeble creatures, but dangerous, the way a cornered animal is dangerous.

"If they are willing to go to those lengths over a nothing organization, what are they doing to the groups they really fear?" One podcaster asked. "What are these people up to? What are they doing right now? These guys are crazy. How many spies do they have? And how many of them are members of Antifa?"

As of today, the sparse mentions of my name came to an end. Left leaning journalists all across the internet have begun writing stories theorizing my personal involvement in the deaths of Morgan Turnbull and Melody Frye. My name is used liberally along with the name of my Party.

The articles refer to Morgan as merely an activist and Melody as nothing more than a woman who had questionable luck with men. It is suggested that the murder-suicide was likely staged as well as any evidence of spying.

"The mere idea that the Democratic Party would spy on such an unproven organization is preposterous," one article stated.

Quoting unnamed sources close to the investigation, the article claims that the scene was "hinky" and "full of inconsistencies". Which, by the way, is complete bullshit. We literally thought of everything.

I open the door to The Noon Siren. A young lady chews gum and stares at her phone while manning the receiving desk of the small lobby.

"I don't have my card. Would you buzz me through?"

"I'm sorry sir, but-" her throat catches and eyes grow wide. "Of course, Mister Waxman."

I hear the lock disengage and I push through.

The room houses a couple dozen work spaces. I don't do an official headcount, but there are at least fifteen people staring at screens and pounding on keyboards.

Scarlet's tense voice can be heard barking out terse words. I follow the sound and find the back of her head. The purple hair is long since gone, giving way to her natural color. She's currently addressing three of her writers. None of them dare look her in the eyes.

"I don't want excuses. We cannot let these accusations stand. I want the police, on the record, setting this straight, today. 'Mister Waxman is not a suspect in this investigation'. Those are the words I want to hear. 'Mister Turnbull's death has been ruled a suicide'. More words I want to hear."

"My defender," I say.

Scarlet turns. Her pretty face is not nearly as soft as I remember it. It's as if some internal tourniquet has tightened every muscle fiber to the eve of snapping.

Her eyes find me and those features only grow harder.

"What the fuck!" she says.

"Good to see you too," I respond.

She stomps past me. "My office!" She barks.

I look to the writers.

"She seems, I don't know… stressed?"

"Now!" She yells from across the space.

"Yeah, I think she might be stressed."

One of the writers actually cracks a smile. The other two don't dare.

I enter Scarlet's office and close the door.

She stares at me from behind her desk.

I stare back.

"Are you going to answer my question?" she asks.

I look at her, unsure. She looks at me, expectant.

"I don't remember you asking a question."

"Sure you do. It sounded like this… what the fuck?"

"You're referring to the articles?"

Scarlet takes a deep labored breath, the way someone does when they're trying to stop themselves from destroying everything within reach.

She says, "Sure. Why not? Let's start there."

She picks up her phone and swipes at the screen. She activates something with the punch of an angry finger. She speaks into her phone.

"Interview with subject William Waxman, November 6th, twelve twenty-three pm."

Scarlet sets the phone down in between us.

"Mister Waxman, what… the… fuck?"

I put my hands up defensively, "Okay…"

I sit down in the seat across the desk from her. I explain to her about my breakfast buddy, Morgan. About how he decided he wanted to set me up with a girl. About how I finally agreed.

"Was it a nice date?"

"It was fine."

"You slept with her?"

I take a breath. I don't want to answer, but do.

"Yes."

"Great! So what happened next."

"She left. That was the end of it."

"Until…"

"The next day two cops came knockin'."

Scarlet asks for their names and I provide them.

"I told them about my neighbor across the street. He has video cameras all around his house. One of them points directly at mine. That alone should prove that she left and that I didn't. She took an Uber, which I assume can be verified as well. They seemed satisfied with that."

"Did they tell you why they were there?"

"Not specifically, but after they got my story, they started asking questions about Morgan. How did I know him? How did we meet? Things like that. They asked me what I did for a living. They asked me if I knew that Morgan was basically stalking me."

"To which you said?"

"No."

"And that was true?"

"Yes."

"He was spying on you?"

"It seems so. They said they found evidence of his extreme interest in all things me."

"And you had nothing to do with anything that happened after Melody left."

"Of course not."

I can't stand lying to her. Not to her.

A truly free man need not lie about anything. I feel the cage clamping down around me. By my own actions, I am a prisoner. For the rest of my life I will be forced to hide from the truth. And I will never again be free.

It is the price I must pay.

She says, "I promise you by tomorrow I will set the record straight."

"Maybe you could hold off on that."

"What?!"

"I see an opportunity."

"Your reputation is being damaged. The Party's reputation is being damaged."

"Like you said, you're gonna set the record straight. What's a few days gonna hurt?"

"What's it gonna help?"

"You said yourself, we're being damaged."

"And…"

"And…" I say. "More damages."

"You're gonna sue? It's nearly impossible to sue the media."

"Who said anything about the media?"

She tilts her head at me and slowly begins to nod.

She says, "Three days, then I'm shutting it down."

"Sounds good," I say. "Enough about that. How's progress? Have you built us an entire world yet?"

"A small one."

"Run it down for me. If you don't mind."

She stares at me, wordless. The anger in her features has yet to subside. I knew she would be mad at me. But I believed, perhaps naively, that it wouldn't last any more than a minute or two.

From the moment we met, our connection was something hard to explain. Often we would find ourselves in a room full of people, yet somehow it felt otherwise. It was like experiencing two realities within the same moment, or existing simultaneously on two different planes. On one plane, there would be a large gathering, people talking, engaging me in conversations, asking me questions, and telling me stories. On the other plane, there was only her and I. We were alone in a room full of people, connected by some mysterious force.

Never in my life had I experienced anything like her. It was exhilarating. It was terrifying.

We were being pulled together like gravity. I never much believed in fate, but this I could hardly deny. Inevitably, we were bound to merge. There was nothing I could do to stop it, except remove myself from her completely.

After election day, I did just that.

And now she's mad at me.

Scarlet opens a drawer and produces a folder. She opens it on the desk.

"My team has established credentials for fifteen different independent news organizations."

"Websites?"

"Correct," she says bluntly.

"Any print?"

"Other than The Noon Siren, no," she says. "Though I knew your old ass would want some print media, so we've established relationships with people at the Daily Oklahoman, The Gayly Oklahoman, The Gazette, The Tulsa World, and a few community newsletters. When the time comes, we might be able to push them to syndicate a story here and there."

"Have any of our publications written about the Mediator Party?"

"A couple mentions, but generally, no. Currently we're just establishing ourselves as reputable news sources."

"Perfect. How's that going?"

"Three are regularly receiving wide distribution. Two hard left, one hard right. You could go on Facebook or Yahoo right now and probably see one of our stories."

"About what?"

"The latest… political… hot topic," she says, annoyed. "Does it matter?"

She really is not happy with me.

"I guess not," I say.

"Anyway, they're doing really well. Those three are actually profitable. We got four more that are improving fairly rapidly. The others are pretty small-time still."

"Sounds like you're doing good work," I say.

The comment is a ridiculously forced sort of olive branch that I immediately hate myself for uttering. From the sneer she throws me, I can tell she feels the same.

178

"Okay," I say. "What else?"

"Blogs. We are currently producing 50 local blogs."

"Political?"

"Ten of them. Two moderate, very little readership. Four hard left, four hard right, with varying topics of concentration."

"Gotcha."

"Those are doing better. And they are each ready and waiting to have a political change of heart."

"Perfect. The other 40?"

"It's a hodge-podge. Movie reviews, TV, foodies, crafting, video games, baking, sports. They each have a tendency to engage their audience in off topic conversations though, so it won't be weird when they delve into politics."

This workmanlike conversation is annoying the hell out of me. Why does it have to be like this?

"Nice," I say. "What's next?"

"Podcasts. We aren't creating any of our own, but I've got a few irons in the fire. Plus we have eight different local podcasts who can be sympathetic to our cause."

"Can be?"

Scarlet rubs her forefinger and thumb together in the universal sign for 'Money'.

"Right, right. Moving on."

Scarlet sighs. She appears to be just as annoyed as I am.

"We have 6500 different social media accounts."

"You've created 6500 people?"

"No. About two thousand people, spread out over 6500 accounts. Like if I had a TikTok, a Facebook, and an Instagram. That's 3 accounts, but only one me."

"Do these accounts have lots of friends?"

"Some do. About a third are very well developed. Lots of details and lots of friends and interactions."

"The rest?"

"The rest… are moving in that direction," she says in the most pissy way possible. "It's a process. We've also created a hundred thousand generic positive posts about the Mediator Party. When it's time, we'll start pushing them out."

"Like what?"

"Like, 'Oh my God, finally a political party that I can get behind. They are going to change everything! Puppies and roses and donuts for all'!"

"Is it gonna read sarcastic, because in real life it felt a little…"

"I'll add an emoji to make it clear."

"Right, because emoji's are never sarcastic."

"We've also written a quarter of a million posts about the disillusionment they feel toward politics in general."

"You're gonna have two thousand people send a quarter of a million posts?"

"No. They'll send some, but the rest will be random bots in various posts on various sites and comments sections and things like that."

"Alright. I like that."

"Oh, I'm so happy to hear it."

"Is that it?" I ask.

"You need more?"

"Only if there is more."

"I think we can call it good," she says.

"Okay, but first, I think we should discuss your attitude."

"My attitude?"

"Your general demeanor."

"You find it objectionable?"

"I find it… less than… cheery."

"Well, perhaps I have abandonment issues," she says, standing to emphasize her point.

"Oh, so this is my fault."

"Of course it's your fault," she says. "I haven't seen you in a year."

"It hasn't been a year."

"It's been almost a year."

"In my defense, you know I'm an asshole."

"But never to me," she says, her voice cracking.

Tears are suddenly streaming down her face.

In all the time we've spent together, in all the moments we've shared, I've never once touched her. I instinctively knew that any physical contact, no matter how innocent, would be more than I could bear.

And yet, before I even know it, I have risen to my feet, gone around the desk, and taken her in my arms.

I hold her tight and she cries into my shoulder. I was right to never touch her. This is a mistake. I just need her to stop crying. Her sadness is unbearable.

Suddenly, I pull back, releasing her from my grasp. I turn and walk back to my seat.

I pretend like the hug never happened, banishing it from existence. I ignore her sadness and begin speaking in an authoritative tone.

"There's something else, but first, I'm gonna need you to forgive me."

"You want me to forgive you?"

"No. I need you to forgive me. It's a required action."

She looks at me like I'm crazy. I hold firm.

She's says, "Just like that? Flip a switch?"

"Yes. Choose to forgive me. Do it right now."

"Really?"

"You don't have to say it. Just do it. Enjoy my company, while I enjoy your company, and we work together to fix the problems of this nation. That is what we set out to do, so let's do it."

Scarlet retakes her seat in a very proper manner.

"Okay. Fine."

"Fine?" I say.

"I'm doing it," she assures me.

"As we speak, you're doing it?"

I look at her with a critic's gaze.

"This is what it looks like where I'm from. Passed down through the generations. From my mother. From my mother's mother. From my -"

"Mother's mother's mother... got it," I say. "Okay then, fine. Let's move on, have you been doing your research?"

"What research is that?"

"I asked you to do some research..."

"You're speaking of eight months ago?" she asks.

"I don't know how long..."

"It was eight months ago. When you called and woke me up at four in the morning."

"I wasn't aware it was four in the morning."

"They make things for that. They call them clocks. Or watches. Or basic recognition of the fact that it's been dark for eight hours. Or... Phones. You know, that thing that was in your hand when you made the call."

"I feel like we've gotten off topic. We were discussing your research."

"Yes! I did the research."

"And."

"And I went down the rabbit hole. I learned everything there is to know about conspiracy theories. I became an expert. How they start. How they spread."

"Do you think you could create one?"

"Of course. It's not a question of can I create one. It's a question of whether people will latch onto it."

"Could you help that along?"

"Sure, I could create an atmosphere where a theory appears to be taking hold, but actually taking hold... no."

"Because..."

"Conspiracy theories serve a purpose, William. They fill a void in the hearts of the weak, the sad, the lonely. They make people feel special. Feel in the know. Feel important. All the while confirming and justifying their original feelings of hate towards... whoever."

"So it comes down to the theory itself?"

"Absolutely. Does it connect? Does it fill that void?"

I think about that for a moment.

I say, "I think I've got one."

"Oh goody. Left or right?"

"Neither."

"Well then who's gonna care about it?"

"The middle."

"The middle doesn't seek out conspiracy theories, William. How the hell are we gonna do that?"

"No idea, That is why I've co-opted the brilliant mind of Scarlet Graham."

Scarlet sighs once again.

I say, "I reject the notion that reasonable people are above conspiracy. When reasonable people are inundated with the unreasonable from both sides day in and day out, the only reasonable thing is to conclude that there is something very unreasonable going on."

"Ya know, I used to enjoy your little tantrums," she says. "Now I'm wondering if maybe I was suffering from some form of Stockholm Syndrome."

"Would you like to hear the theory?"

"I'm on the edge of my seat," she says, leaning back in her chair.

I walk across the room toward the large white board that resides on the far wall.

I stop abruptly and stomp back, "I would like to point out that you are, quite clearly, *not* on the edge of your seat."

Her mouth says nothing, but her eyes say, '*Crazy*'.

I march back to the whiteboard. I draw a small circle about five inches in diameter. I draw a larger circle around the first, this one about twelve inches in diameter. I start to draw a third circle, even larger.

I say, "I want you to imagine a series of concentric circles."

"Am I imagining it, or am I watching you draw it?"

"Both. You are seeing what I'm drawing, but you're imagining it in greater detail."

I look at her and she shrugs.

"For instance, this smallest circle... Do you know what this is? I bet you can imagine what this is."

"This is the conspiracy theory?"

"That is what we've been discussing."

She squints her eyes and thinks for a moment.

"Is it a Cabal?"

"Yes! It is a cabal."

"No points for originality," she says.

"A cabal of powerful people at the highest levels of society and government that all have one common goal. The destruction of the United States. It's Kim Jong Un, and Putin, and Xi, and George Soros, and Bill Gates..."

"Bill Gates! Always a good choice."

"You add it all up, this inner circle is populated by a hundred of the most powerful people in the world. Are you with me?"

"Well I did pass second grade, soooo..."

"The mission is simple. Take the most powerful country in the world and teach it to eat itself. Teach it to pick at its own scabs. To never heal. Convince it to scratch and claw at its own body. To enlarge its wounds until those wounds cover every inch. Let those wounds fester. Let them become infected. And watch as America grows weaker and weaker each day, until finally all that power is a thing of the past."

Scarlet rises from her seat and comes a couple steps closer.

She says, "Believable so far... How long has this mission been active?"

"At least a few decades, but making great strides as of late."

Scarlet nods and moves a few steps closer.

"I'm feeling it."

"The next circle. Now there's thousands of these people here. These are the Agents. People working directly for the Cabal. They know exactly what they're doing and why they're doing it. Trained operatives, ideologically aligned with the cabal's goals. Ten thousand strong, walking among us."

"Exciting."

I move to the third ring. Larger yet again.

"This next ring holds a hundred thousand. These are the compromised. Americans who have sold out their country."

"Compromised how?"

"By these guys, the Agents. Compromised through money, power, fame, sex, good old-fashioned blackmail… or any number of reasons. Whatever that reason, it's enough for them to do as they're told. They use whatever platform they have to spread hate and division to the masses. Most of them probably don't even know why they're doing it. They only know they have to do it, because they're…"

"Compromised," Scarlet says moving closer. "Sounds like we're going big here."

"Yes we are."

I begin to draw a fourth circle, but the white board isn't big enough, so I put partial lines at all the four corners, suggesting the size of the circle.

"This circle holds north of a hundred million."

"Whoa!"

"These are the useful idiots. The people who eat up all the propaganda they've been fed. The bullshit on the compromised left. The nonsense of the compromised right. All the crap. All the hate. They soak it up. They have no idea, none, that they are serving a larger goal. Consequently, they have no qualms about going out into the world or online and spreading that shit to anyone who will listen. And those who listen, spread it further. And further. And further."

I draw a bunch of exes inside the circle, radiating out until the exes begin to populate outside the circle.

"And the circle just keeps getting bigger," Scarlet says.

"That it does."

"So who are these Agents, exactly?"

"I don't know. Who do you think they are?"

"University professors?"

"Maybe. Maybe some are agents. Maybe some are compromised."

"Or just useful idiots."

"They do seem to be that. What about this guy?" I say, writing a name on the board.

I step aside, allowing her to see the name – Ben Shapiro

I say, "I'm certain he lives in one of these circles. Which one do you think?"

Scarlet stares at the whiteboard, her eyes darting around.

"Whoa!" she says, excitement growing in her voice. "It's a game!"

I smile.

"Wait," she says. "I thought you liked Ben Shapiro?"

"I do. But I think of him like a contractor. A man who makes his living building houses. He's very hands on, running his own crew. He builds beautiful houses with strong foundations."

"I think a lot of people would call those houses ugly."

"But that's just a question of style. Just because you don't care for Tudor-style architecture doesn't mean it's not well-built. The kind of house that you know will be there for centuries to come. The problem is, those aren't the only houses he builds. He's got a dozen sub-contractors, out there building another dozen houses with the money he gives them. And most of those houses are slapped together with bad materials and foundations made of shit. Do I think that Ben is out there personally spreading lies and half-truths and twisted facts in an effort to fuel hatred? Not really. But he's a contractor, selling conservatism to the masses, and in this business, you are who you hire."

Scarlet nods, "Agent? He's very smooth. Very well trained. I think agent."

"Yeah, I think so," I agree. "How about…"

I write – Tucker Carlson

"Ohh, Compromised, no question," she says. Scarlet throws up a finger to accentuate a light-bulb-moment. "Hashtag Compromised."

"Yessss!" I say with fervor. "Hashtag Compromised. How about Joy Behar and all those bitches from The View?"

"Idiots. We don't need to talk about them."

"What do we think…"

I jot another name onto the board.

"…Nancy Pelosi has been doing all these years?"

"Agent. Agent all the way. No no, Hashtag EnemyAgent."

I write two more names. Matt Gaetz. Josh Hawley.

"Idiots," Scarlet says with confidence.

"AOC?"

"Idiot. And her squad members too. Hashtag Useful Stupid Idiots."

"Rupert Murdoch?"

She thinks, "Mmm. Got to be Cabal, right?"

I consider, "Hashtag… Cabal?… TheCabal?"

"I think 'the'. 'The', right? Definitely 'the'."

We spend the next hour feverishly filling up the board with names. We energetically debate the merits of each name, determining their level of treasonous guilt. It's quite fun.

Scarlet plops down into a seat in front of the white board. She looks utterly worn out. If someone entered the office right now, they would swear that we just had sex. Not just sex, great sex.

Scarlet says, "Tell me you still smoke."

I pull the pack from my pocket and offer her a cigarette plus a light.

She says, "That was amazing!"

She stares at the white board.

"This is brilliant. I'm not even sure it's not true. The far left and the far right working together to destroy America. It's perfect. And the useful idiot bit…"

She kisses her fingers like a French chef.

"Nobody wants to be that. There's shame in that. Anyone posts something divisive, you just respond with hashtag UsefulIdiot. No need for any other words. You just mark them and move on. It's… absolutely beautiful!"

"But will it work?" I ask.

"Oh it's gonna work," she says, determined. "It's damn sure gonna work. When do we want it to happen?"

"This? Well it needs time to grow right? You can do it right away. Only one rule. It doesn't touch the Mediator Party. We can't be known to be the source of this thing."

"Oh no. Not even a little bit," she says.

I check my phone for the time.

"I gotta get. Is there anything else you need?"

Still staring at the white board, she doesn't even bother to look at me, lost in the afterglow. She raises her hand up in a lazy dismissive wave.

I turn and head for the door.

"Dinner," she says.

I turn back, "What?"

"You asked if there was anything else I need. I need you to buy me dinner. I'll get dressed up. You'll… dress the way you do. You'll take me to some ridiculously expensive restaurant, and we'll eat dinner."

"Scarlet…"

"William…"

"You know I can't do that."

"I've seen you eat dinner, William. You are perfectly capable."

"You are not 25 yet."

"Yes I know, 'my brain is not fully formed'. And yet this fact has never managed to keep me from putting food in my mouth."

I look at her for a long while. I actually lose track of the seconds, lost in her. What is it about her? Is it because she was my first? The very first mind I ever collected. The first inkling that maybe, just maybe, I could change this world. Is she a symbol of what is possible? Is that what makes her so special?

Or is it something more? Is she that thing that naive people dream about? *The one* that was made just for me? A soul mate? If so, why the hell is she so damn young? I need a woman, not a child.

What is she? Twenty-three now? Not quite a child, but still… terribly young.

And yet, I can't deny that the last thing I want to do is leave this room. Removing myself from her was the hardest thing I've ever done. I've never felt so lonely, not even with my wife.

What's the harm? It's just dinner.

"Fine. *Dinner*," I say, with enough emphasis on the word that it sounds like 'just dinner'.

"Yes, *dinner*. That's what I said."

I turn to leave.

"When?" she says.

"When would you like?"

She shrugs, "I eat dinner daily. Strangely enough, I plan on having dinner tonight."

"I have to be in court in an hour and then I'm prepping for my California trip."

"When you get back then."

I nod, "I'll call you."

17

Standing in line at the security checkpoint for the downtown district court is a little like a time warp sending me back to the scene of a former life. It is at once both familiar and so very distant.

For five years I toiled within these walls. As a public defender, I'm not totally sure I ever represented an innocent client. Though many claimed to be, there were only three that I had an occasion to believe. Two of them, I walked out the door, free as a bird. The third didn't get so lucky. He was found guilty of armed robbery and sentenced to five years. His name was Ronnie.

Ronnie was poor and also black. He was a solitary young man who tended to spend his evenings alone watching TV. He had a deep abiding love for science fiction.

The victim was a white man who owned a Liquor Store. While he had a number of video cameras, he'd long ago grown tired of the act of actually recording and storing the footage. Ultimately, that didn't matter. He told the police that he could swear that he recognized the man as a customer who always purchased the same large bottle of Seagram's 7 Crown whiskey along with a small bottle of Jagermeister.

The victim determined the price of those two items, then combed through his credit receipts until he found the one signed by Ronnie West.

As I said, Ronnie was poor. They called that motive. He also lived alone and had no one to verify his whereabouts. They called that opportunity.

The prosecutor, Maggie Jamison, had no physical evidence that connected Ronnie to the crime. She had exactly one eye witness, the victim. Despite the fact that eye witness testimony is at best, flawed, it was the only excuse the jury needed.

Ronnie was a track star in high school. As they led him away, I imagined him running. I Imagined him running so fast that no one could catch him. But Ronnie didn't run that day.

Three months later, he did. Suddenly, he just ran, but not toward freedom, or at least not the freedom I imagined for him. He was in the prison cafeteria when, without warning, he dropped his tray and sprinted across the mess hall. It was a sizable room, giving Ronnie plenty of time to pick up speed. As he neared his destination, Ronnie bowed his head and bent his torso forward. His legs never stopped pumping until he reached the sudden stop of a concrete block wall.

The impact fractured Ronnie's skull and caused his brain to swell. He spent his last three days in a hospital bed before his family decided to let him go.

We pretend as attorneys that we are fighters for justice. The truth is, we are nothing more than fighters for our side, right or wrong. Justice is the extremely flawed by-product of our wins and our losses.

The results of a single case are of little consequence in the greater scheme. The fate of Ronnie West was of little consequence. If an attorney cannot accept that truth, that attorney is in the wrong business. Less than a year after Ronnie's last race, I was working in another profession, staring at stock tickers and playing with people's lives in a completely different way.

Being back in this place brings no sense of nostalgic joy. Like muscle memory, I feel the pressure building in my chest. I'm surrounded by an overwhelming sense of dread. Just another meaningless cog in the dark and dank factory of American Justice.

I make it to the courtroom with a few minutes to spare. My client, Axton Leclaire, is already seated at the table. His brightly colored prison garb clashes with his dark skin.

A man in the gallery gives me a wave. I can't remember his name, but the face is familiar. I approach him.

"Hey man," I say, offering a shake.

"Wax!" he says, accepting my offer. "I saw your name on the docket. Couldn't resist seeing you in action! I'm not the only one. I guess the Iron Lady wanted to get an up close and personal view."

He gestures to the prosecution's table.

I look and find Maggie Jamison sitting there, studying a file.

I give the man a pat on the shoulder. "Well, it was good to see you. I'll try not to let you down."

I squeeze in to the first row of the gallery and sneak up behind Maggie.

"I was just thinking about you."

Her body stiffens. She doesn't look back.

"Your sexual fantasies are of no interest to me, Mister Waxman."

"I wonder if that's true," I ponder aloud.

"All Rise," the bailiff calls the court into order.

The Honorable Melvin Harlow is introduced. He is a black man who worked tirelessly to claim his right to wear the black robe. He was a good draw for me and my client, in part because he's black, but mostly because he's reasonable.

Judge Harlow arrives at the bench.

"Be seated," he says. "Mister Leclaire, where is your attorney?"

I raise my hand from the gallery.

"I'm here, Your Honor," I say. "My apologies. By my watch you called to order two minutes early. I was just taking a moment to say hello to an old friend."

I enter the arena and walk to the defense table. I give Axton a reassuring pat.

The Judge says, "Mister Waxman, oh good. I was of the belief that you had left the legal profession."

"For the most part, Your Honor. But sometimes there's an injustice so egregious it can't be ignored."

"Well, it seems even injustice has a silver lining. We have so missed you in these hallowed halls."

I say, "I'd like the record to show that Your Honor was employing sarcasm in his last statement."

Judge Harlow smirks, not taking my request seriously.

"Could go to bias in these proceedings," I say.

He looks at me, incredulous.

"Really?"

I shrug.

The Judge positions himself to look down on his court reporter.

"Let the record show that His Honor was indeed employing sarcasm," he says. "But he did so in good humor and no bias was apparent."

The court reporter chuckles.

I lean in toward Axton.

"Told you this would be fun."

He looks at me, questioning whether or not I know what I'm doing.

"Well, it's your hearing," the Judge says.

He gives a wave suggesting that the floor is mine.

I stand, "Your Honor, in the state of Oklahoma, a person who is attacked in a place they have the right to be has no duty to retreat. They have the right to stand their ground and meet force with force, including deadly force."

Maggie stands, "Judge, he's conveniently leaving out the most salient piece of the statute."

"And what piece is that?" the Judge asks.

"The statute doesn't just mention 'a person'. It says, and I quote, 'a person who is not engaged in an unlawful activity'."

I respond, "That's exactly my point, Your Honor. I've read the transcripts. In my client's original trial, nearly seven years ago, the prosecution never made any attempt to prove that his actions weren't born of basic self defense. Their only contention was that he was breaking the law in the moments before he defended himself."

The Judge says, "A jury of his peers agreed with that contention."

"Based on what evidence, Your Honor?"

Maggie says, "Enough for the jury to convict, Judge. The defendant had just procured a sizable amount of illegal narcotics."

I say, "If that's the case, then direct me toward the proof. Did anyone see him carrying drugs? Is there video of my client taking possession of these drugs? Were these 'sizable narcotics' ever logged into evidence?"

She says, "The defendant left the scene of the crime, taking the evidence with him. Sadly, it was never found."

"Sounds like a 'no', Your Honor."

The Judge looks at Maggie, "So what evidence did the prosecution present?"

"Multiple witnesses, Judge. The victim was no angel. A stick-up man, known for targeting members of the drug trade exclusively. Such as… the defendant."

"Objection," I say.

The Judge just waves me off.

Maggie continues, "Mister Leclaire was known to have worked for his Uncle, a reputed trafficker of narcotics. Mister Leclaire was seen entering and exiting the apartment of Tito Hernandez, a very well known drug kingpin. He entered empty handed and left carrying a briefcase. Other witnesses saw Mister Leclaire exit the apartment building still carrying said briefcase just moments before the incident."

"Your Honor, by 'incident', I believe she's referring to the moment my client was accosted with a sawed-off shotgun."

"So noted."

"And he was carrying a briefcase? I'm sorry, did briefcases become unlawful at some point? Is this some new statute that I'm unaware of? If so, I apologize for wasting the court's time. But I will call upon the court to arrest that woman, right now!"

I dramatically point to Maggie and the briefcase that resides at her feet.

"A crime is being committed!"

Maggie looks at me the way a teacher does a petulant child.

Judge Harlow tries and fails to hold back an amused smile.

Maggie says, "Your Honor, as you said, the evidence was sufficient for a jury to convict."

I say, "If you think so, then why wasn't he charged with that crime?"

I turn my attention to Judge Harlow.

"Judge, I'm sure you're aware that the prosecutor's office has a long history of stacking charges. If they could've made that case, they would've charged him with it."

The Judge looks to Maggie, "Counselor?"

"Your Honor?"

"What say you? He makes an interesting point."

"I don't believe he does, Your Honor," she says defiantly.

The Judge says, "You say the man is not eligible to claim self defense because he was committing a crime… and yet you neglect to charge him with that crime?"

"We felt the charge of 2nd degree murder was sufficient. We didn't feel the need to add insult to injury."

I watch the Judge closely. He is clearly skeptical of Maggie's assertion.

I say, "I'd like the record to show that the prosecution's last statement was supremely unconvincing."

Maggie's eyes go killer-wide. The Judge turns his attention to me. He appears on the verge of admonishing my behavior, but a change of heart redistributes his features.

"So noted," he says.

"YOUR HONOR!" Maggie cries.

18

I stand in front of a wall covered in writings and drawings from a Sharpie marker. This time it is me who has defaced my property with the results of today's lesson. The multitude of notes and diagrams that I've created all refer to the engineering genius of one specific item – tongue and groove floors.

Astraea sits across the room, facing away from me, unable to see the answers scrawled across the wall.

"Okay," I say. "This is it."

"For all the marbles," Astraea says.

"To determine Decision-Making-Rights on what groceries populate our fridge this week. Are you ready?"

"I was born ready."

"As it applies to the usage of nails, tell me five specific advantages tongue and groove flooring gave the world when compared to its predecessor, simple plank floors."

"Ease of finishing," she says.

"Explain."

"It's hard to sand a wood surface when it has nail heads on that surface."

"Correct. Next."

"No visible nail heads make for a more attractive floor."

"That's two."

"Face nailing tends to be hammered in at ninety degrees, but when nailing a tongue and groove floor the nails go in at 45 degrees."

"I'm sorry I can't accept that answer."

"What?!"

"Those are just numbers. 90? 45? Why is one better than the other?"

"Nails sent in at an angle are more resistant to perpendicular forces, like say, constant foot traffic, keeping the flooring more securely fastened to the subfloor."

"Correct. Three down."

"Uhh, nail pops!" she says with extreme excitement. "Face nails can loosen and pop up, which creates a safety hazard! Trip hazard! Ouchies on your feet!"

I laugh. "That's good, but why aren't we worried about that with tongue and groove?"

"Because each subsequent board covers the nails from the previous board, making them invisible and physically stopping them from popping up!"

"Perfect! One more and you've got it."

"Umm, shit! I know this."

I smile to myself. She doesn't know this, because I only taught her four advantages.

I say, "I can practically taste the groceries I'm gonna pick."

"No, no. I know this. Hold on."

"I don't think you know it. No mac and cheese for you!"

"Wait! Efficiency of materials! Tongue and groove requires half as many nails!"

The answer takes me by surprise.

"I didn't teach you that."

"But it's true. To make each edge secure, simple planks would require two nails every sixteen inches, but with tongue and groove you only need one."

I nod, "Why is that?"

"Because the groove edge is mechanically held down by the tongue of the previous board."

I nod my head proudly.

"I guess you will get mac and cheese."

"Yayyyy!" Astraea screams while frantically clapping her hands.

She turns and looks at me.

"That was a pretty dirty trick though asking for five when you only taught me four."

"Part of being a good engineer is using the information that you have to find the answers that you need."

"Which I did," she says, eyes beaming.

"Yes you did. Good work."

"Now that I've secured my victory, why are you defacing my nice clean wall? You're not gonna make me mud over it again are you?"

"I've decided we're gonna knock this wall down."

"So I wasted all that work?"

I shrug.

She says, "Are you sure that wall can come down?"

"It's not a question of whether it can come down, it's a question of what must be done to make it so."

"And you know what that is?"

"I have no idea. Luckily, I have an engineer on staff."

I look at her.

"Me? I hope you're not talking about me."

"I'm gone all next week. The only job you have in my absence is to determine what must happen in order to remove this wall from existence."

"I don't know how to do that."

"First, you go up in the attic and see what there is to see. Apply thought and common sense and knowledge of gravity… things like that. Second, you do research. Go online. See what you can find."

"How am I suppose to go online? You won't even let me use your computer."

"Halfway between here and your school is a library. I'd start there."

Astraea sighs.

"But first," I say. "Let's go get your winnings."

Evening is just beginning to set in as we exit the grocery store with our bounty. We load the bags into the bed of the truck and set out for home.

Astraea has grown quiet. She seems thoughtful, bothered I think.

"What's rolling around in there?" I ask.

"Huh?" she says.

I tap my temple and leave it at that.

She seems to understand, but says nothing.

I don't press and we continue in silence.

"I read about you the other day," she finally says.

"Oh yeah?"

"Yeah."

The silence returns.

"Are you not gonna ask me if I'm a murderer?"

She says nothing.

"I'm not fragile," I assure her. "If there's something on your mind, we should discuss it."

She says, "That girl. Melody. She was spying on you?"

"It seems so."

"She was tricking you? Trying to make you fall for her?"

"Uhh, that appears to have been the plan."

"That's mean," Astraea says.

"Yeah. I'm sure she had her reasons."

Astraea looks at me with harsh eyes.

"You're defending her?"

"Everybody has reasons for the things they do."

"But it's wrong!"

"According to you it is. She obviously thought differently. She decided that whatever she was attempting to accomplish held more positive value than whatever negative damage she might inflict upon me. Through that thought process, she determined that her actions were righteous."

"What gives her the right?"

"The question isn't what gives her the right, it's who gives her the right? The answer is... She does. She gives herself that right. We all do that to some extent, don't we? We all fall somewhere on the spectrum between the law-abiding and the outlaws. Most of us think it's okay to go five miles over the speed limit. After that I might start to judge myself, but five... who cares?"

"Well that's not the same thing."

"Some people think it's okay to run a red light. As long as it just now turned red. As long as they feel comfortable in their assessment that nobody should get hurt. Personally, I disagree with that. The collective 'we' need to be able to trust that we are fundamentally safe on the road. And the assessments of random people are often far from adequate in achieving that end. Hell, I see near misses all the time. I, personally, never run a red light."

"So you're not an outlaw?"

"No, I absolutely am. After careful consideration, I too choose which laws and moral standards I adhere to. You have no idea how many times I've been screwed over with flawed or incomplete products from the hardware store. And it's not until the product is halfway installed that the flaw reveals itself. Am I suppose to uninstall it and disassemble it and stuff it back into the box and drive back to the store so that I can return it, when I know that I can fix that flaw with a couple minutes and a couple dollars? No, I'm gonna fix the flaw. But I'm also gonna keep a running total of everything it cost me. And when the time comes, I collect what I'm owed from whoever owes it. Some might call that theft. I call it achieving balance."

Astraea laughs.

I continue, "It is never my intent to selfishly put my needs above others. It is my intent to do what's right. Right by myself, but also right by my community. My point is, it's best to judge a person and their actions not by the morals and laws of society, but by a careful consideration of the morals and laws with which they govern themselves. Only then can you truly understand them and properly judge their actions."

"And have you?"

"Have I what?"

"Judged Melody through careful consideration."

"I actually have. And you were right. She was being really mean."

"That's what I said!" She blurts. "My God, how many words does it take to tell someone they're right. Geez!"

"I'm just trying to give you an education."

"On what? How to justify bad behavior?"

"Maybe. It's up to you to determine if the standards with which I live are adequate or if they fall short. If you're passing negative judgment on me, then it's worth exploring where you think I'm falling short, so that when you create your own standards, you can make sure they are better than mine."

"What are you even talking about? It's really simple. Stealing is wrong!"

"Okay. So, who stole from who?"

"What? You just said that you steal stuff from the hardware store."

"Let me tell you a true story."

"Can't wait," Astraea says.

"I buy a twelve-pack of light bulbs from the store. Each bulb is advertised to last about five years with average use, right?"

"If you say so."

"Now I need every one of these bulbs because I just remodeled my home. I screw them all in. I flip the switch. And what do you know, two of the brand new bulbs don't work."

"Shitty."

"So, what should I do?"

"You return the bad bulbs," she says.

"No. I can't return the bad bulbs. I can only return the product that I bought, which was a twelve-pack of light bulbs."

"You have to return all of them?"

"I have to get back on my ladder, dragging it from place to place, removing every single bulb, stuffing them back into the box, and drive back to the store, where I stand in the return line for who knows how long, so that I can get my money back before returning to the light bulb aisle to grab another 12-pack, and hope that when I get home all twelve of those bulbs actually work. So I'm asking you, in this scenario, who is stealing from who?"

"I get your point."

"Thank you!"

"So what did you do?"

"I made a mental note. Next time I went to that store, I forgot to pay for a two-pack of light bulbs."

She nods, "I get it. I could never do it. But I get it."

"You could never steal, huh?"

"Oh no. I really couldn't."

"You do realize that you stole many thousands of dollars from two sisters and a brother who'd just lost their father?"

"What?"

"You think I would've gotten the house we live in at the price I got it, if you hadn't made Swiss Cheese of the walls? Covered them with graffiti? Busted in the back door? Destroyed the floors? Somebody paid for all that and it wasn't me. It was them. Nice people who'd just suffered the loss of a loved one. That's who paid for it."

Astraea appears wounded.

I say, "So this is where you ask yourself... Did I let my anger and my selfish desires rule the day? Or was my behavior justified? We can never stop asking ourselves, 'Am I living up to my moral standards? And are my standards the right standards? Are my motives pure? Am I working toward the greater good? You can never stop asking, because who you are and who you want to be don't often naturally align. It takes work, a lot of work, to make those two people one and the same."

"Did I really take thousands from those people?"

"You absolutely did," I tell her.

"William. William, wake up."

The whispered words penetrate my veil of sleep.

"William."

My eyes flutter open. I hazily look around and find Astraea sitting on the corner of my bed, near my feet.

"What the hell? What's happening? Is everything okay?"

"I can't sleep," she says.

"So no one gets to?" I say, looking at the alarm clock. "It's four in the morning."

"We need to talk."

"What?"

"You were right earlier. What I did to this house, to the people who owned it, was wrong."

"I never told you it was wrong."

"But you implied it. And you were right. You were also right to point it out to me."

I nod, "You're welcome. Can I go back to sleep now?"

"I'm not the only one who was wrong though."

"I thought we settled this."

"You stole."

"They screwed me so I held them accountable. That's it."

"They being?"

"Home Depot," I say, annoyed.

"Those light bulbs come in a box, right?"

I just look at her.

She continues, "And it's taped shut I would guess."

I can tell this could take a while. I sit up, leaning back against the headboard. I rub my sleepy eyes.

I say, "What is your point?"

"Are you suggesting that Home Depot should open every box and test every bulb before resealing the package and selling it to you?"

"I don't know what the hell you're saying."

"I'm saying Home Depot didn't make those light bulbs. They bought them from a manufacturer. So do you expect the Home

Depot to open every package and test every product before they sell it?"

"No," I say, ingesting her point. "I guess I don't."

"And yet you hold Home Depot to be the sole responsible party."

"I never said sole responsible party…"

"But they're the only ones you held responsible. There are three groups involved here. Your solution ends with you breaking even, but-"

"Breaking even is all I'm after."

"That's not true though, is it? You also want to hold the guilty party responsible, right?"

I thoughtfully nod.

She says, "If you had returned the product properly, Home Depot would have given you your money back. You break even. With hassles, yes, but financially even. Home Depot would then return the items to the manufacturer, demanding their money back. It's a hassle for them too, but otherwise breaking even. In the end, the manufacturer, the people who made a faulty product, would be the only ones who suffered a real loss. Your way didn't do that."

I take a moment to play out the scenario.

"My way did the opposite," I regretfully intone. "It actually rewarded the manufacturer. If you think about it, my way actually increased the manufacturer's sales."

"Oh yeah, you're right. They sold fourteen bulbs, not twelve."

"And my way actually hides the problem. There is no indication that they ever made a bad product in the first place. Shit. How did I not see that?"

"To use your own words, it probably has something to do with those selfish impulses. And from what I hear, retailers raise their prices to counteract theft. So a portion of the price that everybody else is overpaying is directly attributable to you."

I shake my head, knowing she's right.

"Now I'm not gonna be able to sleep," I say.

Astraea nods at me empathetically.

"Glad I could return the favor," she yawns. "G'night!"

She abruptly rises from the bed and sleepily stumbles out of the room.

I lay back down, close my eyes, and think about all my guilty actions. Sometimes it's hard to find the truth hidden among the facts.

19

Having ditched me twice in a row, I'm surprised to see Lindsay walking with Robby out of the school. I give them a wave and they hustle over. Lindsey makes Robby get in first, so that she won't have to sit in the middle.

"How was school?" I ask, pulling out of the melee of moms.

"Fine."

"Fine."

"So what do we wanna do today?"

Robby shrugs.

"I have lots of homework," Lindsey declares.

"You can do that when I drop you off. Let's do something fun."

"Oh my God! Why are you trying to ruin my day? Me and Mom need to catch up on The Bachelor tonight!"

The damn Bachelor. I have half a mind to abandon the Mediator cause and devote my every waking moment to ridding the world of reality TV. Something tells me that would be harder.

"I haven't seen you in over a month. I just wanna spend a little time. How about you save The Bachelor for another night?"

"Oh my God! I need to do my homework! What kind of Dad doesn't want their child to do their homework?! Can I not just do my homework? I just want to do my homework!"

And so I drive to the Bethany Library. Astraea may be home and I don't want to have to explain that. Me and Robby play in the park next door, while Lindsey does her all important homework.

I drop them off by seven and drive straight to the airport to catch a late flight to LAX.

206

TUESDAY

If you're looking to lose your faith in society, or America, or humanity in general... L.A. is a special place to be. If you're in the mood for pretentious fakery, you can find that just about anywhere, but nothing like you're sure to encounter here. You can smell it in the air. Feel it coating your skin. Hear it in their desperate line readings. See it in their well developed character traits.

Everybody is acting. Everybody is living a lie.

But the honest truth of this place is becoming more visible each day. The Angel's wings have been sheared off. The blood has leached out past the confines of Skid Row. I see it lining the roadways and spilling out into the streets. Tattered tarps of blue, green, and black are stretched tight over ingenious structures built of old worn out furnishings.

I watch as a greasy leading man pushes a stolen shopping cart filled with another man's trash. A broken damsel stands hunched in the middle of the street, oblivious to the passing cars. The flies have gathered, summoned by the smell of unwashed character actors.

This is show business. And business is booming.

As requested, I arrive early for today's podcast.

Simon sure knows how to pick 'em. It's as if he's gone out of his way to introduce me to the worst possible examples of Americans. Today's host is no exception.

I'm not particularly familiar with this actor's work, but I can tell you that I hate him. This feeling doesn't require any consideration. It just sort of hits me all at once the moment I lay eyes on him. Perhaps it's the clothes. Or the 'look-at-me' glasses he probably doesn't need. Or the floppy hair that I'm certain steals an hour from his life each day. Or maybe it has something to do with his collection of pins and buttons.

He shows them to me as he takes me on a tour of his facilities. A strip of costly fabric hangs proudly on a wall absolutely covered in countless pins and buttons displaying all the causes he selflessly devotes himself to.

He apparently considers it art.

"I've been curating this piece for five years," he says.

The first button I see is a picture of the Earth saying, 'Please don't kill me'.

It's the first of at least a few hundred.

Capitalism = Murder

Save the Trees

Save the Whales

Save the Climate

Hug me I'm vaccinated

Meat is Murder

Black Lives Matter

Health Care is a Human Right

Pro-Choice

Free Palestine

Reparations Now!

Tax the Rich

America Sux

Socialism is Coming

Trans Pride!

I feel like I get the point, so I nod and say, "Alright."

He says, "I call it, 'For a Better Future, Today'."

I nod again, "Alright."

He takes me through the lobby with its wood paneled walls and trendy furnishings. He points out the expensive wall hangings and the massive chandelier. There are shelves and side tables and coffee tables… plenty of surfaces for various useless pretty things to add much needed flair and pops of color.

He shows me the rest of the space, which is currently under construction. In the kitchen/break room, I remark that I like the counter tops.

"Really? They're so played out. It was alright four years ago, I guess, but we're pulling that shit and replacing it with an amazing piece of Carrara marble! All new backsplash. Cabinets. Everything! It's gonna be tight!"

I nod, "Alright."

Across the way I see a painted piece of wood with letters written across its surface. It says, 'Be Authentic'. It's interesting that the more likely you are to use that word, the more likely it doesn't apply to you.

He is a poser, that much is clear, and yet he has many millions of followers on all the different social media sites. It's a disturbing trend that I've noticed for many years now. Why do we choose to love the people who each morning put on a face and slip on a costume and act their way through life? Why do we seek out falsity in our idols?

Perhaps when one looks upon a poser, they see themselves. Posers are popular, because people so badly want to admire their own reflection.

A new hour rolls over and the show begins.

The man leans into his microphone, "So, I was scanning my news feed and, my my, did I read a little something about you. Say it ain't so, Will."

Though I expected this, I take a moment to look offended.

"It ain't so."

"Oh, you gotta give us more than that. This Melody and Morgan tragedy is just too juicy. What is going on?"

I laugh unconvincingly. I've practiced this moment in the mirror. My number one priority is to convey a general sense of unease. Distress. Fear even.

"I'm sorry… it's… it's not something I can talk about."

"Oh," the man says with surprise. "Sounds ominous. Are the articles true? Do you have reason to be nervous?"

"I just can't get into it. I know you want a scoop, but I… I just can't give it to you. I'm sorry. Can we move on?

"I… guess we should," the man says. He looks to the camera and gives his audience a suggestive shrug. "Okay, so, let me consult my list of questions. Oh yes, this is major. Where does the Mediator Party fall on climate change?"

"What about it?"

"How do you plan to combat it? Do you plan to combat it?"

"Does the Mediator Party have specific designs on combating climate change? The answer is no."

"Well why should I vote for your Party if you don't plan to do anything about the greatest threat to our future that humanity has ever seen?"

"The Mediator Party plans to do a number of things that you might like."

"Like what?

"For one, we plan to remove the influence of corporate lobbyists and special interest groups. What you'll like about that, is it will keep oil, energy, and utility companies out of the legislative process. Their desires will no longer be considered when deciding what environmental protections or sustainability measures should be put in place. From there, it will be up to the people to decide what the Mediator Party does. When I say we have no plans to do anything, it doesn't mean we're not going to do anything. It just means we have to wait for the people to tell us what to do… and then we'll do it."

"Seems to me that big business is the only reason we haven't slayed this shit already. We remove that, should be smooth sailing, don't you think?"

His point fits perfectly into my argument. I try to convince myself to agree with him. I fail. The idea of agreeing with this man on anything at all feels like heresy.

"Maybe," I say. "But it's a lot more complicated than that. We're living in a country that's addicted to consuming."

"That's no joke."

"I mean, look at you. You're an Eco-Warrior, right?"

"Of course. You gotta be. We're *all* on the front lines of this war."

"Exactly. It's clear that you *seem* to care deeply about the environment."

"I *seem* to care deeply?"

"When we were talking earlier, I asked if you and your wife planned on having kids. You said you couldn't fathom bringing a child into this screwed up world."

"It's a valid concern, I think."

"Look, it doesn't matter at all to me, but do you know why I asked?"

"I do not."

"Because you'd just told me that you and her live in a five thousand square foot house. Do you realize how much material goes into building a five thousand square foot house?"

"Well, we didn't build it."

"But the material still went into it. And it could be serving a much larger purpose. Instead it serves exactly two people. Let's think about how much furniture it takes to fill it? How much energy it takes to cool it and heat it? How many shingles it takes to keep it dry. For two people. And then there's the fact that you like to remodel every four or five years. You complain about them cutting down the rain forests, why do you think they're doing it? So they can make room to farm the exact kinds of trees that you like to floor your house with. Hell, you're remodeling this place, right now. Completely overhauling a perfectly beautiful kitchen. Tossing the four year old quartz like it's yesterday's news."

"I would never send that to the landfill," he objects. "And I resent the implication. We're not... tossing it. We're going to recycle it."

"Recycling doesn't nullify your actions. It just makes it slightly less wasteful. People act like recycling is some magic bullet. You have any idea how much energy goes into that process? Do you know what has to happen to those counter tops in order to recycle them? They have to be handled and transported multiple times. They have to be cut into a new form and redistributed. Or crushed into aggregate for concrete or underlayment for a highway and then transported again. It's an intensive process, requiring a lot of energy,

211

and it doesn't need to take place at all, because it could serve you dutifully, just like it is, for the rest of your life, and your kids' lives if you were having them. If this is how an Eco-Warrior behaves, we've got even bigger problems than you think."

The man opens his mouth to say something, but nothing comes out. Interestingly, for the first time, I get the sense that there may be a person in there. An actual person.

He leans back in his seat, stunned.

His muscles have gone slack, his face sullen. My interest in him quickly fades, as he is clearly posing again. The transition happened so quickly, I almost missed it. I believe we are witnessing what they like to call the 'aha!' moment. That moment when it all suddenly makes sense. Or a manufactured version of it, at least.

He realized, exposed in his hypocrisy, to continue to argue would not show well. And so...

"Jesus. You're right. I've got a carbon footprint like a Sasquatch! What the hell am I doing?"

I palm my face, "How is any of this surprising? I'm serious. How can you possibly put all this energy into caring about this shit and never once look at the effects of your own behavior? Have we just gone absolutely blind?"

He looks at me, unsure, "I don't know. Maybe we have."

He leans in, eyes pleading.

"So what do we do about it?"

He appears to desperately want the answer to this all important question. The fate of our Earth depends on it.

It is suddenly very clear to me that this man is impenetrable. As long as he is posing, nothing can touch him. His followers will continue to love him as long as he doesn't let his mask slip… as long as he never shows us something real.

I shrug, "Opening your eyes might be a good start. This is a cultural problem. It's wide spread. Used to be that people acquired something they loved with the intent of it lasting forever. Now we're so busy coveting the new, that we've doomed ourselves into a perpetual state of unhappiness. And the only way to cure that unhappiness is to buy more shit. People travel across the ocean to marvel at five hundred year old buildings. Then they come home and sneer at a five year old piece of stone because it's dated."

I shake my head and continue, "I was talking to this young guy the other day. He, like you, liked to claim his support for socialism. He was bitching about how hard it is to make it in this country. Saying, 'How could I ever possibly hope to own a home?'."

"That's actually a good question," the host says.

"He was standing in front of his new SUV, the latest iPhone in his hand, an Apple watch on his wrist, 5 or 6 tattoos on his arms, Oakley sunglasses over his eyes, Jordans on his feet, a Starbucks coffee on the hood… Here's an idea, how about we discontinue the never-ending battle to stay on-trend? Stop letting the world convince you that what you've got is trash. You complain about the big evil corporations, but can't you see that you're the problem? Trendy is their business model to keep you coming to the dinner table, but you're the one who never fails to throw a bib on and gorge yourself. Look, industry is good. It's necessary. We need houses. We need clothes. We need a lot of things. But there's a reason for the sheer volume of trees being cut down. The mountains being flattened. The mines being dug. And all the energy that goes into all those processes. Capitalism may be the means by which that happens, but it is not the reason. The reason is you."

The man sits slumped in his chair. I can see his mind churning through a million different thoughts, but he's not thinking about my words, not really. He's determining the proper pose.

20

WEDNESDAY

A cold shower forces me to liven up before heading out for another plunge into the world of podcasting.

I reach the studio with time to spare. After brief intros, I am made to wait. I refuse a powder from the make-up girl and pass the time by checking the response to yesterday's show.

My time with the EcoWarrior has not gone unnoticed. The comment section is filled to the brim with hateful messages directed at me. Interesting, but clearly I'm not reaching my intended audience. These podcasts are nothing more than pulpits, places where the faithful gather to listen to their chosen preacher.

The volume of comments is impressive, though. I check the EcoWarrior's previous show with a much more agreeable guest. The comments are spare and civilized. As expected, that show has been viewed less than half as many times.

I am both heavily consumed and uniformly hated. I ponder the significance. Hate isn't always a crowd-pleaser, but it always draws a crowd.

I think back to the year before the midterm elections, recalling all those TV interviews and podcasts and online news articles. I was the picture of agreeableness, approaching discussions with love in my heart. I was the seeker of compromise, the voice of reason, the man who sought to bring us together through thoughtful consideration and kindness and understanding. I never raised my voice. I never approached the controversial. And I certainly never drew a crowd.

I've often heard the phrase 'a labor of love', but never have I heard 'a labor of hate'. Perhaps because hate is a well built machine requiring very little maintenance and its fuel so easy to find. It runs unrestrained through the hearts of mankind. But again, love is a labor and its tank so very hard to keep full.

I send a text to Scarlet.

Check out the podcast comments. Tell that story. Take their side. Make me the bad guy. Focus on the hate!

This is how I will reach my people. I will make them hear the hate. Where hate is, people follow. My people will see me saying the words they've never spoken. They will feel a kinship, a bond. They will hate that I am hated. A well built machine will be constructed.

The show begins and across from me is yet another example of tribal idiocy. It doesn't matter the argument, the conservative view is clearly the right one. I decide to throw him a bone.

"I was absolutely on the side of the Republicans in that particular debate."

"Well I'm glad to hear it. That is a breath of fresh air. Would you like to tell our audience why the Republicans were right?"

"Sure. The Republicans were trying to accomplish two things in that moment. One, raise the debt ceiling, because we gotta pay our bills. And two, cut costs for the future. Both positive endeavors that should absolutely need to take place. The Democrats, meanwhile, only wanted to do one of those things. Let's raise the debt ceiling and pay zero attention to the fact that we are constantly driving our country closer and closer to the edge of bankruptcy."

"Wow! That's great! I couldn't have said it better myself. Is it too much to ask for a little fiscal responsibility?"

"I don't know. Who are you asking?"

"I'm asking Biden. Just like I asked Obama. And every other damn Libtard that somehow got the keys to our country."

"Well there's no doubt those guys fall short of fiscally responsible."

"No doubt at all."

"But did you ask Trump? Did you ask W? I didn't hear you bitchin' when those guys wanted to raise the debt ceiling. To suggest that Republicans are any better is a joke without a punchline."

"Republicans are a lot better."

"The last Republican to balance the budget was Eisenhower, over 60 years ago. Since then, Lyndon Johnson, a Democrat, did it once in '69. Bill Clinton balanced his entire second term. It was pretty damn impressive. And in case you've forgotten, he was a Democrat. Fiscal responsibility is just like this... *thing* that Republicans like to talk about. They talk about it... They don't actually do it. And when they pretend to do it, they never cut the costs of conservative causes, only liberal ones. So what do we call those people? Conservatards?"

My second podcast of the day was mostly uneventful. It consisted of two people speaking rationally and discussing differences in a civil manner.

Will wonders never cease?

I have to admit I was a little disappointed. But the Hate Train will not be derailed. My third stop of the day has given me exactly what I need.

I speak loud and proud, pumping my fist into the air with each revolutionary statement.

"The right to vote is fundamental to a working society! The importance of it cannot be overstated! I will not be silenced!"

Suddenly, the exuberance drains from my body.

"Wait," I say, deflated. "You expect me to show a photo ID?"

The black woman across from me is livid. In her eyes, I am everything wrong with this country.

She says, "That law is designed to suppress the black vote."

"That might be true, and if so, it is offensive."

"Not might be true, it is true."

"But from a legislative point of view, I just don't care."

"You don't care?" she says, taken aback.

"I can't really speak to the lawmaker's intent. What I will speak to is the content of the law. Should you have to prove that you are who you say you are when voting to determine the future of this country? Yes! Yes you should! Stop complaining and go get a damn ID!"

"They ain't got no money, they ain't got no license, and they ain't got no car. How they suppose to get there?"

"Well, you got all these activists selflessly engaged in voter drives. Why not an ID drive? I'll tell you why not, because that would actually fix the problem and there would be one less thing to complain about. And we certainly can't have that."

"That's a low down lie."

"In the world of activist propaganda, victimhood is so much more productive than actually being productive."

"You are really trying, aren't ya? Are you actually so dead-headed that you think you're going to convince me that you're right?"

"Is that what you think? Understand, I'm not trying to convince you that I'm right. I'm trying to convince you that your argument is not the only argument. We've got two people here, and we do not agree."

"Oh, honey, you don't need to convince me of that."

"And yet if you had your way, you'd have legislation written that fully encompasses your opinion and completely ignores mine."

"Well, hell yeah! Because you wrong!"

THURSDAY
10:00am
I say, "Look, they've come up short on multiple occasions. I will grant you that. The hospital reporting was damn near criminal if you ask me. But that's not what we're talking about. Why does this particular issue bother you so much?"

"Why does it bother me that the BBC refuses to call these people terrorists?"

"Yes. Why?"

"Because terrorists is what they are. They've taken people hostage. Executed people on video. They've killed women and old people. Babies!"

"And did the BBC fail to report those things?"

"They failed to report them properly."

"No. I asked a simple question. Did the BBC report those things?"

"They did. But they didn't call them what they are. They are terrorists. It's a fact."

"It's not a fact. It's a determination."

"Oh, please. It's a simple determination."

"Yeah. Simple for me. And simple for you. So why is it necessary that the BBC tell us what we can easily determine on our own?"

"Because words matter. It's important that we all stand up against these horrible acts. We must all condemn these actions."

"It's important that *you and I* condemn these acts. It's just as important that proper news organizations maintain their neutrality. Their job is to report the news, not how you should feel about it. What you're arguing for is exactly what gave birth to Fox News. That's where MSNBC came from. Where CNN lost their way. Don Lemon, Tucker Carlson, Rachel Maddow… these are the kinds of idiots who rise up from the ashes of neutrality."

12:00pm
"I'm telling you zombies are real. And any zombie movie should start with the advent of social media."

2:30pm
I say, "Collecting the thoughts of the constituency should be the ultimate aim of politics. The goal of silencing voices is the polar opposite of what we should be doing."

"No one's trying to silence anybody."

"Really? You're gonna make that claim? You also claim that institutional racism is a myth, but when your politicians gerrymander the black voice into non-existence, what do you think that is?"

His mouth opens, but nothing comes out.

I say, "Now, I live in a predominately white neighborhood, but not all that far away sits a black neighborhood. If you were to magically pick up my house, take it one mile north and two miles east, it would lose forty percent of its value on the way there."

"That's not institutional. It's a less desirable area. That's the law of supply and demand. That's got nothing to do with our government."

"I'm with ya, but what happens when you base public school funding on the property taxes collected in the immediate area? Do me a favor and play that one out in your head. You cannot claim that black people have achieved equality, while nullifying their votes. Nor can you do it while actively ensuring that their children receive a lesser education than your own."

4:00pm

"I don't understand how you can be so callus," the host says. "Look at all the poverty. It's like twelve percent."

I shrug, "See, that's where we differ. I prefer to see the glass as 88 percent full."

"We're talking, like, 40 million people living in squalor, and you're making jokes. Can you really have that little compassion for your fellow man?"

"Look, the thing is, I've met a lot of people in my life. And for every hundred people, there's at least 12 that are lazy as all hell. You can make of that number what you will."

"Wow! Just... wow!"

"How many times do we need to see humanity struggle in the name of socialism before we declare it a failed experiment? Hitler fancied himself a certain kind of socialist, building off of bad ideas. Stalin, Mao, Pol Pot. How many dictators? How many famines? How many mass killings? How many Muslim Uyghurs need to be enslaved, today? Just give me a number. What's it gonna take before you're like, 'Oh damn, that shit just doesn't work'?"

6:00pm

"But we've all paid Medicare taxes," the host says. "Of course we want to collect on that when the time comes."

"Medicare tax is 1.45%, 2.9 if you add in the employee match. That's still less than a quarter of what we pay in Social Security tax. Now guess which one of those programs costs more."

"Medicare or Social Security?"

"Yeah," I say. "Take a guess."

"Well, based on the point you're making, I'd guess it's Medicare."

"And you'd be correct. It is now the single largest expenditure in this country. That tax doesn't even put a dent into the actual costs. These people are taking exponentially more than they ever put in. And before you say it, that's taking inflation into account."

"So it's about dollars and cents? You don't believe that healthcare is a human right?"

"Healthcare is not a human right. It's a service like any other. It's knowledge. It's labor. It's equipment. All things that cost money. And, yes, someone has to pay the bill. That someone should be the consumer. But no, they think they've earned it because they paid a tiny portion of their paycheck. To that I say, yes, you've earned the right to have a tiny portion of your medical bills covered. That's it. That's all you've earned. By all rights, Medicare benefits should be cut by 80% across the board. That's what they paid for, that's what they should get."

"I gotta tell ya, Mister Waxman, that is not going to be a popular opinion."

"Whatever," I shrug. "The Medicare/Medicaid program is far and away the number one reason this country is going broke. It's not even close. People like to talk about how entitled this new generation is, and they're not wrong, but I'll tell you this, the geezers got 'em beat. They've got plenty of time on their hands, and they're spending it digging this country's grave. Why? Because they're entitled. Today's generation ain't got nothing on them."

"And what do you say to those who accuse you of ageism?"

"It's not ageism, it's behaviorism. We've got a large contingent of people who are banding together in an effort to take more than their fair share. That's wrong, no matter who the group is."

"The elderly are banding together?"

"What are the two largest circulating publications in the United States?"

"Uhh, to be honest, I don't know."

"AARP Magazine and AARP Bulletin. That's a nonpartisan political lobby that every politician in this country is scared to death of. Nearly forty million dues-paying members are sending out their lobbyists every day. Pushing for more benefits. More this. More that. More everything. And who's gonna tell them 'no'? Not the left. Not the right. Not much of anybody. Every one of these politicians knows what's driving the bulk of our national debt. They know it. All you gotta do is look at the numbers and ask the obvious questions. What are these people actually entitled to? And what are they actually getting? These numbers don't match up. Not even in the vicinity of close. Everybody knows it. But they're not gonna say it. Look, I don't have a problem with old people. I hope to be one someday. What I have a problem with is old people taking advantage of their kids and their grand kids. I have a problem with the non-productive members of society devising ways to steal from the productive members of society. And I have a problem with a governmental system that allows that to happen out of fear."

"So your contention is that the Mediator Party would fix this problem?"

"Maybe. Maybe not. People love their parents, their grand-parents, and, of course, people love themselves. And some of them even have the forethought of their own impending old age. It's quite possible, maybe even probable, that nothing would change at all. But it won't be because of a lobby that's holding the entirety of Congress hostage. It will be because the people chose it. At that point, so be it."

FRIDAY

I've found my way onto a popular political talk show. The host is a comedian who sits firmly on the left. He does this while managing to somehow hold on to basic reasoning skills, proof that those two things can exist simultaneously.

He comes off a bit douchey, with every joke drenched in sarcasm and built with the intent of making any detractors feel stupid.

I'm no stranger to the tactic, but this guy has it down to an art. That said, I genuinely like him… kind of.

My purpose here today is to participate in a panel discussion.

Today's discussion is focused on the education system.

Joining me on the panel is a middle aged man who has taught in the public school system his entire adult life.

We're mid-discussion and I've about had my fill.

"The fact remains we need our educators to feel more valued," the teacher says. "Teacher pay is abhorrent."

I say, "Well, there's plenty of information on teacher pay rates, is there not? It's not like you're getting blindsided by this. You chose to enter a field where the pay is not particularly good. Now you complain about it?"

"That's no reason to just accept the status quo."

"Did you know that a starting teacher's salary, first day on the job, is more than that of a career factory worker's? We're talking someone who has been doing it for thirty years."

"A career factory worker wasn't forced to attain a college degree," he says.

"Forced is a strong word. You wanted to be a teacher, so you did what was necessary to enter that field. That's a choice. Now let's compare that thirty year factory worker to a teacher straight out of school… Which one of these people is better educated to do their respective job?"

"Well, your argument goes both ways, doesn't it? That factory worker chose that job."

"You're absolutely right. And I'm not complaining about his salary. You're the only one here fretting about how much you make."

He says, "Well, it's a question of priorities, isn't it? These are the people entrusted with the development of our children. Their futures."

"In every other job in the world, a raise usually comes as a result of good work. We just got done talking about how poorly the school system is performing. But you're saying, 'No, you're right, maybe we're not doing a very good job, so consequently you should pay us more'. Why would we do that? Rewarding poor performance has never been a good strategy."

"The teachers aren't the problem."

"Right, I forgot, it's the administration and it's the parents. The teachers don't shoulder any of that responsibility. You ever think that maybe the shirking of responsibility is a big part of the problem?"

"We are not shirking responsibility," he says with high offense.

"You admit that there's a problem. Okay, how do you fix it? How do *you* fix the problem? What can *you* do to improve the situation? That's the exact question being asked here today. And your answer is… 'pay me more'."

"That is not what I said," he protests.

"You didn't say a lot of things. One of them being anything at all about what you as a teacher can do to better educate your students."

The host chimes in, "This is interesting. Most people say, 'well there's only so much money. Teachers definitely deserve more, it's just not in the budget'. But you're actually saying that they get paid just fine."

"I am. Let's return to our factory worker, shall we? Your average teacher, over the course of their career will make 600,000 dollars more. And they'll do so while enjoying 10 years – that's years – more vacation time. Nor will they endure the same level of physical distress as those engaged in constant manual labor. If you ask me, the teachers are doing just fine, especially when you consider the quality of work."

The teacher says, "I take exception to your suggestion that we do poor quality work. We are doing the best we can."

"Would you agree that the fundamental purpose of schooling is to prepare our children for adulthood?"

"That's an easy one. Yes."

I dig my wallet out of my back pocket.

"So why is it our kids are going to school six hours a day, five days a week, for twelve years and their teachers aren't gonna find the time to tell them how this thing works?"

I hold up my credit card, careful to cover the number with my finger.

"We have personal finance classes."

"And when I went to school it was taught by our wrestling coach. An elective course that next to nobody took. And even in that course, you're not gonna teach them how it really works. You're not gonna teach them how to calculate interest rates or hold discussions on revolving debt or what it really means to make the minimum payment. We're not gonna talk about the pitfalls, or how to recognize the trap, or how that trap is constructed. What we're gonna do is we're gonna let them fall in. And ten, twenty years down the line, maybe they'll dig themselves out of that hole. And maybe they'll learn a very expensive lesson. A lesson you chose not to teach them in the twelve years you had them. My question is... Who's writing this curriculum? Visa?"

To say I'm ready to leave this state is an understatement. I feel like I'm suffering from some sort of infection, like the aura of this place is beginning to penetrate my soul.

Luckily, I fly out on the red eye this evening with an unfortunate layover in Dallas. But first, one more podcast.

The podcast is streamed live on Friday night in a studio made up to look like a bar. A producer asks me my drink of choice and I opt for a margarita.

The host is a pretty woman in her late forties, with bleached blond hair and a bit of a southern accent. Despite the bleached hair, I can tell she's quite intelligent. She manages to dress sexy, while remaining professional. She also possesses a disarming smile that I'm sure she uses to great benefit.

Her drink of choice appears to be straight bourbon. She has a side-kick, who doubles as the bartender. She keeps him busy.

"So how's the Golden State treating you Mister Waxman?" she asks with a flash of that smile.

"Truth be told, I'm a little homesick."

"Well you're from Oklahoma, so I don't blame ya. You got things pretty good over there. You don't understand what it's like living in a liberal wonderland."

"No, we got a different kind of wonderland going on," I bow my head and press my hands together in prayer.

"Well that's the kind of wonderland we should all be so lucky to experience. What I wouldn't give to have my state run by God-fearing men. Your governor has been a little soft on crime, but otherwise I'd say you've got it pretty good. Hell, I'm jealous. Minimal welfare. Anti-trans laws. A ban on baby killing. Sounds like paradise to me."

"You know, I've been thinking about how Governor Stitt might turnaround that 'soft on crime' image."

"How's that?"

"By far the worst committers of crime come from one particular subset of society. Now what if we could minimize that subset and in the process make the world a happier place, while lowering crime rates and the prison population all at the same time?"

She narrows her eyes at me.

She asks, "What subset are we talking about?"

"Unloved and unwanted children. What if we could remove them from existence before they actually exist?"

"Oh, now you're just being ornery."

"Think of all the benefits. Population control, check. A less burdened court system, check. Less substance abuse. Less violent crime. Less child abuse. Less children raised by the state, which leads to a lower tax burden on the average citizen. I could go on and on. And let's be honest, the incidents of unwanted pregnancy increase exponentially the lower your income and the lower your IQ. Are these really the people we want reproducing? If you want lower taxes, try making less needy people. In effect, abortion protects our

225

evolutionary progress and the future of humanity itself. Plus, it's easy. All Governor Stitt has to do is make it legal again and those people will self-regulate their population. They want to do it. It's not like we'll be forcing them."

"That is the craziest thing I have ever heard."

"You wanna hear crazy, there's been like 65 million abortions since Roe v Wade. That's 65 million unwanted children that you say should be here, right now, walking among us. And those babies would of course have babies too. We're talking at least a hundred million people, minimum, added to our population. That's a 30 percent increase. And not a good 30 percent, a predominantly disadvantaged, poorly raised, angry-at-the-world 100 million people. What do you think that does to your 'Tough on Crime' agenda?"

My host gawks at me for a moment before speaking.

"I don't even know what to say. This never happens to me, but I'm at a loss for words. You know what, Mister Waxman, I think you're a lunatic."

Once again, it's time to predictably circle back and drive home the Mediator Party line.

I say, "But the idea is sound. Everything I said makes perfect sense. And yet I can tell you… that kind of thinking is a rabbit hole that, yes, leads to lunacy. Not just personal lunacy, but societal lunacy. This is why the ideas of one person or one group should not be the decider of an entire society."

"So you don't actually believe what you just said?"

"No, I definitely do. But I should not be the decider of society. That's the whole point. You make me an authoritarian leader, I will fuck shit up, guaranteed."

"Hence the need for democracy," she says. "Which we already have."

"But democracy only works if we can trust our leaders to practice it. In the state of Oklahoma, polling shows that a little more than half of the population believes abortion should be somewhat legal. Regulated… but legal. Less than a third support an all out ban. And yet our governor and our lawmakers decided to do just that. They've usurped the people's will and replaced it with their own. That is not a government for the people, by the people."

In the interest of southern hospitality, my host offered to take me to dinner. Dinner being a late night diner amid all the other drunks Los Angeles has to offer. As hospitality sounded nice, I accepted, rescheduling my flight for tomorrow afternoon.

Her name is Ellie.

We share a cigarette in her bed, wrapped up in each other's flesh. Though I am a free man, I feel somewhat dirty, as if I've broken a promise that I've yet to make.

"Is there a Mrs. Waxman?" she asks, taking a deep pull on our cigarette.

"No."

"Too bad. I prefer my men to be otherwise engaged."

"Really?"

She shrugs, "Makes it easier. You seem like someone who's otherwise engaged."

I nod, "There is someone. We're not together though."

"On again, off again?"

"More like never been on at all. We've just kind of been... circling each other, I guess."

"Like sharks."

"Not like sharks. Like something, but not sharks."

"So why the circling, Mister Waxman? Why not just stop and let her come to you?"

"She's young. Too young."

"Mmm," Ellie says with a slight edge. "But it's just so hard to say no to a sweet piece of young ass."

"It's not about that."

She raises her head off my chest and brings her eyes to mine.

"I'm gonna have to call bullshit on that one. You got a picture of this thing?"

I laugh, "I'm not saying she doesn't have her charms. I'm just saying it's not about that."

"Come on then, show me. Let me take a look at these charms."

I sigh and grab my phone off the night stand, while Ellie settles back into my chest. I find a group picture from election night, celebrating our first victory. I hold the phone for Ellie to see.

Ellie looks, "As I suspected, quite the charmer."

Ellie touches the screen and zooms in on a girl whose name I've forgotten.

"That's not her," I say, adjusting the zoom to frame Scarlet.

Ellie stares at the screen for a long moment.

"Hmm. Not what I was expecting. A little plain, wouldn't you say?"

I furrow my brow and look at the picture.

"You think?" I ask.

"She's… objectively average."

Her words surprise me. I shake my head a little.

"That's not what I see."

Ellie again adjusts to look at me. She squints her eyes, studying.

"I suggest you stop circling then."

"Yeah, I don't know about that. I keep telling myself I don't want to play with her mind, but I'm not even sure that's it. I think maybe I'm afraid she'll get bored with me."

"You don't strike me as a boring man, Mister Waxman."

"Hmm."

She studies me further.

"You've had your heart broken," she says, before again resting her head on my chest.

I take a drag and think on it. I blow out the smoke.

"Maybe."

"Oh honey, I've broken enough hearts to know it when I see it. Ain't no maybe about it. Who did that to you?"

I nod, "That would be my ex-wife."

"What did she do?"

"She made me fall in love with her. And then she made me her Settle Fish."

"Settle Fish."

"It's a reference to 'plenty of f-' "

"Oh, I get the joke. Tale as old as time."

"It fuckin' hurt," I say, surprised by the crack in my voice. I blame the alcohol swimming in my veins. I feel things differently when I drink. Not more deeply, just... differently.

My eyes start to well up. I try to push it down.

"It sucks, man," I say. "You fall in love. You give that person everything. All of you. That's a lot of power to give someone. And then they use that power to rewrite you into something else."

"Why would you give someone power you don't want them to use?" she asks. "Sounds like a fine way to break stuff."

"It's not something you can help, is it?"

"Sure you can."

"You've never given power to someone?"

"I keep the power for myself," she says softly.

She says the words, but I don't believe them. Hearts aren't naturally made of stone. They get that way through a process.

Ellie raises her head and looks at me. She reaches up and softly wipes a finger across the corner of my eye. A tear falls out onto her fingertip. She brings it to her lips and tastes my emptiness.

"You're a sad man, Mister Waxman."

She's not wrong, but I don't want to be sad right now. I reach up and graze her cheek. She leans in to my touch. My hand pushes forward, wrapping around to the base of her skull. My fingers flex into a fistful of hair.

"Call me Mister Waxman again."

Her eyes brighten with mischief and a dirty smile forms.

"What can I do for you, Mister Waxman?"

21

NOVEMBER 18, 2023
353 DAYS UNTIL ELECTION

It's been a long trip home. Usually I make use of the time, pencil in hand, jotting down the makings of my next book. Today I spent the whole of two flights plus a long layover thinking about Scarlet. Once again, she holds me captive, unable to shake loose of the mere thought of her. It's already dark when the plane finally lands.

I collect my bag from the carousel and make the trek to long term parking.

I point my truck toward The Village and listen to the highway moan. One good thing about Scarlet, at least for the day, she has pushed Melody out.

But one thought is all it takes. My ghost has returned, a sorrowful dead-weight upon my chest.

I spend the entirety of the drive home in her dreadful embrace.

I unlock the front door to find Astraea waiting for me on the other side.

"You're home!" She screams.

My heart warms and Melody disappears into nothingness.

The place looks different. The wall. It's gone.

"What the hell," I say.

"I figured it out," she says with a shrug.

"How? Was it non-weight-bearing? I could've sworn it would be weight-bearing."

"It was. But I fixed it."

She smiles proudly.

"You fixed it?"

"You're skeptical," she says, handing me a flashlight. "Why don't you go up and see for yourself."

She says it like a challenge, supremely confident.

I accept her challenge.

In the garage, I lower the attic ladder. The garage is different too. The big pile of eight-foot long two-by-fours is all but gone.

I crawl through the attic until finally the roof line gives me enough space to stand like a hunchback. I shine the flashlight ahead and see Astraea's work. She appears to have made a very complicated fourteen foot long truss system out of eight-foot long boards. I move closer, studying the choices that she made.

I find myself fearful, scared that my weight will cause the ceiling to give way. But everything feels solid. I take a close look at each transfer of load, paying particular attention to the scabbed seams of the eight-foot boards. I examine each notched joist. The attention to detail is impressive.

Every decision makes perfect sense, while at the same time being completely unexpected. It's brilliant. It truly is.

"So what do we think," Astraea asks as I descend the ladder.

"I think it'll work."

She throws her hands up triumphantly.

"Yay!!!"

"But… the material costs are a problem."

"How so?"

"The same job could've been done with a couple sixteen-foot long two-by-twelves. The sheer number of two-by-fours you used is cost prohibitive."

"But that's just lumber costs. In your method, you'd use metal joist hangers, wouldn't you?"

I give her a look, surprised that she even knows what a joist hanger is. She really did do her research.

"I guess I would."

She says, "The cost of those hangers alone is equivalent to ten two-by-fours. I did the math."

I think about that and nod my agreement. I offer her a congratulatory high-five.

She reaches out and grasps my hand instead of slapping it. It's a little awkward, but heartfelt.

"Good job, Astraea."

"Thank you."

"Oh wait," I say. "I've got something you're gonna like."

"You got something for me?!"

"It's in my room, hold on."

We go inside and I retrieve the box from my room.

"Oh my God!! You got me a computer?!"

I hold up a tempering finger and say, "No. I got myself a computer. This is what I wanted to show you."

I set the box on the dining table and open it.

Astraea looks at it, crestfallen.

"You got me an empty box?"

"This isn't just any box. This is an engineering marvel."

"You don't say," she says, absent of enthusiasm.

"For many, many years these things have come in boxes supplemented with molded Styrofoam to protect it in the shipping process. You know what molded styrofoam does when compared to cardboard?"

Astraea shakes her head, annoyed.

"What?"

"It costs more. It takes up more space in the warehouse. It doesn't recycle. Nor is it biodegradable. But this…"

I motion to the so-called empty box. A piece of cardboard inside the box has been manipulated to perfectly nestle the laptop computer, while providing ample cushioning from all sides. It does so through a very complicated endeavor resembling something like cardboard origami.

"I mean look at this," I say, unfolding the masterful piece of engineering to reveal a single piece of cardboard.

"Slots and scores and folds and notches and tabs and perforations all working together. Hugging and securing and stabilizing this fragile piece of equipment. All of this accomplished through one piece of inexpensive, lightweight, recyclable material. It's a thing of beauty!"

Astraea looks at it and inhales deeply.

She says, "Okay, you're right. This is pretty cool."

"Exactly! Most people just see a box. But you and I know better. This is inspiring stuff!"

Astraea nods.

"When you're right, you're right," she says. "Hey, you know what?"

"What?"

"I bet the person who designed this… did so on a computer!"

A short drive from the Capitol sits a popular little deli by the name of Someplace Else. They have killer meatball subs. Before me, sit the remnants of one such sub. By remnants, I mean crumbs on a sheet of deli paper. I consider ordering another, but decide against it.

Across from me sits an Oklahoma Congressman elected to one of the few competitive districts in the state. I tend to eat like my life depends on it, so he's still got half a sandwich.

I say, "I know you're a centrist at heart. I know it. Your voting record doesn't show it, but I know it."

"Voting record isn't everything."

"But you'd agree it's a pretty big thing."

"I can't legislate if I'm not a legislator. That's a pretty big thing. If I don't vote with my team I'll get primaried right out of office."

"And what would it matter when all you ever do is walk the Party line, just like the guy they'd replace you with."

233

The Congressman wipes his mouth with a napkin and throws it down onto his unfinished sandwich.

"Don't start acting like you know my job. You've never been in these shoes. You ever legislate? You ever even run for office?"

"I have not."

"I don't tell you how to be a cult leader, do I?"

"It's not a cult."

"Whatever you say, your excellency," he says with a smirk. "My job isn't to cross the Party line, it's to move the line. Ever so slightly, I push it just a little bit closer toward center. Through negotiation, through understanding, through constant dialogue, and soul crushing effort. I never stop. And I do all this before the vote ever takes place."

I nod, "I can appreciate that, but you never actually win, do you? By win, I mean accurately represent your constituents."

"No," he says with frustration. "I never actually win."

"I've designed the Mediator Party so that it can win every time. Every time."

He laughs.

"What's so funny?"

"You've got one man in the House. One guy. One lonely worthless guy. You know how miserable that dude is? How many times has he won? He won an election and not a damn thing since. My team actually listens to me. They even try to accommodate me from time to time. Don't no one listen to your boy. Not a soul. He's a joke. He starts talking, all anyone hears is Charlie Brown's parents. You call that winning?"

"If we can get a majority, then we-"

"Oh, is that it? Is that all you need? Just a majority of Congress, that's all! A third party majority! No big deal! Why didn't you say so? Sign me up! I'd love nothing more than to switch parties, make myself irrelevant, and almost certainly go job hunting this time next year! Sounds great! I don't know about you, but I'm excited. Let's do this thing!"

He stares at me and just shakes his head.

He says, "You know, if I'm honest, I feel sorry for you. I really do."

Without another word he rises from his seat and exits the restaurant.

I sit at a French restaurant in downtown OKC. It's an intimate little place with a candlelight burning. Scarlet looks beautiful, the light flickering off her features.

I take a bite of my braised short rib and continue ranting on.

"I want memes, memes, and more memes! I want a meme factory. I want you pumping them out every hour of the day. Every stupid partisan activity on the planet, I want you to shine a light on it in a way that makes people laugh, or cry, have steam coming out of their goddamn ears."

"We are in public William," she says in a hushed tone.

"We need to wake people the fuck up!"

"Shhh"

"Make them feel something again. We're all sleepwalking through life. We gotta break through this social media fog, this medically induced haze, and make them feel it."

"Jesus, William!" she snaps, scolding me in a whisper. "You're not just some random asshole anymore. People know who you are. You need to keep it down."

"And I wanna bring back the political cartoon. The old time political cartoon. That's important."

"Really? My God, how old are you?"

"And I got our first one. You ready?"

"Sure. Fine."

"I wanna see a trans woman standing there in a sun dress. She's got the front of her dress hiked up, and her own fat cock in her hand, pissing on Rosie the Riveter, down on her damn knees. And that dude's just looking at us, red lipstick, eye lashes, full beard, just smiling."

Scarlet looks around, nervously.

She says, "You know that'll get taken down, right?"

"So you put it back up. Put it everywhere. Text it to random numbers. I don't care, just get it out there. Make it a part of the conversation. And we can make different versions. Instead of Rosie, make it JK Rowling. The Statue of Liberty. Gloria Steinem. Just flood the market with it."

"You really think the whole trans thing is gonna help us?"

"This is what it's all about! A tiny group that wields an ungodly amount of power within our government because they're very very loud, and an entire party has decided that anything they say is gold. A group that's literally changing the rules by which we all live, regardless of the fact that the vast majority of Americans disagree with it. No group should have that kind of power. They should have as much legislative say as they have members and allies, but that's it. Nothing more. And that's not nearly as much as they want, because outside of the 'I'm a leftist retard' contingent, most Democrats are actually reasonable people. If given the chance to say how they truly feel in the privacy of our survey, they're not gonna say, *'Yes, I want my child to have the absolute right to make life and body altering decisions at nine years old. Yes, I want my first grader to be given vivid lessons on gender and sexuality, regardless of the teacher's qualifications or personal leanings. Unless, of course, those leanings are conservative, and then they absolutely can't. Yes, I want to be required to say a person's pronouns, no matter how confusing they may be, under penalty of law. Yes, I want women and young girls to be forced to change clothes in a room where cocks are swinging. Yes, I want my daughter to be forced to compete against biological men. To hell with her ability to compete for a scholarship.'* Your average Democrat is not going to say these things, because they're not down with some of the crap these people are trying to pull. Hell, even the LGBs are a little suspect of the Ts, if you know what I'm saying."

Scarlet looks around again, embarrassed.

"I think everybody knows what you're saying."

"You talk to April lately? She hates this crap. And she's not alone. This could be our secret weapon. We're not gonna win many conservatives on it, because they got it covered, but liberals... maybe. Their leadership have got their heads so far up those Tranny skirts, someone's gonna lose an eye. Joe Biden's gonna look like a pirate come election night."

I bang my fist into the table to emphasize my point. Several dishes shake.

"What the hell is wrong with you?" Scarlet asks.

"What do you mean?"

"Why are you so pissy? Did something happen?"

I shake my head in frustration.

"I don't know."

She squints her eyes and studies me.

"Did you talk to that bitch from polling?"

"Our numbers are shit, okay? We're stagnant. We're going nowhere fast. It's total bullshit. Cause I've been hitting it hard. Have you been hitting it hard?"

"Yes! We've been killing it. And getting great response. Our articles are getting read... a lot. The comment sections are full. The reporters' emails are filling up with love letters and death threats. It's amazing! The Party's name is everywhere. Your name is everywhere. We're doing better than I could've possibly imagined."

"Well it's not showing up in the polls."

"It'll show up in the next cycle. Even our conspiracy theory is taking off. Hashtag UsefulIdiot has been trending for the last week. I even got a game designer to turn it into an app you can play on your phone. It's coming out next month. We are making a dent, William. I promise you, it's working."

I sigh.

"If you say so."

"I do. Just calm down and enjoy your food."

"Aghhh, I hate that bitch from polling."

"Maybe we can talk about something else."

I say, "Okay, let's do that. How's your sex life?"

237

"What? My sex life? I don't have a sex life, William. I'm too busy doing your bidding and resurrecting the political cartoon, apparently."

"Don't blame your lack of social life on me."

"I'm not blaming. I'm perfectly happy the way things are."

She looks down at her plate and stabs at her crepe.

"Have you thought about what's gonna happen when you turn twenty-five?" I ask.

Scarlet looks up at me.

"Nothing," I say. "Nothing is going to happen. I have no interest in being with you, Scarlet."

She blinks at me.

"Why do you think I haven't pursued this? Because I know it's wrong, that's why. It's wrong for me. It's wrong for you. I told you twenty-five, because I thought if you spent that time actually living, actually experiencing, going on dates, meeting people, having fights, making love, learning all the things that life can teach you… then maybe… maybe it wouldn't be wrong anymore. But you're not living. You're just holding a candle and watching the sand run through the hourglass. So when you turn twenty-five you're gonna be the same goddamn idiot I met three years ago."

"Astraea!" I yell from the couch.

"What!"

"Get in here."

"Ughh. Coming!"

Astraea enters the living room.

"What is it?"

"Grab a chair," I tell her.

She does as I ask and pulls a chair from the dining room. She places it across the coffee table from me.

"What are we talking about today? World domination?"

"Unless otherwise stated, all conversations are about world domination."

"Cool," she says and takes a seat.

The coffee table is covered in a host of electronic gadgets.

She says, "Looks like a fifth grade science experiment."

"Well somebody's gotta teach our eighth graders how to do fifth grade work. Can't depend on our schools to do it."

"Something tells me I should be offended by that."

"It's that fourth grade education paying dividends."

"Yeah... yeah. I'm definitely feeling a bit offended."

I set a couple 9-volt batteries on the coffee table, side by side. I grab a nail and hold it for her to see.

"This is a copper nail. Copper is an excellent conductor. It's what you'll find powering the outlets in any modern home. So, I lay one nail across both positives and another across the negatives. These two batteries are now hooked together in parallel."

"This is riveting stuff," Astraea says.

"How are they hooked together?" I demand.

"In parallel, Jesus! Is it me or are you a bit testy today?"

I point at the multimeter that sits on the table.

"Check the voltage."

Astraea grabs the multimeter. She flips the dial to measure voltage as previously taught. She touches the leads to each copper nail.

"Shows nine volts. Aren't these already nine volt batteries?"

"Yes they are, but now twice the amperage, allowing for a larger load or simply last twice as long on the smaller load."

She shrugs, "Makes sense to me."

I remove the copper nails and snap the two batteries together, offset from each other. They are made to go together, the negative terminal from one fitting perfectly into the positive terminal of the other.

"This is lining up in series. Negative to positive. Again a doubling effect, but in a different way. Now we're increasing the voltage."

I add a third battery.

"Measure that."

She does.

"Twenty seven point two."

"Right. Because three times nine is…"

"I think you can handle that one on your own."

I throw her an expectant look.

"Twenty seven," she says.

"Good. So, what if we had twenty-four of these bad boys?"

Astraea reaches for my phone.

"Nope," I tell her, blocking the phone.

"Where's a pen and paper?"

"You don't need it."

Astraea sighs, unsure of the answer. I let her think, while I begin to assemble the 24 batteries into one large battery pack.

"Ummmm." she says.

I ask, "What's nine times ten?"

"Ninety."

"So nine times twenty would be twice that."

"One eighty."

"Twenty batteries would be 180. That leaves four left over."

She says, "180 plus 36."

She thinks, frustrated.

I say, "They really don't teach you how to think do they?"

"Again, I feel like I should be offended."

"Except you're not smart enough to be offended. Take twenty of that thirty-six and add it to the one eighty."

"Two hundred."

"And how much is left over?"

"Sixteen. Two hundred and sixteen."

"There we go."

"You do math weird," she says.

"But I never said 'Ummmmm', like some voluntary retard. I worked the problem. I found a solution."

She points to my phone.

"I tried to work the problem."

"You're gonna have to trust me here," I say, pointing to my temple. "Knowing how to use this is way more valuable than knowing how to use this."

She sneers a bit as I gesture to my phone. I have no proof from her sour expression, but I get the feeling she actually appreciates my tutelage.

I snap the last battery into place.

"So we should have somewhere in the vicinity of 216 volts. Go ahead and check. But be careful, this level of voltage could kill you."

"Is that a joke?"

"It's only dangerous if you touch it. Go ahead."

Astraea nervously does as I ask.

"Two seventeen, point eight."

"Perfect. Now look at this very simple system that I've put together. We've got the power lines, which the batteries will provide. They lead to this old-school dimmer switch that effectively eats up voltage allowing us to adjust what gets fed to this light socket. All make sense?"

"Yes."

I point out the threaded metal side wall of the simple light socket.

"This threaded portion here is where the neutral wire makes its connection. Go ahead and look down into the socket."

"What am I looking for?"

"Dead center at the bottom of the socket, you should see an isolated metal tab."

"Yeah, I see it."

"That's where the hot connects. So tell me why the body of the socket is the neutral and that metal tab is the hot."

"How the hell would I know that?"

"Because you're an engineer and this is an engineering question."

Astraea looks at it, thinking.

"Because it's tucked away?"

"Say more."

"Because it would be easy to accidentally touch this part of the socket. And so it should be the negative because it's much less dangerous than the positive. It's a safety feature."

I offer a high five and she accepts.

"Go ahead and throw your testers into that socket. We're looking for 120."

Astraea aims the leads of the multimeter into the socket. She touches one to the body of the socket and the other to the tucked away tab on bottom.

I turn the knob on the dimmer switch to a lower setting.

"What do you got?"

"Uhh, ninety-two."

I slowly increase the voltage.

"108... 124... back a little... there! 120."

I mark the location on the dimmer.

I open a package of light bulbs.

"These are twenty-five watt bulbs designed to function optimally at one hundred and twenty volts."

I screw the bulb in and it immediately lights up.

"We made light!" Astraea squeals.

She claps her hands in an enthusiastically sarcastic way.

She says, "So I have a question. Not about this, about the other thing."

"Okay."

"It sounds like you're trying to create a whole new system of government. How feasible is that?"

"That's not what I'm doing at all. Any changes the Mediator Party brings will be done completely within the bounds of the system we've already created. We remain a republic. We just elect people who've agreed to actually represent the whole of the constituency."

"Democracy 2.0"

"It's just the logical step forward. The only reason we wouldn't take that step, would be to keep the current power structures in place."

"Actively keeping that power from the people."

"Talk about engineering…" I say, "We've been engineered to think in this very narrow way. So much so, that anything outside that narrow band is the work of a kook."

"So our job, as kooks, is to re-engineer society?"

"Yes. How do we purge the Two-Party System from the collective mindset of America? You know, if you want a brilliant example of social engineering, look no further than the liberal movement over the last few decades."

Astraea laughs, "Wow! You really hate those liberals, don't you?"

"Hey, they're not lying when they call it a progressive movement, it just keeps getting progressively more stupid. We've always had our issues, but only after the last ten years or so did they solidify their position on my shit list. Where was I?"

"Uhh, If history has taught me anything, you were about to give a lecture on the pitfalls of the liberal agenda."

"Right. So, imagine you're making a plan to infiltrate and eventually rule over the various social power structures. Where do you start?"

"I have no idea."

"Come on," I say. "I need you to participate."

"Do I get a trophy?"

"No," I tell her. The girl really knows how to push my buttons.

"Testy," she says.

"Come on, give me an answer."

"Uhhh, Hollywood?"

"Why?"

"Well, they're our storytellers," she says. "They get to determine who the good guys are. Who the bad guys are. Who we root for. Who we don't."

I say, "Every time someone sits down to watch a movie. Every time they check out a new TV show. Every time a parent puts their child in front of a cartoon. These are opportunities to spread your ideals to the masses. To redefine the values of America."

Astraea nods.

"Who else?" I ask.

"The media?"

"Absolutely. The people who tell us what's actually happening out there. The people who have the opportunity to frame what's happening and suggest how we should feel about it. Powerful stuff. Who else?"

"Ummm, Ms. Jeffers?"

"Who the hell is Ms. Jeffers?"

"My history teacher."

"Public schools! Hell yeah. Get them while they're young. Build them into what you want them to be. If you're playing the long game, there is no better target audience than the next generation. Which leads to our institutes of higher learning. Molding the minds of our young leaders before sending them off into the corporate landscape."

She says, "I tell ya, these liberals sure are smart!"

"I told you. A brilliant example of social engineering. You gotta give it to 'em. I got another one for ya. The mental health field. How do you rebrand a delusional behavior as perfectly normal?"

Astraea gives me an annoyed look.

I continue, "You set yourself up to be the ones that write the book. Or, more accurately, *rewrite* the book. And then you call it science."

Astraea thinks about that.

I say, "This is war, Astraea. It really is. It's psy-ops. It's tactical positioning. It's propaganda. It's winning hearts and minds through constant reinforcement, through multiple avenues, attacking you from all sides. It's a non-stop, always churning, thoughtful overthrow of the status quo."

"Well, that's not all bad, is it?"

"Not at all. I'm no defender of the status quo. But as of late, it has become a comedy of excess. The fight for equal rights has evolved into a culture of victimization."

I turn the dial on the dimmer switch beyond the 120 mark. The bulb burns brighter.

"A race to declare yourself oppressed, sniffing out injustice in the form of microaggressions and the mere existence of people more successful than you."

I turn the dial. The bulb grows even brighter.

"We've fertilized this culture of entitlement through the thoughtful dissolution of historically good traits like personal responsibility, accountability, self-sacrifice, stoicism, work ethic… That's all nonsense now. On top of all that, we so very badly want to remove the stigma of mental illness, but never for a moment stop and say, 'Wait. Mental illness is bad, right?'. Maybe some of that stigma is not only accurate, but a healthy deterrent."

"What? Are you kidding? You wanna hold on to the stigma?"

"I'm not saying we should shun people who have a mental illness. We should practice a certain degree of understanding, but we should never teach people that being a whack job is A-OK. We shouldn't instruct the masses to lean into it."

"Oh come on! Bringing it out into the open is a positive step. It's better that we talk about these things."

"For sure! The other day I saw a crackhead giving mental health advice to an alcoholic, and I thought… this is good! This is progress! We're all talking about it. We're removing judgment. And of course mental health has vastly improved."

Astraea looks at me and sort of nods, unsure.

"That is if you consider an increase in mental illness an improvement. Less gumption with which to attack it… also an improvement, I suppose. You ever notice how people don't *have* depression, they don't *battle* anxiety, they don't *contend* with ADHD. What do they do? You know this. Tell me what they do."

"They suffer," she says.

"They suffer from it. They always suffer. I *suffer* from depression. I *suffer* from crippling anxiety. *Crippling* anxiety. We can't forget the adjective to further highlight the extent of my victimhood. This is our common language now. We used to applaud fighting through adversity, now we talk about how brave someone was for quitting. Did you know that Time Magazine named Simone Biles *Athlete of the Year*… Specifically for quitting. In the biggest moment, on the biggest stage, she quit on herself, on her teammates, on her country. Time Magazine bypassed every athlete who fought, who dug deep, who scratched and clawed their way to the finish line and said, 'Screw you. We no longer value that kind of tenacity. We've chosen a quitter to be our Athlete of the Damn Year.' You want to rewrite the mindset of the next generation? You want to create a country of weak, fragile little individuals whose only strength lies in their ability to blame others for their misfortunes… that's how you do it."

With a single brilliant flash and a popping sound, the light bulb extinguishes.

"See? It burnt up. Why? Because it went too far."

Astraea says, "I'm sorry, but that sounds like bullshit. Why would anyone do that?"

"You tell me. Why would someone purposely create a culture of complete powerlessness?"

She thinks, "China?"

"That's one explanation. I'm sure they are happy to lend a hand, but I don't think China is the architect of this movement. I'm thinking a little closer to home."

"Who then?"

I shrug suggestively.

"The liberals," Astraea says with an eye roll.

"All I can say is, socialism will never succeed in a country full of strong, independent-minded, productive people."

Astraea considers that.

She says, "But a country of weak minded victims…"

"Who just want to be taken care of," I interject.

"…And it's a Brave New World."

I throw my hands up emphatically.

"That's what I'm saying!"

Astraea unscrews the burnt out light bulb from its socket. She replaces it with a new one. It burns bright. She immediately reaches over to turn the dimmer down to 120.

"So the cure," she says, "is to keep it at 120."

"Exactly," I say, taking over control of the dimmer.

I turn the dimmer way down. The filament appears as nothing more than a tiny ember.

"We're talking about a system that doesn't leave you in the dark and straining to see, but also doesn't seek to destroy itself."

I turn the dimmer to max power. I am forced to look away from the blinding light.

"We're talking about balance."

I return the dimmer to 120.

"Balance," Astraea says with a nod. "I'm curious, how many different ways are you gonna teach me this lesson?"

"As many as it takes."

"Okay, but you've completely lost track of the original question."

"What was the original question?" I ask.

"What are we gonna do? How do we engineer this system of balance into actual existence?"

"Well, that's the question, isn't it? What can we do? What are we willing to do? To what lengths will we go to save this country of ours?"

22

My last scheduled visit with the kids got canceled because 'The Ex' planned a two week long Thanksgiving trip. I'm looking forward to seeing them. Or at least one of them. I suspect Lindsey will find a reason to not show.

Somehow, I need to repair that damage. We are badly in need of a heart to heart. She needs to know that I divorced her mother, not her. She needs to know that her father loves her.

My heart gets a little jolt when I see the two of them walking out of the school together. They are walking the wrong path, so I give the horn a little honk and wave my arm out the window. They both look my way and then immediately look down as if they didn't see me. If I'm not mistaken, their legs are moving faster than before, still traveling the wrong path.

Something's wrong here. I step out of my truck and weave through the gridlock just in time to witness my children hustling into the backseat of an over-sized SUV.

It is, of course, my ex-wife's over-sized SUV. I hadn't seen it before, my view blocked by all the other over-sized SUVs. My feet pick up speed and I begin to run.

A tire squeals and the SUV lurches spastically forward. A hard turn narrowly avoids a fender-bender as the SUV escapes out onto the roadway. My run slows into a jog as I reach the space where my children once were, just moments ago. I smell the lingering scent of burnt rubber and watch that mammoth of a vehicle get smaller and smaller until it is gone.

I return to my truck and immediately send a text. After several minutes, I send another. And another. And another.

I drive to their house, but no one appears to be home. The lights are all off. No one answers the door.

It's Thursday afternoon and my plane has just touched down at the world's busiest airport. It's a vivid reminder of how much I hate people. I didn't bother to check a bag, so I happily skip past the crowded spectacle of the baggage carousel.

I flag down the first available cab and read off an address saved on my phone.

The driver puts his foot down and I watch Hartsfield-Jackson Atlanta Airport slowly drift away through the rear windshield.

Watching it disappear reminds me of the kids. It's been three days and still I've heard nothing.

"What brings you to town?" The cabbie says.

He is a black man with a welcoming smile. His eyes meet mine in the rearview and I instantly feel just a little bit less on edge. Strange how some people can do that to you. Something about their energy, their aura, their welcoming nature… something.

"My continued efforts to save the world," I tell him.

"Oh, A superhero, huh? Where's your cape?"

"I only wear it on special occasions."

"Saving the world ain't a special occasion?"

"Not really. Every hour of every day."

The cabbie throws me another smile and again I feel another lift.

He says, "I hear ya. So if you a super hero, which outfit you with? DC or Marvel?"

"Oh I'm not part of the big two. Isn't there one called Dark Horse or something?"

"Yeah, Dark Horse Comics. They pretty good."

"That sounds like a more accurate analogy."

"So really, how you saving the world, brother?"

"What's your name?" I ask.

"Darrell."

"Do you vote, Darrell?"

"From time to time," he says.

"Democrat or Republican?" I ask.

"Shii-iit. What do you think?"

"I think whichever answer you give is bound to be wrong. You know that voice inside your head that tells you 'this is bullshit. There's gotta be a better way'? Do you know that voice, Darrell?"

"Yeah, I got one of them."

"Well, that's me. I am the personification of that voice. And I'm telling you there is a better way."

Darrell pulls the cab into an office park.

"Oh shit. You doin' the 'Rascal and Big T' show? That where you going?"

"Yeah."

"Those are my boys, One of my favorite podcasts!"

Darrell pulls the cab into a parking space.

"Really? Well we're about to go live in less than an hour. Maybe you can do me a favor. I want you to listen to this podcast and then I want you to call me."

I hand him a business card.

"Like me or hate me, I wanna know exactly what you think. Will you do that for me?"

On the way inside the building, I receive a text. It's my ex-wife.

HER – I'm taking the kids and moving to Canada.

ME – What? When?

HER – Now!

ME – You can't do that. You can't take my kids to another country!

HER – My fiance is being transferred. I've already cleared it with the judge.

ME – How can you do this?

HER – Simple, I asked myself... WHAT WOULD JESUS DO!

Shit.

ME – It was an innocent conversation.

HER – My son is a Christian. You told him he worships the devil! That is not an innocent conversation.

ME – I think you may be missing some context.

HER – What possible context could excuse you making your son think that he kneels at the feet of Satan?

HER – Just so you know, I took Robby to talk to the Judge.

HER – Interesting tidbit, he's a pastor at his church! LOL

HER – He personally amended our custody agreement!

HER – LOL!!!

HER – You should be getting something in the mail!

HER – Bye

I stare at the screen, thumb poised. But what is there to say? There is nothing left.

Perhaps it is better this way. They aren't even my kids. Not really. They were that other man's kids. And that other man is dead. No more will I mourn his passing.

I take a breath, silence my phone, and enter the studio.

I sit in a small room with four other people. Two of them are basically invisible, sitting quietly monitoring the camera feeds and sound board. Across from me are Rascal and Big T.

I can already tell that Rascal is the comic relief. He's loud and obnoxious and has no filter. He's more show than substance.

The substance comes from Big T, a stout man with intense, militant eyes. Moments ago, on first contact, he stared me down as we shook hands. His grip went a step beyond firm, delving into the realm of intimidation. I sense that he derives no small amount of joy from the fear that his presence inspires.

Posters of Malcolm X, Black Panthers, and Olympic Fists of Freedom hang on the wall. Stickers saying Black Lives Matter, I Can't Breathe, and Defund the Police are liberally displayed.

One of the invisible people counts us down. Three... Two... One...

"And here we are again. Welcome my Brothers and Sisters to the Blackhole. We got a special treat for you today. Whiteboy in the house. Joining us now is William Waxman. Willy, my boy, what brings you to the Blackhole?"

"I was just wondering the same thing."

"Oh yeah?" Big T says.

"Ah shit! Boy don't even know why he's here!" Rascal says. "You did know you were comin' on a show today, right?"

"I did. But my whole deal is that I'm trying to bring people together. I'm trying to reach the reasonable people. So I'm wondering if I'm on the wrong show."

"You trying to suggest we ain't reasonable," T says. "What you see that says we aren't reasonable? I saw you checkin' my wall."

"To be honest, I think you've carefully crafted an unreasonable position. So I hardly think it comes as a surprise. I believe you've found your niche in the marketplace and now you're playing it for all it's worth. The problem is, it's not real."

Big T laughs. It's not a real laugh, it's a tough-guy cool laugh, all pretense and no heart.

"What's not real? You think my anger ain't real?"

"I think we'll never have a meaningful conversation as long as you treat me like the enemy."

"Boy, I aint treated you like nothin'."

"I think that's the third time you called me 'boy'. How would you like it if I called you 'boy'? You'd be okay with that? Or what if this was my show, and you were my guest, and I said to my audience, 'we got a special treat for you today. Blackboy in the house!' Does that sound like someone welcoming a friend? Does that sound like someone with an open heart or an open mind?"

Rascal looks nervous. He's not saying a word.

Big T just glares at me, silent. He appears to be on the verge of exploding.

I say, "Can I tell you what I think?"

He says nothing.

"I think you're a Teddy Bear, dressed up like a Grizzly. And don't take that wrong. I ain't saying you're a pussy or some shit like that. I got no illusions, Teddy Bears are still bears and they can tear shit up if they get pushed. But violence and hate and anger, that's not where a Teddy Bear lives. If given the option, a Teddy Bear will choose love and kindness and understanding. He feels anger, rightfully, but he doesn't choose it. He's got hate eating away at him, but he fights that shit with every bit of love he can muster."

I gesture to myself.

"This Teddy Bear wants a friend, not a foe. We can be enemies, if that's how it goes. But why don't we try it the other way first?"

Big T continues to stare at me. I see the slightest of nods. For the first time his militant posture relaxes to a minor degree. Not much, but something.

"Where you wanna begin?" he says.

"Well, I see that 'I can't breathe' sticker behind you. You wanna start there? Let's talk about Eric Garner."

"You gonna try to justify his murder?" Big T asks.

"I'm suggesting we watch the video," I say. "We break it down moment by moment. You tell me what you see. I'll tell you what I see. We debate it. We discuss it. Understanding what you see when you watch that video would be valuable to me. And I would think the inverse would be true for you."

Big T seems to be chewing on the idea.

"Nah man, I done watched too many niggas get murdered. I ain't about to watch that shit again. Break it down like video playback or somethin'. Nigger killin' ain't no spectator sport. That shit's disgusting. That's some sick shit you talking 'bout right there."

I digest his point and nod a bit.

"Maybe so, but this is a chance to educate me. To educate yourself. And not just yourself, every one of your listeners and viewers could learn something real today. I don't claim to speak for the entirety of the white community, but I can tell you that I'm not alone. You'll be gaining knowledge of not just my feelings, but a good subset of the white population. With greater understanding on all our parts, we might be able to take some positive steps forward. That's what I'm trying to accomplish here. I'm not trying to make light of Eric Garner's death, but I'm trying to make it mean someth-"

"Murder, motherfucker! That ain't death! That's murder, bitch! Call it what it is!"

Big T's militant posture is back in full force. Any trace of a Teddy Bear has been forcefully eradicated. He is a Grizzly and I am his next meal.

"Get the hell out of my studio, boy! You come up in here and disrespect everything we fought for? I oughta beat your ass!"

"Yeah, bitch!" Rascal joins in. "Get your scrawny ass outta here. Fuckin' bitch ass Teddy Bear lovin' cracker!"

I stand up and walk to the exit. I hear the continued taunts and bravado and laughter until finally the soundproof door shuts behind me.

I step out into the parking lot and use my phone to order an Uber. Before I complete the order, my phone rings.

"Hello."

"What the hell was that? That was some crazy shit!"

"Darrell?"

"Yeah man. That was crazy! And disappointing. I was looking forward to hearing what you were gonna say."

"Well maybe you still can. What are you doing right now?"

23

Darrell insisted that I join his family for an early dinner at his home in Mechanicsville. Upon hearing those words, visions of fried chicken danced through my head. Instead, we had spaghetti, which managed to be quite good and disappointing all at the same time. The garlic bread was amazing, but it wasn't fried chicken.

I try to help clean off the table, but Darrell's wife shoos me away.

"Grab your chair," Darrell says. "We ain't got enough seats."

Darrell's son sets up a single cell phone in the living room, angling it to capture everyone. I take a seat in my relocated dining room chair.

On one couch is Darrell, his wife Sheila, and his brother Carl. On the love seat are Talia and Javon, Darrell's nineteen year old daughter and fourteen year old son.

I look at Javon, "We rolling?"

"Yeah."

"Why don't we start with the next generation? What are you hoping to get out of this conversation?"

"I don't know," Javon says with a shrug.

"Any questions you wanna ask me?"

"So I know who I'm talking to, how 'bout you tell me if you recognize your white privilege."

"I'll say this… I recognize that you *think* I'm privileged."

"Ahhh, I see. I see you. I know who I'm talking to now."

I ask him, "Do you recognize your privilege?"

"Open your eyes. I'm black."

"Not white privilege. Just... privilege."

"What privilege?" he says, face scrunched up in disbelief.

"I see a young man with freshly cut hair, wearing nearly new clothes, stuffed to the brim from a big spaghetti dinner that he ate in a clean, well-kept home with his mother and his father. Is that privilege? You ever go over to a friend's house and notice how dirty it is? How when he opened the fridge it was nearly empty? How he only has one parent in the home? How his clothes seemed a little too big for him last year, but this year they fit pretty good, probably next year they'll be a little too tight? You ever notice anything like that?"

"Sure," he says, nodding.

"When that happened, did you recognize your privilege?"

"I did," he says with pride.

"Did you declare it out loud?"

"No."

"Did he ask you to?"

"No."

"Would you have respected him if he did?"

Javon looks at me hard. He leans back in his chair, clearly offended by the implication of my words.

I ask, "Does this privilege you have make you less of a man? Does it devalue your accomplishments? Should the A you got in Algebra get dropped to a B?"

"It's not the same thing."

"Okay. How so?"

"Don't act like you got no white privilege," Talia says. "Ain't nobody assuming you gonna rob their store when you walk in the door."

"That's true. I have the privilege of belonging to a race that is statistically a lot less likely to do something like that."

Carl says, "You think you're hot shit don't you?"

I say, "Why do you think we call it 'white privilege'? We clearly aren't the privileged few. We're not the one percent, or even the ten percent. We're the majority. How can 62% of the population be privileged. At that point, you just call it normal."

"Majority rules, huh?" Darrell says. "Might be true, but it damn sure don't make it right."

"It's not about majority rules. I think we can all agree that *my* normal should be *the* normal. In a perfect world nobody would be assumed to be a criminal just by walking through the door. Isn't that right? You're not really complaining that nobody thinks I'm a criminal. You're complaining that they think you are."

"That's true," Carl says. "I'll take me some white privilege. I'll have a big steaming bowl of it, thank you very much."

"So it's not really privilege. It's the standard we should all be judged by."

"But we're not," Javon says.

"So why don't we call it what it is? Why don't we call it Black Disadvantage?" I ask. "That's a lot more accurate, but I guess that wouldn't give you the opportunity to cast aspersions on random white people every time you say it."

Sheila says, "Damn, are you really twisting this into some reverse racism bullshit?"

"You're saying that I'm doing something wrong, because I walk into a store and no one thinks I'm going to rob the place. Exactly what have I done wrong? Ultimately, you're saying I'm guilty of being white. Which is the exact opposite of what you should do if you're trying to heal the divisions between the races."

Talia says, "Well who do you think is causing this 'black disadvantage'? It's not racist to call you out on the systems that you created."

"So should we call it 'white judgment'?" I ask. "That doesn't strike me as all that accurate either. Store owners of all races put a strong eye to the black man. White store owners, brown, yellow, and, yes, even black store owners… Strangely enough, they all seem to agree on this subject. Not really a white thing, is it?"

"It's the system you created. Racism is instilled in its very existence."

"Racism is instilled in the local corner store? Exactly what system are you talking about?"

"The system of American life. The way we're portrayed in the media. In movies."

"Or rap music," I say. "Which if I'm not mistaken are produced by… who exactly?"

"Wow, you just spoilin' for a fight, aren't ya?" Carl says. "Just rolling around in your generational wealth. Nothing better to do than pick a fight with the black man. I heard the way you talked to Big T."

"Did you hear the way he talked to me?"

Carl just sneers.

I say, "Let me tell you about my privileges. I got all kinds of privileges. I had the privilege of roofing houses all summer in the hot Oklahoma sun. I had the privilege of delivering pizzas on the weekends. I had the privilege of giving all those earnings to my institute of higher learning, while I got by eating cheap Bar-S hot dogs on plain white bread. I had the privilege of maintaining a full time job while school was in session and getting a second for summer and Christmas breaks. These are the kinds of privileges I had through nine years of schooling."

"You paid your own way?" Darrell asks.

"I guess all that generational wealth didn't quite make it to my door."

Carl grunts his disbelief.

"The truth is, most of us white people don't know shit about generational wealth. We don't much care about generational trauma. We don't hold a lot of generational guilt. And we simply ain't offering any generational pity."

"Ain't nobody asking for no pity!" Darrell's wife Sheila says.

"Really? Cause that's not what it sounds like when I listen to your leaders. Sounds like you want a whole hell of a lot."

Darrell says, "So what? You just don't give a damn about us?"

"I care. I care about you. The here. The now. The past happened. I didn't do it. I can't change it. Nor do I accept the responsibility of trying to make up for it. We learn from the past. We exist in the present. We strive for the future. That's the way of things. Or at least it should be."

"What the hell do you think we're doing?" Javon says.

"Honestly, I think you're living in the past. Striving to somehow correct what can't be corrected. We're living, right now, in the time of equal rights. This is exactly what your forefathers dreamed of. They fought for it and they got it. For you. This is your time. And you're wasting it."

"The fight ain't over," Carl says. "You want it to be over, but it ain't over."

"See, I think you're the one who should want it to be over. I'm telling ya, you guys are stuck. I don't know what the hell you're doing. I mean, look at the Mexicans. Those guys are fighting like hell to get over here. And by the time they get here, they've got nothing in their pockets. Less than nothing. Less than you've got, that's for sure. You've got citizenship. You can go get a proper driver's license. You don't have to look over your shoulder for immigration. You're not worried about being deported. You don't have to learn a new language. And you're not sending money back to Africa the way they send it back to Mexico. In the here and now, these people have it so much harder than you. And yet their poverty rate is less than yours. Compared to them, you guys should have built some generational wealth. Why haven't you? Is it because you spend so much time stewing in generational trauma? Imagine a world where you said, 'This is my time to make good. And whatever generational trauma I have, I'm gonna keep that shit to myself and not pass it on to my kids.' Wouldn't that be something?"

Javon shakes his head.

"How we suppose to do that when we see all this stuff on TV, social media, everywhere we look another black man's getting murdered."

"Look, if I'm telling it honestly, the majority of white people… if we were to see a video of a white guy resisting arrest, refusing to do the things he's been told… and then that white guy ends up dead… I promise you the majority of us would be saying *'What an idiot. What did you expect?'* And then we'd just shake our heads and move on. I guarantee you the majority of the blame would be put on the guy who… A – committed a crime, and then B – didn't follow orders. That's where the blame would go."

"You'd just give the cops a pass?" Javon says.

"That depends on the situation. I'm not saying we would hold the police completely blameless. What I'm sa-"

"But ultimately, you gonna blame the black man?" Carl says.

"Ultimately, I'm gonna blame the person or persons responsible."

"Why don't you give us some examples," Carl says. "We all know the names. Do you?"

"I know a few. Where do you wanna start?"

"Well you from Oklahoma. How about Terence Crutcher?"

I put my hands up in the air and repeat the rallying cry.

"Hands up, don't shoot."

"That's the one."

I shrug, "That guy wasn't following orders."

"His hands were up!" Carl says.

"They were... until they weren't. Anyone who watches that video and doesn't see that he lowered his hands just before getting shot, isn't looking hard enough. Either that, or they just don't want to see."

"That's bullshit."

"They'd rather live on a lie and spread those lies throughout the land. They'd rather declare that lady cop a racist and a murderer than admit that the guy was behaving really strangely and then made a move that would've scared the shit out of any one of us if we were in her position."

Carl looks very unhappy with my take on the situation. He looks to be on the verge of saying something, but Darrell puts a hand out to stop him.

"What about Walter Scott?" Darrell asks.

"That one's more complicated. Walter is definitely guilty of creating a very bad situation. If he had behaved differently, he'd probably be alive today. That doesn't change the fact that the cop who shot him is a murderer. No question in my mind, that was murder. You don't shoot some unarmed man while they're running away from you."

"George Floyd?" Sheila asks.

"Pfft... Clearly murder... with the same prerequisite though."

Talia says, "Prerequisite? He was higher than a kite. He wasn't in his right mind. That cop could see that and yet he dug his knee into that man's neck for eight damn minutes."

"And forty six seconds," Javon adds.

"In no way am I forgiving what Derek Chauvin did. It was disgusting. My only point is that had George not broken the law the encounter would've never taken place. But he did commit a crime. Even then, had he not resisted arrest, he'd have ended up in jail, still breathing. We make choices in this life. For that matter, one of those choices is whether or not to get high in the first place. Or get drunk. Or whatever. These are choices, and our choices don't get to also be our excuses. I don't go in for this idea that you carry less blame when you're not in your right mind. Especially when having that wrong mind was a decision you willfully made. If I beat my wife when I'm drunk, those are drinks I decided to take. Consequently, those are blows I decided to give."

"Personal responsibility," Darrell says throwing a look at his kids.

"It's in short supply these days," I say. "Look, I'll run through 'em real quick. Sam Dubose is another one. Another dumbass and the cop who straight up murdered him. Now the cop says his hand was stuck on the handle inside that door, so he was afraid he was gonna get dragged or run over, and I'd love to get that model of car and see if that's even plausible, but my gut tells me that's a bullshit story. Alton Sterling, that was a good shoot. Rayshard Brooks, same deal, good shoot. You don't get physical with a cop, steal his taser and make a run for it while shooting the taser over your shoulder. The guy got what he got. I'm sorry he's dead. I really am. But there was no injustice."

Carl groans, "I can't believe I'm listening to this shit."

I say, "Personal responsibility goes both ways, though. The guy who killed Akai Gurley. You remember him? He got shot near a stairwell. The cop got startled, didn't even mean to fire his gun. The bullet ricocheted and killed Mister Gurley. Do I think that cop should go to prison for manslaughter? Yes I do. You decide to put that gun on your hip, you don't get to just make mistakes."

Javon says, "Spiderman's uncle said it best, 'with great power comes great responsibility'."

"Thank you Spiderman's uncle. Truer words were never spoken." I agree. "Then there's that reserve cop, also from my neck of the woods, who accidentally pulled his gun instead of his taser. He was like 73 or something, but I don't give a shit. Send his ass away. There's no room for 'oops' in this thing."

Javon says, "How do you confuse your taser for your gun?"

I shrug, "Poor training, I guess."

Darrell says, "Maybe whoever's in charge of that training should serve some time."

"Maybe they should," I agree. "I've heard that the reserve program was a joke. But they still let them wear a badge. They still let them wear a gun. A portion of that death is on whoever was in charge. Maybe some heads oughta roll. And roll hard."

Sheila says, "What do you think about Tamir Rice?"

"That's a really sad one, but I can't fault a cop for shooting somebody who was in the act of raising a gun. I just can't do it."

"The boy was twelve years old," Carl says.

"Right, because there's no history of twelve-year-olds shooting people in the hood."

Sheila says, "But it wasn't even a real gun."

"It was a replica of a real gun. There is no training someone to know the difference, because visually, there is no difference."

Carl says, "On the podcast you were gonna talk about Eric Garner. Is he a dumbass too?"

"Without question. Total and complete dumbass. This is the one that I think most encapsulates my, and a lot of other people's, recoil from the activism that's been taking place."

"Why?" Carl asks.

"Because it's so full of lies. There's been a lot of lies told about a lot of these situations, but if you ask me, this one takes the cake."

"What lies? Ain't no damn lies."

I raise my voice in mock outrage. "They killed him... for selling cigarettes! They choked the man to death! That cop is a racist murderer! Eric Garner didn't even do anything!"

I look at Carl, annoyance seeping from my pores.

"First of all, let's talk about the economics of this man's business plan. How much you think you're gonna make selling individual, overpriced cigarettes? In order for this plan to pay off, you need one of two things: Either some major volume, or up-charging like crazy. So who is your customer base? Smokers don't want individual cigarettes. They buy by the pack and they damn sure aren't gonna overpay. That takes us to non-smokers. They don't want what you're selling in the first place. That takes care of 98 percent of the population, leaving the people who don't really smoke, but every once in a while, they like to sneak one. And then you gotta get them at that perfect moment when they're like, 'hey, a cigarette sounds really good right about now'. You've got next to no customer base. It's a terrible business model. It doesn't work. Unless... You happen to be six and a half feet tall, four hundred pounds, and a terrible salesman. You're just really bad at it. You take up the entire sidewalk, so they can't even walk past you. That's annoying. Worse yet, you're a close talker, invading people's personal space, making your customers feel uncomfortable. You never smile. You've got this deep snarl of a voice. An absolutely terrible salesman, but for some reason, the people seem to respond. Your customer base has gone through the roof! Smokers, non-smokers, one dollar, two dollar, five dollar... it doesn't seem to matter. The people want your product, because you're not really selling cigarettes anymore, are ya? You're selling safety. And people value their safety."

"Is that really what happened?" Sheila asks.

"You tell me. Does anything else make sense? There is no customer base. So what was he doing out there? The man was a menace. You can try to make a saint out of the guy if you want, but there's a reason why shop owners complained about him. Legitimate business owners, trying to make a legal living, were losing their customers. Your average person doesn't want to be harassed every damn time they go someplace, so eventually they start going elsewhere.

"Even if that's not what was happening, which I'm almost certain it was, Mister Garner was still breaking the law. He'd been arrested for that very thing, in that very place, on multiple occasions. He knew he was doing wrong and he did it anyway."

"That ain't no reason to kill somebody," Javon says. "You can't choke a nigga for trying to make a dollar."

"Hey," Darrell says. "Not in this house, boy."

Javon lowers his head.

"Look, I got a lot to say and this is not my house, I know I'm not in charge of shit, but I'm gonna suggest that you guys just let me say it. This is that moment, when a guy just starts talking and talking and won't stop. That moment when, if you don't interrupt him, he'll show exactly who he is. So let me show you."

Sheila says, "You want us to give you enough rope to hang yourself?"

"That's exactly what I want."

"Shit, boy. It's your funeral."

"Javon is right. It's not a reason to kill someone, but it is a reason to arrest them. Which is all that would've happened if Eric Garner had simply accepted responsibility for his actions. Instead, he refused all orders, acting like a victim, like he couldn't understand why the cops keep bothering him every damn time he breaks the law. When that cop tried to take his arm, Mister Garner shook it off violently. He started yelling, getting worked up, and waving his arms erratically. The facts are simple, there's only one thing that can happen at that point. The cops can't, cannot, under any circumstances, reward a person for resisting arrest. They can't do it. They start doing that, compliance will be a thing of the past. The cops had no choice but to arrest that man, and yet he refused to be arrested. So force was absolutely necessary and Eric Garner was the one who chose it.

"Now, if you watch the video, the cop tried to control him with a safer maneuver, putting one arm under the armpit. Garner's reaction was violent. Nearly put both of them through a window. The man weighed 400 pounds. That cop was probably half his size. If you think a man's size is irrelevant then you know nothing about physical altercations. That cop was in real danger at that moment. That glass could've broke. They fall through that glass, who knows what he hits his head on, and with an extra 400 pounds of weight carrying him through, it may not be something he gets up from. Hypotheticals aside, I'm certain that shit hurt, and he probably got the wind knocked out of him. So yeah, he switched to a more effective hold. An illegal hold, yes. Should he be punished for that, maybe. But he did it in an attempt to gain control of a violent man and a dangerous situation. If I'm honest with you, I would've done the same. And I'd venture to guess that anyone in this room would have too. One thing is for certain, he didn't do it because he felt like killing a black man. To suggest that is beyond disingenuous. It's a bald faced lie. And, to suggest that that police officer actually choked him to death is also patently false. Yes, he had him in a choke hold for 15 seconds, which he released as soon as he gained control. And he wasn't blocking his airway. Restricting a bit, maybe, blocking it, no. A man cannot speak loudly and clearly, 'I can't breathe'... loud enough to be easily heard above all the chaos... Eleven times. That is not something a man can do when his airway is blocked. He felt like he couldn't breathe, because he was having a heart attack.

"At the end of the day, Eric Garner was breaking the law. He got unnecessarily worked up when someone tried to hold him accountable for his behavior. He was severely overweight, due to his own choices. He had a history of hypertension and diabetes, due to those same choices. He was a heart attack waiting to happen before he practically demanded to be in a violent situation. Did the illegal chokehold contribute to his medical emergency? I'm sure it didn't help, but it was his own choices that did most the work.

"Most importantly, I think it is a real problem when you canonize a man like that. Police brutality is a real thing. Racial factors within that realm are real too. But when you make that man and that situation the poster child of your cause, you're making a mockery of it all. If you want a lot of white people to tune out, that's how you do it. You want someone like Trump to win an election… it works for that too."

I shrug in a way that lets everyone know that I've said my piece.

Sheila says, "You think that's why Trump won?"

"I think it played a big part."

Darrell looks at me.

"You voted for Trump?" he asks.

"I didn't vote for anybody. Til we get a candidate that's worth a damn…"

Sheila says, "I don't think you give enough weight to the black experience out there. This world that I grew up in. This world that my kids are growing up in. You don't know that world. Not the way we do."

"I'm sure you're right. I know that equal rights alone don't necessarily add up to equality. I know that black people, in general, have a harder road than white. Then again, there's a lot of help for black people that's not available to white. And I also know a white girl whose father raped her for the first time at age seven. He continued to do so until she outgrew his interests at fourteen. Now, I don't know if you've been through something like that, but I'm guessing on a one-to-one basis, that white girl had a harder road than you. And I feel for the girl, I really do, but I still expect her to practice civilized behavior. And if she fails to do that, I expect her to pay the consequences. She doesn't get a pass."

"We're not asking for a pass."

"You are if you don't make non-compliance an important part of the issue. If you just forgive bad behavior and attribute the whole problem to racist cops… that sounds to me like asking for a pass. We've been bringing up a bunch of names, well, I've got a few more. Loren Simpson, Tony Timpa, Daniel Shaver, Brandon Staley, Dylan Noble, Andrew Thomas. These names have experienced very similar situations to the ones we're talking about, several of them on video. The difference is, you've never heard of them. Why? They're all white."

"Cops just wanna pull that trigger," Carl says with a shake of the head.

"When weighed against their chances of going home that night, yes they do. It's amazing to me how quick people are to say, 'just wait until you see a gun!'. You do realize that the time span between seeing a gun and feeling a bullet can be quite small, right? Do you really think these people should take that risk when the subject has already shown a willingness to break the law? To disobey orders? To put others in harm's way? I'm betting you wouldn't take that risk. They do something hinky, you're gonna pull that trigger."

Carl says, "Don't start thinkin' you know me."

"I wouldn't dream of it. I'm only guessing that you'd rather be alive than dead. Am I right on that score?"

He doesn't answer.

I ask, "Do you know who Roland Fryer is?"

"Another white guy?" Carl says.

"No. He's a black man. An economist out of Harvard. He was so disturbed by all the racial police violence he was seeing on the news, that he decided to statistically prove that it was a real problem. And he succeeded."

"Damn right he did," Carl says.

"He found that on any given police interaction, black people were 53 percent more likely to be treated with some measure of force."

"Sounds about right," Sheila says. "Tell me there ain't a problem."

"I can't say there's not a problem, because there is one. He also found that even in cases of compliance… where the subject was noted to have been compliant, even then, blacks were 21 percent more likely to have been treated with some kind of force."

Carl says, "Then what the hell are we talking about? The evidence is clear."

"Now here's what surprised Mister Fryer, in the cases of officer involved shootings, he could find no difference between white and black at all."

"Now that's some bullshit."

"That's what the numbers said."

"Uh unh. No way," Carl says.

Darrell says, "I gotta agree with Carl. My people getting killed a lot more than your people."

"Proportionally, that's true. In absolute numbers, it's not. When it comes to people killed by cops, more whites end up in the morgue. Mister Fryers numbers aren't based on either of those things. They're based on actual police interactions."

Sheila says, "Well shit. Cops creep on us all the time. They just let the light skins roll on by. Of course those numbers are skewed."

"More interactions... More chances to kill us," Carl says.

I nod, "I agree with you. It's a problem."

"Finally."

I say, "We need some reforms, better training, and... better citizens."

"What the hell!" Carl says.

"Hold up!" Sheila says. "You saying this is our fault? We bring it on ourselves?"

"I'm saying that's a big piece of the pie."

"Damn. This white boy's crazy," Javon says with a whistle.

I say, "If you want things to get better, you have to address the problems. All the problems."

"Alright, we've been pretty patient with you," Darrell says. "We've listened up to this point, but damn."

"Look," I say. "We can't ignore the facts. A sober look at the entirety of the situation tells me that the inequities of racial force in policing is mostly due to bias, not racism."

"Man, racial bias is just another word for racism."

"That's not true," I say.

Darrell stands up.

"Alright man, maybe we need to call it a night."

"Can I say one thing? Let me make one attempt to get you on the same page. After that, if you still want me to go, I'll go."

Darrell crosses his arms across his chest. He stares at me and gives a little nod.

"Okay. Imagine for a moment that you're a cop. You've been sent to a scene with very little information. All you know is that yelling has been heard. That's it."

"Alright," Darrell says, patience wearing thin.

"You get to the scene. You find two people, both white. One is a man, the other a woman. Now as a policeman, you have no choice but to always be on guard. Always be ready. Always be evaluating potential danger, right?"

"I'm with ya."

"So while you're doing that, while you're evaluating potential danger, which of these two people is getting more of your attention? Who are you clockin'?"

"The guy."

"Why?"

Darrell shrugs, "Because he's a man."

"Men are more likely to seek out physical conflict, right?"

"Yeah."

"Statistically more likely to commit murder too."

"For sure."

"In this situation, you've allowed these facts and all that you've witnessed in your life to make you biased toward that man."

Darrell thinks about that.

I ask, "Do you think masculinity is toxic?"

"Nah man."

"Do you hate men? Do you look down on them?"

"No."

"So you don't hate men, but you do have a situational bias against them?"

Darrell thinks and sort of nods.

"Our brains are just poorly functioning computers. They're designed to recognize patterns. It's how we learn. It's how we grow. It's how we avoid danger. And yes, it's how we develop biases. Racial bias and racism are not the same thing. Every year we crown an American city as the murder capital of the U.S. And every year it's a city with a gang problem. More specifically, a black gang problem. You can go to your computer right now and print off two lists. One – the cities with the greatest percentage of black population. Two – Cities with the highest murder rates. I'll save you some time, it's basically the same list. Somewhere in the realm of two-thirds of all robberies in this country are committed by black people. 56 percent of all homicides are committed by black people. That's in a country where you make up 13 percent of the population."

"And why do you think that is? You're ignoring the socio-economic factors," Sheila says.

"I know that plays a part, but it's not the whole story. The fact is, there are nearly twice as many whites living beneath the poverty line as blacks."

"That ain't true," Carl says. He looks at Darrell. "Is that true?"

Darrell shakes his head, "A lot of white people in this country."

Carl says, "And because of that, they runnin' the damn thing. And don't tell me they ain't doing it with race in mind."

I say, "Okay, how about this? Black people in proportion to their percentage of the population are 5 times more likely to be incarcerated than white people. You believe that?"

"Hell yeah, I believe that."

"And it's because white people are running this thing?"

"Damn straight."

"And they don't like black people?"

"Don't seem like it."

"Okay. So explain this... white people – the people running this thing – are 2.3 times more likely, by percentage, to be incarcerated than Asians."

Carl says nothing.

"By your own logic, white people must *really* love Asians. Just some weird fetish we have, I guess. Otherwise, why would we treat them better than we treat ourselves?"

Carl says, "Man, I don't know about any of that. White people's fetishes are outside my field of expertise."

"I think if we're honest about it, we'll find our answer," I tell him. "Asians have a strong culture of family. Comparatively, there are very few single parent homes in the Asian community. That's compared to whites. They tend to stress education, more so than whites. They are actively involved in their children's development of knowledge and work ethic, compared to whites. And so, in a country run by white people, Asians somehow manage to be more successful. On average, Asian families in this country earn twenty-five percent more than white families. How the hell does that happen? They earn it, that's how. The deserve it. From the day that child is born, the parents are putting in the work. And then the child is made to put in the work. And when that child has a child, they put in the work. That's how they go from being immigrants with nearly nothing, to being the most successful race in this country. The least incarcerated. The most financially secure. There's no nice way to say this... the problems within the black community have to be solved within that community. Until you latch on to that truth, you'll always be in this same boat. The cops are the people on the ground. They see what's happening every day. There is an extremely large and violent subculture at play within your community. Until that shit changes, biases are going to be formed in the minds of human beings. It's unavoidable."

No one says anything for several moments.

"And your shit don't stink?" Carl says. "I don't see a whole lot of black men going to schools and grocery stores and killing everybody in sight."

I nod.

"You got me on that one. Whitey's got problems too."

Everyone relaxes a bit when the subject turns to white people. Smiles begin to bloom, spirits begin to flow, and laughter echoes off the walls of the family room.

The merciless roast of all things white continues for at least half an hour. It's great fun, actually. We talk about Proud Boys and Oath Keepers and QAnon and January 6th and Red Hats and Helicopter Moms and Serial Killers and Suburban Anxiety and the overwhelming need to touch black people's hair.

The taboo subjects of politics and religion lead to lengthy arguments that find no winners, but plenty of losers. I tell them of the Mediator Party and the hope of a better way. They listen. They ask questions. They seem interested. But sadly, they remain Democrats.

Stories are told and dreams explored. I become the butt of several jokes, but so does everyone else.

We ping-pong from one subject to the next in an ever evolving exploration of this crazy fucking world. Before we know it, hours have passed. For a moment, I allow myself to forget that this is not my home. I curl up in their familial embrace. I find it warm and inviting. In a weird way, I love them. I pretend that they love me too. And I am happy.

24

There are times when I just want to be alone. But I am not alone. I am never alone. She is with me. I ended her and so she is mine, always and forever.

I think of her smell. Her smile. Her freckles. Her soft lips. Her fragile strength. Her warm body as she received me. Her... all around me.

But mostly I think of her face, shock and confusion morphing into horror as she finally realizes exactly who I am.

She sees me in that moment, stripped bare. The lines of her face define me like no string of words ever could.

I am her monster.

And now she is mine.

Still, I'm finding it hard to accept her definition of me. She's too close, too biased on the subject at hand. How can she judge me? She was the one who preyed on a man's loneliness, on his desire for human affection. She was the one who attempted to worm her way into my heart, all the while, intent on betraying me. Perhaps she is the only monster here.

Perhaps not.

I hate that I seek out these excuses. I wish nothing more than to be at peace with my decision. Having chosen to live in service of society, I must concede that the service of a mere man is bounded by limits. In such, the decision to avoid the monstrous, is a decision to leave great wells of potential untapped. Monsters have no such limits.

Perhaps it is a matter of self-realized evolution. Each of us have a monster gestating inside of us. And yet, we are not all monsters. It is only through our own chosen actions that a monster is born. Why must that birth be an ugly thing? Why can't it be beautiful, as births often are? The birth of a fully realized human being.

Is it not possible to be both a monster and a man? After all, the distance between the two is so small and tenuous. Can we not occupy both spaces and all the breadth in between? Can we not embrace the monstrous while leaving our humanity intact? There must be a balance that can be achieved. A balance that allows us to be something more, something valuable, something worthy of a calling?

Melody never leaves me on our two hour drive to the Oklahoma State Penitentiary. We are as one, two monsters entwined. Together we wait for Axton Leclaire to step out of the confines of his prison.

Two years ago, I donated a copy of *A Love/Hate Letter To America* to every prison in the state of Oklahoma. I quickly forgot about it. That is until I received a letter in the mail. A prisoner by the name of Axton Leclaire had read my book and he wanted to talk about it. Over the ensuing months we exchanged many a letter. Self-educated behind bars, he's a strange mix of half street and half scholar. Hidden behind the language of the streets, lies one simple fact – he is possibly the smartest person I have ever met.

Ten minutes and a world away from his prison cell, Axton and I slide into a booth at Captain John's. We order something called Cajun Toothpicks as well as Catfish Bites and Crab Stuffed Shrimp. That's just the appetizers. For the entree, I dive into my Crawfish Etouffee, while Axton throws down a healthy portion of Cajun Jambalaya Pasta.

I'm enjoying our meal, but I can't imagine how it tastes to Axton. After seven years of cafeteria food, he might just believe he's in heaven. He lays down his fork, an empty plate before him.

"I can't thank you enough Mister Waxman. I don't know how I'll ever repay you."

I look at him. He's lost in heaven still, staring at his empty plate. I wait for him to look up.

"Yes you do," I say.

He nods.

"Yeah, I guess I do."

"So tell me."

"Tell you?"

"Tell me how you're going to repay me."

"Okay. So you say you want me to help you get the black vote, but you're thinking too small."

"Really?"

"For sure. The Mediator Party can be the voice we've never had. Democrats don't speak for us. They pretend to. They give us plenty of lip-service. But they talking down, see. Even when we taller than them, they talking down. Trying to be the fathers we ain't got. You ain't my damn step-daddy, nigga. Let me ask you something, you think we pro-Democrat?"

"All evidence points to it."

"Hell no. We anti-Republican. That's what we are. You said it yourself, there's only two choices. We ain't no fans of step-daddy, but we'll take him over some hood wearin' motherfucker. We been stuck with these niggas. We more than primed for a better option."

"And the Mediator Party is that option?"

"It is when I'm selling it. You don't know what I'm capable of. But I'm gonna show you. You get the black vote, in the right way, with the right message, it will bring so much more."

"Explain that. Tell me about the more."

"You ever heard of trickle down economics?"

I smile, "Sure. Gotta be honest, I wouldn't have pegged you as a fan."

"I'm not a fan, because it only works if the people at the top want to share that wealth. To some degree they do, because they want to expand, grow their business and that creates jobs and what not, but they also want to put a whole bunch of that cheddar in their pockets. And their pockets ain't like the pockets where I'm from. They ain't got no holes in 'em."

"So no trickle."

"Not even a drop. The idea is sound. Not liquid, sound. We don't trickle down, we echo out. When we, the black people, claim our voice, we'll speak loud, we'll speak proud. And that pride and that joy will echo out beyond the confines of the black community. Finding its way to the white community. And that shit will sound like a symphony orchestra to the ears of white guilt."

"You're gonna sing the praises so loud that white guilt can't help but sing along?"

"You damn right!"

I love this man. I really do.

"We're talking about liberals," I say. "Like for real liberals?"

"Oh yeah."

"That's not a segment of the vote I expected to pick up."

"I know. That's why I said you thinkin' small."

"I like this idea, but… what percentage of the white population feels enough of that guilt to drop their Party loyalties?"

"Yeah, I read some studies about that guilt… It ain't pervasive, but it's somethin'."

Axton points at my water glass.

"Is this glass half full or half empty?"

"Half-empty."

Axton nods, then shrugs, "Maybe two percent."

"Of the white population?"

He nods.

"That is something," I say, pondering the implications of receiving an extra two percent of the white vote. I'm greedy, so I ask, "What if this glass was half full?"

"Somewhere between four and eight," he says.

"Okay, that's really something," I say. "So, here's the big question. I'm trying to figure out if black people would really want the Mediator Party."

"You don't think so?"

"Well, you guys make up 13 percent of the population."

"So?"

"Which means, according to my Party, your cumulative vote will only get 13 percent of the say in legislative matters."

"What? You think we want more than our share?"

"Everybody wants more than their share. And black people might just be able to get it. They might be able to bend an entire Party to their will, like they already did in the summer of 2020. Had governments allowing violent protest. Even had them defunding the police for God's sake. Let me tell you something, that's more than your fair share."

"That was an anomaly."

"And it ain't happening with the Mediator Party. You'll get your thirteen. That's all you'll ever get."

"We might get to fourteen."

"Maybe. You stop killing each other in the streets. Stop snuffing out your unborn."

"No sign of that," Axton says, with a hint of regret.

"So… thirteen it is. How you gonna sell that to them?"

"As an improvement. Page 74, *A Love/Hate Letter To America*. Remember that shit?"

I shake my head, "Not a clue."

"You wrote that shit, what's wrong with you?"

"Why don't you refresh my memory?"

"It was two pie charts. The first was a demographic breakdown of the populace. Black, 13 percent slice of the pie. The second chart though, that's the real pie. The Political Influence pie. Twenty percent to the rich, AKA white people. Twenty percent to special interests, mostly white people. Forty percent to the corporations, damn near all white people. The populace, well, they get the final twenty percent. And here's my people, getting thirteen percent of twenty percent."

"What is that, three percent?"

"If you wanna round up. But in reality it's two point six. All we've ever had was a little bit of sway. Just a sliver. With the Mediator Party we got the say, not the sway, the say. That's 13%

ownership of the legislative process. That's some shit we ain't never had. To hell with the sway. It's all about the say."

Melody likes to visit me best when I'm driving, but with another live body in the passenger seat, she stays away. It's a welcome change.

I say, "Hey, I almost forgot, I got you a gift."

"Yeah?" Axton says.

"Yeah. Open that briefcase between your legs."

"Wow, a gift. I can't remember the last time that happened."

Axton opens the briefcase and just stares at the contents. Over the last year, he's been sending me essays in the mail. Every week, without fail, I would find a new thought provoking treatise on the state of our society. Some weeks, it was the only thing that made me smile. There is something truly beautiful in the way his mind works.

Axton reaches into the briefcase and pulls out a hardcover book. He looks at me and I see the water forming in his eyes. He looks down at the book and runs a finger over the author's name – AXTON LECLAIRE.

"The Dying of the Guard," he says, referring to the title. "Where'd you come up with that?"

"Are you kidding? You wrote that shit, what's wrong with you? You expect me to remember page 74 of my book, but you don't even remember the concept behind one of your greatest essays? That one stuck with me for weeks, plus it felt like a good title. I'm half jealous that I didn't write it myself."

Axton flips through the pages.

"Did you publish this?"

"No. I plan to though. Just as soon as you approve it. And then you'll be going on a publicity tour."

"I can do that. Maybe I can go on Darrell's Family Time Podcast."

"The what?"

"You know, Darrell… and his family… in Atlanta."

"Oh, yeah. That was fun. We called an audible when Big T threw me out. Is it an actual podcast now?"

"Yes sir. They've turned it into a whole thing. Your visit got so many viewers they've started up a whole new family business, upped their production values, the whole nine."

"That's awesome! Good for them. I like Darrell. I guess you listened to my time with them?"

"I did. Used up all my computer time on that shit."

"What did you think?"

Axton takes a moment to think about that. He takes a thoughtful breath.

"I think you're the wrong messenger."

I nod, "Maybe."

"That wouldn't be that big of a deal, except I think you knew it when you did it. And you did it anyway."

I take my eyes off the road and look at him. His gaze is unmistakably accusatory. He's a very smart man. No sense bullshitting him.

I say, "...'This killing is not based upon poverty; it is based upon greed and violence and guns'. Who said that?"

Axton squints his eyes in thought, but the answer eludes him.

"I'll give you another one. Same guy. 'There is nothing more painful to me at this stage in my life than to walk down the street and hear footsteps and start thinking about robbery, look around, see someone white, and feel relieved'."

Axton nods his head, realizing the answer. He says, "The Reverend Jesse Jackson."

"I'm guessing that's what you might call the right messenger. I was a kid when he said that. Thirty years and ain't nothin' changed. How long are we suppose to stay quiet about this? Waiting for the next right messenger to fail to make any difference at all. Maybe some outside pressure is exactly what you need."

Axton shakes his head.

I continue, "There are clips of that podcast on YouTube that have gotten over 20 million views."

"I saw that."

"Now Ax, I think you know, I'm not just after the black vote. White people been wanting to say that shit to black people for a very long time. There's millions of 'em, right now, living vicariously through me. And I'm not talking about racists. I'm talking reasonable people who've seen the problem, because they'd be blind if they didn't. They're finally getting to say it, through me. That's millions of potential voters."

"But it don't play right comin' out of your mouth. Not to my people. Can't you see you've made my job harder. I've gotta repair the damage you've caused."

"I never said your job would be easy."

"But it is my job, right? It belongs to me?"

"It is."

"Then as of right now, you're gonna leave my shit alone. You don't talk about my people. You don't go on black podcasts. You don't meddle in my business. It's mine. You gonna back the hell off."

There is a part of me that reflexively wants to bow up, the alpha male refusing to be pushed around. But the rest of me is dancing a jig. This is music to my ears.

"You want full ownership?"

"Do I need to say it again? This shit is mine."

"I understand what you're saying," I tell him. "Do you?"

I look at him, demanding an answer. He looks at me.

"I do."

"Being 'the man' means you got no one to complain to. No excuses. No one to blame. Any failure is yours and yours alone. That sound like fun?"

"More than you know."

"Then it's yours, Axton. That briefcase and everything in it is yours. There's a phone, courtesy of the Mediator Party. My number's already programmed in. You'll also find a deed to a commercial property on the Northeast side. You are free to use that property as you please. It's a bit of a trash heap right now, but we cleared out an area for you to shut your eyes. Threw a bed in there, plus a fridge. You have a bank account with twenty grand in it. An additional ten grand will be deposited every month. If you need more, I suggest you knock on doors, make phone calls, make friends. Ultimately, your entry into this family should increase the Mediator Party's donations. Your existence should make us money, not cost us money. You understand?"

"I've already got irons in the fire."

"That's what I like to hear," I say. "You thought about opening a charitable organization? Ways to become a pillar of your community?"

"I got some ideas."

"Like what?"

Axton stares out at the road, thinking.

"You know, before my Daddy got shot, he decided he wanted a shed in the backyard. We didn't have any money, so that summer we drove around white neighborhoods during big trash pickup. It was always big trash somewhere. All the scrappers wanted was the metal, but there was so much more than that. Worn out couches, broken down tables and chairs, night stands, bar stools, old wood fencing. We focused on the fencing. The slats were rotting on the ends, but they were six feet long. You cut off the rot, you still got four or five feet of good wood. We glued and screwed those slats together, three thick, then used 'em like two-by-fours. Framed out an entire shed that way. My dad was one hell of a builder. He used a router to transform more of those slats into wood siding. We asked a roofer if we could take the trash shingles they were pulling off a house. They didn't care. A lot of those shingles was fine. We cut off the damaged portion and used the left overs. The inside of that shed never saw an ounce of water. And I bet what you're imagining looks trashy, but it wasn't. It was beautiful. Truly beautiful. Artfully done and every decision made with care. That so-called trash cleaned up real nice."

"That's pretty cool."

"Imagine all the things we could make from other people's trash. I looked it up, an eight by ten shed goes for more than five thousand dollars. And those are the cheap ones. I can make that with next to no material costs. You don't think there's some people out there that'd be happy to have a zero-waste shed? Construction companies tend to throw away any piece of wood less than two feet long. You ever look at a dining room chair? It's just a collection of small pieces of wood. We're only limited by our imaginations. Take an old couch, for instance. A lot of the upholstery is worn, but the back and the sides are usually fine. Tear that off, save the framing, the padding, the zippers, the springs, the feet. All those raw materials available for other projects. More than enough padding and fabric to supply an entire set of seat cushions for dining chairs. And that fence wood, I can make almost anything out of that. Outdoor dining table, a bench, Adirondack chairs, planters, whatever you want.

"Get this, professional fence installers are expected to remove the old fence and haul it off. It costs them seventy dollars or more to take it to the dump and that doesn't include the time. What if I told them they could drop it off at my place for only thirty? Or hell, give me the address and I'll come get it, same day, for only sixty? They'd be crazy not to take me up on one of those options."

"A truly eco-friendly furniture store."

"Not just furniture. Decor items too. Picture frames, lamps, wall planters, clocks, coasters, those stupid signs with words and phrases stenciled on them. Have you seen all the shit people buy? Bird houses, whatever. There's no end to what we could make. Industrial items as well. Eco-friendly pallets would be easy to produce. Wooden stakes for concrete workers."

"You've really been thinking about this."

"What can I say, I've had plenty of time. I also want to connect with artists. Imagine all the stuff we collect through this process. All the different items that could be used to create art. Sculptures. Mixed media pieces. A trash piece of plywood can serve as a perfectly good canvas. What about that worn out upholstery I was talkin' about? Why can't that be a canvas? A warehouse of free materials available to creative people who just want to express themselves. We'll have showrooms and galleries to display and sell those creations. And when they do sell, we'll cut the artist a check."

I say, "We could hold paint drives through neighborhoods, collecting the half-used paint cans sitting in everybody's garages."

"We'd end up with a surplus of grays and beiges."

"Yeah, but we could dump any surplus into five gallon buckets and make a new beige or gray. Sell five gallons for forty bucks to people remodeling their homes. You can barely get one gallon for forty bucks these days."

"That's true. A lot of people have unused tile or laminate floors in their garage too."

"That they do."

"Think of the ecosystem we could create. Employees and builders and artists and customers and scrappers and donaters and volunteers all functioning together to build this environment of creativity and recycled goods."

I take a moment to imagine what that could look like.

I say, "Enriching our black neighborhoods by selling white people's trash back to them. I like it. I could see an operation like that in every state of the union."

"I don't see why not," Axton agrees.

"Now all you gotta do is prove it."

I drop Axton off at the Mediator Party's new Northeast Side Headquarters.

He shakes my hand in a meaningful way and gives me a little nod before stepping out of my truck and into his new life.

"Mister Waxman, Mister Waxman!"

I speed up my gait through the halls of the courthouse.

"Sorry, can't talk. I'm late… for a very important date."

I immediately veer toward the men's room and push the door open.

The man pursuing me follows me in.

"You can stop playing coy, Mister Waxman. I know you're looking for a settlement. You should really want to talk to me."

"And yet…"

I enter a stall and take a seat.

283

The man's name is Cary Clark. He sighs loudly.

"Why don't you want to talk to me?" he asks through the stall door.

"Because I think you're mad at me."

"Mister Waxman, I don't even know you. Why would I be mad at you? Not counting that smell. Jesus!"

"I just successfully petitioned to have your client's accounts frozen. To put that another way. I won. You lost."

"It's one hearing. Slow your roll."

"I think you're mad at me. And I think you have a desire to be mean. I don't like mean people."

"Well that's surprising, because I read your book last year and you were pretty mean in that."

"Which book?"

"The one about Murray Rothbard."

"Ahh, you're a Libertarian. Now I know you're mad at me."

"Former Libertarian."

"In my defense, it would be impossible to write a book about the beliefs of Murray Rothbard without being mean. The man was an idiot."

"Or he was a genius."

"You did read my book."

Clark recites, "Our friend Murray is either an idiot for not recognizing the innumerable pitfalls that exist within his system of non-governance, or he is a genius for understanding that there are countless morons who will happily make him rich if he just keeps spouting nonsense."

I flush the toilet and exit the stall.

"Wow. I don't think I've ever had myself quoted back to me. I quite like it."

"Well that makes one of us."

"You didn't like being called a moron?"

"Not particularly."

Clark stands in front of the mirror, checking his hair. I wash my hands.

"Look, I don't blame you for being attracted to Murray's idea. It's a beautiful idea. Like an open marriage or a healthy dessert. It's an idea that could never possibly exist outside the confines of a fantasy riddled mind. You can't define away society's existence, Mister Clark. Let me ask you something, if a man is murdered who has no friends and no family, has a crime even been committed?

"What?"

I head for the door. Clark follows.

"The answer is… not in the world of Murray Rothbard."

Back in the hall, I have to walk around a large gathering of people who seem to think hallways are for visiting.

I continue, "He never says it, but his words add up to it. The only victim is dead, so essentially, it's a victimless crime. Hell, in his world, I could build a hundred story skyscraper right next to a functioning airport and I will have done no wrong. Or I could buy all the land surrounding your house and forbid you to enter my property."

"He addressed that issue," Clark says.

"He suggested we would negotiate easement rights."

"That's right."

"But as a land owner, I'm under no obligation to offer you easement rights."

"Well in a civilized society…"

"No no, don't forget, society does not exist. Murray was very clear. This idea of 'society' is just a bunch of hooey."

We reach the exit and push our way out into a chilly winter day.

I continue, "We're just a collection of individual property owners looking out for our own best interests. And this property owner…" I say, gesturing to myself, "…might just be an asshole? Maybe my interests are best served with a 'Screw you, Mister Clark'. That's the thing about Murray's system, it only works if there are no assholes in the world."

"A fundamentally naive system."

I smile, "I gotta say, I really do like it when you quote me."

We cross the street and weave through the massive lot of parked cars.

I say, "So what is a former Libertarian doing working for the Democratic Party?"

"I don't work for the Democratic Party. My client is a Political Action Committee."

"Sure, let's pretend that's true."

"My client is prepared to offer you a settlement."

"Oh? This'll be fun."

"Firstly, I must warn you, we're considering a counter suit."

I stop unexpectedly and he nearly runs me over.

"For what?"

Clark shrugs.

I say, "Okay, let's review, shall we? It was your guys who got their hands caught in the espionage jar. It was your guys who hired a love-struck, mentally unstable, card carrying member of Antifa to perform this illegal act. And it was your guys who, in an astounding act of victim-blaming, decided to convince every left-wing organization in existence to paint me as a murderer…"

"There is no proof my clients were behind that."

"What could you possibly sue me for?"

"You can read all about it when we submit the suit, but we have cause and we will be filing on Monday unless you accept our offer."

"Which is?"

I turn away from him and continue my march in the general direction of my truck.

"Two hundred thousand dollars, plus a standard non-disclosure."

"You seem to be under the impression that my damages are minor."

"Oh please, your damages are everything you wish you could have accomplished on your own. Everybody's talking about you and your Mediators, and making it seem like maybe you're something to be taken seriously."

"Well, why would you spy on someone you don't take seriously?"

Finally I reach my truck. I stop at the tailgate and turn to listen to Clark's answer.

"The truth is, when that douche bag decided to burn himself in effigy... that was you getting lucky. It kick-started your fifteen minutes. But this is the majors, Mister Waxman, and luck only goes so far. You're a little league player who made it to first on an error. You'd do well to remember who you are."

"Hmm. Would you like to hear my counter?"

"All I can do is take it to my client."

"I don't give a shit about your client. I give a shit about that other contact in your phone. The one that goes straight through to DNC leadership."

"I have no such contact, but my client would be happy to hear your counter."

"You ever heard of the Stasis Institute?"

"I'm not new to this game. I've done my research Mister Waxman."

"So you know who I am. I'm the guy who has several hundred people willing to devote their time to whatever I say will create a better world. That's who I am. I don't have a labor shortage and you will never drown me in paperwork."

I turn to the tailgate and drop it down with a thud.

"With that in mind, I got two offers for you. And I don't care which one we do."

I hop up, taking a seat on my lowered tailgate.

"I'm listening."

"One, we go to trial. I depose everyone. I subpoena every financial transaction, every email, every phone call, every text, of anyone who ever had the pleasure of working for your client. I will make connections between your client and DNC proper. If there's one thing you can always count on, it's the human penchant to get sloppy. I have no doubt that resources were shared. Emails were sent. Calls were made. Your client and the Democratic Party are not two distinct organizations, but one group working in concert. I will prove this on TV. On YouTube. On social media. For all the world to see."

Clark's tough demeanor softens. He thoughtfully relaxes his stance. He walks to the tailgate and hops up to take a seat beside me.

"Or?" he says.

"Or, maybe the Mediator Party and the Democratic Party are both victims in this ordeal. Victims of your client, a rogue political action committee. Maybe we both make public statements to that effect."

"You'll hold the Democratic Party blameless?"

"Why the hell not?"

"You'll say so, officially?"

"That can be arranged."

"In exchange for…"

"As I said, my damages are substantial. So I'm gonna need every frozen dollar. Eight point one six million of them, to be exact."

Clark nods slowly, digesting. If he's surprised, he doesn't show it.

"I'll talk to my client."

He dismounts from the tailgate and begins to walk away.

"One more thing," I say. "That statement, the one the DNC will make… I'm gonna write it myself."

"Oh fuck off! That's never gonna happen!"

Clark turns and strides away.

I yell after him, "Option number one then!"

25

JANUARY 19, 2024
291 DAYS UNTIL ELECTION

Sitting in my office at Stasis Headquarters, I eagerly stare at the television set. On screen is nothing but an empty podium, littered with countless microphones.

The camera pulls back to reveal a group of five people walking toward the podium. Several bright flashes light up the room in succession as photographers capture the moment. One person in particular takes center stage behind the podium. I recognize him as the DNC Chairman.

"Hello Everyone. Thank you for coming today. This should just take a few minutes."

The Chairman's face is doing a poor job of hiding his disgust. It makes me all the happier.

"I am here to announce that our independent investigation into the events surrounding the deaths of Morgan Turnbull and Melody Frye have concluded. These are our findings."

I listen as he reads the very words that I wrote. I savor every moment, every syllable, every poorly disguised grimace. I let my thoughts drift to the casualties that allowed this moment to happen. I think about what was sacrificed and what was gained. Eight million to the cause and the DNC Chair as my own personal wind-up doll. In terms of value realized, it's hard to imagine a better outcome. Their deaths were not in vain.

I lean back in my chair and bask in the glow of a job well done. After a couple minutes, I have to remind myself… No Great Man is ever successful, for the moment he decides that he's a success is the moment he stops being Great.

Back to work.

I hear a knock at my door.

"Come in."

Roland Vanderbilt enters. He's a good looking guy, with traces of gray just beginning to tell the story of his age. He's the kind of guy you like from the moment you lay eyes on him. Then you talk to him and you like him all the more.

I suspect he could've been a movie star. The old adage of the leading man – *Men want to be him, women want to be with him* – seems accurate enough.

Roland holds a piece of paper in his hand and reads from it.

"The Mediator Party is a legitimate organization, fulfilling a legitimate political need."

Roland lowers the paper and stares at me, mouth agape.

"How in God's name did you get them to say that?"

"I think they just like me. It was practically their idea."

"That's amazing. Validation from the enemy. You can't buy that kind of publicity! I don't know how you did it, but nice work man. Nice work!"

"Thanks brother. Why don't you shut the door and have a seat?"

Roland does as I ask.

"Do you have your Stasis membership card on you?"

"I'm sure I do."

"May I see it?"

"Uhh, yeah. Is everything all right?"

He pulls the card from his wallet.

"Mediator card too," I say.

He worriedly pulls another card and hands it across the desk. I take them both and walk across the office.

"Have I done something wrong?"

"Not at all," I say, pushing his membership cards into the blades of the shredder.

Roland watches me, confused.

I say, "Do you remember what I asked of you when you first joined."

"Look, William, if someone tagged me in a post, I had nothing-"

"Relax Roland. I'm not accusing you of anything. You do remember, yes?"

"You asked me to never advertise my involvement with The Institute or The Party."

"And yet others, people you know, post freely on social media every day."

"I have noticed that, but I haven't broken my promise."

"My point is, we all have our parts to play, and yours is different than theirs."

Roland slowly nods.

He says, "So it's happening? I have an assignment? It's finally happening? I'm ready, William. So very ready."

"You sure about that?"

"I want to make a difference. I've been waiting."

"Do you believe in the Mediator Party?"

"With everything I am," he says.

"Me too," I say. "I believe it is the obvious evolution of a democratic society. But that is not why we will succeed. We will succeed when people have finally had enough of the crazy. The way I see it, the Proud Boys work for us. Antifa works for us. The Trans Activists, The Woke Police, The Religious Nuts, they all work for us. With every stupid act they perform, we grow that much closer to the tipping point. There is a tipping point somewhere, but sadly, unbelievably, we still haven't reached it. And so it is our job to find that tipping point."

"How are we gonna do that?"

"There are certain lines that the crazies haven't quite crossed. With that in mind, I want you, Roland, to be the face of a movement."

"The face of a movement?"

"A movement that can have no connection to the work we are doing here. Your records will be purged from the system as if you never existed. Is that something you can live with?"

Roland leans back in his seat. His heart is breaking a bit.

"You're asking me…"

"It's a big ask."

"This place is my life."

"I know. And it gets worse."

I proceed to inform Roland about the movement he is destined to lead. By the end of our conversation, Roland's face has gone ghostly pale. He sits there, suffering from a sort of shock.

He says, "You really believe this will help?"

"I have no doubt. Look, Roland, in our dreams we imagine ourselves performing these amazing feats and the world looks upon us with pride. But that's not reality. In reality, it requires lots of heroes working together in various ways, most of them thankless. Some get spat upon by the very people they save. We'd all prefer to be that other kind of hero, but I'm asking you to be the kind of hero we actually need."

Roland's eyes are cast down to the floor, seemingly darting from one speck of carpet to the next. His head begins to bob a bit in the affirmative.

"Okay," he says, reluctantly. "I'll do it."

I console him as best I can. After several minutes, Roland takes his leave, his head hung low.

My next appointment is already waiting in the hall.

"Lisa! Good to see you. Come on in. Did you bring your membership cards with you?"

I step out onto the stage at a local TEDx event. The entire night is dedicated to environmental issues and awareness.

I look out at the audience. It's a full house.

"Ladies and gentleman, your presence here tonight is just further proof, there is a lot of environmental support out there."

The crowd claps with enthusiasm.

"Yeah, yeah… Give yourselves a round of applause, if you like. If you think it's warranted, by all means…"

The applause quickly dies.

"I don't know why you would though. Because we're failing miserably, But hey…"

I dramatically clap my hands.

Clap, clap, clap.

Aside from my clapping hands, the auditorium is dead silent.

"Look, there are, in fact, a lot of people who care about our planet, our air, our water, the place that our kids and grandkids will have to call home. A lot of people care. This has been true for a very long time. You can look at polling going back to the seventies. A large percentage, a majority in fact, of the population wants to see our environment protected.

"That said, in recent years, that percentage has actually gotten smaller. Why? The call for change has gotten so much louder, so much more urgent. And yet the percentage of the population that supports environmental protection has lessened. Why would this be the case? Well, I suspect we all know why. Money. The oil companies. the utilities…"

A smattering of boos can be heard.

"…the car manufacturers, the wood producers, the farmers, the fisheries, and the literally thousands of other businesses directly affected by this topic. And so, the inevitable political war began. The Democrats chose to land on the side of the environment, at least publicly. The Republicans sided with the corporations. And you, if you're here out of love for the environment, chose your side as well. Raise your hand if you vote Democrat."

Nearly the entire auditorium raises their hands.

"Surprise, surprise," I say.

A good amount of laughter reaches my ears. I've got their attention. They are along for the ride.

"Let's do a quick review of our past, shall we? Better yet, let's do a quick preview of our future. Doesn't really matter, because they're both the same thing."

I walk to the far end of the stage and turn around so that the length of the stage is before me.

"Where I stand is where we currently are."

I point to the other end of the stage.

"All the way down there – the opposite end – that's where we want to go. That's the finish line."

I take two steps forward and stop.

"Now, why did I take two steps forward? Why only two steps? I will tell you why. Because for the purposes of this exercise, I am the personification of environmental legislation. And I can only go as far as the government wills me to go. And our government has to balance a lot of different facets of society. No, no. Booing is not appropriate. We have to face facts. No one likes it when the economy tanks. No one likes it when our world comes to a screeching halt because there isn't enough fuel… of any kind. We can take a step forward. We can even take two steps forward. But then we need to let society catch up. At which point we can make our next move. So, why did I take two steps forward? Because the Democrats had a good election. So, two steps closer to our goal. That's pretty good. Next election rolls around, guess who wins… The Republicans."

A collection of boos bounce around the auditorium.

I look to the audience and smile.

I take a single step back.

More boos. I wait for the silence to return.

"Next election. It's a photo finish, but the… Democrats win the day!"

I hear cheers and begin to take a step forward, but stop. I pull my leg back, replacing it on the stage exactly where it began.

"It seems the Congress can't agree on a path forward. Strange, I know, but believe it or not, sometimes that happens. As I said, it was a photo finish, so nobody has the absolute power to make anything happen. It appears we're at a standstill."

More boos.

"So that's exactly what I'm gonna do. I'm just gonna stand here."

The boos are getting louder, spreading like a virus through the audience.

I stand, waiting. I say nothing. I do nothing. The audience is growing restless. I wait for that restlessness to become nearly unbearable.

Finally, I speak.

"I've performed three actions. Two steps forward, one step back, and stand perfectly still. This is a fairly accurate representation of our past. It is also what we can expect from our future. Three actions and I've moved exactly one step forward. Are we happy?"

I hear a lot of "no" and "hell no" mixed in with the continued boos.

"What if there was a way to do this?"

I hold one finger up and take a single step forward.

I hold up two fingers…

"Two," I say.

…and take another step forward.

"Three."

Another step forward.

"That's three actions. Three steps forward. Would you like to see the fourth action?"

I take another step forward.

"How 'bout the fifth?"

Another step forward.

"Does this sound like something you'd be interested in?"

The audience is with me. I am treated to cheers and numerous fist pumps. I look to the wings of the stage. Tucked away, just out of the view of the audience is Astraea. She gives me a smile. I give her one in return.

"As I said before, there is great support for increased environmental protection among the population. This divisive atmosphere has lessened that support, but you are still very clearly winning the battle for hearts and minds. In a just world, that fact alone should send me forward. Unfortunately for all of us, this is not a just world."

The audiences anger rises to a crescendo.

I raise my voice to be heard above the fervor.

"But I'm here to tell you that it can be! IT CAN BE!!"

Astraea sings along to a terrible tune on the radio as I attempt to navigate my way out of downtown. For reasons I can't begin to justify, I let her pick the station. I rarely listen to the radio anymore, but when I do, it's always KOMA – All oldies, all the time.

The song crescendos just as I'm finding the entrance to the highway. Astraea mercifully reaches out and turns the knob, lowering the volume.

"That was fun," she says. "Thanks for taking me with you."

"I liked having you there."

"I'm growing on ya, huh! Like a fungus!"

"You strike me as more bacterial than fungal."

"Ha ha. I am in the presence of comedic genius."

"Careful now. Last time someone made fun of my sense of humor, I had her killed."

Astraea crooks her neck back and gives me a harsh look.

"That's not funny."

"That's what she said."

"Come on, really. It's nothing to joke about."

I nod, "Yeah, you're probably right."

We drive in silence, reaching the sunken bit of Lake Hefner Parkway. I roll the window down and listen to the sounds of all the numerous vehicles traveling at high speed. They reverberate off the high walls and meld into something that sounds like music.

"Is it a joke?" Astraea asks.

"I'm sorry?" I say, pretending not to understand.

"You allude to this thing as something beyond politics. It's war. And she was an enemy."

Astraea stares out at the road ahead.

I say, "Astraea. Look at me."

She looks.

"It was a joke," I assure her.

"I just... I don't know. 'What are we willing to do to save this country of ours?' That's what you said. And like a domino effect from the events of one night, suddenly you get all this press, speaking engagements, people are tuning in to your podcasts."

"You think I wanted that press? Those accusations?"

"People had no idea who you were... Now they do. You get vindicated. Your opposition gets exposed. The Party gets noticed, legitimized even. All while dispatching an enemy combatant. Sounds... engineered, you might say."

Out of the corner of my eye, I can see her turn and look at me. I keep my eyes on the road and say nothing. I listen to the music of the highway.

I flip my turn signal and take the Britton Road exit.

"We also got eight million dollars in damages," I say. "But don't tell anybody. I had to sign an NDA."

Astraea's eyebrows rise.

"Eight million?"

"Yeah," I say. "I'm still trying to decide if it was worth it."

Astraea seems to ponder that for a moment.

"It won't be if we lose." she says.

Astraea has drifted off to bed. We didn't talk much after that. I wish I knew what she was thinking. My statement wasn't an outright admission, but it was suggestive.

I need to relax. I decide to go for a midnight jog.

I try to let my mind go blank, to drift off into a meditative state. I focus on my muscles churning, my lungs inflating, my blood pumping...

It won't be if we lose, she said. We. She specifically said 'we'. Does she consider herself part of my team?

I would like that.

Muscles churning, lungs inflating, blood pumping...

I stop.

What did I just see?

At the curb of each house in this neighborhood stands a solid brick mailbox. I turn around and step closer to the mailbox I just passed. On the little hinged door to the box are a collection of weatherproof stickers. They are the letters of the alphabet. Specifically, they are W E S T P H A L.

Westphal.

As in… Astraea Westphal.

We have never discussed her parents in any specific way. I don't know their names. I don't know where they live. At least I didn't. Perhaps now, I do.

I open the box and remove the few pieces of mail.

I see what looks like a credit card solicitation addressed to Lydia Westphal. A couple bills are addressed to Lonnie Westphal. The rest is junk mail.

I look at the house and wonder if Lonnie is Astraea's father. Is he the man who did the things I read on that wall? Is he inside this house, right now, safe and sound?

I put the mail back in the box, shut the door, and jog away.

26

Around here, DHS doesn't stand for the Department of Homeland Security. Around here, DHS is the Department of Human Services. These are the people whose job it is to rescue children from unsafe environments, put them into temporary shelters, and eventually place them into a new home.

Around here, if a person is lucky, they know very little about DHS.

I enter the building.

"Hello sir," A woman with kind, but tired eyes says. "Is there something I can help you with?"

"Yeah. Do you have pamphlets or anything on fostering, adopting, things like that?"

"Sure. I can get that for you. You know, all that information is available online."

"Yeah. I'm a bit old school."

Pamphlets in hand, I leave DHS and head toward my scheduled meeting across town. I'm ahead of schedule, so I stop at an office supply store to buy some printable mailing labels, plus some ink for my printer.

I arrive for my meeting right on time.

A smattering of cars, trucks, and a small collection of Harleys populate the lot of the Red Dog Cafe.

It is an OKC institution, a rite of sleazy passage to the young men who call this city home. It's been a couple decades since I've stepped foot on this hallowed ground. For the most part, it looks the same as it ever did.

I step inside and confirm that very little has changed. As always, it's dark, even at 11:30 in the morning. A collection of neon signs help to illuminate the large space and high ceilings.

A dancer twirls lazily around a pole on center stage. Red and green swirling lights accentuate her sweaty, glittered curves. Several men in business suits sit silently watching at the edge of the stage. Pervert Row, we used to call it.

I pass by a currently uninhabited human-sized birdcage hanging from the rafters. A half dressed girl smiles at me from the bar. I skip past her and make my way to the pool tables.

I approach as Glenda lines up a shot on the 3-ball. She's tall and skinny, dressed in jeans and a flannel. Her hair is the female version of a curly-haired mullet. She takes her shot and misses.

"Son of a whore!" she says.

"How's the wife?" I ask.

She turns and looks at me coldly.

"She's a bitch."

"And the girlfriend?"

She points her cue stick toward the stage.

"Ask her yourself."

I shift my eyes to the stage. The girl looks barely old enough to be here, shaking her ass in a man's face for a dollar.

"I can't afford it," I tell her.

"You want a game?"

"I can't afford that either."

"You should order a burger. They're amazing."

"Yeah, I'd hate to break my forty-three year streak of not eating at strip clubs."

"All business, huh?"

"No offense, you're just my least favorite person in the world."

"But I come bearing good news!"

"That's what you said last time."

"And it was true last time."

"I don't consider going from the basement to another area of the basement good news."

"But closer to the elevator!" she says with a grin.

"A broken elevator... I believe was the analogy you used."

"Yeah," she says with a sullen nod. "It's definitely broken. First of all, 40 percent of respondents have still never heard of the Mediator Party."

"Jesus. Forty?"

"That's down from 48! Of the people who have heard of you, 52 percent really like what you're doing. Up from 39! It's really good news, except yes, the elevator's still broken. Of those 52 percent only one in ten will actually consider voting for your Party."

"Still!"

"It's Wasted Vote Syndrome, man! No one wants to cast their vote for a loser."

"Son of a bitch."

"The way I see it, you got a couple things to do. One – You can't have forty percent of the population saying, 'who?'. You gotta find a way to reach them. They gotta know you exist! Two – You gotta make them believe that you can actually win. That's how you fix the elevator. Making them want what you're offering isn't enough. They have to believe it's actually realistic."

I bury my face into my hands and tell myself to breathe.

She says, "Wasted Vote is the law of the land. It's insurmountable. There's only one exception."

"What?" I say quickly.

"You ever see the kind of people who play the lottery? Some of them are just degenerate gamblers, but most…"

Glenda shakes her head sadly before lining up for another shot.

"…They've lived through their past, they know their present, and they've seen their future. It's all bad and there ain't no escaping it. They know that. They know it deep in their hearts. But maybe, just maybe, if they spend what little they have on a lottery ticket. Maybe they break the cycle of suck. Worst odds you can possibly imagine, but the dream is alive. It's this crazy hope that's so faint and so far off, and yet they keep grasping for it. Day in, day out, those tickets get sold… to sad, desperate people. Desperation is the only exception."

I point the truck towards home and think about Glenda's words. I am a desperate man in need of a desperate populace. I have to believe it's close, so close.

We are living in an emotional war zone, hate being lobbed like mortar shells each moment of the day. Ugly words getting fired like bullets everywhere we turn. Radio, TV, social media, newspapers, the workplace, home… nowhere is safe. We are surrounded by anger and distrust. We are living in a world of hall monitors, watching our every move, cameras at the ready. How can any sane person not feel the desperation seeping in?

I can see it in the sheer volume of our kind turning to psychiatric drugs, the anti-this and anti-that medications gobbled up by nearly one in every four Americans.

And they aren't the only ones.

I ease my foot onto the brake. The car in front of me is having trouble maintaining a constant speed. I consider passing, but instead slow my truck to 32mph. After a couple blocks of low speed travel, the vehicle accelerates back to 45. The car manages to mostly stay between the lines, but barely. A sudden pointless swerve and correction is accompanied by another drop in speed.

I can only assume that the driver of that car is just another one of the self-medicating masses, escaping into a haze of alcohol or opioids or tranquilizers or… whatever.

It's clear to me that the people are already sad and desperate. We are lost, teetering on the precipice of internal annihilation. And so we cope. Some with alcohol, some with sex, some with drugs, some with pharmaceuticals. Beyond that, most all of us have turned to the worst coping mechanism of all, ambivalence. We shrug our shoulders and accept the things we cannot change. We accept our impotence.

How can I harness the desperation of the masses if they can't hear me through their self induced haze? Somehow, I need to break through. But how?

I ponder the question, while The Wax Man screams from his cell.

I pull into the driveway of my home. I throw it into park and let the engine idle, surrounding me in its stench.

My eyes move to the roof full of worn out shingles that need replaced. Stasis has two members who own roofing companies. Hiring one without offending the other will be tricky, but I'll figure it out. I think I'll wait til after spring and hope for a hail storm to put my insurance company on the hook. The home insurance rates in this state are the highest in the country. Might as well try to get my money's worth.

I find myself staring at one of the vent pipes poking out from the rooftop. It's larger than the others at three inches in diameter. That's a sure clue that it runs straight down a wall in direct proximity to a toilet.

Drainage systems need air pressure. Without it, they won't drain properly. My Dad taught me that in one of the few good memories I have of him.

Those memories all have one thing in common – Mom wasn't around. The opposite is also true. Every good memory I have of my Mother – Dad wasn't around. It sounds strange, but I always envied my classmates from broken homes. I used to daydream about being shuttled between them, never being forced to endure their constant bickering and screaming and fighting.

I have no doubt they loved each other. They must have. Otherwise, why would they stay together? They were always together. And I endured their love. I endured it for thirteen years, until one day she was gone, lying peacefully in bed, an empty bottle of pills standing tall on her bedside table.

It was a sad day, but somewhere in the forefront of my mind, it gave me hope. No more snide remarks. No more screaming. No more threats. No more slamming doors.

Those dreams came true. There was no more screaming, no more slamming doors, no more anything. My Dad became an empty shell of a man, sleepwalking through life. He rarely spoke. He never smiled. He barely ate. It was as if his wife had swallowed enough pills for the both of them. Two people died that day, one quickly and peacefully, the other, agonizingly slow. It took twenty-three years for those sleeping pills to finish the job.

Still, a few good memories remain. I have no idea how old I was... Seven? Eight? ...but I remember us sitting at a restaurant called Harry Bear's. We were grabbing a bite to eat before going bowling right next door. As always, I ordered the Chicken Delight plus an Upside Down Shake. The waitress dramatically flipped the shake end over end before delivering it safely to our table. I thought it was pretty cool.

"You think that's cool?" Dad said. "Check this out!"

He reached out and took hold of the straw that rested in my glass of Coca-Cola. He lifted the straw straight up and then lowered it back down. He did this once, twice, and then a third time. But the third time was different. The Coca-Cola stayed in the straw! It was defying gravity! It was magic!

Actually, it was science. I hadn't noticed that on the third lift, he had used a finger to cover the hole at the top of the straw.

He smiled at me.

"Now watch closely."

He lifted his finger, equalizing the air pressure, allowing gravity to do its job. My Coca-Cola slipped harmlessly back into its glass.

This is why we have open pipes poking out from the tops of our houses, so that air pressure can help carry our shit and piss downhill toward city sanitation.

The front door of the house opens and Astraea pokes her head out. She looks at me, sitting quietly in my truck.

"What are you doing?" She yells.

"You ready for your lesson?" I yell back.

I can hear Astraea hard at work across the house. I instructed her to remove the sheetrock from the wall above the toilet. She has chosen to do so in the most violent way possible – hit it with a hammer until it's gone.

I print out a couple of mailing labels and affix them in place. I run out to the truck and throw my 'mailers' into the glove box.

Back inside, I pull open a kitchen drawer and find the trash bags. Using a pair of scissors, I cut out a section of the bag, providing me with a simple sheet of plastic.

On the way to the bathroom, I seek out and find a roll of tape.

By the time I reach the bathroom, the sheetrock has been annihilated. The stark white vent pipe that travels up through the wall is no longer hidden from our view.

"Alright, next we want to cut out a foot-long section of this pipe," I tell Astraea.

I gesture to the reciprocating saw that sits on the ground, an eight inch blade jutting from the end.

"This is what they call a Sawzall. You ever use one of these?"

"No."

"Well let's change that."

I hold the pipe steady to minimize vibrations, while Astraea struggles to make one cut and then another. She ends up damaging the other side of the wall, but whatever.

With the section of PVC pipe removed, I wrap the thin plastic around the empty space. I make it as tight as I can before taping it down at each cut end and also at the seam. This should create a nice tight seal. For all intents and purposes, I have reconstituted the vent pipe. For the most part, it should function no different than before.

"Moment of truth," I say. "Give it a flush."

Astraea reaches out and flushes the toilet.

The thin plastic sucks inward momentarily before puffing back out and then relaxing to its original state.

"You see that," I ask. "That's either a change in air pressure or air flow or probably both."

"So?" Astraea says, unimpressed.

"So both those things are measurable. That's confirmation that something specific is happening inside that vent pipe every time we flush the toilet. Come on. Let's go to the store."

I march out of the bathroom and toward the front door.

"Why? What exactly are we doing?" Astraea yells.

Traffic is shit. This trip to the store could take a while.

"That is a weird question," Astraea says. "Why would you ask something like that?"

"It's a famous moral quandary. Some of the smartest people in the world have considered the implications of this very problem. Now it's your turn."

Astraea sighs.

She says, "Okay, so there's five people on a railroad track?"

"Yes."

"Why are they on a railroad track?"

"I don't know. Maybe they fell asleep."

"So can't I just go wake them up?"

"No. They're too far away. The runaway trolley will get to them long before you ever could."

"Why are they sleeping on a track? Are we sure they're not dead already?"

"Yes. We are sure. Maybe they're not asleep. Maybe they've been tied to the tracks by a mad man."

"So there's nothing I can do?"

"Well, as I said before, you realize that you're standing right next to the lever that switches the tracks. You can save them by pulling that lever."

"But there's another person tied to the other track?"

"Yes. There is one person tied to the alternate track."

"Well who is driving this trolley? Can't they use the brakes."

"Nobody's driving the damn trolley! It's a runaway trolley! Would you please just surrender to the facts at hand? You don't get to change the story to suit your desire to not make a decision. You have two choices. What do you do?"

"I don't like this game."

"It's not a game. It's about real life choices."

"This would never happen in real life."

"Why is this so difficult?"

"You're asking me to kill somebody."

"No I'm not. You don't have to kill anybody. You are free to do nothing at all."

"But then five people die!"

"Right," I say. "You can choose to let five people die, and take solace in the fact that you were not the one who made it happen. Or you can actively save those five people, but forever know that your actions straight up killed that other dude. A guy who would absolutely be alive had you done nothing."

"Ughhh," She grunts. "You're wearing me out. Who the hell thinks of this shit?"

"People who are trying to understand their own minds. The nature of humanity. Of goodness. Of morality. Of sound decision-making."

"Well what would you do?"

"I'd pull the lever," I tell her with a shrug.

"That easy?"

"It's the greater good. It's a mathematical inequation. One is clearly greater than the other. The only issue at stake here is the issue of my emotional well-being. Am I willing to take on the emotional turmoil of knowing that my actions directly caused a person's death? Yes. Yes I am. Will I always remember the pull of that lever? Will I never stop thinking about that innocent person that I sentenced to death? Yeah. I'm sure that would stick with me. But the fact remains, all I'm really choosing between is what's best for the world at large, or what's best for my level of mental anguish. Which one of those things is more important?"

Astraea squints her eyes and ponders my words.

"So to do nothing would really just be a way to protect yourself?"

"Is there any other way to look at it? It's the selfish choice."

Astraea nods.

"That's crazy," she says, shaking her head. "But I guess it's right."

"You guess?"

"I know you're right. I just... I don't like it."

"Of course you don't like it. The question is... what would you do?"

"I suppose I would pull the lever," she says with an unsure grimace.

"How 'bout this? Runaway trolley on the track. You're watching it come directly toward you. It will soon travel directly beneath you, because you're standing on a bridge. On the other side of the bridge, tied to the tracks, are those same five people."

"They're tied to the tracks again?!"

"Yes they are."

"These people are ridiculous!"

"They are going to die, but you realize with a hundred percent certainty, that if you were to throw something big and heavy off that bridge and onto the tracks, it would stop the trolley before it gets to them."

"Okay. Let's do that."

"You look around, but there's nothing to throw down there."

"So what are we talking about?"

"Well, you're not alone on the bridge. There's another guy, standing right there next to you. A big fat dude. No question, his enormous body would stop that trolley."

"Are you serious?"

"Do you push him off?"

"That's different!"

"No it's not. It's the same circumstance."

"It is not!"

"It's a more heightened level of mental anguish! That's the only difference. What do you do?!"

She looks at me, doe eyed.

I say, "Those people are gonna die! Five of them! What do you do?!"

"I can't do it. I can't push somebody off a bridge."

I shrug, "Okay."

The drive is silent for several moments.

She says, "Well, what if you were big and fat?"

"I'm sorry?"

"What if you had to make this decision. You are on the bridge, but you, yourself, are also big and fat? What would *you* do?"

I take a moment.

"Honestly, I think I'd still push the other guy. It's a one to one equation. I have to admit I'd probably give myself the benefit on that one."

"But what if you're the only one on the bridge?"

"I see where you're going. An even greater level of sacrifice."

"Do you jump?"

"Hold on," I say, thinking. "Give me a second."

"You don't have time! The train is a comin'. Do you jump?!"

"No!"

"No?"

I shake my head, "No."

"Well how do you justify that? It is an inequation, right?"

"From a strictly numbers standpoint, 'yes', but…"

"But what?"

"But in this case, I have more data to consider. I'm intimately familiar with the circumstances of my life. I know that I'm on a mission. And the Mediator Party has yet to grow strong enough to survive my death. If I die, so does the mission. And the mission is more important than any five random people."

"Oh my God," she's says, wide-eyed. "You actually believe that!"

I shrug, "Only because it's true."

I stop at a red light and search for my opening to turn right on red. It finally comes and I accelerate into the turn.

"William."

"Yes?"

"What actually happened to Melody and Morgan?" Astraea asks, her quiet voice absent of any humor. "Did you do it?"

I take a deep breath and slowly exhale.

"They were a threat to the mission, so yeah, I pulled the lever."

I take my eyes off the road and turn to look at Astraea. She keeps her eyes forward, staring out at the road ahead. She doesn't even appear to be breathing.

I return my attention to the path in front of me and try to figure out why I would admit to such a thing. Why did I say that?

Astraea says, "You ever think that maybe you're just crazy?"

"All the time," I tell her.

"I'm serious," she says. "My uncle is saving money to go buy land in the middle of nowhere. He said, 'I don't want a neighbor for as far as my eye can see'. He's certain that this country is going to fall into some kind of race war or something. That nobody will be safe. That anybody living in the city will be living in a war zone. Crazy."

"Is it?"

"You don't think so?"

"I don't know. On some level, it's amazing that we haven't fallen into chaos long long ago. Somehow, we've maintained order in this country for hundreds of years. You know if you add up every law enforcement officer... federal, state, city, county, all of them... there's still only one for every five hundred citizens. And each one of those guys are on duty about a quarter of the time. So at any given moment, it's two thousand to one. That's not enough. One cannot control two thousand. They just can't. They do what they can, but ultimately, they are not what maintains order."

"So what does?"

"Trust."

"Shit. I don't trust anybody."

"I don't believe that's true. How do you get on the school bus every morning?"

"Umm... I use my feet."

"But how do you know that driver isn't a maniac with a plan to kidnap dozens of kids all at once? How do you know he's not gonna drive that wagon off a cliff?"

"Why would I even think that?"

"I thought you said you didn't trust him."

"Well, I don't think badly of him."

"Isn't that, to some extent, trust?" I ask. "And how could you possibly agree to enter an enclosed space like that, knowing you'll be trapped in there with fifty or so kids that you don't trust? That's a lot of kids. It's not a far stretch to think one of those kids might have the desire to beat you half to death or rape you or who knows what."

"You just said there's like fifty people there. I'm sure one of them would pull him off of me."

"You *trust* that someone will rescue you?"

Astraea tilts her head and sort of nods to herself.

"Despite your history, you trust in the basic decency of your fellow human beings. You trust in the established systems and decorum."

I point at the road ahead. We are coming up on a green light.

"How could I ever roll through this green light, if I didn't have trust? I can't confirm that the other lights are red. Not from this angle. Has the city properly programmed and maintained these lights? Is one of my fellow citizens going to say 'screw it', and run through a red. My life is literally on the line, multiple times a day, and yet I trust.

"When we get to the store, we're gonna find hundreds of thousands of dollars worth of products – millions maybe – just sitting there, unprotected. How do these corporations get away with that? How can they just lay it all out there, free for the taking? Trust. It's all just trust. Our society is built on it.

"But then we take a closer look at recent developments. We see flash mob robberies picking stores clean. We see inventory shrinkage, which is just another word for theft, at an all time high and growing by astounding margins every year. We see District Attorneys refusing to prosecute criminals who were caught red-handed. We see entire police forces abandoning their stations so that rioters can come in and burn it down. We see Autonomous Zones being created, and the police refusing to help the lawful citizens who get caught up in the crossfire. We see a president desperately try to steal an election, actively seeking to overturn the results based on emotion and rhetoric, but no real evidence. We see his supporters busting through the doors and windows of our Capitol. We watch them chase down cops and yell for the heads of our elected leaders. And then we listen as the RNC describes it, and I quote, as 'legitimate political discourse'.

"Every day we're further exposed to an ever growing culture of narcissism. A general disrespect for rules-based systems or decorum of any kind."

Astraea says, "That sounds like something old people say based on emotion and rhetoric. Where's your proof?"

"I just gave you proof."

"By cherry-picking major events. We're talking about society as a whole, not pockets."

"I have the perfect example. You remember our lazy Sunday?"

"Cash Cab!!!" she yells, excitedly.

"Exactly. We watched that shit for four hours straight. The first two were on TV. Reruns from 2007. When it was over, we were upset. We wanted more. So we found more On-Demand. Only those shows were from recent times. Same show, just fifteen years later. You notice any difference?"

"Ben's hair is more stylish now!"

"Yeah, he's got that floof at the front now. What else?"

She shrugs, "I don't know."

"The old shows almost never had to bleep anyone out. Everyone knows that nationally televised game shows don't allow cussing. So guess what? As a general rule, the contestants didn't cuss. At least not on the older shows. On the newer shows, nearly every group of contestants got bleeped out multiple times."

"Crabby old man," she says, shaking her head.

"In the older shows contestants would celebrate their correct answers for a short time before quickly returning their attention to the host. New shows, they celebrate and talk amongst themselves, and celebrate some more… meanwhile Ben is struggling to find a way to even ask the next question. That happened multiple times. One guy even turned around, mounted his seat, and twerked for the camera."

"That was funny."

"We're gonna have to disagree on that," I assure her. "The point is, this is just one example of the general breakdown of situational decorum. It's happening everywhere. In grocery stores and libraries and movie theaters and Congress and every other place you bother to look."

"So you think we've lost track of what acceptable behavior is?"

"It's worse than that. I think we don't care. I think we've decided that the rules don't apply to us. That somehow we are special."

"Well, how's that different than you?"

"How do you mean?"

"If I'm understanding correctly, you set two people on fire, William. Or you had someone else do it, I don't know. Either way, that sounds like a breach of societal decorum to me."

"That's… a very good point. See, this is why it's good to have someone to bounce your thoughts off."

"You needed a sounding board to realize that setting people on fire is-"

"I'm not saying I agree with you, just that you made a good point. And like all good points, it deserves consideration."

"Perhaps an adjective is in order. How about *intensive* consideration?"

"They used to fight wars with spears and swords," I say.

"Are we changing topics?"

"If they tried that today, they would lose. If you're going to war, you must at least attempt to match your enemy's arsenal."

"Because they feel entitled to break the rules, you should too? Is that what I'm hearing?"

"Or maybe a certain level of crazy can only be defeated with a certain level of crazy. Regardless, you have to remember, I'm existing in a state of war. In times of war, the rules change."

"Do you really believe you're in a war?"

"That's the one thing I'm certain about. My question is... How do you not see it? We've got footage from the front lines being broadcast every night. It's on TV, on YouTube, TikTok, everywhere you look. How does a guy like Trump end up in the oval office? For that matter, how does a man like Biden become 'The Big Guy'? We've populated the halls of Congress with liars and cheaters and snakes. The exact kind of people you'd want fighting for you in a dirty ugly war.

"We're all out for ourselves or our tribe, and nobody gives a shit about anything. We certainly don't care about The Truth. All we care about is Our Truth. All that matters is that Climate Change is a hoax and you can take all that evidence to the contrary and shove it up your ass. Or being a woman has nothing to do with having a vagina, you Fucking Terf Whore! So let's start electing the people who are willing to spout those lies and Fight-the-Good-Fight. Let's go to fucking war... every day... with our neighbors and our family and our friends. You ever wonder why doom-scrolling has become our national pastime? It's not a mystery. None of us trust each other. And for some strange reason, we kinda like it. We love reading the shit that pisses us off. You ever go doom-scrolling and find nothing much of concern? It's annoying isn't it? Why did I just waste all this time reading all these mundane headlines? Not one of them infuriated me! What a waste of time!

"But lucky for us, trust is a thing of the past. We don't value that anymore, and that opens the door for a new breed of journalist. A journalist that doesn't give a shit about the basic tenets of journalism. They don't even require for the things they write to be true. And, you know what? We're okay with it. Why? Because they're giving us what we want. We want war, Astraea. We want it! We crave it! Peace is boring. A society of different cultures and ideas living together in harmony... that's boring. Let's fight! Deep down in our ugly little hearts, that's what we want. We want to fight. We want to complain and hate and view ourselves as superior.

"You know what happens when someone has the gall to say, 'Why can't we all just get along'? We laugh, that's what happens. We turn it into a punchline. Because it's stupid and naive and would require that we rise above our tribal natures. It would require that we create a system of trust and acceptance and mutual respect. And why the hell would we want to do that, when war is so much more fun? Every time I get depressed about my blasé existence, all I gotta do is hold tight to my intersectionality and jump online and the endorphins come rushing to the rescue. It's so easy! Why would I ever want to live in a time of peace?

"This is where we are, Astraea. So who do we trust? Our institutions? The Catholic Church became a pedophile factory. The FDA cosigned the opioid epidemic into existence. Our Congresspeople are getting rich. We got corporations putting profit over the environment, over Chinese children, over foreign slave labor, over general safety of the American People. We got freedom of speech hanging by a precarious thread… So who do we turn to? Who do we trust? Each other? Hell no! You can't trust me, I'm an able-bodied-straight-white-cis-gendered-male. And I sure as hell can't trust you, you're a part of the Alphabet Brigade."

I point out the windshield at a black man walking down the street.

"Can't trust that guy. Look what color he is. According to a recent survey, half of 'em don't even think it's okay to be white. Which makes them a hate-group according to a cartoonist I know."

I move my attention to a Mexican man in the parking lot of McDonald's.

"And look at this guy, damn sure can't trust that piece of shit. Over here stealing our jobs, raping our women. Where the hell is that wall anyway?"

Astraea shakes her head.

I point at a person with gray hair.

"And check out this untrustworthy prick. Fucking Boomer!"

I sigh and rub my tired eyes.

Astraea says, "Oh and there's Karen!"

I look.

"Yeah, there she is. Ruling the world upon her hill of white privilege."

"Wrapped up in Lulu Lemon."

"A cunt of the highest order," I say

"Oh no," Astraea says. "Does that guy look Muslim to you?"

"Where? Oh shit. Yeah he does. And his jacket's zipped up!"

"You know what that means…" she says.

"He's got a suicide vest for sure," I agree.

"That is what they do," Astraea says with a shrug. "All two billion of them."

"Facts!" I say, "And somewhere there's a Jew orchestrating all of this."

Astraea laughs.

I say, "So, no, I guess what I'm saying is, I don't think your uncle is crazy. There's plenty of reason to be scared."

Astraea says, "I wasn't really asking about my uncle."

"I know that," I tell her. "You want to know if I'm crazy. And, unfortunately, I can't tell you the answer. I've convinced myself that the majority of us would rather live in peacetime. Perhaps, naively, I believe that most of us don't want this conflict. We are stuck in this war zone, surrounded by all these nutty factions with their endless hate and strange alliances. The white nationalists and the black freedom fighters and the people who call themselves educators and the pro-this and anti-thats with their corporate sponsors and government funding, all coalescing into left and right… and it's all just too much. There's too many trains barreling down too many tracks. And those tracks are filled with people… most of them good, honest people. People who would love to put an end to this war. They just don't know how. And here I am standing in the train yard, watching it all happen. Has that made me crazy? Maybe. I don't know. And if I am crazy, is it the kind of crazy that is necessary? The kind of crazy that allows me to run around this train yard making insane choices, figuring out which levers I should pull? Is that crazy? You tell me. Am I crazy?"

She shakes her head.

"I don't know. This is just... I don't know what it is," she says. "Why are we going to the store?"

"I told you this. To buy measuring devices. We need an anenometer, and a barometer."

"I know, but why do we care about atmospheric changes inside our plumbing vent? Is this one of those levers?"

"Okay, so," I take a deep breath. "I suspect that the nearby injection of waste water, also known as flushing the toilet, will cause a measurable temporary reaction inside the vent pipe. I also suspect that reaction will be noticeably different than every other interaction within that drain system. Whether it be the draining of a bathtub, the dishwasher pump activating, the flushing of an upstream toilet, whatever... They'll all be different. That nearby toilet will have its own particular fingerprint or signature, if you will."

"Okay?"

"Now, what if we could program a computer, like a little one the size of my thumb, to recognize that signature? That signature could then be converted into a trigger."

"A trigger," Astraea says with alarm.

"And if there's one thing we know about toilet flushes, it means there's either someone on the throne or standing before it."

"You're talking about planting a bomb?"

"I'm talking about *easily* planting a bomb. A quick sneak up on the roof. We've analyzed the situation from afar. We've cut fishing line to the proper length. We've attached our purpose built measuring and triggering device. We just feed it down the pipe and attach it to the rim with a little fishhook that's practically invisible. And that's it. It just sits there, waiting to do its job. We just set it and forget it. We never even have to enter the house. We don't even have to wonder if our target is in the right position. Eventually, they will use the bathroom."

"And pull the trigger themselves," she says.

"Exactly."

"Jesus Christ," she says. "Who are you trying to kill?"

"It's not any particular person. We just need to wake people up."

"Hold on. Hold on."

Astraea wraps her face up in her hands and appears to be trying to squeeze something out.

I say, "Look, we have a government that is corrupt in so many ways that I can't delineate them all. Which has led to and allowed a corporate environment where profit is routinely placed above basic societal obligations. This environment has led to ideological divisions so large that it has developed into a literal war being fought on every street corner, every workplace, every website in this country. And nobody trusts anybody unless they are the exact same intersectionality as themselves."

"I cannot listen to this anymore."

"It all stems from one place, Astraea. It was born out of our government's failures. And it just keeps going. It's a perpetual motion machine. It just keeps churning. Our government is the engine that is driving this thing. It's a locomotive. It is the runaway train. There's three hundred and thirty million people tied to the track."

"So you wanna pull the lever."

"Of course I do."

"How many people are on that other track?"

"I'm not sure. We'll have to play that by ear. Does it really matter if it's a dozen or a few hundred or a thousand? There's *three hundred million* on the main track."

"No, no, no. No!" Astraea says. "You're talking about killing people. Our government is not killing three hundred million people. That's a... what do they call it? A false equivalence. Maybe they're giving them a life that's less good, in a society that's less than ideal, but they're not killing them."

I say, "Well it's not 300 million, is it then? It's their future children, their children's children, and on and on and on. It's generational. We're talking about billions of lives being lived in an emotional war zone. Billions of lives being lived in a society fueled by hate and distrust. Eventually, it will implode on itself, but there's gonna be a lot of victims before that day. And when that day finally comes, this country will be reformed... through actual war. Many will die. Not a small number. My plan exists specifically to avoid all of that. We're talking about a cycle of pain that is being inflicted on the entirety of society over and over and over again. The longer we wait, the more victims we create. I see the solution, Astraea. It's right there, we just have to be willing to do the hard thing. There will be collateral damage. It will be ugly. *We* will be ugly. We will look in the mirror and we will see a monster. But then we will look out the window, and we will see a better world."

Astraea shakes her head.

"I don't think I can do this. I mean, I don't even understand what you're doing."

"I'm trying to wake the people up. Every single one of them knows there's something wrong. Even if they can't put their finger on it, they know it. They feel it in their blood. In their essence. All the way down to a cellular level, they know. But they're sleepwalking and we need to wake them up. We need to scare the ever-lovin' hell out of them. So how do we do that?"

"We blow them up in their bathrooms?"

"Yes! Yes. That is what we do. In their own homes. In the most private and personal place within that home. If you can't hide there, you can't hide anywhere."

"So who would be the target?"

"Well, the people dividing this country is the obvious choice. But which ones? My gut tells me it should be the populace itself. Not the Senators, or the rich, or the news makers... it should be the nobodies, the facebook friends, the TikTokkers with a few hundred followers. We have the biggest database ever created right there at our fingertips. These retards will happily tell us exactly who they are and where they live. And we'll have all the evidence in the world to know that they are, in fact, one of the dividers of this country. And so... what happens, happens."

I pause to light a cigarette.

"Imagine seeing that happen all across the country. It's a scary thing to think about. Just the kind of scary we need. The kind that pierces the haze of existence and strikes at the very heart of our fears.

"I imagine people across the country terrified to go to the loo. I see a mother refusing to visit the daughter that just posted some far right nonsense on Facebook. I see a girlfriend who won't go to her boyfriend's house anymore… because she knows he could be a target. I see entire families afraid to go home because one of them is a loud-mouthed left-wing crazy. I see people on rooftops, staring down pipes, paranoid and on edge. I see a country broken of its ambivalence."

She says, "But that would be weird wouldn't it? Left and right being blown up through the same method?"

"True. We would obviously need to limit the attacks to one side. If only right wingers are attacked, people will assume it's Antifa, Black Lives Matter, or some other group of insane lefties. If we attack exclusively left wingers, MAGAs and white nationalists will likely get the blame. Clearly, if we attack both sides, we in the middle will become the suspects, so that's a no go. So… which side do we commit to?"

She says, "How about we blow up a bunch of Trump-loving douche bags?"

"Okay and after a few conservatives bite the dust, I can imagine that the narrative would allow for those assholes to retaliate. Obviously using a completely different method. Easiest thing would probably be sniper attacks. A single shot outside of a Planned Parenthood, an ACLU office, a school board meeting, Google… There are countless potential targets. Imagine the chaos! Imagine the desperation!"

Astraea shakes her head.

"You are way to excited about this. You actually look happy."

"Because the solutions are materializing. We can fix this. We really can."

"No," Astraea says, shaking her head. "Just… no."

"You don't think you can pull the levers that need pulled?"

"No. Nor do I want to. Nor should you. Seriously, you're really scaring me."

We've finally reached our destination. I pull into the lot and park the truck. We sit in silence for a long time.

I say, "Alright Astraea, our conversation got a little off track there. Truth is I have something I need to talk to you about. I didn't mean to get into politics."

She shrugs uncomfortably.

I continue, "Do your parents live in our neighborhood?"

"What?" she says.

"I mean, it makes sense. When you decided to run away, you picked a house you'd already seen. Something you knew was abandoned."

"Why are you asking this?"

"Because I went for a jog the other night. I saw a mailbox with the name Westphal on it. Is that your parents?"

Astraea says nothing, just staring into her lap.

"I looked in the mailbox. Is your father's name Lonnie?"

Astraea looks at me.

"Why does it matter?"

"Do me a favor. Look in the glove box."

She gives me a quizzical look, but then does as I ask.

In the glove box she finds two pamphlets. One of them provides information specifically on adoption. The other is about becoming a foster parent.

On the surface of each pamphlet is a mailing label. The recipient is listed as Lonnie Westphal.

I say, "I've never gotten anything like that in the mail. I'm guessing that kind of thing comes on request."

She looks at me, a lot sad and a bit confused.

I say, "Looks like he's trying to replace you."

27

FEBRUARY 3, 2024
276 DAYS UNTIL ELECTION

My Amazon order came on time, as usual. It was an expensive order, comprised of a 14 inch gas powered concrete saw, a 4.2 cubic foot concrete mixer, a 1000 watt power inverter, two hard hats, a couple of construction vests, and a pair of work boots for Astraea.

Last night, around one a.m., I pulled over at the tail end of some road construction. I proceeded to load five tall traffic cones into the bed of my truck. Three cars passed as I did this. They never questioned what I was doing, and if they did, they kept those questions to themselves.

It's early morning as we load all the stuff into the truck bed along with an old 55 gallon drum filled with water. A few days ago I drilled a hole near the bottom of the drum and installed a spigot for a water hose.

The jobsite is located on the main entry road of a neighborhood in northwest OKC. I noticed the pothole several weeks ago while visiting a friend in the area. It's a nice neighborhood, quiet and well-kept, with half million dollar homes. The kind of place you'd expect a Congressman or Senator to call home.

I instruct Astraea to set up the traffic cones while I prep the saw for use. I hook the hose to the saw, the water working to protect the saw's diamond encrusted blades.

Astraea watches as I cut a three foot square around the pothole. We use sledge hammers to break it apart and throw the broken pieces into the truck bed.

I drill ¾ inch holes into the side walls of the concrete and install metal dowels for added stability.

We pour the concrete mix into the machine, add some water, and then let it run.

Astraea says meekly, "I didn't sleep too well last night."

I nod, "Yeah. I get that. Do you regret it?"

"I don't know. It doesn't even seem real," she says.

"You know, every one of us has something ugly inside. In that way, your dad was no different than anybody. The truth is, I don't judge him for having those desires. Personally, I don't get it. I think it's disgusting. But it's not like he set out to develop those desires. They were just there and he had no choice but to contend with them. The way I see it, he could have been a hero. Not the kind we see in movies. A different kind, but no less admirable. He doesn't save you from some bad guy. He is the bad guy, but he saves you from himself. He fights against his demon… every hour of every day, never allowing himself to create victims through his selfish desires. It's a hard choice to make, denying yourself. Not just today, but tomorrow and the next. Day in, day out… No… No… No. It's a hard job. A hero's job. He could have done that job. He could've made the hard choice, but he made a different one.

"His choice left you no choice. Knowing what you know, you made the only decision you could. Somewhere out there, there's a seven year old girl who will never have to meet that monster. And that's thanks to you being willing to make the hard choice. You ask me, you should sleep like a baby."

"What did they do to him?"

I shrug, "I couldn't tell ya. Beyond the plan me and you came up with, I didn't give them any parameters. They're the professionals. They did the job. The job is done."

She nods.

My security team has a number of specialists. One of them is an impressive hacker. She was able to infiltrate Lonnie Westphal's computer in no time flat. Within two days, she had gained access to his email, social networking accounts, online banking… basically everything.

Through this access she was able to spin a transactional tale of a man in the midst of a midlife crisis. A study of his online interactions would convince anybody that he simply decided to fly the coop.

Physical evidence will support this conclusion. His bank account – empty. His car – gone. His suitcase – gone. His clothes – gone. His jewelry – gone. Even his toothbrush – gone.

The only requirements I gave were that it appear that he simply split town. And, of course, that his body and belongings are never found.

"Did they torture him?"

"I doubt it," I say. "They're very professional. But who knows? I told them why it was happening, so… maybe."

"A part of me hopes they did. Is that wrong?"

"Like I said, we all have our own ugly. You had every opportunity to ask that torture be a part of the plan. Did you do that?"

"No."

"Well, there you go. You didn't feed your ugly. That's all we can do. We evaluate. We make the right choice, even if it's the hard choice. And we don't feed our ugly. That's the job."

I stop the mixer and we pour the first batch into place.

Four batches later, the hole is filled. I smooth out and level the surface until everything looks right.

After a bit of finishing work, we cover the cold-weather concrete with an insulating blanket and weigh it down with a piece of plywood.

We load up our equipment and head out. I drive out to the main road and wait for a gap in traffic that allows me to drive directly across the street.

I pull into the parking lot of the Indian restaurant and park my truck with a view of the street. We are perfectly in line with the entrance of the neighborhood. We can see the distant traffic cones that we left in place to protect our work.

I reach into the little duffel bag that sits between us. I remove something from the bag and hand it to Astraea.

"This is a range finder. See if you can tell me how far away the third traffic cone is."

After taking a moment to figure out how it works, Astraea determines the answer.

"Nine hundred and thirty six feet."

I pull up a satellite image of the neighborhood on my phone.

"Look at this. This subdivision has four main entrances. You see that?"

"Yeah."

"Now, if we knew that someone lived, say… in this house here. And we also knew that they worked downtown… What would be the most obvious entrance they would use when coming home?"

Astraea points to the southernmost entrance on the satellite image.

"This one," she says. "That's this one, right?"

She gestures out the windshield to the actual entrance before us.

"That's exactly right," I tell her. "So, unless this person has an errand to run that takes them further north, we can predictably assume the path they will take."

I look to see an SUV turning into the entrance to the neighborhood. I gesture to the SUV.

"Go ahead and track this guy here. Tell me when you get to nine-thirty-six."

She does as I ask, lifting the range finder and pointing it at the SUV.

"Seven hundred, eight hundred, nine… thirty six."

I press my thumb into my fist as if pushing a button on a remote.

I say, "So if we knew what car they were driving and we had a zero-delay transmitter, activating a receiver…"

"Easy peasy," Astraea says.

"Easy peasy," I agree.

325

She says, "I get how we could've easily planted a bomb under the concrete we just poured, but would the receiver be able to do its job covered in concrete?"

"Good question. I'm not really sure. Very likely, no. But, you see those storm drains?"

"Yeah."

"What if we did our 'repairs' very near a storm drain like that one. We could cut a thin channel the width of a saw blade running to the storm drain. We run a wire through that channel and set up a waterproof receiver to just hang out in the storm drain, below the surface, where no one can see it."

"Would the channel be suspicious?"

"We fill it with tar, it'll look completely normal."

Astraea nods.

"Yeah," she says. "It seems like that would work. It's so crazy that nobody ever said anything to us. A hundred cars must've driven by us."

"And a cop car even."

"Oh dude! I was freaking out! Thought we were going to jail for sure!"

"All that equipment, the proper uniforms... People just assume you are who you say you are."

"But don't you think a Senator's neighborhood might be different? More vigilant?"

"You remember that house I pointed to on the map?"

"Yeah."

"Not quite a Senator, but a member of the US House."

"Really?" she says. "Is that the target?"

"Oh no. This stuff will be strictly out of state, far from the Mediator Party."

Today is a special day. Axton is beginning his nationwide book tour, and it's kicking off with his very first podcast.

I tune in, nervously. Smart or not, you never really know how someone will fare in the broadcast world.

The show begins and so far he's holding his own. It's a black-owned podcast, geared toward a black audience. My research of the host suggests that he won't take too kindly to some of Axton's ideas. I sit through the calm, certain that the storm will come.

"We've gotta recalibrate our M.O." Axton says. "We ain't gotta let these people rule our streets. We call them out. We call the cops. We make a stand. We take the stand. We do whatever we gotta do."

"Ahh shit, brother... You talking about being a *snitch*? Boy, you done lost your mind."

"Snitch..." Axton mumbles to himself. He shakes his head in frustration. "Man, you gotta hand it to the criminals. A lotta dumb ones, but as a group they ain't so stupid."

"What are you goin' on about?" the host asks.

Axton says, "They create a system to enrich themselves. Then they create a lore around that system... For you... Mr. Law-abiding. Then they create words to enhance that lore and protect that system. And here *you* go, buying every inch of it. Do you hear yourself? These boys got you wrapped up."

"I ain't wrapped up in shit."

"Well then why'd you say it like you did? You said that word like it was the devil's brew. With every ounce of disgust you could gather. You hate that word. And you love that you're not one. They actually got you *feeling yourself*... cause you ain't a snitch."

"Man, you crazy. You gonna come up in here and try to rebrand the word snitch like it's a good thing?"

"I dare a dealer to throw some white boy on a white corner and see how long before the phones start blowin' up at the local cophouse. How long before the squad cars come light that boy up?"

The host laughs, "Oh you wanna be like those Karen-ass motherfuckers?"

"We ain't talkin' about dimin' out your neighbor for having an unsanctioned poker game. We talkin' about pimpin', and dealin', and killin'. We talking 'bout honest men handing over their paper at the end of a gun. We talkin' about moms and dads going to the

327

graveyard to visit their kids. We talkin' about law abiding citizens... like you... convinced that they owe their allegiance to the very criminal enterprises that are ravaging their community. You know what I call that? A con job. You know what I call you? A chump. How'd we decide to let the worst of us destroy the rest of us? And how'd we determine to feel proud while we do it?"

Axton pauses to let his host chime in. The man just looks at him, eyes narrowed, churning on Axton's words.

Axton says, "Look here, I want you to do something for me. Next time you rollin' through your ma's hood and see some shit you know is hurting your people, I want you to take a moment and look at your phone. Just look at it... for a moment. And when you decide not to use it, I want you to check yourself in the rearview. And when you see those eyes staring back at you, I want you to know exactly what you lookin' at... A fuckin' sucker."

The host takes the shot and sits there, stunned.

Axton says, "What are these assholes giving you? They give you fear. They give you the constant need to take precautions. They give you a reason to buy an alarm system... bars on your windows. What else they givin' ya? Dead bodies. Broken homes. A broken community. What else? A bunch of other races thinkin' we animals. Boys in blue thinkin' the same... that they damn sure give ya. What else?"

Axton looks at the host, begging for an answer.

The host says nothing.

"They give you nothing you want. And you give them everything they need. You look the other way. That's all they need and you give it to them... freely. Proudly even. And you think I'm crazy."

It's been two months since the hostile takeover.

In a large room at Brighton Technology, I have gathered around me the team that will give birth to our greatest creation. All around me I hear voices tackling problems and the clickity-clack of fingers on keyboards. Meanwhile, others sit stone silent, staring into the abyss of their computer screens.

We have experts on all things government policy providing the genesis of our survey questions. Linguistics professionals to hone those questions, making them easily understood and non-biased in the asking. Web designers and programmers translate it all into a pleasing, yet functional environment, building the architecture of a new world.

"Everybody stop!" I yell.

The place goes silent.

I hold my tablet up high for everyone to see.

"I have here the most up to date version of what you all are working on."

I turn and throw the tablet hard into a wall. It crashes down leaving a sizable gash in the drywall.

I turn back and look at my audience.

"What are we doing here?"

No one says anything. I point at a man whose face I know.

"Lonnie. What are we doing here?"

"We're building a website?"

"Jeanine! Where are ya!"

"I'm here, sir," she says. She steps forward and meekly raises a hand. "Here."

"What are we doing?"

"We're giving the people their voice."

"That's an improvement," I say, throwing eyes at Lonnie.

Someone chuckles.

"Don't you dare laugh," I point at the man who chuckled. "You. What are we doing?"

"Umm…"

"Nevermind. I'll tell you what we're doing. We are building the foundation of a new America. That's what we're doing. When you complete this work. When I send out my army and we sign up 2.5 million Oklahomans… Those 2.5 million people will become the envy of the entire country. Every citizen of every state will wonder why they don't have a voice. A chain reaction will take place. And a new America will be built."

I walk over to my broken tablet and collect it from the floor. I hold it up, its cracked screen clearly visible.

"Construction 101. You don't build on a shit foundation. *This* is everything. Without *this*, the Mediator Party is nothing. Out there beyond these walls lies a world where 'good enough' is actually good enough. But within these walls 'good enough' is a death sentence. 'Good enough' is a house of cards. 'Good enough' turns our dream into a nightmare.

"Out there, 80 percent effort, 80 percent quality, hell, that's pretty good. Out there, 90 percent is really damn good. You can make a pretty good life for yourself doing 90 percent. But not here. Here, 90 percent finds nothing but failure. Get me that last ten percent. Every piece of the puzzle. Every building block. Every step of the way. Get me that last ten percent. I don't care what you're doing, whatever it is, get me that last ten percent. It may take twice as long to get the last ten than it did to get the first ninety, but you GET IT! The last ten is harder than the first ninety, because it's the last ten that sets it apart. It's the last ten that changes the world. It turns good into great. And those two things are light-years apart. Get me that last ten percent!"

I look out at the people. Very few of them meet my eyes.

"Linguistics! Where are ya?"

"Here sir," Ronald raises his hand.

"Section 5, question 8. Don't tell me that question doesn't engender bias."

Ronald scrambles to find the question on his computer. I can see that he's found it. His face sinks.

"What the... I'm sorry sir, that must've slipped through."

"Nothing slips through! Do you understand? Nothing!"

"Yes sir. I understand."

"Get me that last ten percent!"

I turn and walk toward the door.

"Kevin!" I bark as I'm walking out.

Just a few seconds later Kevin finds me in the hall.

"Yes sir," he says. "I'm really sorry about the-"

"Stop. Kevin, it's fine," I say reassuringly. "It's coming along well."

"Really?"

"We just need the last ten percent."

He nods, "Okay. I will get it for you."

"Good. I have an additional request. It'll suck, but it's important."

"Name it."

"Every question needs to have its own index of information attached to it. If a voter wants to understand the question better, they need to be able to quickly access a non-partisan clearly stated explanation as to the purpose of that question and the ramifications of any particular answer."

"Like a help button?"

"Maybe. Play with it, see what you come up with. It should have stages to it though. If the quick and concise answer doesn't satisfy them, they should be able to expand that further. Maybe get examples of how that policy can directly affect the people within a society. Pros and cons, all that."

"You want it to be educational?"

"Yes. A thousand times yes. Not only should they be able to learn more about the question, I want them to be able to learn more about the varying opinions. Click here and you'll get a little snippet about how each of these relevant groups feel about this subject. The opposing viewpoints... All of it."

"So... for every viewpoint, we need the opposing viewpoint?"

"Correct. And we need to make sure that we get the best version of the argument from each side. We should actually submit a request to each of the parties."

"...For their official stance on each question?"

"Sure. They'd be crazy not to want their opinions represented."

"You said relevant groups?"

"If it's a civil liberties question, you could consult the ACLU. But also…"

"Seek out the opposing viewpoint," he says, finishing my thought.

"You got it," I tell him. "Now, I'm not expecting you to write a book about each question. Just a general understanding. After that, there should also be resource links that help lead people to where they can further their education off-site. We don't just want voters. We want informed voters. We do this right, we will end up with the most politically involved and educated populace in the history of this country."

28

I've made it to primetime in the podcast world. My host today has an audience of 11 million tuning in to multiple shows a week. He hosts long one-on-one three hour discussions about anything and everything under the sun.

I've seen quite a few episodes and suspect we'll get along famously. He grills me from the start.

He says, "The other day, I watched you argue that black equality hasn't yet been achieved. The next day, you went the other way. I've heard you argue for abortion... I've heard you argue against abortion. One minute capitalism is beautiful, the next minute it's a major problem."

"What can I say? I'm a complex guy."

"Or you're a liar."

"Every argument I make is based in fact."

"Well, no shit. Somehow, you won both arguments. So you're not just a liar, you're a very good liar. I'm not sure we need more of those in politics."

I laugh.

"I'm serious," he says. "You're trying to win people to your movement, but how are we suppose to know who you are? How can we even know what you believe?"

"What I believe is that both arguments have merit. There are two different kinds of conversations I have on these podcasts. Discussions and debates. You can have a hard-core position, but if your argument has nuance... if you treat the issue as complex... then we're gonna have a discussion. But if you hold an extreme opinion and express it as fact, then we're gonna have a debate. I don't care which side your on, if you're trafficking in the extremes... and throwing complexity out the window... you're gonna lose the argument. Every time. These issues are not black and white. They are varying shades of gray. So, yes, I can argue both sides of an issue, because both extremes have a tendency to have their head up their ass. People think I'm this great debater, but really I just pick and choose the battles I know I'm gonna win. That gets a lot of hits on YouTube, but the reality of it is this... there's only one argument I ever truly care to win."

"What's that?"

"That whatever my ultimate opinion is... even at the extremes... it deserves to be considered. It should be taken into account. That's it. Every day, our leaders utterly dismiss the opinions of the people they are charged to represent. Why? Because they don't like that particular opinion. AOC doesn't give one iota of credence to the thoughts of her non-liberal constituents. Not one. Matt Gaetz wouldn't listen to a liberal if his life depended on it. You wanna know what I believe? I believe that is wrong. Ultimately, I intend to share where I land on every subject... with our leaders... through a survey. Beyond that, what I believe is immaterial. This isn't about what I believe. It's about what you believe. And by 'you', I mean every voter who tunes in to this podcast and the other quarter of a billion that don't. Let's collect those opinions. Every damn one of them."

The man looks at me and nods.

He says, "I never thought I'd say this, but you're making me wish I was an Oklahoman!"

Ninety minutes in, the talk has turned to COVID-19 and all its aftermath.

He says, "So, in your book, you were struggling with whether or not to get the vaccine."

"I was."

"The book never answers that question."

"That's because I was finishing that particular book right around the time when the Covid vaccines first came available. I published it still not knowing the answer."

"But you know now, right? Did you get it?"

"No. I never did."

"Why not?"

"Honestly? The phrase 'safe and effective' is what ultimately did it for me. To this day, those words scare the shit out of me."

"Explain that."

"Everyone was saying it. Every website. Every paper. All the TV stations. Every traditional news source. Safe and effective. Safe and effective."

"Like a broken record."

"I must have heard it a million times. It was coordinated messaging. It was a mass marketing campaign."

"Propaganda."

"Exactly. Not once did I hear the words 'long term side-effects'. Not once. It was as if long term side-effects weren't even a possibility."

"Well who cares about that?"

"Historically, the FDA does. Suddenly, not so much. They usually watch drug trials for ten to fifteen years. They track the phase 1 participants from a decade earlier… why? To watch for long-term effects. Why? Because it's their job to make sure it's safe. They'd been testing this vaccine for a sum total of eight months at the time they approved it for emergency use. And that's fine, we were in a bad spot, I get it, but be honest with me. Be honest with the American People."

"Oh no. They can't do that. It would stop people from taking it."

"Some, sure, but that's so much better than the alternative. I now know for a fact, that my government is more than happy to lie to me about things that are integral to my well-being. I now know that my government doesn't trust me to make my own decisions about my own life. I also learned that the fourth estate, the group that should be my most ardent defender against government overreach, is more than happy to do the government's bidding."

"The fourth estate being the media."

"Correct. The media. They were all in. Social media... same deal. Censoring people that didn't toe the line. And then an entire political party falls down on the side of censorship. The Democratic Party, my God, they demonized anybody who decided to question whether the vaccine was right for them."

"You don't have to tell me. I'm an OG demon."

"Yeah you are. You're like the Devil's favorite General. If we could see your true form, you'd probably be a centaur."

"A centaur? That's a half man, half..."

"Horse."

"Ahh, I see where you're going. You think you're funny. Alright, that is pretty funny." He shakes his head. "Fuckin' CNN."

"CNN. MSNBC. Your local corner store. It's everywhere. This, 'You're a bad person' propaganda, bullshit. It's really scary. Even when the Twitter Files provided proof that the government was pushing for censorship, in some cases factual information, the Democrats acted like it was no big deal. They kept with that same worn out line, 'These are private companies, it's not a First Amendment issue'. Really? When it's happening at the behest of the government, it's not a free speech issue? Still?"

"What about the argument that the government was only making suggestions? They never actually *ordered* Twitter to censor anything. In fact, Twitter said no to a lot of those suggestions."

"Okay, let's imagine I'm a hot shot movie producer and you're a beautiful young actress."

"That will take a healthy imagination."

"Now you know that I'm currently casting for the role of a lifetime. The kind of role that could change your life. Your career. Your everything."

"I'm with ya."

"Is it okay for me to suggest we go have drinks and discuss your future? It's just a suggestion. I'm not ordering you to do it. What if I suggest you stop by my hotel room later? Is that okay?"

He says, "Mister Producer, I do believe you're operating from a position of power."

"What if you said 'no' when I suggested you go lie naked on the bed and spread those legs?"

"I would definitely say no."

"But then maybe you'd say yes when I downgraded my suggestion to a simple blow job. After all, we are talking about your hopes, your dreams, and your livelihood. We all weigh our options in the face of pros and cons. Does the fact that you had the agency to say 'no' to some of my suggestions absolve me from the wielding of my power in the first place?"

"Hmm. That does have the ring of truth. The 'MeToo' of it all. It really is the same thing, isn't it?"

"It's the exact same thing. Just a much bigger scale. We're talking about the United States Government. They have the power to regulate Social Media or leave them alone to count their money. When the people that regulate you make a suggestion, is it really just an innocent suggestion? Or are there undeniable power dynamics at play? And then the question is, is it somehow okay for the government to regulate our speech as long as it's done through a private intermediary? Or does that fly in the face of the very concept of free speech?"

"I think it does exactly that."

"Me too. The best way to counteract one side is to tell the other side. More conversation, not less. Not censorship. We can't silence voices and still claim to be free. We have to trust each other to make our own decisions. To live our own lives. We can't control everyone around us."

"Nor should we want to."

"It takes a special kind of asshole to feel so superior that you believe you should have the power to dictate what other people can and can't say. This is one of the many reasons we need the Mediator Party right now."

"Dude! I'm so into it. I've been watchin' you. Been keeping a real close eye. I love what you're doing! I think it's exactly what we need at exactly the time we need it."

"Well, maybe a decade or two ago would've been better."

"Maybe, but they would've laughed you out of the room a decade or two ago. We needed all this crazy shit to happen to make us listen. We needed Woke. We needed Identity Politics. And Evergreen. And Trump. And January 6th. And Covid. And Vaccines. And Cancel Culture. It's like this perfect storm of stupidity that comes along and tears up everything in its path, clearing the ground for something new and revolutionary."

"It boggles the mind that this idea is somehow considered revolutionary."

"I know. I was thinking about that when I listened to your book. It's so simple. It's such a simple idea. And yet, it is revolutionary."

"That just shows how bogged down we are in this system we've created. We have the technology and have for a while. Imagine if our leaders had decided on their own initiative, 'Hey, with all these advances, maybe we should build a system to see what the people really think. And maybe we should let that drive how we run this thing'."

"That'll never happen," he says. "They'd be giving away their power. I used to have this little tiny ray of hope, but I've realized, that's just not real. They will never freely give their power to the people. It will never happen. If the people want that power, they have to take it. *We* have to take it from *them*."

I say, "I've yet to hear one Senator or member of the House come out in support of this idea. Not one has said, 'Collecting the thoughts of the American People is a fine idea'. Quite a few have called me a crank though."

"That's interesting, isn't it. It pisses me off, but you know what really pisses me off? You're doing all this, and I'm completely out in the cold. And so is 98 percent of America. If you're not in Oklahoma, all you can do is watch. I want skin in the game! Bring the game to Texas!"

"I don't know what to tell ya, man. It's early times. Oklahoma will serve as proof of concept. We pull that off, I promise you, the Mediator Party will be coming to a theater near you."

"You know what you should do? You should run for president. Then we'd all be in it."

"Me? No."

"Why not? Come on, just do it. Run for president. I mean, seriously, what is it?... You fill out some paperwork. You say a few words. What's the big deal?"

I shake my head.

"I'm not the right guy. I'm the guy who finds and supports the right guy... or gal."

"So do that."

I laugh, "Sorry, brother, it's not really in the budget. I can't steal from one goal to support another. That's a good way to fail at both."

"Well I've been talking to some people," he says with a suggestive tone. His eyes are wide open and dancing with excitement. "People are talking. Believe me, people are talking."

"What are they saying?"

"That they want to be part of the revolution!"

My plan to avoid an overnight trip has been foiled. After a productive three hour conversation, the host suggested that I go to dinner with him. He has someone he'd like me to meet.

"Who's that?" I asked.

"I've been sworn to secrecy," he said. "But I promise you, it'll be worth your while."

I manage to find a hotel room on short notice, so I check in and take a quick shower. I have no change of clothes, so I throw the old ones back on.

I turn on the TV and flip it to the first news channel I see. Ivy Leaguers are chanting "From the River to the Sea" in an an effort to promote a peaceful world. It's more stupid than interesting, so I open my laptop.

I search for 'Bulgur Swine', the restaurant where we will be eating tonight. It looks to be one of those fancy-douchey type establishments that charges by the appendage. They likely serve a Chef's Tasting Menu that leaves you broke and starving at the end of the night. According to the website, service opens at 5pm, Thursday through Sunday.

Interestingly, today is Monday, and they are clearly closed on Mondays.

Something I hear on the TV catches my attention.

On the screen is video surveillance footage of what looks to be a wide shot of a workout facility floor. Everything appears normal, men and women running on treadmills and stair-steppers. A sweaty fat balding man rows a boat to nowhere. A bearded brute lifts twice his weight on the universal machine. All is well.

One man shuts down his treadmill, wipes his face with a towel, and exits the screen. Another man steps off an elliptical and also takes his leave. The bearded brute has had enough. He rises from the bench press and makes a hasty exit. These normal behaviors begin to appear coordinated, as if it's all a part of some plan. The row-boater and two other men quickly join the exodus.

The news broadcast switches to footage from a different camera. The six men walk in single file down a hallway. The very familiar man at the front of the line veers to the right, and pushes his way through a door. Each of the five men follow. As the door closes, it's easy to read the sign upon its surface – WOMEN'S LOCKER ROOM.

A two week old booking photo from a North Carolina jail pops up on the screen. It's the leader of the group – my friend Roland. He was arrested that day after being forcibly removed from the women's locker room of a North Carolina YMCA. Having broken no laws, he was released shortly after.

The news anchor speaks to the camera.

"Rollin' Roland has just added a new stop on *her* much talked about tour of the country. Today, *she* and *her* five friends visited a YMCA in New Jersey."

Footage is shown of Roland exiting the New Jersey YMCA and walking through the parking lot. Police are there, keeping the peace. Several people are carrying signs calling for women's rights and safe-spaces. Boos and hisses and name-calling can be heard.

"What are your pronouns, Roland? What are your pronouns?" A reporter yells.

Roland turns and looks squarely at the reporter. He makes no attempt to feminize his movements or disguise his general manliness.

"I'm a she," he says in the unaltered voice of a man. "I'm a her. I'm a woman! I don't know why this is so hard to understand. Why am I being persecuted? For simply being me? We should all be allowed the freedom to be our most authentic selves! I have a human right to be my true self! All of us do!"

He gestures to his five friends, all of whom are as far from womanhood as could possibly be imagined.

The protesters continue their sneers as Roland and his friends each mount their Harleys and ride away.

That's entertainment!

I listen to the broadcast for a little longer, enjoying the verbal gymnastics the anchor must perform to maintain her veneer of political correctness.

It's clear that everyone knows it's bullshit. But the left can't say it. They are boxed in by their own policies on the subject. They have no choice but to accept and support Roland for exactly what he says he is. Excuse me... for exactly what *she* says *she* is.

I've been following Roland's progress around the country for weeks. And I'm not the only one. He has fan pages and hate pages on X, TikTok, Facebook... you name it. News articles supporting *her* rights, or condemning *his* actions are released every day of the week. The comment sections never cease to be filled to the brim... and an absolute blast to read.

Recently, several copycat groups have gotten in on the fun. There's even a group of pretty young girls in sundresses traveling the country, violating men's private spaces. To the chagrin of the men in those spaces, these girls never remove a single stitch of clothing. They just stand there and watch with judging eyes.

It's amazing!

I arrive at the restaurant at exactly eight o'clock. I am led to the only table in use. My new friend is already seated and waiting for me. He looks over and gives me a chin nod as I approach. Seated diagonally from him is the mystery guest. I recognize him immediately. He might just be the most famous entrepreneur in all the world. He might also be the richest man who ever lived. I'm not quite up to date on those numbers. Either way, he makes Simon look like a pauper.

Over the last few years, the man has become the target of much hate. They hate his success. They hate even more that he's earned it.

The first course arrives just as I take my seat.

The food is pretty good, but the conversation is surprisingly dull. He has a way of smirking for no apparent reason, as if he thought of a joke, but neglected to speak it out loud. The few times he does speak it, the joke falls flat, a victim of poor timing and dismal delivery.

Still, he's an interesting man. I'm quite certain he has a motive for this meeting, but he's keeping it to himself.

We eat our food and dabble through this topic and that. I get the distinct feeling he's taking my measure. I also get the feeling he's underestimating me.

I think I know exactly why he's here. Tiring of the cat-and-mouse, I decide to cut through the bullshit.

"Fifty million dollars," I say.

He looks at me. For the first time, I feel his full engagement.

"Fifty million dollars?"

"That's what I need."

He smiles at me like I'm a child, "Why would I give you fifty million dollars?"

"Look, let's be honest. Shall we?"

He shrugs.

"You don't give a shit about the Mediator Party. You think it's gonna fail. Scratch that… You think it's gonna fail miserably."

He sort of nods.

"But we're here for a reason," I say, sizing him up. "And that reason is… You like my survey. You believe it has real potential."

His condescending smile disappears.

I continue, "Hell, with your connections, you've probably infiltrated my organization, and already seen a draft of the website."

"I wouldn't put it past me," he says with a smirk.

"See, even if the Mediator Party fails… if in the midst of that failure, I can manage to sign up an entire state… to a policy survey of all things… well, that changes the game, doesn't it?"

The billionaire leans back in his seat and studies me. He silently stares at me, a million or so calculations rattling around his overdeveloped mind.

I say, "Now, I don't know why you're so interested. Maybe you think it's a change that leads to a better world. Or maybe it serves some unknown purpose in some master plan you've concocted. Truth is, I don't care. All that matters is that we both want this survey to succeed. You have fifty million dollars. And I need fifty million dollars."

"What does fifty million buy?"

"It buys success."

"I need specifics," he says, all humor gone from his voice.

"There's about four million people in Oklahoma. 2.2 million of them are registered to vote. What if I can get more people to sign up than are even registered? What if I can get 2.5 million voting-age Oklahomans? That would be inarguable success."

He nods, "That would be impressive."

"The plan is simple. I'm gonna give the money to them."

He squints at me and sort of shakes his head.

"You're gonna pay people to sign up? 2.5 million people. Fifty million dollars. That's twenty bucks each."

"Yes it is."

He shakes his head again, "It won't work."

"No?"

"Twenty dollars is nothing. You have to make them care. And they don't. Third parties don't matter, because third parties are a laughing matter. They are, frankly, pointless. Consequently, no one cares. And twenty dollars isn't enough to make them care."

"Does that mean you want to give me more?"

"I don't want to give you the first fifty, I'm certainly not gonna give you more. It's a ridiculous idea. Your average person isn't gonna leave his house and go stand in line for twenty measly dollars."

"Did I give the impression that I'm trying to attract the average person? Because that is not the case."

"Then what?"

I smile. I try not to make it condescending. I fail… miserably.

"Come on man, think about it. Who would be willing to leave their house and go stand in line for twenty dollars?"

He looks at me, a flicker of realization informing his features.

"Poor people," he says. "But that's only like fifteen percent of the population. You expect me to give everyone twenty dollars so that you can get one out of every six?"

"You know… People may not believe in this thing. They may, like you say, think it's a laughing matter. But there's always that flicker of doubt. And what happens when that flicker of doubt goes online, or visits social media, or flips on the local news? What happens when every day you see stories about how well the sign up is going? You see pictures and videos of lines going around the building? What happens when you realize that those lines consist almost exclusively of the under privileged class? Can you think of any collection of individuals who wouldn't want the under privileged in the driver's seat on policy decisions?"

He nods thoughtfully, "The rich."

"Sure. I think the rich might want to cancel out a few of those votes. Who else? Anti-welfare Republicans maybe? Yeah, I think so. There's our next big wave. And just like the poor people before them, those people will make the news. I wonder how the liberals will feel about that?"

"The Snowball Effect," he says.

"My whole system might be built around breaking this stalemate and bridging the divide, but in the meantime, let's put that divide to work. Young versus old. Black versus white. Rich versus poor. Urban versus rural. Democrat versus Republican. Before I'm done, I'm gonna have every single Okie scared to death to not be a part of this thing."

"And all you need is a catalyst."

I shrug.

"You can call it anything you like. I call it fifty million dollars."

After our dinner, the three of us make our way outside. We end up talking for an additional half hour, leaning against our vehicles and sharing a joint.

We debate an uncertain future where Artificial Intelligence might just help us move forward, or enslave us, or destroy us.

The billionaire says, "You ever notice that the biggest proponents of AI are almost always on the far left, blindly moving forward without fear?"

I take in his words and let them settle uneasily into the spaces of my mind.

"Why do you think that is?" I ask.

He says, "Every time the topic of socialism comes up, they always lose the debate. They, of course, hate that. They never admit defeat, but a simple look at history tells a story that can't be ignored. Time and again we've proven that humanity can't be trusted to lead a Socialist System. *Humanity*... can't be trusted to lead it."

He leaves the implication unsaid, allowing us to fill in the blank. On that lovely note, the billionaire takes his leave. I watch him go, fearful that he might be onto something.

My new friend shakes off the thought and lets a smile form.

"Dude. You just made fifty million dollars."

"My community just made fifty million dollars."

"Even better," he says. "Leave your truck and come with me. I got someone else you need to meet."

He neglects to inform me that our destination is more than an hour away. Despite the three hour podcast and the subsequent dinner, we never struggle in our continued exploration into each other's minds.

Eventually, we end up at a huge estate nestled in the woods along Lake LBJ. A lean silhouette strides toward us as we pull into the drive. As with the billionaire, I recognize the man instantly. He is a movie star of the first order. One of the last of his kind. His good looks and southern charm have been celebrated for more than 30 years at this point.

We step out of the car and he greets me warmly with a handshake-hug combo.

He leads us inside.

"Welcome to my humble abode," he says. "I'd give you the tour, but the wife and kids are catching some Zs."

"No problem."

"Plus, I'm afraid I might be judged for having a carbon footprint like a Sasquatch."

"Well, if it makes you feel any better, I suspect Sasquatch has a fairly low carbon footprint."

He nods thoughtfully and wags a finger at me, "I like that."

He pulls a twelve pack of local brews from the fridge and hands us both one. He leads us through his opulent home and out onto an expansive balcony overlooking the woods and the water. He gestures to some seats and takes one for himself, setting the remains of the twelve pack at his feet.

"I do struggle with the realities of my existence," he says, looking around at his kingdom. "All this. It's a bit more than one man and his family needs."

He stares off into the distance thinking thoughts unsaid. It's a familiar image. I've seen it many times on both the silver screen and my living room TV. Some people just have an undeniable magnetism.

I watch him, waiting for what he will do or say next. He never says or does anything, which is somehow just as interesting.

I decide to break the silence.

"You know, I dabble in Real Estate." I say. "And to be honest, I think you could use a bigger house."

"Really?" he says with a grin.

His piercing eyes shift toward me. He really is captivating. A beautiful man who is adored by women and yet approved of by men. A rare combination.

"Alright," he says. "I'll bite. How big a house do you think I need?"

"To my understanding it's about fifty-five thousand square feet. Located at 1600 Pennsylvania Avenue. I can arrange a tour if you'd like."

The man just stares at me, digesting my words. He slowly begins to nod.

"I told our friend here that I'd be interested in meeting you. What you're doing is important. I think you might have something. Something meaningful. Something real. I was wondering if your Party would support me in a run for Congress."

"You'd be wasted in Congress. You're a star. We need your voice to be the voice people hear. Not drowned out by a symphony of idiots."

"Yeah. I'm not sure I'm qualified for what you're suggesting."

"Was Donald Trump? Let's face it, being qualified isn't particularly valued at this point. In fact, a lot of people see it as a detriment. You don't fix a rotten system by promoting from within."

He nods, "I can see that."

"Here's what I'm thinking. This country needs a change… badly. We're traveling a bad road to an even worse place. I believe the Mediator Party can turn us around. But in order to succeed, we need to prove it can be done. Oklahoma is our opportunity to do that."

"I'm with ya. It's a fine plan. Last thing I wanna do is muddy the waters."

"I need people to see me. To see The Party. To know what we stand for. To understand what we are offering them. Your average person doesn't give a shit about local politics. The things that affect our nation… *that* they see… *that* they hear. A man like you running for President under the banner of the Mediator Party... *that* they'll see... *that* they'll hear."

"Hold up. Let me make sure I understand you. You want me to run for President as a publicity stunt?"

"Why the hell not? The movement needs you. Nobody cares about some crazy, kooky, local movement. Not even the locals. We need to be taken seriously. We need legitimacy. We need you, mixing it up on the presidential stage, telling everybody that we are no fucking joke."

"So you don't even intend for me to win?"

"I would love for you to win. But my intent is for your campaign to lift us up out of anonymity. I want you to speak to the people of this country, but most importantly, to the people of Oklahoma. I have plowed the fields. I have laid the seeds. And if you do this, I promise you, we will make it rain. We will take that state. People all across the nation will see that it's not just a dream. It's a reality. A reality that will change the very fabric of the system. So even if you come up short, your work will have ignited the revolution. Not only that, you will have the inside track in 2028. Proof of concept complete, there'll be no stopping you that year."

The man moves his attention over to our friend, who has been quietly listening to our conversation.

"What do you think?"

"Dude! I'm practically jumping out of my skin over here. I might want this more than you guys do! I got butterflies churning, ya know? Seriously, I'm gonna be so pissed if you say no."

The actor shakes his head.

"I play to win, William. That's the only way I play."

"I'm glad to hear it."

"We're nine months from election day. It's too rushed. We can't start from zero this late in the game. Nah. It doesn't feel right."

"I'll make you a deal."

"What's that?"

"You go on a show this month. Any major talk show or podcast that you deem worthy. You can promote your charitable foundation or something."

"Alright?"

"While you're on that show, you hint at a general interest in what the Mediator Party is doing. This prompts questions from the host. You lay out a few talking points. The inefficiencies of the Two-Party System. The growing division. The corruption. Bringing power back to the people. We got more than enough talking points. The host starts needling you. Asking you if you're gonna run for office. What office? Is it the presidency? And while you never say you're going to run, you never say you're not going to either. And then you say something like this, 'All I can tell you is that I love this country. But I don't want to play spoiler or just run out of vanity. That doesn't interest me. If I'm running, it's because the American People have told me they need me'."

"And then what?"

"That's it. Either the response proves that you should run or it doesn't. Simple."

"And what if it does?"

"My suggestion would be to follow the template set by Ross Perot. You go on another show. You say that the call for your candidacy has been strong. And you would like to state for the record... if your supporters can get you on the ballot in all 50 states, you will run to be their President."

"As an independent?"

"Yeah. We're a little late to get The Party on all the ballots, but a single candidate running as an independent... that we can do. Plus it gives you the opportunity to make that call to action. That's a powerful tool. Perot proved that. It really affected people when they saw his supporters knockin' on doors, makin' calls, shakin' every tree. It moved people. Made them think, 'Man, I need to look into this Ross Perot guy'."

The actor nods and stares at the floor. He looks over to our friend.

"When could you get me on your show?"

"Name it. Let's do it this week."

29

Astraea is spending the night with a friend. I am alone and the house is quiet. I tell myself to be productive, but my arguments are unconvincing. I deserve a break. A movie. I love movies.

Correction – I used to love movies.

I haven't watched a movie in months and yet I can't find a damn thing that looks good.

The quality of films has taken a major hit over the last decade. I remember when I was younger, every Tuesday I would drive to my local Blockbuster and peruse all the new releases that came out that day. It was rare that I wouldn't find something I was excited to see. I was a Gold Member, which allowed me a free older movie for every new release I rented.

They were some of the happiest times of my life. Me and my wife would turn down the lights and curl up on the couch, getting lost in the story and each other. This was back when I still loved her and when I still believed she loved me.

The memories are tainted now, ugly. But every once in a while, I get a little flash of a memory that felt so real that it's hard to believe it wasn't.

When the credits would roll, we would find ourselves half naked in the kitchen. We would cook up some Ramen, or microwave leftovers, or slice up the pears she liked to keep on hand. I specifically remember an episode involving Kraft Macaroni & Cheese. It's a memory that never failed to make me smile. Until it didn't.

We would talk endlessly about the film. How it made us feel, our favorite lines, the moments that took our breath away.

Eventually we would find ourselves back on the couch ready for the second half of our double feature.

Sometimes we would make it through... Sometimes we wouldn't, so caught up in each other, we decided that story-time could wait.

We would make love, exploring one another's bodies, often tenderly, other times ravenously, but always careful not to wake the child in the next room.

Such simple pleasures, but it was all I ever needed.

We seemed to fit so well together. I adored all her little flaws and quirks and weird vices. I believed the inverse was true as well.

She used to get such a kick out of my eating habits. Laughing incessantly at my voracious appetite, my tendency to eat with my hands, my disdain for chopsticks. She seemed to enjoy my little foibles. Until she didn't.

One day, sitting across from each other at a nice Japanese restaurant, I caught her glancing around mortified as I used a fork to eat my Sushi.

I don't know what happened exactly. I don't know why she became obsessed with home improvement shows. Why she felt a sudden need to upgrade my wardrobe. Why my personality became an embarrassment at parties.

One evening, we were scheduled to meet a few friends at a nearby bar. She disappeared into the bathroom and took longer than usual to get ready. I sat and waited on the couch, annoyed that we were going to be late. When she finally materialized, I hardly recognized her. She looked like a clown. Less than human.

Sadly, everyone told her how beautiful she looked. She seemed to like that.

I'm convinced that if the earth is ever invaded by a Star Trek style alien race, the first wave will consist of the more effeminate members of that society. They'll insinuate themselves into our everyday lives, walking among us, studying us. We'll be oblivious to their arrival, the tools for their deception being readily available on nearly every corner of every city.

I can't even be sure it hasn't already happened. Maybe that's why women outnumber men in this country. I suspect the second wave would seek to send the more masculine members of their alien race. But how would this second wave hide themselves from our eyes? If somehow they could further normalize this strange behavior of hiding in plain sight... that would make the job easier...

Hmm. Now that might make an interesting film... I'd pay to see that.

I sigh in frustration.

Goddamnit. I'm so fucking lonely. I hate feeling this way. Desperately nostalgic for the lies that nearly destroyed me.

On top of everything, I still can't find a movie that sounds remotely good.

It's 8pm and the lot at The Noon Siren is nearly empty. Only one vehicle remains. It's an old beat up little Honda Accord with peeling red paint. It's always here, every time I look. Last night, I drove by around two in the morning and there it sat, collecting dust.

She's killing herself for me. We haven't spoken since that night at the restaurant. Every night I peruse the online news feeds, seeking out the articles I know she fostered into existence. I miss breathing the same air as her. Hearing her voice. That warm feeling when she laughs.

I sit in my truck and stare at the building, knowing she's inside. I can't seem to convince myself to step out of my truck, so I just sit here.

The phone rings.

"Simon," I answer.

"I hear you had dinner with a billionaire."

"Oh Simon, don't be jealous. You'll always be my first."

"You need to be careful with that guy. I don't trust him."

"If it makes you feel any better, I'm just using him for his money."

"So you're a whore?"

"I'm a high priced whore."

"How much did you get?"

I tell him about the 50 million and my plans for spending it.

"Hmm." he says. "That might actually work."

"It will work. I'll make sure of it."

Simon says, "You know how you're always begging me to shift my capital into the Stasis Fund?"

"I do recall making suggestions. I never beg."

"Well, I've been thinking about that, but now I kinda wanna hear you beg."

"That seems a bit petty, Simon. Even for you."

"If I'm going to invest 500 million into your fund, I wanna hear you beg."

I sigh.

"Please Simon," I say with zero passion. "Will you please, please, please make a sound investment into a proven fund that has the added benefit of helping to finance a political cause that you ardently support? Please."

"You're an asshole."

"You took the words right out of my mouth."

"I'll call Paul in the morning and set up the transfer," he says.

Billionaires competing for my affection… there are worse things in life.

"Happy Valentine's Day," Simon says, before disconnecting.

Valentine's Day?

I look to the building where Scarlet remains. I can't go in there on Valentine's Day. That would send a weird message.

No. I can't do this to her.

I shift the truck into gear, preparing to run away.

What is wrong with me? All these risks I'm willing to take with my life, but not this one? Why am I so afraid of her?

Why am I such a coward?

I unlock the door and enter the building. It's mostly dark, save some security lights. I move past the reception desk and use a card to access the work area.

It's quiet. I walk toward Scarlet's office. Her door is open. The lights are off, but I see her face lit by the glow of her computer monitor.

Her eyes shift to find me. A terrified look comes over her. It is quickly replaced by recognition.

"What the hell?! You scared me half to death."

"I'm sorry. That wasn't my intention."

Her body relaxes and she lets out a tension releasing sigh. She looks at me and a different kind of tension takes hold.

"What are you doing here?" she says in a slightly hostile tone.

"I wanted to talk to you about something."

"Okay," she says, rising up and grabbing her jacket off a hook on the far wall.

I see now that she's wearing a dress. A nice dress. Strange attire for a late night at the office.

She says, "Can it be quick? I have a date."

A date? On Valentine's Day? I realize I told her she needed to date, but Valentine's Day? That sounds serious.

I say, "Yeah, absolutely, I'll be quick."

She looks at me as she slips on her jacket.

"Okay then. What is it?"

"I want you to look into manufacturing a grass roots movement for a run at the presidency."

"The Presidency?! Are you serious?"

I tell her about my meeting with the actor.

"Oh wow, that's... that's amazing! When is this happening?"

"The insinuation of possible interest will happen Sunday. We need a groundswell of constantly growing interest, nationwide. If we succeed at that, after a month or so, he will challenge his supporters to get him on the ballot in every state of the union."

"Oh wow! Geez!"

She looks around, confused as to how to move forward with this information.

"Oh man! I need to cancel my date."

"No, no. You should go on your date," I say unconvincingly.

I take a breath and try again.

"Go on your date," I say with more conviction. "Tomorrow, I need you to start developing a plan."

"Are you sure?" she asks.

I may be imagining things, but I get the impression that maybe she wants me to make her cancel that date. Maybe she wants nothing more than to sit here with me, burning the midnight oil, breathing the same air, making plans for the future.

"I'm sure," I say. "You go ahead. I'll lock up."

She stands there, perfectly still, for several moments. She nods her head and walks past me without another word.

I turn and watch her walk away from me, toward the exit. I move to the desk and lower myself into her seat. In the silence of the empty office, I hear her exit out the door. Though she's gone, I can still smell the lingering scent of lavender.

I close my eyes, lost in self-hate. Frustrated tears well up under the lids of my eyes. My cowardice knows no bounds.

I open my eyes. My gaze is drawn to a silhouette in the doorway. She watches me, silently. How long has she been standing there? She must've never really left.

"I don't wanna go," she says.

"Then don't," I tell her.

She steps into the office and I am on my feet. I am carried in her direction by some unseen force. Our bodies collide, fitting together like long lost broken pieces of a whole. Our lips meet and the world and all its damage disappears. The emptiness in my chest... The cold dark spaces in my soul... I feel none of it. There is only her.

30

FEBRUARY 18, 2024
261 DAYS UNTIL ELECTION

Poetry is not thought or written or even spoken. Poetry holds my face and gives me a kiss. Poetry grips my hips and pulls me deeper inside. Poetry walks naked to the bathroom and sends me a smile before she disappears.

I sit naked in bed, leaning back against the headboard. I take a drag off my cigarette, listening to the voice on the other end of my phone.

"No," I say. "I need you to make that decision... No... No. Mary, I want you to take a second and tell me why I put you in charge of this project... No, I put you in charge, because I trust you. So now I need *you* to trust you... There is no better person to select our candidates, all one hundred and twenty-nine of them!... Right... Right... I just talked to our security team. They feel confident about their assessments of each prospect... who?... I don't care if he's a good public speaker. We are not selling the candidate. We are selling The Party. By our own rules, they aren't even allowed to raise money. They aren't allowed to make those phone calls. They aren't allowed to hold those events. Our legislator's are going to spend their time legislating, strange as that sounds. That's their entire job. Campaigning is the Party's job, not theirs. We don't need silver tongues. We don't need winning smiles. We need the best people for the job... Are you going to trust yourself?... Should I expect *another* call in *another* hour?... I hope that's true... Okay, bye."

I hang up.

I project my voice toward the open bathroom door. "Why do I have to hold these people's hands?! Don't they know I'm busy? Very, very busy!"

A naked Scarlet appears in the open doorway. She has a phone to her ear and holds up an index finger, telling me to wait.

I happily do as she asks. I'm happy to wait. Happy to just sit here, watching her. She is beautiful. From her head to her ankles, she is perfect. Just not her feet. There is something very wrong with her feet.

I smile.

I love all of her. Especially her feet.

She says, "If your contact in Colorado is dead, I suggest you make a new contact... Yes, preferably someone with a pulse... Great... And-don't-forget-the-Wisconsin-thing!"

She looks at her phone.

"Shit! He hung up."

Scarlet looks at me and smiles.

"What were you saying?" she asks.

"I forget."

"Oh good. I was hoping you'd forget."

She comes to me and we do what we've been doing for days now. We silently explore the depths of each other's souls.

I forget a lot of things when I'm with her, things I'm happy to lose, if just for a while. That isn't the only thing she does for my memory. I'd long ago forgotten what the word 'home' could feel like, but with her... I remember.

We lie in bed, exhausted, wrapped up in bliss. I feel her heart pounding against my chest, syncing with my own. Sometimes I think this world is ugly, then I look at her and know that I am wrong.

She rolls away from me, onto her side. She shimmies back until pressed against my chest. I wrap an arm around her, pull her tight, and kiss her neck.

"I love this painting," she says.

On the wall beside the bed stands a large canvas.

"Yeah," I agree. "It's actually a print. The original is much, much smaller. I took a picture of it and had it blown up."

"It looks like a black sun, peeking out from storm clouds. And yet there's something... beautiful about it. Is that what you see?"

I nod, "Something like that."

My phone chimes.

I look to find a text from my podcaster friend in Austin.

Just dropped the episode. I think you'll like it.

Another text comes through. This one is from my actor friend.

Time to get to work.

We put our clothes on and leave the bedroom for the first time all day.

Astraea says, "Well, looketh what the cat druggeth in. Did you two run out of fuel for whatever you're doing in there?"

Scarlet blushes.

"Did you do your homework?" I ask, changing the subject. "What about your math test on Monday? Did you study?"

"Yessss, Daaad! I have officially studied like the Dickens!"

Scarlet says, "Like the Dickens, huh?"

"Yeah," Astraea replies. "I like to use the phrasing and lingo from his time. That way I can be sure he understands."

They both laugh. It's very funny.

"She's very thoughtful," Scarlet says.

"Yeah, she's great!" I agree.

The Dad joke has worked its way into frequent usage, the word 'Dad' drenched in sarcasm. It could be my imagination, but the level of sarcasm seems to be lessening over time.

I say, "Why don't you make yourself useful, and cook us up some popcorn? We have a show to watch."

"What show?" Astraea asks.

"A podcast," Scarlet corrects.

"You mean... THE podcast?" Astraea says, excitedly. "Three tubs of popcorn, coming right up!"

I call up the Spotify app on the TV and me and Scarlet settle in on the couch.

Astraea arrives with three bowls of popcorn. She has a dish towel draped over her forearm and serves us in a formal manner.

"Sir," she says, handing me my bowl with a silly bow. She moves her attention to Scarlet. "Madam."

Scarlet looks at me, "Are we supposed to tip?"

"Tips are customary," Astraea assures her.

Scarlet says something, but I don't quite catch it. Astraea laughs, and the two of them share a smile as Astraea plops down on the couch beside us.

A wave of emotion rises up in me. It originates from somewhere in my chest, swells up, and then spreads throughout my body. It radiates through my extremities, to my toes, my fingertips, and the scalp of my head. A strange mix of cold tingle and warm rush crawls across my skin.

I push play on the remote as my eyes begin to water. The show begins but I hear nothing of the conversation. I hear only my own thoughts, swirling inside of me and all around me. I feel them as if they are a tangible, physical force interacting with each part of me... My heart, my mind, my soul, my body... All of me. They engage each of my senses and hold me captive. A million thoughts collide together into one simple story.

This thing that I've been searching for, everything I ever desired, all I ever truly needed, it is with me now. It is here in this house... in this room... on this couch.

I am whole.

Scarlet leans into me and my mind slowly begins to settle. The words spoken on the TV begin to make sense.

Our actor friend is on a roll.

"Well that's the thing... we aren't a society. Not really. Not anymore. I mean what is a society? A society is a collection of people, living amongst each other, in an ordered community. You can't have order, unless there's some agreement on at least a baseline of what is considered appropriate behavior. So, what is our baseline? I'm taking a good hard look, but I can't find it. We don't agree on anything. Nothing! Not even the most fundamental things, like 'Love of country'. That's gone, blowin' in the wind somewhere. We haven't always agreed on who our President should be, but we always agreed that his job was to bring us together, not drive us apart. Where'd that go? Short of a handful of complete assholes, we eventually all came to the agreement that segregation was not the America we wanted. That's on its way out the door, my friend."

"Freedom of speech," the Podcaster adds.

"On the next train out of town. If we're a society, we're a broken society. A society at war with itself."

"A cold war."

"A cold civil war. So very cold, indeed. And how has it served us? Are we happier? You people, camped out on the far right side of the battle field… Are you happier? And over there on the left… Are you happier? Boy, I'll tell ya, the misery index is on the rise. Even me, sitting squarely in the center… I'm not a soldier in this war, but I still have to dodge the bullets. I still see the carnage. I still feel the cold, deep in my bones."

"So how do we turn it around?"

"Maybe we suit up. Maybe we join the fight," he says, raising a finger. "But, we don't fight like they do. We don't go out of our way to tear each other down and destroy everything that's been built."

"How do we do that, exactly?"

"Well, you had a guy on this show just this past week. What's his name… Waxman."

"William Waxman."

"Yeah. I liked that guy. That guy sees what I see, and he has a plan to fix it."

"The Mediator Party."

"Damn straight. The Mediator Party. Because that's what we need, a mediator. A whole army of mediators, working to repair all this damage that surrounds us, that's wormed its way into our souls. Can't you see how damaged we've all become? It's so slow, you don't even realize what's happening to you. You adapt and it becomes your reality, but it doesn't need to be. We can beat this thing."

"With a third party?" The podcaster says with skepticism.

"Why not? I'm serious, why not? Sure, it's unheard of, but so are the times we're living in, brother. It's gonna take all of us. Every moderate, every centrist, every single one of us that's had all we can stand of the noise... we gotta stand up, suit up, and fight. Every Mother who's sick, every Father who's tired, every son of a bitch who votes for the lesser of two evils. Cause let me tell you something, when you pick the lesser of two evils, evil wins the day my friend. If we can all just agree that enough is enough, a third party might just save us from ourselves."

"And what are you gonna do? When you suit up and go fight, what do you see your role as?"

"It's whatever it needs to be."

"Would you run for office?"

"Do you want me to run for office?"

"I'd love you to run for office. And not Governor... You know what I want? I want a President."

"Okay, that makes one. Anybody else? I think back to 1992, when Ross Perot challenged his supporters to get him on the ballot in every state. He said in very clear terms, 'if you want me, show me'. I like that. That seems like a pretty good indicator of support."

"Wait a minute! What are you saying? Are you issuing that challenge now?"

"Well, why the hell not? A change is desperately needed. If I'm not alone, America, let's talk. Let's do more than talk... Let's do."

Scarlet rises from the couch.

"Oh shit!" she says. "I thought he was gonna tease a little interest."

"That... was the plan," I say.

Scarlet turns to me. "We've got work to do!"

The response was immediate. There wasn't a talk show, news outlet, or podcast in America that didn't have an opinion. For once, the left wing media and the right wing media were in total agreement – This man is a problem.

The attacks came hard and heavy. He was a right wing plant, meant to split the vote. Or, he was a left wing plant, meant to split the vote. Some painted him as a threat to this country. Others claimed he was an absurd joke, barely worth mentioning.

And yet they never failed to mention him. Each day there was a new monologue, a new skit, a new column detailing all the ways in which his candidacy would be a disaster.

Endless memes and hashtags spread like wildfire through social media. Seemingly every day, our man would appear on a new magazine cover or talk show or podcast. He even began his own podcast, where every Tuesday he would talk to any activist or politician willing to debate with him in front of 20 million viewers and listeners.

Donations to the Mediator Party began to flood our bank accounts. Organizing a base of supporters in each state was easy work. Today, a mere two months after his call to action, every city in America with a population over 100k has at least one Mediator Party office. At last count, we have 512 satellite offices across the nation.

The people are speaking.

I watch on the TV as our man approaches the podium. There's something unmistakable in his eyes, in the way he's holding himself. He is a fighter, entering the ring.

He reaches the podium and looks around at the reporters in attendance.

"Ladies and Gentleman, thank you for joining me today. I think we all know why we're here. Just about this time yesterday, it became official that I am on the ballot in all fifty states. So what now?"

He brings his intense eyes to the camera lens. He locks in on his real audience, stares into us, and holds us captive.

"Well, I intend to be your president, that's what's now."

It feels as if he's speaking directly to me. And I believe every word.

He breaks our connection and speaks broadly to his audience.

"I told the people of this country to show me what they want, and they have spoken loud and clear. Not just with words, but actions. And we all know that actions speak loudest."

Once again, he returns his eyes to me, drawing me in.

"I'm here to tell you now… that I hear you. I hear you."

He looks out across the gathered crowd and points at someone.

"I hear you. And I hear you. And I hear you," he says, singling out members of his audience. "I hear all of you. But I've been hearing something else too. I've been hearing a lot of doubters. People telling us that we don't stand a chance. That nobody wants to cast a wasted vote."

He returns his eyes to the camera and pulls us all into his gravity.

"You know what I say to them? The only wasted vote is a vote for the Two-Party System."

I watch as an anger rises from within him.

"You want more of the same, you just go ahead. That is your right as a citizen of this country. But we have other rights too. We have the right to demand more from our leaders. We have the right to see a corrupt system and say that it should be no more.

"There's something truly bonkers about that system. They've done their best to build it so that at the end of the day we only ever have two choices. Just two. They've tried to convince us that those two choices are all we get. All we deserve. It's insanity. And yet, regretfully, they have succeeded. That is the world we live in."

He shakes his head in frustration.

"Let me tell you something, the first casualties of an insane world will be the sane among us. We don't stand a chance. So, in an effort to merely survive, we've all gone off and lost our marbles. We've accepted our fate. We've accepted our impotence."

His eyes return to that magical lens, and he speaks directly to me, nobody else.

"Well I don't know about you, but I want my marbles back."

Timed to the word 'marbles', he reaches down, grabs his crotch, and gives it a strong tug. He turns away and strides off stage with the confidence of a fighter who just landed a knockout punch. The reporters beg him to say more, but he never breaks stride. He said what he came to say.

A smile grows across my face.

Previous to the speech, I sent the man my notes. Many of the words he used were, in fact, my own. But the magnetic performance, that was all him. The crotch grab was a stroke of genius. Blocked by the podium, it managed to avoid seeming obscene, but the point was made.

It spoke so loudly and said so many words. We have, all of us, been neutered by the very system we created. We are nothing more than working animals, choosing which trough to feed from. We are the mass emasculated, powerless to determine our own path.

Perhaps it's time we grow a pair.

It's always a risky proposition to accuse someone of being emasculated. Offense will surely be taken. That offense will lead to anger. And that anger will block your words from ever reaching their target. But it wasn't so much an accusation as it was an admission. He himself had been castrated. And he was angry about it.

Something about that spoke to people, or at least a certain type of person. They were the people of strong will, of independent spirit. They were the people who naturally fought against the overbearing weight that the system brought to bear. They fought it for as long as they could, but the weight was constant and the clock never stopped ticking. They lost an inch at a time, day after day, year after year, until eventually they were on their knees, like everybody else.

It was these people who were awakened.

Just walking around town, I can feel it. Something is different. I can see it in the upright posture of a once broken man. The bright eyes of a formally worn-down woman. Something dead has come back to life.

Hope has risen with the spring. As summer soon approaches, my people have answered the call.

They are the leaders of their families, of their workplaces, of their communities. They will take the hope I give them, and they will pass it along to their followers.

I feel it myself. Perhaps that's why I've ditched the old truck and gotten a new car, an electric vehicle no less.

With each new face I see, the pessimism drains from my soul. Across the street, through the pristine windshield, I watch them, standing in a line wrapping around a building. They don't appear angry or annoyed or impatient. They know why they're here, and it is worth the wait. One by one, they go inside and sign up for the right to take a political survey.

I shift the car into drive and head home. It's Astraea's birthday and she wants to go to Top Golf.

31

It's fair to say that I am not the best golfer in the world. If I'm not hooking the ball to one side, it's a good bet that I'm slicing it to the other. Every correction I make turns out to be an over-correction. It would be frustrating if my two competitors weren't just as bad as I am.

To watch us compete would be a comedy of errors. And yet, for every group, there must be a winner. And so we compete for the dubious honor.

The important part is that we are together. That, and the fact that I won two out of our three games. Astraea won the other. Scarlet has brought up the rear in each of the three contests. She is a sore loser, which only adds to our fun. At least I think so. Scarlet may not agree.

By the time we leave, night has fallen. My electric vehicle whizzes down the road as I sing along to a song on the radio. It's a Meatloaf song, which is to say… very dramatic. I belt out every word while Scarlet and Astraea judge both my singing voice and my taste in music.

"Oh no. Are you speeding?" Astraea suddenly asks from the back seat.

I check my rear-view to see flashing lights pushing up on me. I check my speed – three miles over the limit.

I groan and pull the vehicle over.

"Be cool. No big deal," I say.

The squad car follows me to the curb. Two officers step out and approach from each side.

One approaches my window, while the other shines a light into the car, searching for anything of interest.

I roll down my window as the lead officer arrives. He shines a bright light into my eyes, robbing me of my vision.

"Do you know why I pulled you over?"

"Driving while blind?" I ask.

"What?"

"I can't see! Though I promise you, it's a very recent affliction. Could have something to do with that flashlight."

"License and insurance," he barks.

"Okay. I'm gonna have to reach for my wallet," I tell him.

"Do you have any firearms or weapons on your person or in the vehicle?"

"No sir."

"Go ahead. Slowly."

I've got a bad feeling about this guy. Most cops are decent people, but every once in a while…

I put my right hand on the steering wheel, then angle my body so that he can watch my left hand as I reach for my wallet in the ass pocket.

Wallet in hand, I pull my driver's license and insurance card. I make a point to keep my hands in clear view.

The cop looks at my insurance card and returns it to me. He studies my license.

"Mister Waxman. Where are you headed?"

It would be easy to just answer the question. To be honest, I would like to. I really would. I just can't.

"I don't believe that's any of your business, officer."

"Is that right?"

"No offense intended. I'm traveling legally down a public roadway. My destination is simply not your concern."

"You call swerving all over the road 'legal travel'?"

I shake my head.

Scarlet leans over from the passenger seat. The cop points his flashlight at her.

She says, "Is your squad car equipped with a camera? He was not swerving and I will use the Freedom of Information Act to prove it."

I look at her, "Let me handle this."

The cop squats down and gives her a creepy grin. I notice his name-tag, Sgt. J. Rifkin.

Rifkin says, "That's a good idea. Maybe you should let us do the talking."

I look at the body-cam pinned to his chest and wonder if it's active.

"Officer," I say. "What is this about?"

He sniffs the air.

"What is that? Have you been smoking weed?"

I sigh, "No sir."

"You realize 'medically legal' doesn't give you the right to operate a vehicle under the influence?"

The other cop knocks on the passenger window.

"Ma'am, roll your window down."

With a frustrated huff, Scarlet pushes the button and the window glides down.

"Yep, I smell it too," the other cop confirms.

Rifkin reaches in and uses the inside handle to open my door.

"Step out of the vehicle, sir. Keep your hands where I can see them."

I am asked to face my vehicle and lay palms flat on the car. After a thorough frisking, I am given a sobriety test, which I pass with flying colors.

I am escorted to the squad car, cuffed, and placed into the back seat.

"This is just for your protection while we sort this out," Rifkin assures me. "If we search your vehicle, what are we gonna find?"

"Nothing."

"If that's true, we can clear this up and you'll be on your way. Would you like that?"

"I'm not sure how to answer that question."

He just stares at me, annoyed.

I say, "You just asked me two different questions. Would I like to be on my way? Yes. Do you have permission to search my vehicle? No. No you do not."

"Well that puts us in a rough spot, doesn't it Mister Waxman? I can always call the K9 unit, if that's what you prefer. May take a while. And your lack of cooperation will be noted."

"You know what? Whatever. Fine. Search to your heart's content. I've got nothing to hide."

I watch as Scarlet and Astraea are cuffed and made to sit on the curb. Rifkin searches the cab, while his buddy checks the trunk.

More squad cars are arriving. Three, in fact. Scarlet and Astraea are taken to one of them and placed into the back seat.

Rifkin approaches. He opens the driver door and leans down to look at me through the metal cage.

"This is the part where I read you your rights," he says.

"On what charge?"

"Let's start with possession," he says. "You have the right to remain silent…"

After completing my Miranda Rights, I tell him that I do, in fact, want my lawyer.

"That is your right," he says. "We've got some things to wrap up here, then we'll drive you to your doom. Sound good?"

"Sounds wonderful."

Twenty or so minutes later, it has become apparent that the things they need to wrap up involves a lot of standing around, talking, laughing, and telling stories.

The stories being told don't quite reach my ears, but I do pick up the name of Rifkin's partner, Officer Bruner.

A few pats on the back later, Sgt. Rifkin and Officer Bruner return to their vehicle, intent on driving me to my doom.

Rifkin says, "Sorry to keep you waiting."

"It's no problem," I say. "I'm just sitting here making money. It takes a lot of that to run a political campaign and I've got over a hundred of them to think about. If I can make the city pay for it… All the better."

Bruner says, "Well this guy's got delusions of grandeur."

I say, "Can I tell you what's gonna happen here?"

"You're going to prison, that's what's gonna happen," Rifkin says, blaring his siren and pulling out into traffic.

"He's not wrong," Bruner adds. "After what we pulled from your car."

Bruner turns in his seat and looks at me.

"The lab will have to confirm, but I've seen Fentanyl before and that was enough to kill my entire family tree."

"If only we were that lucky," Rifkin chuckles.

I nod.

"So where'd you get it?" Rifkin asks. "Who's your supplier?"

My eyes find him in the rear view mirror.

"I think I might be looking at him."

"Oh really?" Rifkin says. "That defense has been tried and failed so many times… it's nothing but a joke at this point."

I say, "Here's what I think is gonna happen. I think the local press is going to catch wind of my arrest. I think it's gonna be all over the ten o'clock news. All over the papers. All over social media. And then I bet the story goes national. I think that I, and The Party that I represent, are going to be pummeled in the court of public opinion long before my arraignment on Monday."

"Sounds like a bad deal for you," Rifkin laughs.

"Party you represent?" Bruner says.

"That's a bell that can't be unrung," I say. "Which means, I'm going to suffer major damages. And not just me. The Party and anyone connected to it will suffer similar damages. And that's when I'll own you. I don't mean you specifically. I mean the badge. This car. The building we're headed to. I'll own it all."

"Wow!" Rifkin shakes his head. "I have heard some shit in my day."

"Who's the biggest dog in your building? Chief of Police? Someone like that? That's where you should be taking me. Straight to their office."

Bruner laughs, "It'll be empty. The chief don't work after dark. Not unless something big has happened."

"Something big has happened," I tell him.

After several hours in a cell, I am led down a hallway and to the office of the Chief of Police. The Chief sits behind his desk. Across from him is another man. His name is Trevor Fulton, the one man I was able to get elected to State Congress.

I'm ushered in through the door by my two uniformed escorts.

"I hardly think the handcuffs are necessary," the Congressman says. "He's not charged with a violent crime."

"Neither was Al Capone," the Chief responds.

"Al Capone?" I say. "I would never not pay my taxes, though I would have every reason to, considering how those dollars are being spent."

I look at the Congressman.

"I assume you're working on that."

"It's an uphill battle," he says. "I could use a few teammates."

"Reinforcements are scheduled for January," I assure him.

"Sure about that?" The Chief says with skepticism.

"It's all but assured."

"So... no," the Chief says.

I shrug.

The Chief gives my escorting officers a nod and they remove my cuffs. I rub my sore wrists as the officers step out and close the door behind them.

The Chief says, "Mister Waxman, I don't make a habit of entertaining criminals in my office."

"Oh, let's not start out by lying to each other," I say, while taking a seat next to the Congressman.

He continues, "I'm making an exception out of respect for the Congressman."

"I appreciate that, Chief. I too have respect for the Congressman. With that in mind, I think it'd be best if he waited outside with your fine officers."

Trevor seems surprised by this.

"In the interest of candor," I say.

The Congressman rises from his seat.

"Oh," I say, grabbing his arm as he passes. "I'll need your phone."

"I need to return a couple emails."

"Do it later."

He appears unsure.

"It's necessary," I tell him.

He nods and hands over his phone before heading out the door.

I do a quick search on the phone.

"Pardon me Chief, I'm just checking something."

"Of course. My time is hardly worth considering."

I smile, "I wouldn't have pegged you as a pouter."

"You know how many times my phone has rang over the past two hours. I finally had to turn my ringer off."

"What can I say? I know a few citizens, and they are concerned."

The Chief shakes his head, but says nothing.

"Shit." I say. "The news broke. This is what I was trying to avoid, Chief. One of your boys in blue has been blabbing to the press."

The Chief shrugs, "Sounds like the kind of problem that falls squarely in the category of 'Not Mine'."

I say, "You sure about that? This article mentions me, my Party, and the future president."

The Chief stifles a laugh.

I say, "You don't believe he's our future president?"

"He's got about as much chance as me bedding down Aaliyah."

"Aaliyah? The singer? Isn't she dead?"

The Chief tosses his hands, "Hence the slim odds."

373

"No offense Chief, but the day that plane crashed, I don't think your odds changed at all."

He holds up a finger, intent on correcting the record.

"I was really something in my younger days. You can't discount the possibility."

I nod, "The road not traveled."

He nods as well, wistfully.

I check the phone.

"This is taking forever. What's your wifi password?"

"All caps, no spaces, G, O, F, U, C, K..."

"YOURSELF?" I ask.

He points at me, "You got it."

I type it in and try it.

"It didn't work," I say.

"Perhaps you should try again," the Chief suggests.

I sigh.

"Good things come to those who wait, I suppose. At least that's what they tell me."

I watch the status bar slowly progress.

I ask, "Did you know that I recently acquired a new vehicle?"

"Did you know that I can hardly pretend to care?"

"You should absolutely care. Ask me why?"

He just stares at me.

"Okay, we've got a minute, so I'll tell ya. It's all-electric, but otherwise it seems like a completely normal car. To look at it, you'd never know that there are, quite literally, 22 pinhole cameras installed to capture every conceivable angle in and around the vehicle. In case you were wondering, this is an aftermarket feature, and it was not cheap."

"I was not wondering."

Despite the Chief's words, I've clearly gotten the man's attention.

"You're probably asking yourself, 'How does that work?'. Well, it's got a sizable battery that recharges itself every time I drive. And it's always recording, 24/7, to an onboard hard drive. Every time I drive, it's constantly recording new footage and deleting old footage. It's just recycling constantly, right up until the moment that I open an app and push a little button. Or, as was the case this evening, when I activated the hazard lights on my vehicle. At which point it uses its own hotspot or something like that to begin uploading everything it has recorded and everything it's still recording to my own little cloud in the sky. And it will continue to do this until I stop it or it runs out of battery."

I show the phone screen to the Chief.

"You see this? This is the view from my car, right now. If I'm not mistaken, that's the impound lot."

The chief sighs, "I'm this close to ordering you back to your cell, Mister Waxman."

"Like I said, there's a lot of angles here. It's my first time seeing this footage too. We're just gonna need to practice a little patience. Wait… I think this is it… Yes… Yes! Check this out."

I rise from my seat and walk around the Chief's desk. I kneel down beside him. He seems perturbed by my invasion of his personal space, but he doesn't stop me.

I hold the phone so we can both watch. I decide to narrate for the fun of it.

"That appears to be Sgt. Rifkin beginning his search of my vehicle. Hmm, that's strange. Why is he contorting his body like that? It's almost as if he's trying to manipulate what his body cam sees."

We watch as Sgt. Rifkin pretends to be searching the crease between the seat and backrest of the passenger-side backseat. With his other hand, he pulls something from his pocket. Careful not to move his chest, he swivels his head and looks toward the front passenger seat beside him. He stuffs the object deep under the seat and then returns to his previously begun search.

Rifkin continues searching various areas of the vehicle. Eventually he finds his way to the front passenger seat, where he finds the three baggies of what Officer Bruner suggested looked like Fentanyl.

I stop the video and look at the Chief.

He's just sitting there, stunned.

I wait.

Eventually, he says, "What can I do for you, Mister Waxman?"

I pick up the phone and return to my seat.

"Well, the opportunity to make this quietly go away has passed. I will be making this video public. What you can do for me is prosecute this man to the fullest extent of the law. What you can also do is invest significant resources into finding out who put him up to it, because I would really love to know."

The Chief nods.

"I think we can do that. Is there anything else?"

"There is one other little thing. You seem like a good guy, and I'm very sorry to tell you this, but my interest in police activity didn't just begin tonight."

The Chief's eyes slowly close and his jaw flexes.

I continue, "See I've been funding a… I guess you'd call it a Law Enforcement Watch Dog Association. Basically it's just a group of enthusiastic individuals who enjoy following your cops around at a distance and recording everything they do."

"You think you're pretty fucking cute, don't ya?"

I open another folder on the cloud. Several sub-folders are visible. The folder names are… General Misconduct, Excessive Force, Black Interactions, Hispanic Interactions, Female Interactions… And so on.

"Like I said, these guys love what they do, so they're very affordable, but after a year, the bill has gotten substantial. There's a total of 383 videos on here and if it's not damaging, it doesn't make its way onto my cloud. So feel free to click around. Whatever video you pick, I feel confident it will make you unhappy."

I hand the phone across his desk and he sadly opens a video. I watch as his face slowly explores the depths of misery. He sets the phone down as if folding his cards, defeated.

"What else can I do for you, Mister Waxman."

"I think the real question is, 'what can I do with all this footage'? At first I was thinking of the nightly news. Channel 4 would love this, right? They could rule the airwaves for months with this."

"Just tell me what you want."

"I like to imagine a world where if someone wants to get to me, the police won't help them do it. Where the police love their citizens, and I'm a citizen, so they love me. A world where the police serve me and protect me, because that's just what they do."

"You want us to *serve* you?"

"And *support* me. I think the Mediator Party would very much welcome your support."

I am accosted by reporters outside the Mediator Party's Oklahoma City offices.

"Yes, the reports that I was arrested last night are accurate. That said, I assure you, I am innocent of those charges."

"Why are you not in jail? Are you currently on bail?"

"Is it true you were trafficking narcotics?"

"Reports suggest a large quantity of Fentanyl. How did you secure your release?"

"Clearly, this is a sensitive matter and I can't go into details at this time. What I can tell you is that I fully proclaim my innocence in these matters. A press conference is being organized as we speak. Monday, I expect. Until then, I've said all I can."

I escape their ravenous clutches and seek shelter inside the office. My team locks the door behind me.

An online video shows more reporters having the same luck with the Police's Media Relations Department.

"I'm afraid we can't comment on an ongoing investigation." The Captain says, tight lipped.

When confronted, our presidential hopeful tells them, "I've been made aware of the situation. I feel confident that Mister Waxman will be vindicated. My understanding is that there will be a press conference on Monday. Perhaps we should hold our respective horses, and practice a little patience before we jump to any conclusions."

Throughout the weekend, I am skewered by the press. After having their hands slapped over their handling of the Melody and Morgan Affair, they were all chomping at the bit.

Sitting at the breakfast table, Astraea recites to me one of the many articles she finds online.

"Sources in the police department say that a large amount of Fentanyl was discovered in Mister Waxman's vehicle. It's been suggested that such an amount could and should lead to charges of Intent to Distribute. 'We are very obviously venturing into the area of large-scale dealing', a source said. 'One wonders if the proceeds of such dealing might be the means with which Mister Waxman finances multiple political campaigns'."

Astraea looks at me, mouth open.

"This is nuts! You really need to nip this crap!"

"I'll do it tomorrow," I tell her with a dismissive wave.

"By tomorrow you're going to be Pablo Escobar," Scarlet says.

"I could've nipped this in the bud right from the get, but that wouldn't protect us from future slayings."

Scarlet says, "Most people never see the retraction, Honey. Hell, these days most reporters don't even print the retraction."

"It's your job to make them see it," I say. "The bigger they go, the more trust we can gain from the voters when I, yet again, prove them wrong. Shit like this will make us impervious to their attacks. And we can transfer that earned immunity to our boy running for the oval. You better believe they're making plans to assassinate his character, right now. We're just weeks away from all the women he raped twenty years ago finally stepping forward and bravely telling their story."

Astraea says, "He raped women twenty years ago?!"

"Well not yet... but he will. It'll all be okay though, if nobody believes them. Our enemies are destroying their own credibility. The trick is to let them do it."

"Well," Scarlet says, "If you wanna make your girlfriend's job harder, I suppose that's the way to do it."

"My girlfriend's a trooper. She can handle it."

"Mmm hmm. Speaking of…"

Scarlet grabs her bag and gives me a kiss.

"I'll see you when the sky stops falling!"

"Love you!" Me and Astraea say in unison.

"Love you too!" Scarlet returns, walking out the door.

Astraea looks at me. She appears to have something on her mind.

"What?" I ask.

"Do you know what the date is?"

I look at her and chew my food. She waits impatiently for a response.

I swallow.

"Is it really necessary that I stop eating in order to answer rhetorical questions? Perhaps you could just, I don't know… keep talking."

She says, "All winter long we were creating scenarios and weighing effects and creating a path to victory, then suddenly that all just went away."

"Well, we've been a little busy."

"Engineering doesn't work if you never actually build anything."

"Yeah," I say with a sigh. "What if we don't need to build those things? This presidential bid has changed the game. We're on a good trajectory. What if we don't have to do all that?"

"Are you kidding?"

"No. I think we can do this. The right way. We've got a real chance."

"A chance?" she says. "Since when are you happy with a chance?"

She looks at me and tilts her head.

"You've lost your nerve," she says.

I exhale and slump into my seat.

I say softly, "This isn't about what I've lost. It's about what I've gained. People go their whole lives searching for what I've finally found. I knew there was something out there, something worthy of all this bullshit. I knew there was something. But you can never quite put your finger on it, until you finally do. And when you do, everything changes."

"What the hell are you talking about?"

"I'm talking about you. I'm talking about Scarlet. I'm talking about being whole. For the first time in my life."

I shake my head, searching for the words.

"I can't be that man anymore. I can't jeopardize what I've found. I have to be worthy of her."

"But you are that man," Astraea says.

"No. Not anymore."

"You're pretending. This isn't you, William. Aren't you the one who told me that to find your real family requires that you be your real self? And here you are, playing a part."

"I'm not playing a part. I'm choosing to be a better man. I'm making a decision."

"But you're making it out of fear. You're afraid she won't love you if she knew the real you."

"And I'm afraid she'll be right!" I say, with unexpected force.

"But can't you see that she already doesn't love you."

"You need to stop talking."

"How could she? She doesn't even know you."

"That's enough!" I bark. "I've made a decision. I can do that, Astraea. That's who I am. I'm the guy who made a decision."

"A selfish decision."

"Astraea, stop. You need to stop. It's not happening. That's the end of it."

Astraea shakes her head and stomps to her bedroom.

Astraea's words keep spinning around my head. The air in the house is heavy, thick with all the words we want to say, but can't. I make my way to her bedroom door.

380

She's lying in bed, staring up at the ceiling. I stand there in the doorway, waiting for her to acknowledge me. She doesn't.

I say, "We can fight the fight, but we can't take it there. Not there. That's too far. I see that now. I'm sorry I went there. And I'm sorry I took you with me. But I've realized that, just like a lot of us, I was lost. I'm really good at seeing when a person is lost. It's harder when that person is you. But I see it now. I was lost."

"And now you're found?" she says, still staring up at the ceiling.

"Yes," I say with a shrug. "Yes."

"Maybe you're lost right now."

"No. I know exactly where I am and exactly who I want to be. Who I need to be. I need to be worthy of your love."

A slight flinch intrudes on her stillness, but her refusal to look at me remains.

I say, "As of right now, that's who I am. Innocent lives are off the table."

She doesn't move. I turn to leave her to her thoughts.

"And what about that runaway train?" she asks.

Walking away, I throw my hands up in a helpless gesture, "We're just gonna have to do the best we can."

32

JUNE 1, 2024
157 DAYS UNTIL ELECTION

It's morning. I lie in bed, thinking. Astraea has hardly spoken to me in nearly two weeks. The air is so miserably thick that I can barely stand to breathe it.

I close my eyes once more and try to hide from the day. It doesn't work. It never does.

I rise with a groan. I feel old. Worn.

The hot water rushes down onto my stiff muscles. My legs feel weak, so I sit down on the floor of the old tub. I breathe in the steam and want to cry. But no tears come. There is no release. The sadness, the anger, the confusion… it all stays right where it belongs. It is mine to keep.

I hear whispered voices as I walk down the hall. The voices go quiet as I enter the room.

Scarlet and Astraea sit at the dining room table. They look at me.

"Good morning," I say.

"Sit down," Scarlet says. "I have something I want to read to you."

"Okay," I say, taking a seat.

Scarlet looks down at the open book on the table before her.

She reads, "A man recently asked me, 'Why do you smoke, when you know it could kill you?' My response was simple, 'Something's got to. It might as well be something I enjoy'."

I recognize the words.

"What is this?" I ask.

She ignores me and continues reading.

"In the time since, I have had the occasion to ponder the subject more thoroughly. These are my findings:

"We are a species obsessed with living. Not living in the sense that we desire to drink every ounce of nectar from every possible moment, that is not the living that I speak of. We are obsessed with the simple act of being alive. We wish our hearts to continue pumping. Our lungs to continue breathing. Our brains to continue producing electrical impulses. This is how we define life. The simple act of continuation. This is what we so desperately cling to.

"It is a battle that each of us will eventually lose. It is not a question. It is only a question of when. So... When should we lose? When we're 90? 95? 100?

"In many ways, we have succeeded in our obsession. With each passing decade, life expectancy rises. A hundred years ago, the average life was a mere 68 years. The middling retirement age was 65. A person would enjoy a few golden years and then move along, leaving the world to the next generation. Today, life expectancy is 81. The average retirement age is 64. And so the average person lives 17 years past the date on which they willfully decided to become unproductive members of society.

"For 17 years, they eat our food and burn our energy and buy our products. We send them clean water. We filter their waste. We pick up their trash. We sell them all the trees we killed in the form of furniture and flooring and cabinets and picture frames. Meanwhile, we foot the lion's share of the bill for the constant and continued monitoring of their health. We buy them pills to lower their blood pressure, to level out their cholesterol, to regulate their metabolism, to stimulate their urine production, to treat intestinal issues, and bacterial infections, and arrhythmias, and... and... and... They bleed us dry.

"Social Security and Medicare alone eat up 62% of our federal tax revenues. And we wonder why we can't balance the budget. This year, the gargantuan thing we call our federal deficit is almost exactly the same as our medicare expenditures. And with each passing year, it only gets worse. Through healthy living and a never ending string of medical breakthroughs, life expectancy continues to rise. What doesn't rise is our ability to keep fighting, to keep working, to keep being productive members of society. This is the world we live in. You'll have to pardon my French, but fuck that."

Scarlet looks up from the book and sets her hard eyes on me. She holds me in her cross-hairs for a moment before returning her attention to the pages of the book.

"I, for one, have no interest in being the reason this country goes bankrupt. I want not to be a financial weight upon the shoulders of society's productive members. I have no desire to exploit the labor of future generations. I do not wish to enjoy the fruits of a bounty I played no hand in harvesting. I will not eat their food, or drink their water, or enjoy their electrical output. Instead, I will work. I will be productive until the very day I can do so no more. And on that day, I will make plans to be no more. I will not languish in retirement. I will not make you my beast of burden. I will simply bid you farewell.

"In the meantime, I will eat the food I enjoy. I will drink as I may. And yes... I will smoke."

Again, Scarlet looks at me, offended.

I shrug, "What's the problem?"

"You plan on leaving me."

I exhale, frustrated, "There's no such thing as the perfect man, Scarlet."

"I know that."

"This isn't the first time you've read that book. This isn't exactly news. This..."

I point at the book.

"...This is who you chose."

"You're right. It is. This..."

She pushes a hard finger into the words on the page.

"...is the man I chose. A man of principle. A man who is willing to do whatever is necessary to create a better world."

I shake my head, "What the hell are we talking about?"

"Astraea told me that you're backing off of what you deemed to be necessary plans to accomplish our goals. *Necessary* plans."

"Scarlet, look, I'm not sure you understand what…"

"I understand completely, William."

Astraea says, "I told her everything."

My eyes shift from Astraea back to Scarlet. My worst fears are coming true. She can see me. All of me. I feel like a child, scared and needy and pathetic.

She says, "Do you know how old my great grandma is?"

I blink, her words making little sense.

"What?"

"She's ninety-four years old. You know how old my other great grandma is? Ninety-three. I'm gonna live a long time, William. And you're twenty-two years my senior. It's not a stretch at all to imagine I might have to live the last half of my life without you. I know that. I know who you are. I know you've got a date with death. And I accept it. But if you're gonna leave me, you can't leave me here, in this world."

Her words are coming to me in jumbled bits. I'm struggling to translate them into something meaningful.

Scarlet abandons her chair and comes to me. She cups her hand along the side of my face. The tears begin to stream down. I look into her loving eyes through a love-soaked haze.

"You've got to leave me in the world you promised me," she says, nodding with a reassuring smile.

I nod in return.

She says, "You cannot cancel necessary plans. You just can't."

She wraps her arms around my head and pulls me into the warmth of her chest.

"I know it's hard. I know," she says, kissing the top of my head. "But you've got work to do, baby. And I'm trusting you to do it. Not just for me, but for her, for everybody. It's time to be productive."

385

I weep into her chest, my tears drenching her skin. Another set of arms closes around us and the three of us meld into one blubbering mess.

There are no more secrets here.

We are one.

A team.

All members of a team must be used to that team's advantage. Their particular skills must be recognized, honed, and kept at the ready. Our darker selves are no exception. To ignore them, is to weaken ourselves. If we ever wish to be our best selves, we must reckon with our darkness.

Deep in the corridors of my mind, I imagine myself turning a key. I open the door and stand aside, letting The Wax Man out of his cage.

33

Another day, another flight, another podcast.

It's evening when the plane lands at Dulles International Airport. I skip the baggage carousel, bringing nothing but the backpack I carried onto the plane.

The podcast isn't til morning. The cab drops me off at a corner store several blocks from my evening plans.

I rarely wear hats and I never wear glasses. Today, I've made an exception on both counts. I need to be inconspicuous.

Under the cover of darkness, I walk the three blocks to a little house in a little neighborhood. I give the door a knock.

Philip Gates, a young man just shy of his 26th birthday, answers.

"Man," he says, with a growing smile. "It is good to see you."

I return his smile and step inside. We embrace the way old friends do.

Philip squeezes tight and I reciprocate. His hands begin to wander, as do my own.

With Philip, reciprocation is key. It was key to gaining his trust. It was necessary just to keep him alive.

It's a difficult thing, having sex with a man. With no attraction and a fair amount of repulsion, it requires that I escape into another realm. As I taught myself to do in the fall of 2021, I allow myself to drift off into a sort of trance.

For a time, I believed I would be incapable of this act. My nature wouldn't allow it. Then again, gay men have been taking wives since the dawn of time. However repulsive to them, they performed their husbandly duties. Fear is a powerful motivator, but no more powerful than my quest to right what is wrong.

Training my mind and body to perform these actions turned out to be quite interesting. Ultimately, I relied on the human tendency toward self-love. After all, I am a man... and yet I am not repulsed by my own body. If puberty taught me anything, handling a penis is well within my capabilities.

And so, with a fair amount of projection and a dash of transference, I took a lover.

I lounge on the couch in post-coital regret, while Philip bakes up some goodies in the kitchen. I study the framed pictures that adorn the fireplace mantel. Philip smiles for the camera, his arm around the shoulder of Chuck Schumer. He shakes hands with Nancy Pelosi. He shares a laugh with AOC. There are many more pictures with names less famous, but no less powerful.

Philip has spent the last two years cozying up to Washington's liberal elite. He buys their dinners and donates to their causes and hosts their fundraisers. Each day for two years he has won their hearts through the words he says, the actions he takes, and most of all, the money he spends.

They love him.

Philip pulls the frozen pizza rolls from the oven. He dumps them onto a plate and joins me in the living room.

I take another pull off his THC vape pen. I imagine the vapor entering my lungs, dispersing into my blood, and flowing to my brain.

The pizza rolls are amazing.

"Did you see the news this morning?" Philip asks.

"What news?"

"They caught the guy... that paid the cop... to set you up."

A couple days ago, news broke that Sgt. Rifkin had been paid to plant those drugs in my car. The police were on the hunt for the real culprit.

"Oh, that news," I say. "Well, they didn't quite catch him."

"No, I guess not," Philip says. "He put a bullet in his brain. That sucks man, I wanted that Republican dick-wad to suffer in a cell."

I shrug, "Doesn't make a difference." I raise my arms to the heavens, "I've been vindicated."

"Shit. You've been more than vindicated. It's worked out perfect for us, right? That dude was an Oklahoma right-wing darling. Had half of the State Congress in his contact list. That doesn't just vindicate, it validates. Plus it makes the whole damn GOP look like shit."

I nod and wave my hand through the air in a wide arc, "Perfect."

Philip gives me a side-eye.

"Wait… That guy was like the right wing version of me. Was he a friend?"

I smile, "He was a great friend."

"Oh shit! Are you kidding me? The guy that paid the cop to set you up was on our team all along? Now I'm totally jealous of that dude."

"Jealous? I promise you, I wouldn't touch that guy with a ten foot pole."

"Oh, I know that. I know your type and he was not your type," Philip says with a knowing smile. "I'm jealous of his contribution. He just martyred himself for the cause. And look at all he accomplished! Seriously, I am jealous, man! Plus, it's all over for him. That's what I'm most jealous of."

"Really?" I ask, in a sad tone.

"Yeah man. I think about it every day."

I nod, "You've been here two years. Created a life for yourself. I wouldn't blame you if you were having second thoughts."

"No," he says emphatically. "No second thoughts here. You see that little table over there?"

He points to a side table sitting in the corner. It holds a single drawer.

"In that drawer is a loaded .45, and not a day goes by I don't imagine using it. The only thing that stops me is you. Knowing that

389

I can make my death mean something, that's the only reason I'm still here. But it's getting hard, William. It's a struggle."

"I know. I'm sorry I've put you through it, but we're there now. If you're ready, it's time to start the process."

"Seriously?" he says, eyes wide with excitement.

"There's work to do, but yeah."

"Just tell me what's next," he says.

"Do you have the packages I sent you?"

"Yes!" he says, with sudden excitement. "Unopened, as requested."

He jumps up and finds three small cardboard boxes, hiding behind the couch. He sets them on the coffee table in front of me, along with a utility knife.

"I've been looking forward to seeing what's in these," he says.

"Question," I say, cutting the tape of the first package. "Politically, what is the demographic significance of the older population."

"Well, they're more likely to vote."

"True. What else?"

"They're more likely to be conservative."

"That's exactly right."

I remove the contents of the first box. The label declares it to be fiber pills.

"Fiber pills?" Philip says, his face scrunched in confusion.

"Who is the main user of this product?" I ask.

"That would be… the aforementioned old people."

"Right. And these aren't just any fiber pills. They are the generic store brand. A 'store that has over two thousand locations all across this country."

"Okay?"

"Question two. If we can root out conservativism by age, can we also do it by location?"

Philip chuckles, "Uhh, clearly. We could go to a red state."

I say, "An old person, in a red town, within a red state."

Philip nods, "Very likely conservative."

"How about by color?"

"Color?"

"Race," I clarify.

Philip thinks it through, "An old person… in a red town… in a red state… in a white neighborhood."

He watches as I remove the contents of the next box. 1. A collection of unused safety seals, nearly identical to those used on the fiber pills. 2. A zip-lock bag full of clear empty capsules. 3. A tiny scoop used to fill the capsules. 4. A tool to bind the capsule halves together.

"Holy shit," Philip says. "Is this for real?"

I look at him, "You tell me Philip. You having second thoughts?"

"No, I just… I didn't expect… this."

Out of the next package I remove a bottle that is labeled Diatomaceous Earth. It is not Diatomaceous Earth. It is a potent poison that has been processed to look a lot like Psyllium Husk, the ingredient in fiber pills.

"This, Philip, is what is necessary. A darling of the Democratic Party, that's you, goes on a killing spree, targeting likely conservatives."

"Jesus Christ," he says, looking to be in shock.

"Is that list you gave us still good?"

"What?"

"A year ago, you gave us a list of fifteen names. People you've built a strong relationship with. Congressmen, lobbyists, Party leaders…"

"Yeah, yeah. I'm still good with all those people."

"You talk, you email, you text?"

"Yeah, sure, they like me."

"Okay, well, my security team has managed to penetrate eight of the fifteen's digital worlds. We have complete access. Four of them have personal self-run brokerage accounts. We've gotten into those too."

"What does that mean?"

"It means, you're going to take a road trip. You're going to visit white neighborhoods, in red towns, in red states all across the country. You're going to leave exactly one tainted bottle, with exactly one tainted pill in every store you visit. Afterwards, you're going to go online, and sell short this company's stock."

"I'm gonna try to make money?"

"Yes, because you're an asshole. And so are your four friends. You're going to send each of them a cryptically worded email at a prescribed date and time. We will intercept that email and delete it, so that they will never actually see it. But any future forensic searches will confirm that they did, in fact, receive it. Shortly after receiving that email, each of those four people, two of them sitting Congressmen, will also sell that stock short."

"Because you have access to their brokerage accounts?"

"Correct. We've already bought and sold on their accounts, just to see if they would notice. They didn't seem to."

Philip nods, "So… a liberal psychopath, killing conservatives, and trying to profit from it. Some of his political friends appear to know about it and also try to profit from it. Is that right?"

"That's exactly right. We've got madness, corruption, a willingness to throw our system into chaos. These people are crazy. There's not much scarier than our product pipeline being so easily breached. We can't even trust the shit we buy at the store. What happens next time I have a headache? Can I trust those pills? It's going to be pandemonium. We gotta wake these people up, Philip. This is a necessary piece of that puzzle."

"Okay, but what I don't get is why I would try to profit from it. I'm obviously going to get caught, what good does money do me?"

"You're not obviously gonna get caught. We'll make sure you make some mistakes that lead to you getting caught, but you're trying to get away with it. Do you understand?"

He nods a bit.

"You're gonna wear a disguise. Good enough that people won't easily recognize you, but not so good that they wouldn't know it was you once they had reason to think it was you. You'll also use a car that isn't yours, too stupid to realize that a rental car will easily trace back to you. Just to be safe, you'll park it toward the back of the lot, where you think cameras won't see it. But then, of course, you'll drive pass the cameras on your way out. You're not too bright. Once people catch on to what's happening with these pills, it won't take long for them to find you."

Philip nods. His face is slack, lost in thought. I recognize the look. I may have lost him. This is more than he bargained for.

"Philip."

He looks at me.

"We always knew this war would have collateral damage."

"Is that what you call it? This is intentional damage, not collateral damage."

"It's the only means we have! It's the only way! Don't you think if I could talk my way to a solution, I would? No one's listening! We have to open their ears and open their minds! This is how we do that!"

"Are you listening? To yourself? Do you even hear what you're saying? Do you understand what you're asking me to do?"

"I'm asking you to put an end to all the damage that's being caused to every man, woman, and child every goddamn day, day in, day out, with no end in sight. We're surrounded by lies and corruption and hate. Why do you think you wanna die so bad, Philip? Because this world is too ugly for some people. Because this shit has rotted your soul from since you were little. You never stood a chance, and it's only getting worse. Are we gonna cause short term damage? Yes, but the end will be in sight. We'll create a better world where the next Philip does stand a chance. We can't give up now. We can't."

Tears are streaming from Philip's eyes.

He says, "I don't think I can do this."

I study him. He means it. This is new. He has never denied me before.

"Do you love me?" I ask.

"What?"

"Do you love me?"

"You know I love you."

"And yet you plan on leaving me," I say. "I get it. I know you've been fighting this for too long. Too many wounds that will never heal. I understand that and I accept it."

I remember Scarlet's words and my eyes well up with tears.

"What I can't accept is that you're gonna leave me here, in this world. Do you have any idea how much it meant to me that you were willing to make this sacrifice, so that I don't have to keep living in this world? This world that broke you? It meant everything, Philip. Everything. That's how I knew you loved me."

Philip looks at me, crestfallen.

"I do love you," he says.

He takes a step toward me. I step back.

"Fuck," I say, hurt and confused. "I can't believe this. I actually believed you. My heart is breaking right now. I can't even look at you."

Philip comes to me.

"No," I say.

He attempts to wrap me up in his arms.

I turn away from him.

"Stop, no, it's meaningless."

"Please, William, I'm sorry. I'm sorry. I made a mistake. I was scared. I got scared. I'll do it. Of course I'll do it. I'd do anything for you."

I slowly turn into him and return his embrace. Once again, I allow myself to slip into a trance.

34

I sit in a large newsroom. The woman across from me holds herself in a very serious manner. Her reddish hair is pulled tight into a severe bun and her eyes make no secret that she intends to destroy me. I've watched her show on several occasions and she is far from dumb. I'd do well to be careful here.

We exchange a few nice words, she throws me a couple softballs, and then she reveals herself...

"Seeing that you're not a fan of black people, I wonder if you've thought-"

"I'm sorry, I'm gonna have to interrupt you there."

"Excuse me, this is my interview, you are not running the show here. You need to listen the entirety of the question."

"Whatever the question is, I am not opposed to it. I am, however, opposed to the statement that preceded the question."

"Really, because I've listened to quite a few of your interviews, and that statement strikes me as completely accurate."

"Well, it's not inaccurate, but it's certainly not completely accurate.

"It's not inaccurate?" she asks. "Are you admitting to racial bigotry?"

"What I'm admitting to is that the word fan is short for fanatic. I am not a fanatic of black people. Nor am I a fanatic of white people, or Asians, or Arabs, or any other race or ethnicity or cultural demographic you could come up with. In that way, your words were absolutely correct. But your suggestion was that I am somehow against the whole of black people. Which is absolutely false. I am against an unfortunately sizable subset of the black population that sees fit to exist in a state of lawlessness. I am against an even more sizable subset that excuses that behavior by suggesting that calling it out is somehow tantamount to racism."

"Would you like to hear some of the names of people who have parroted your words in recent weeks?"

"Do I deny that there are racists who will use my arguments? No. Of course they will. It's a good argument. Using the argument doesn't make them racists. Hating black people is what makes them racist."

"And you don't hate black people?"

"I can't think of a single good reason to hate an entire race of people. It's the act of an idiot."

"And you're not an idiot?"

I laugh, "I like to think not."

"But apparently you're not sure. So we both have our doubts."

I stifle a laugh and shake my head.

She says, "May I ask my question now?"

"Please."

"Your system of governance, I believe you call it Democratic Mediation…"

"That's correct."

"Yes, well, throughout our history, and one would assume our future, there have been moments that required decisive action. So what do you say to the criticism that Democratic Mediation is by its very nature indecisive?"

"Hmm, I'm not sure I would agree with that characterization, but please give me an example to consider."

"In this country, we once held black people as slaves. Can we agree on that? Do you agree to the validity of that statement?"

"Sure. Please continue."

"In 1865, Abraham Lincoln made the decisive action to outlaw slavery. Do you agree this was a positive development?"

"Absolutely."

"And yet, your system of governance would not have accomplished this positive step forward. Your system would have said, 'well, there's a sizable contingent of people who wish for slavery to remain intact, so we have to consider their opinion when writing this law.' Your system may have taken baby steps. It may have made black people slightly more free, but it wouldn't have made them actually free. You might say it would have loosened their chains, but not removed them. Can you not see that there are issues where compromise is simply not the proper answer to the question?"

I nod my head slowly, ingesting her point.

"This is interesting. One of the better questions I've been asked."

"So what is your answer?"

"You know, I'm not altogether certain that Democratic Mediation would have been the proper system at that time."

"That sounds like a fine way to avoid the question."

"No, I don't wanna avoid it. I'm just considering the facts of the era. I mean, we're talking about a system that attempts to give an equal voice to all citizens. But the times themselves wouldn't have allowed for that. You realize, at that time, the majority of the population wasn't even allowed to vote. An actual majority. All the black people – No vote. Half the white people – No vote. It's a little mind-blowing to think about, really. Would Democratic Mediation have been the proper system at a time when equality was hardly even a consideration? That's a complicated question. Can we kind of talk it through? In all seriousness, I'd like to explore this."

"Sure," she shrugs, annoyed.

"My first thought, and I have many, is that you might be guilty of simplifying the matter."

"Am I?"

"Well, yes, because you're suggesting that our current system of governance performed wonderfully in this particular situation, when in fact it failed miserably. The divide was so pronounced that we literally went to war. Hundreds of thousands of people died. Entire family trees were wiped off the planet. So to suggest that the current system is without fault is, well, lacking in evidence to say the least."

"But ultimately that system allowed for a decisive righting of a wrong, while your system would seek endless compromise with that wrong."

"I get your point."

"Don't you think that's a problem? Don't you think that slavery is wrong no matter the degree to which it's enforced. 'You're only sort-of a slave' is not a good answer to a crime against humanity."

"I can agree that it's not a good answer, but it could be the beginning of a process that ultimately leads down the right road."

"The Emancipation Proclamation did, in a day, what your system would drag out for-"

"In a day? Come on. The tensions over slavery go back at least to the 1830's. So we Mediators can assume that we would have about three decades of those compromises taking place before the civil war even began. Three decades of arguing in your system, would have been three decades of progressive improvements in my system. Or as you say, loosening of the shackles."

"But how substantial would those improvements have been? And can they compare to the decisiveness of the Emancipation Proclamation?"

"Hard to say, but I can tell you that at the beginning of the civil war, the North had a population of about 21 million people. The South, 9 million. Seventy percent of the populace was in the north. So we can expect that the Northern sentiment would've played a large role in the Mediation of legislative matters."

"But… States Rights."

"With an issue like this, I suspect the people would've been tasked to determine whether the issue should be federalized fairly early on. Now what percent of the vote do we need to federalize an issue? A basic majority? 60 percent? Two-thirds? This is something that needs to be determined, but I suspect even the two-thirds would've happened and this issue would've become a federal one."

"There's a lot of suspecting going on here."

"Well what else am I suppose to do? That's all we can do. We take the facts as they are known and try to determine what may have unfolded. I can't know for certain what would've happened."

"No you can't. Obviously the north had numbers, but I've got news for ya, not all Northerners were abolitionists."

"And not all Southerners were pro-slavery. Your average Southerner never owned a slave. They never made money off of black people's backs. And if you asked them, 'should black people be owned as property and forced to work without pay?', I bet you a lot of them would've said 'ehh, that doesn't really sound right'."

"Well then why'd they go to war?"

"Not all of them did. And the ones that did weren't recruited through the message, 'Fight for the Confederates and you can own slaves!' They were recruited through 'Fight for the Confederates and stick it to those damn Yankees who are always looking down on us and telling us how they think we should live! Fight for Southern Pride!' That's what got 'em. The Confederate flag was never about slavery. It was Southern Pride. It was 'Screw You Yankees'. Truth is, there's not a whole lot of difference between that flag and a Make America Great Again banner. They don't love Trump because of his political views. They love him because he hates you. And even better, you hate him! They'll agree with him no matter what he says, because every time they do, it's a spit in your eye. Conservative Pride! 'Screw You Liberals'."

"Well... that's about all I need to hear to know that I'm on the right side of history."

"Don't get carried away. The tactics may be the same, but the issues are quite different. Let's not make you the equivalent of an Abolitionist just yet. One fought to end slavery. The other is fighting for a man's right to practice misogyny in a dress."

Her face tightens into a ball of anger. Her eyes are on fire.

I speak, rapid-fire, "The point is, I can look at the facts as they were and say with very little doubt that in an environment of Mediation, black lives would have improved long before the Civil War ever even took place. A large portion of the population wanted black people to be afforded more freedoms. And so, the Mediator

Party would have made it so. Year after year, little by little, survey after survey black people gain more freedoms and move closer to equality. Eventually they would get the right to vote themselves. And then the survey numbers would improve even more. Freedoms and equalities come ever faster. Lives are constantly improving."

"But they're still not free!"

"But at some point they would be! You can only move closer to freedom for so long, with the votes still calling for more freedom, before full freedom becomes the only solution."

"But wouldn't it be better to simply do what's right like Abe Lincoln did in 1865? Just one decisive decision to do what's right!"

"Okay, can we be a little more genuine about what happened in 1865."

"I know exactly what happened in 1865!"

"It was a big deal, yes, but let's not pretend that it decisively solved black problems. This is a pretty convenient time for you to forget all the things that happened after 1865. If we were having a different conversation, you'd be screaming words like Plessy versus Ferguson, Indentured Servitude, Jim Crow Laws! But for this particular conversation, you're gonna pretend like all that stuff and a million other things didn't happen. It was a literal hundred years before the Voting Rights Act was passed. And in that hundred years, a whole lot of congressional infighting played tug-o-war with black peoples' lives. The Emancipation Proclamation was a great thing, but it was only the beginning of a hundred year legislative war for Black Equality. It was anything but decisive. I suspect, and yes I'm suspecting again... I suspect that a Congress of Mediators would have slowly but surely provided that freedom and all those equal rights in less than a hundred years. I also suspect that process would have begun 30 years earlier. I also suspect that the slow incremental progress of legislators working together, rather than waging war, may have avoided six hundred thousand dead Americans."

35

I've made my way to Stillwater, Oklahoma, a college-town. Driving across campus, I am surrounded by the young. Stopped at a light, I watch them. I see leaders and followers and those that go it alone. Some are scared of their own shadows, others are kings and queens of their own little worlds. None of them are what they will become. The world will whittle away at them, forming something new.

They'll dance and sing and throw caution to the wind. They'll collect lessons and scars and emotions that threaten to end them. They'll fight for what is right and what is wrong and change their minds about which is which. They'll fly, at times, high above the storm. They'll wallow, at times, in the deepest wells that a soul can create.

In short, they will live a life. All the while, they will be shaped by the environment in which that life is lived. Will it be a place of sorrow? Shut in, dark, dank, and ugly? Or will it be a place where the sun can shine and the flowers can bloom?

I want to give them that place. I want to see them thrive, untouched by an ugliness that serves no real purpose.

I think about the storm that I've been brewing. Will it be strong enough to wash the slate clean? How much is too much? How much is not enough?

I pull into a neighborhood and park the car at a small house surrounded by an amazing array of beautiful flowers.

I knock on the door and am greeted by the smiling face of Lizde Hernandez. She gives me a warm hug and welcomes me inside.

"Julio is upstairs. He'll be down in a minute. Food's almost ready."

"Great!"

Two young girls bang their way into the room. The one with pigtails screams at me as if we were separated by a great distance.

"We got a new Dog!" She declares. "Do you want to meet him?"

"Sure," I say. "I'd love to."

"Come on!"

She grabs my arm and leads me into the den, where a cute little puppy is trying so very hard to climb the barricade that keeps him there.

We sit on the floor and play with the excitable young thing. I make monster faces at the younger girl. If I remember right, she turned five last month. She laughs at my scary face and then I growl at her. She screams and playfully hides behind her sister who valiantly protects her. She vanquishes me with the mighty swing of a cheap plastic sword. I dramatically fall to the ground and my eyes slowly close.

"Noooo! Don't die! Don't die," she demands, tugging at me. "I'm a doctor! I'm a doctor!"

The girls perform surgery and bring the monster back to life.

"You need to be house-trained," they inform me.

Through a complicated set of training exercises, I become domesticated. They ride me like a horse from one side of the room to the other. The puppy nips at my heels the whole way.

"Dinner's ready!" Their mom declares.

I stuff myself full of carne asada in homemade tortillas with an avocado, jalapeno, and lime salsa. It is amazing. I have to talk myself out of a third trip to the bar.

After dinner, Julio leads me out the back door.

We walk through the expansive garden full of onions and peppers and tomatoes. Julio stops and picks a caterpillar off a leaf. He tosses it to the paved walkway and grinds it into nothingness under his shoe.

We enter the large shop in his backyard. I look around and can't imagine how much he must've spent on the endless tools and machinery and measuring devices.

He offers me a beer from a little mini-fridge and I accept.

"I believe this is what you've come to see," Julio says, pinching a shop rag and lifting it to reveal what lies beneath.

On the work bench is a little plastic black box, about the size of a small TV remote. A small rod extends about two inches from one end leading to a tiny little set of encased fan blades. On the opposite end, two unused wires protrude from the otherwise nondescript black box.

"I was able to get it small enough to be used in a two inch pipe as well as a three inch."

"That's gonna be a big help. And it works?"

"It works great. I've tested it on seven different drainage systems. Flying colors every time. I actually added an additional input."

"Really? What?"

"Sound."

I crane my neck and throw him a look of disgust. "Are you kidding me? How did I not think of sound?"

"Don't be too hard on yourself. Some things require a doctorate."

"Right, like toilet flushes are loud and sound travels really well through an enclosed pipe. That's some PHD stuff right there."

"Exactly," he agrees.

"So how's it work? There's no buttons. No screen."

"Those things just take up space," he says, grabbing a nearby cell phone off the table. "This is how you operate it."

"With a phone?"

"Not a phone, this phone. It isn't even a phone anymore. I just repurposed the casing and screen."

Julio connects the two devices with a mini-USB cord. A little screen pops up displaying exactly four lines. The first line is the date. The second is the time.

"First, you're gonna wanna make sure the time and date are correct."

"Got it."

The third line says WAKE-UP DATE. The fourth, ARM DATE. Both lines have an entry field that is currently blank.

I ask, "What is the difference between wake-up and arm?"

"Well, every drainage system is a bit different. I was having trouble creating parameters large enough to encompass all possibilities without risking the eventuality of false triggers."

"Yeah, I thought that might be a problem."

"So, through many long hours and sleepless nights, I applied vast levels of brilliance."

"Understood."

"And appreciated?"

"Yes, Julio. Your dedication and brilliance is very much appreciated."

"Ahh, thanks boss. You didn't have to say that."

"So what is the difference between wake and arm?"

"The difference is they are five days apart. Whichever one you put in, the other will auto-fill."

"What if I set it to arm four days from now?"

"It won't accept the entry. It needs five days."

"Understood."

"Okay, so, basically, this device has enough battery power to rest for up to two months, doing nothing but keeping track of the time and date. At two months of rest, it will still have enough battery power to complete its job. Beyond that, there's a risk of failure."

"Understood."

"When it reaches its wake date it will do exactly that. It will wake-up and begin recording all of the different inputs and how they work together. It will do this for exactly five days. At which point it will analyze all of this data and determine which particular combination of factors constitute the proper trigger."

"It can do that?"

"As I said, brilliant."

"And that's when it arms?"

"Correct."

"How many of these can you make?"

"Uhhh, if I'm put to task, I suspect I could make one every… two days."

"Untraceable? Some of these things might get found intact."

"No problem. Completely untraceable."

I nod.

"Okay," I say, placing a hand on his shoulder. "I'm putting you to task."

36

Every other month, a poker night is held at the law offices of Burnett & Crowell in St. Louis, Missouri. From all around the nation, the eight of us travel to sit around a table and try to take each other's money. But mostly it's a chance to catch up on our pending and active cases.

"You haven't gotten a settlement offer?" I ask Scott, our lawyer based out of Louisiana.

"No," he says with a shrug. "I thought we didn't want to settle."

"We don't, but an offer would be nice. An offer tells me that you're scaring them. Why aren't you scaring them, Scott?"

"Because the case is a loser."

"If there's a loser here, it's not the case. I could win that damn case."

"Raise," Tracy says throwing in five blue chips.

A couple players fold.

The action is to me, but instead I hold my stare on Scott.

Scott shakes his head, frustrated, "They aren't even taking the case seriously."

I say, "Body dysmorphia and gender dysphoria are two representations of the same damn disorder. So why is body dysmorphia considered a negative diagnosis that requires therapy, while gender dysphoria is a positive step toward finding your true self? This is blatant discrimination against cis-gendered people who were born in the wrong body!"

Tim chokes on his drink, while Dexter tries not to laugh.

I continue, "If I'm a pretty person who was born in the body of an ugly person, why doesn't insurance cover my nose job? Every time I look in the mirror, I fucking hate myself, because that's not the me I know. I know who I am and this isn't it! And unlike some people, who have it easy, I can't hide. I can't tuck away this big honking snout. I can't stuff a sock down my pants and play pretend. I can't throw on a stuffed bra and convince the world this nose doesn't exist. There is no hiding from this thing on my face. This is my public facing representative and it's not me. This thing that I was born with, this thing that society hatefully forces me to showcase... You won't even let me drive without taking a picture of it and forcing me to carry it around everywhere I go. You make me pose it for you from two angles every time I get arrested. And then you tell me, 'That's you', but it's not. It's not me. That's not who I am! Every time I see those pictures all I want to do is fucking kill myself. And you're telling me that it's cosmetic! How 'bout a little freakin' empathy, huh? Would you rather I take a handful of pills, slit my wrists, and take a bath? Is that you want? You wanna put me in the ground? Don't tell me this is cosmetic. This is a medical emergency! And insurance should damn well pay. That's what insurance is for, right? For the health of the patient? And you can keep your conversion 'therapy' to yourself, you stupid bigot, I know who I am. I'm the guy with a cute fucking nose. All I want is a little fucking affirmation, is that too much to ask?"

I stop and look at Scott, who just stares back at me.

"Should I go on," I ask. "I can do the same thing with flat-chested women, thin lips, tiny inadequate butts... you name it."

"I think I'm good," Scott says.

Dexter says, "I kinda liked it. I wanna hear one about a fat person wanting liposuction."

"I can do that," I tell him. "Hell, we can make a parallel between hormone therapy and Ozempic... easy."

Scott says, "So you want me to make a mockery of the insurance industry's treatment of gender affirming care?"

"It's already a mockery. Every time I pay my health insurance bill, I'm buying some lucky guy's brand new pair of Double Ds. Me.

I'm doing that. I'm paying for some twelve year old girl's puberty blockers. A fourteen year old boy's hormone replacement. I'm doing that. I am guilty... of screwing these kid's lives, because I'm the one paying for their undoing. I don't need you to make a mockery of it, Scott. That's been done. I need you to make a parody of the mockery that already exists. Every argument that the gender warriors make about dysphoria, I want you to create a perfectly aligned argument about dysmorphia. You won't even have to try, really, because they're the same damn thing. I want a stack of affidavits, this thick, of licensed therapists and psychologists saying that dysmorphia and dysphoria go hand in hand. Dysmorphia and depression, hand in hand. Suicidal tendencies, hand in hand."

Josh says, "You know I'm sitting with a straight over here, you think maybe we could play this thing?"

"You don't have a straight," I declare. "My two pair is gonna annihilate that straight you don't have."

I match the bet and call.

Josh frowns and predictably folds.

The betting is done and Tracy shows her cards.

"I think you might've been looking over my shoulder, Josh. Maybe that's where you got confused."

Tracy lays down her straight and rakes in her winnings.

"Jesus Christ!" Scott moans. "The femi-nazi again. This is some bullshit."

"That's one lucky bitch, I'll tell ya." Dexter says.

"Hey!" Tim scolds. "That's not cool."

"I can't help it," Dexter says. "I'm a good person trapped in the mind of an asshole."

"We're all good people," Tim returns, dealing out the cards. "trapped in a room with an asshole."

Tracy just smiles as she stacks up the huge pile of chips that dwarfs each of her competitors'.

"We need to talk about Roland," she says.

"Mmm, how's he doing?" I ask.

"Not good," she says, sadly. "He's not holding up well."

"Just tell him to be cool. We'll figure it out. Just hold tight."

"I'm trying, but he's about had it. He wants you to come see him."

"In jail? That's not gonna happen. I can't be connected to him. I got too many eyes on me."

"I told him that. He doesn't care."

"Just tell him you're gonna win the trial, and in the meantime, be cool."

"They're throwing the book at him. Peeping Tom laws, indecent exposure, exposure to a minor… multiple counts. He's worried he's going to serve time and spend the rest of his life as a registered sex offender. He thinks that you knew this was gonna happen to him."

"We all knew there were risks, including him. He agreed to play his part."

"He's threatening to talk," she says, matter of fact.

"He what?" I say, on edge.

"He says he'll tell the whole story."

I lean back in my chair and struggle to find balance… It's taking a while.

"What do you want me to tell him," Tracy asks.

I work a kink out of my neck and think about that.

"I want you tell him that the story right now is that he is a transwoman. As such, according to the gym owner's own policies, he did nothing wrong. According to the preferred policies of the NBA, the YMCA, the President of our United States, and millions of other stupid people… he did nothing wrong. Sounds pretty good to me. That's a lot of support to take with you to court. The moment he tells that other story, all of that goes away. He is, and always was, a man. A man who willfully entered a women's locker room. A man, who in that process, looked at women in various stages of undress. A man who looked at young girls in various stages of undress. A man who proceeded to change his clothes, revealing his willy to said children. In this story, all of the crimes he has been charged with are 100% accurate. And all those supporters will quickly disappear. But that's not it, there's more. He is also a man who has already spoken in court. A man who declared himself to be a woman. A man who committed perjury. Again, we're not done. He is also a man who performed these same lewd acts in dozens of gyms all across the country. Performances that were inexplicably allowed to take place for one simple reason – he claimed he was a woman. Was! Not anymore. I'm pretty sure we're well within the statute of limitations on all those crimes too. So here's what you can tell him – he can be a man and make his voice heard, or he can be a woman and shut the fuck up!"

Tracy receives my words with disapproval.

"Can I leave out the misogyny?" she asks.

"You can, but it's much funnier if you leave it in. Am I right?" I look around the table, "Tell me I'm right."

"He's right," Josh assures Tracy.

"Totally," Dexter agrees. "A lot funnier."

"He does have a point," Scott says.

Tracy doesn't appear to agree.

Josh says, "See, this is why women can't do comedy."

Tracy yawns and stretches her arms out.

She says, "You guys... make me so sleepy."

She lays her tired head down on the huge stacks of chips in front of her.

"But my big giant pillow... It's so hard and lumpy."

I laugh.

Dexter shakes his head, "That wasn't funny,"

"Not even a little bit," Josh agrees.

Scott points at me, but looks at Tracy, "That was a pity laugh! He feels sorry for you."

"I feel sorry for us," I say. "Look at the size of that pillow!"

Tim breaks out the cigars and the game rolls on. Losers re-buy and winners gloat and laughter surrounds us.

"Here's what I don't get..." Dexter says, drunkenly. "How come so many of those dudes get top-surgery but not bottom-surgery?"

"Yeah," Josh says. "It's an overwhelming majority of 'em. What's that all about?"

"Bottom-surgery is much more complicated," Tim says.

"Yeah, but if being a woman is that damn important... if your life depends on it... that cock has got to be a problem, right?"

I say, "Maybe they don't actually mind the cock. How do we know these people aren't just dudes with major boob fetishes?"

"Hey, hey!" Josh says, "That'd make my morning shower a lot more fun! That's brilliant! I ain't mad at 'em!"

Tracy says, "*Check our website today to see if your kink is covered!* And we wonder why health Insurance is out of control."

I say, "Are you listening to this Scott? These people are giving you pearls!"

We play deep into the night, discussing plans and drinking spirits and immersing ourselves in a camaraderie that can only be forged in a time of war.

The stage is set.

We are ready.

Next week, I'll have another meeting, not much different than this one. I'll meet with my security team and we will finalize our battle plans.

The next day I'll meet with Scarlet and her team. There will be long days, weeks, and months ahead. The time of work-life balance has come to an end.

The Oklahoma City Police and the local chapter of The Fraternal Order of Police have wholeheartedly endorsed the Mediator Party. Each and every candidate. Each local campaign is already in full swing. Funds are being allotted and the word is spreading.

Just this week, the survey sign-up has broken through the million-user barrier. One million users... and rising.

Our run for the presidency is gaining steam. His opponents on the left and the right continually throw mud, but he expertly sidesteps and never returns fire. In fact, he never even mentions their names. He only ever speaks about the system they inhabit.

This puzzle that I've been studying for so long is finally beginning to come together.

37

A STUDY IN CHAOS
(Study period: July 18th - October 17th, 2024)

Our plans for inter-party mayhem have all gone off without a hitch. #Bathbomb has been trending for months[1]. As hypothesized, the *Fear Creation Index* (FCI) was exceptionally high, as was the *Anger Creation Index* (ACI)[2]. Considering the target base *(Vocal Conservatives)*, it was fully expected that the bulk of that fear and anger would be felt on the conservative side of the equation. What was unexpected was the need to formulate another index. The *Jubilation Creation Index* (JCI) was much higher than anyone would have theorized. Most visible online, a sizable portion of *Liberal Americans* found vast amounts of joy in the bombings[2]. Memes and jokes and hallelujahs spread like wildfire through cyberspace. It was reminiscent of the celebratory dancing among some Arab classes when the towers came down, or more recently when Hamas terrorists viciously killed many hundreds of Israeli citizens. I had feared that these bombings of American citizens might backfire, creating universal disgust and fostering unity between the members of the two parties. Those fears have proven to be unfounded.

At last count #BathBomb has resulted in 33 dead and 19 wounded[3].

When a new variable was introduced (*Laced Fiber Pills*), the poop related humor skyrocketed[2]. *ex. Talk about explosive diarrhea! / Now that's a 'movement' I can get behind / To flush or not to flush, that is the question.* The use of the internet term 'lol' in conjunction with the use of the poop emoji rose by 863%[4]. The ACI among the subgroup of *Conservative Americans* continued to grow substantially[2].

At last count, the actions of Philip Gates, alternatively known as *Fiber Fatale* or *The Constipation Killer*, have resulted in the deaths of 16 and the hospitalization of 14[3]. Philip Gates became the 17th related death, killed in a shootout with police on August 19th, 2024[3].

The revelation that several highly respected Democrats (1 lobbyist, 1 activist, 2 sitting Congresspeople) appeared to have prior knowledge of Philip's actions[5], caused another correlating uptick in the ACI among the *Conservative American* cohort[2].

In an unsponsored event, a spate of retaliatory vandalism soon followed and continues to this day. It appears to be an organized effort, as it spawned simultaneously in all fifty states of the union. The most common targets of said vandalism has been vehicles. Many of said vehicles displayed bumper stickers supporting liberal causes and organizations[6]. ex - *ACLU, NAACP, Pro-Choice, Reduce Reuse Recycle.* Electric Vehicles and Hybrids have also been targeted, no bumper stickers necessary. Recently, homes and businesses have been gaining the vandal's attentions. These efforts are still ongoing and have shown no signs of abating. The JCI among *Conservative Americans* has risen, though no subsequent drop in ACI has been observed[2]. Vandalism is up 1172% from this time last year[4]. *Note – recent activity suggests a growing counter-offensive, targeting conservative vehicles, homes, and businesses*[5].

The planned targeting of *Liberal Institutions* via use of a sniper rifle was deemed unnecessary by the creators of this experiment. This is such due to the fact that someone beat us to it. The campaign began on August 12th, 2024. On October 5th, 2024, that someone was identified as John Holcomb. He was arrested that day and is charged with the murder of 12 and the attempted murder of 28[3]. During his campaign, both FCI and ACI climbed among the *Liberal American* cohort[2]. Upon his arrest, he uttered the now famous words, "Can you blame me? We can't even take a shit anymore!"

On September 8th, 2024, a street-embedded IED exploded in Missouri, killing a Congresswoman. Twelve days later, a similar explosion occurred in Massachusetts[3]. Both Congresswomen were of the far-left variety[5]. JCI among the *Conservative American* class experienced a temporary uptick[2]. ACI among the *Liberal American* class rose significantly[2].

Incidences of random violence between citizens have become commonplace[3]. Reports of domestic violence have nearly doubled from this time last year[3]. Active arson cases have quadrupled[3].

Throughout the timeline of this study, the *Independent American* cohort has seen a steady rise in both ACI as well as FCI[2]. No observable JCI has been recorded[2].

In mid-September, "Mostly Peaceful" protests began to pop up in large cities throughout the country[6]. By late September, "Completely Destructive" riots had taken their place[5].

A new trend in Flash-Mob Robberies has organized online. Hundreds of participants hit dozens of stores simultaneously at a pre-prescribed time, limiting the ability for police to respond[5]. They methodically pick stores clean, while chanting "Reparations Now! Reparations Now!"

Many conservatives have taken up arms to defend themselves, their neighborhoods, and their businesses[3].

Gun sales are up by 273%. Most shops have activated a waiting list[3].

Insurance rates have risen exponentially[7].

ACI has been observed to be extremely high among all cohorts[2].

FCI has been observed to be extremely high among all cohorts[2].

JCI has been observed to be extremely low among all cohorts[2].

---

[1] As reported by Hashtagify
[2] As determined through constant monitoring of social media and IRL social interactions
[3] As reported by multiple sources
[4] As determined by ChatGPT
[5] As reported by Fox News
[6] As reported by MSNBC
[7] As observed on my bill

38

OCTOBER 18, 2024
18 DAYS UNTIL ELECTION

I walk through the neon darkness, passing the empty birdcage, the dancing girl, and Pervert Row.

Veering around the stage, I push past the bar toward the billiard tables.

I stop.

Glenda is not playing pool just now. She sits beside a table, her lap straddled by a young girl with long red hair whipping in high fanning circles.

The girl arches her back, falling away. The ever-changing colored lights reflect blindingly off her porcelain skin. Her long hair dangles just above the floor as her fingertips drag lightly across her navel, rib cage, erect nipples. Muscles contract and she rises up to smother her prey.

I pull a nearby chair, drag it close, and watch from the seat's edge. The redhead glances my way nervously. She also takes note of my two-man security team, standing awkwardly nearby. Her seductive, snake-like movements have lost their charm.

Glenda turns her head and acknowledges me with an irritated huff.

"Alright, thanks honey," Glenda says. "That'll be all. Very nice though. Very, very nice."

Glenda stuffs a twenty into the girls garter and gives her a little smack on the butt.

Glenda says, "You're very impatient."

"What do you mean? I was just marveling at the unfolding of events. It's strange, that stuff never happens at my place of business."

Glenda pretends to laugh for half a second, before pulling her briefcase from the floor. She opens it on the table and pulls out some papers.

"It's lunchtime. You guys hungry?" She looks at me and my security detail. "You guys look hungry."

Gathered around a table of political polling data, strip club burgers, and pitchers of beer… I seek balance.

I empty my glass and quickly refill it. I drink some more and light a cigarette.

My balance is precarious.

I look toward the bar and meet eyes with a disheveled man in a rumpled suit. He quickly looks away.

It could be one of those awkward moments when two people just happen to look in each other's directions at the same exact time, but I don't think so. I get the distinct feeling that he was watching me.

FBI maybe? They've been lurking around lately. Half the new members of the Stasis Institute are affiliated with one government organization or another. It's annoying.

The man doesn't look like FBI though. He looks… odd. Something about him is off. Familiar, even. Have I seen him before? In other places? How long has he been watching me? Maybe I'm just being paranoid.

I take another drink and return my attention to Glenda.

"How can these numbers possibly be accurate?" I ask.

"Are you questioning the validity of my work?"

"I'm questioning everything. You told me desperation could counteract your 'Wasted Vote' thesis."

"And I stand by that," Glenda says.

"Then why are these numbers shit? According to this, we'll be lucky if we win ten races."

"Desperation isn't the only factor here," Glenda argues.

"Have you watched the news lately?" Redfield asks. "All I see is desperation!"

"Yeah," I say with the force of an accusation.

Glenda sighs, "The situation has gone beyond desperation. It's looking like war out there. You know what happens when the big dogs go to war? People pick a side. Name me a European country that remained neutral through World War II."

"Switzerland!" Redfield says.

"Yeah," I say.

Glenda picks up one of her papers and points to a number.

"Switzerland," she agrees. "That's the fifteen percent that your guy vying for the oval is projected to get. That's Switzerland. Now name me another one."

"Fifteen percent," I say, shaking my head.

"Sweden!" Redfield says.

I nod along and throw Glenda a pair of challenging eyes.

"Sweden supported Finland, an Axis power. They allowed the German Army to march through their lands to Norway. They supplied Iron ore to the Nazis. Sweden wasn't neutral."

"Spain?" Redfield says, unsure.

"Spain organized the Blue Division, Spanish volunteers to fight for the Axis powers. Plus they supplied tungsten ore to, guess who, the Nazis. Is that neutral?"

Redfield just looks at her.

Glenda continues, "Ireland allowed the Allies access to their Naval yards. Portugal gave them a military base. Turkey claimed neutrality, but ultimately, declared war. Iceland, Estonia, Latvia, Lithuania... All declared neutral and all of them were occupied at some point or another. When you're surrounded by war, neutral is a hard position to hold. People want to side with somebody."

"So why can't they side with us?"

"With the Mediator Party?"

"Yeah."

"Because we're at war and you're not an army. You preach the individual, not the collective. People want to join a team. They want to know someone has their back."

"We do have their back," I say. "We're a 'team' of individuals."

"But you don't look like a team," she says. "You walk into a room. You look to your left. You see a group of people. They're all kind of bunched together and commiserating with each other."

"Okay?"

"That's a team. You look to your right. You see the same thing. A group of people lumping together. That too, is a team. Now you step back and you take in the whole of the room. You notice that there's a lot of people standing by themselves, dotted randomly around the space. You know who they are?"

"That's us," I say, understanding.

"No," Glenda says, shaking her head. "It's not us. There is no 'us'. It's Tommy and Suzy and Jasper and Jennifer and Bob. They are individuals. They do not stand together. They are not aligned. They are not an 'us'. They are not a team. Do you understand?"

"But they all believe that those other two teams suck, so when given the choice to prioritize the individual…"

"But they're not commiserating!" Glenda says. "Don't you get it! They're invisible to each other. All they know is that they are standing alone."

I move to another table where I can stew in my misery. A couple tables over, my security detail drink their beers and watch the girls in silence. Their mood looks to be a mix of anger, dejection, and the kind of horny that leads to rough sex.

I have failed them. Of all my followers, my security team has given the most. They deserve better.

I scribble angry words onto the back of Glenda's polling results. I have a speech this afternoon. In just a couple hours, in fact.

"Hey William!" A voice says. "William."

I look to find the familiar man approaching.

418

Like a light, my security detail is on him. They have him flanked from both sides. They block his path, while trigger fingers hover near their concealed weapons.

"It's me," the man says. "Gary!"

I squint my eyes at him and try to recall.

"Your muse!" he says.

And with that, it clicks.

"Oh shit. Gary! What the hell? Let him through."

"You sure, Boss? He seems a little… Something."

"Thanks," Gary says.

I say, "I'm sure he is a little something, but I think it'll be alright."

My security detail reluctantly lets Gary through.

Gary shakes my hand and accepts the seat across from me.

"You look different," I tell him.

"I've made some changes," he says, patting his flat belly.

The extra forty pounds he used to carry has disappeared. So has a fair amount of his hair. Either that or he's stopped trying to hide it. I'm betting a little bit of both.

"How's the mediation business?" I ask.

"Oh, I got out of that business. Like I said, I've made some changes. Our time together, however brief, it left a lasting impression. Made me think, you might say."

"In a good way or a bad way?"

"Good way. Great way!"

The man really does seem a little off, but who am I to judge?

He says, "I've been monitoring your progress, Mister Waxman. Very impressive. Got to be honest, I never woulda thought you'd make it this far."

He looks at the paper in front of me.

"What are you writing?"

"I have a speech later this afternoon."

"May I?" he says, reaching forward.

I shrug.

He eagerly snatches up the paper.

Gary reads my words. I watch for the minute changes in his expression as his eyes scroll down the page.

"Interesting," he says, placing the paper back to where he got it. "Not exactly the 'win one for the Gipper' I was expecting."

"Fuck the Gipper. The Gipper can kiss my ass."

"I guess things aren't going all that well?"

"That's a good guess, Gary. We're eighteen days from the election and apparently the votes I'm courting... they just don't know how to come together."

Gary points at my speech.

"And you think that will help?"

"You tell me."

"Maybe," he says, noncommittal. "It does have a certain call-to-arms-ness. Maybe with the right ending."

"You don't like my ending?"

"Ahh, it's fine. I was just thinking..."

His eyes track something behind me.

"Look at that."

I turn to find one of the pretty young waitresses carrying a tray of drinks. She's wearing a tight T-shirt that accentuates her curves. Across the chest are the words, *I Want My Marbles Back*.

"See all the difference you've made?" Gary says. "If not for you, that girl would be topless."

"It's a topless bar. I don't think anyone would mind."

"What I'm saying is..."

"Doesn't matter what you're saying. What I heard was 'if not for me, she wouldn't be wasting her vote'."

"Is that how you really feel? You think it's a waste?"

"I think I wanted to win."

"You've signed 1.6 million Oklahomans to your survey. You don't call that a win? You've started a conversation that needed to be had and people are actually listening. You don't call that a win? You've scared your enemy. They thought they were untouchable, but you've shown them otherwise. They can't just go off the rails, further and further to one side or the other. That creates a vacuum and somebody's gonna fill it. You've shown them that. Mark my words, those guys are gonna start veering back toward the middle to protect themselves against guys like you. If you wanna fight extremism, that's a win!"

"It's not a win, Gary. If what you say is true, all I've done is teach a bunch a corrupt human beings how to better stay in power. It's a failure. A colossal failure!"

Gary takes in my words and looks on the bright side.

"Something to build on though. Things keep going like they are, you're bound to win at some point."

I shake my head.

"Yeah," I say in a slow exhale. "I'm not sure I have the energy for all that. I'm tired Gary."

"The guy I knew was willing to die for what he believed in."

I snort.

"Dying for what you believe in is a hell of a lot easier than living for it."

Gary looks at me sadly. He nods.

"Well," he says. "I just wanted to say hello. This isn't goodbye though, maybe I'll come see your speech today."

I nod my head, but say nothing.

Gary stands and offers a hand to shake. I grasp his hand and give him another nod.

Gary turns to walk away.

I yell after him, "You never told me what you're doing now."

Gary turns, "I'm a lobbyist."

"Get outta here. For who?"

"The NRA!"

"Serious?"

Gary shrugs a smile. He turns away from me and walks toward the exit.

I bury my face into my hands and massage my eyes. So damn tired.

"Ready to go, Boss?" Redfield asks.

"No. I want another drink."

39

Redfield takes the wheel and we set off for our fundraising rally. The image of Daniel Wellman enters my alcohol-soaked mind. I first saw his face just a few weeks ago. I hadn't meant to see him, but there he was on my TV screen. A news program was doing a profile on one of the many victims of this war. Daniel managed to survive the initial blast, an over-the-toilet cabinet absorbing much of the shrapnel that would have eviscerated his chest and face. His abdomen wasn't so lucky.

Daniel survived in the hospital for over a week. He had seemingly beaten the odds and his prognosis was good, that is, until an infection took hold. His funeral was held at a small church just six blocks from the explosion that cut his life short. In attendance was his wife, his child, his mother, his father, his friends and co-workers and relatives and classmates from years past. By all accounts he was much loved, and he will be missed.

Daniel is just one of the many monsters that I've added to my collection. I see him regularly. He joins Melody, and Morgan, and Philip, and a young woman named Rebecca. There are dozens more whose names and faces I've managed to avoid. And while they are nameless and they are faceless, they are with me nonetheless. I can feel them. They are so very heavy and take up so much space.

I look to Redfield in the seat next to me. He silently navigates the vehicle to the site of our next battle for hearts and minds. Redfield is a different kind of monster. A monster of flesh and blood. I think of Julio and Sarah and Diego and Scarlet and Astraea and... me. Can't forget me. So many monsters. One look at my database and I could name a few dozen more.

What have I done? And for what?

In a time of need, I accepted my monster and allowed him to serve me. But maybe I only thought he served me. Maybe I served him. Perhaps a monster's greatest calling is to create more monsters. To be fruitful and multiply. If that's the case, The Wax Man has surely done his job. He started with me – his host – his greatest assistant. With my help, he created an army. Will each of my creations – each member of my army – now feel their own calling?

Be fruitful.

Multiply.

How many monsters will ultimately be born of my actions? Will it continue on through generations, The Wax Man's legacy living on through the ages? Where will it end? Will it ever end at all?

I've always wondered if I could ever truly make a difference in this world. In this moment, sadly, I am sure that I have.

But they were necessary monsters, weren't they? So very necessary. For even just a chance, it had to be worth it, right? Did I really even have a choice? The only other option was to do nothing and quietly accept failure.

For whatever it's worth, I tried. No one can say I didn't try. But it was all for naught. The levers that need pulling have not been pulled, nor will they be. That train is still barreling down the track.

I have failed.

The only one to come out ahead will be The Wax Man.

In the middle of northwest OKC sits a city within a city. They have their own council, their own police force, and their own building standards. Nichols Hills is an exclusive sort of place, serving as home to about 4,000 of Oklahoma's richest residents.

With Redfield behind the wheel, I enjoy the scenic drive past houses big and beautiful. We travel along the gently curving streets passing parks of sloping green grass and mature trees too numerous to count.

For now, the grass is green and the leaves are too. I try to imagine what it'll look like in a month, when the grass fades and the leaves begin to turn with the season.

We arrive at one of the 31 parks this little city has to offer. We step out of the vehicle and walk the path toward the event, already in progress.

My sulking need for another drink led to another and then another. As a consequence, we are late.

It's a pretty October day with the temperature hovering just short of seventy. The grill is fired up, serving burgers and dogs to a decent crowd of supporters.

Scarlet and Astraea are somewhere among the crowd, but I don't see them. I shake a few hands on the way to the temporary stage erected for just this occasion.

Our host sees me and runs over excitedly.

"Oh good! You're here!" she says, glancing at her expensive watch. "Did you run into some trouble?"

"A meeting went long. Couldn't be helped."

"Well that's just fine. We managed, as you can see!"

She laughs in the practiced way that some people do. She immediately dives head first into the story of her day, her life, her everything, and yet somehow manages to say nothing at all. The most annoying people I know are the ones described as having 'the gift of gab'. They talk ceaselessly. I'd much rather they just say something.

I endure the small talk for a few more minutes.

She says, "Well, I suppose we should get this show on the road. Let me just go whip these people into shape!"

The woman approaches the podium, tests the microphone, and gets everyone's attention. She tells a few God-awful jokes and then finally introduces me.

I step to the podium and look out at my audience. Standing among the crowd, I see Gary Trindall with a glass of champagne in his hand. He gives me a little smile and a champagne glass salute. I return a little smirk and search out Scarlet and Astraea. I find them, beaming at me with cheesy grins. My sour mood lifts a bit.

I look back to where Gary was, but I don't find him. Instead, I catch a glimpse of another familiar face. Familiar, but I can't quite place her. I squint my eyes and rack my brain… Della Hooper. Wow, if she hasn't met her goal weight, she must be close. Her eyes meet mine and I give her an approving nod. She puts a hand on her heart and mouths 'thank you'.

The sight of her success energizes me. I imagine her friends and coworkers and family members will all be impressed. They'll say, 'Wow! You look amazing! What is your secret?' And she will lead them to me.

This thing is not over. We may lose this battle, but the war is far from done. And my army grows stronger everyday.

Next to Della stands her daughter, Penny. I find myself drawn to the shirt she's wearing. It looks to be a plain white t-shirt with a hand-painted figure on it's surface. It is the figure of a capital M with two dots over the top of it. The two dots are referred to as an umlaut, but many people prefer to call them 'rock dots' considering the colorful usage of bands like Mötley Crüe and Blue Öyster Cult. The individual dots hover directly over the top of the M's legs. I quickly realize that the M with an umlaut is actually two stick figures shaking hands.

Would you look at that? Our little artist is already paying dividends. I do believe we've just found our new logo.

My gaze drifts across the gathering and I realize that these are not the people I wish to speak to. The people I wish to speak to are not at a rally or a donor party or any other such event. They are at home. They are at work. They are living their lives and doing their best to ignore the shit that surrounds them.

I find Nick, my videographer, set up in the back, his camera lens trained on me. This is where I intend to focus my energy.

"Thank you everyone for having me today. I'm very happy to be here."

I talk for what feels like forever, saying all the things that you have to say at events like this. I am thankful and gracious and completely full of shit.

It's time to get down to business. It's time to say what I came here to say.

"You'll have to pardon me, but I'd like to take a moment to speak to the people who are tearing this country apart."

I level my eyes upon the camera.

"You know who you are. You are the rich that bleed us. You are the poor who gnaw on our carcass. You are the privileged. You are the pitiful. You are the powerful. You are the weak. You are the parasites, one and all.

"With each passing day, you break something or someone and leave us to pick up the pieces. Every day, your behavior gets plastered across our news feeds and we have no choice but to just keep going.

"As your corruption leaches into every facet of our lives, we keep our heads down and simply do our jobs. We mow your beautiful lawns, we build your fancy cars, we balance your dirty books.

"As your peaceful protests infect our communities, we keep our heads down and we do our jobs. We pave the roads you march across. We craft the glass you shatter. We raise the buildings that you burn.

"We walk among the hate, surrounded by cameras and informers and friends we can't trust. We keep our heads down and we do our jobs. We work, as we always have, shelling out the taxes that you squander. We work, as we always have, feeding and housing and cutting checks to those who choose not to. With each hour we toil, we watch as you take your cut.

"We put on a uniform and protect you on the very streets you make unsafe. And then we listen as you declare us murderers. We put on a uniform, fly to a strange land, and protect you from outside forces. Then we listen as you call us killers.

"We say nothing as you poison the food we eat, the water we drink, the air we breathe. We say nothing as you push the drugs that keep us compliant. We say nothing as you declare us Straight White Males, or Karens, or Race Traitors, or Uncle Toms. Then we listen as you call us racist. We say nothing as each dollar we earn feeds back into your rotten system. A system that doesn't see us, doesn't know us, doesn't care for us.

"We stand idly by, while you file your next complaint, or hatch your next plan, or steal just a little more. We take it in stride. We do as we're told. We continue feeding your system, for that is what we do.

"Soon, we will 'Build Back Better'. Or perhaps we'll 'Make America Great Again'. We'll check one of your two prescribed boxes, we'll thank you for the choice, and we'll pretend that it makes us free.

"After all, we only want to be of service. For this service, we require nothing in return. To the people at the top, we ask nothing of you. We only wish to be a cog in your machine. To the people at the bottom, we ask nothing. We only wish that we could give you more.

"We are the silent majority! And we are at your service!"

I look out onto the crowd, silenced by my words. I send out an accusatory glare, meant for all those who deserve it.

The silence is suddenly broken by a thud followed by a loud bang in the distance. My torso is flung back by some force unseen. I fall to the stage, disoriented and confused. I look down at my shirt and witness a red stain blooming across the fabric.

I scramble to my feet and stumble across the stage. I teeter off the edge and fall into the grass. I land among the blades, staring up into a cloudless blue sky. I hear a symphony of screams accompanied by the percussive stampede of panicked feet.

Another shot rings out. More screams. A warm feeling is brewing in my chest. I try to sit up, but can't.

I lay here, thinking so many thoughts, but none of them stick. They all seem to just float away from me, unexamined and quickly forgotten.

In this moment, staring up at the bluest sky I've ever seen, I suddenly know exactly what has taken place. Somehow I just know. I knew there was something off in the way he was acting. This was the work of my muse.

I remember the story of the fawn he held in his sights. The way he matched his breathing to that of his prey. The connection he felt. It was the greatest and worst day of his life.

I wonder if he felt that connection with me? Did he hear his own heartbeat and imagine it was my own? Did he feel at one with me as he pulled the trigger?

He must have overcame his fear of dying. I imagine that's what the second shot was. He flipped the joke. It was suppose to be me committing murder-suicide.

My body begins to tremble. I can't stop it. I'm getting cold.

An angel appears, hovering over me. No... two angels.

I can barely hear what they're saying.

"Put pressure on it. Hard! Look at me! Look at me! Don't you dare leave me! Stay with me, honey!"

I try to speak.

I don't want to leave you.

I don't want to leave.

I don't want to.

My muscles aren't working anymore. My head limply slumps over to the side. My angels have left my vision.

Come back.

I try to get them back, to lift my head and look at them one last time. I fail.

All I see is the manicured grass stretching out before me. It is a beautiful shade of unwavering deep green.

40

One evening, when I was young, my parents decided I was old enough to be left on my own. I can't remember how old I was. Nor can I remember what event they were attending... A play, a movie, dinner with friends... something.

Shortly after they left, a thunderstorm began to brew. The wind began to whip and howl, and sudden bright flashes of light penetrated the curtains, painting oddly shaped shadows across the walls.

I decided to take a bath. I filled the tub with hot water, as hot as I could take it. I submerged a towel and placed it under my neck, adjusting the thickness so that all of me was below the surface of the water except my nose and my mouth.

Filtered through the water, I could still hear the raging storm, but the flog of the wind and the endless torrential spray felt distant, pleasing, soothing even. The lightning crashes no longer prompted me to jump out of my skin. They were nothing more than oddly timed percussive movements in an atonal orchestra. I listened to the music, feeling warm and safe.

Another bang of the drum prompted the red tinged darkness behind my eyelids to lose its color. Black, the blackest of black. I raised my head up out of the water and opened my eyes, but there was nothing to see. The storm had knocked out the power. I was in the dark, surrounded by a ferocious wind, a driving rain, and terrible bolts of unspeakable power. I lowered my head and listened to the orchestra play.

Eventually, the music faded, leaving a silence so pure it was unnerving. I raised my head, but the odd silence remained. It's strange, all the things we don't hear. We rarely notice the air moving through the vents, the buzz of the lights, the hum of electricity that surrounds us. We only notice when it's gone.

Silence. Complete and utter silence.

I lowered my head back into the water and listened to the quiet.

It feels like that now. As if there is nothing in this world. I see nothing. I feel nothing. I hear nothing. I am nothing but a collection of thoughts and memories.

Do I even have a body anymore? Have I been reduced to a soul living in a void? Is this the death I've been courting? Is this what we become? Senseless?

Wait.

I hear something. Talking? Or are those the thoughts of another? Is there another spirit with me in this void?

I strain to listen.

I hear distant voices. The squelch of rubber soles on a polished floor. I try to yell out, but my throat is raw. My throat! I can feel my throat. My senses are returning.

I open my eyes.

41

MARCH 18, 2025
FOUR MONTHS POST-ELECTION

Redfield stands over me, staring down at me.

"Jesus," he says. "You're awake. I can't believe it."

He helps me sip water from a straw.

"Where am I?" I manage to ask.

"Baptist Hospital," he says. "You've been here for five months."

Five months. I have no memory of any of it. What has my brain been doing? What have I been thinking? Where have all those thoughts gone?

I ask, "Where are the girls?"

"Scarlet is in Kansas City, organizing an event. I called her though. She's on the road back. Astraea is in school. I've got someone picking her up when school lets out. She should be here in a few hours."

I nod.

"Five months. What happened?"

"You got shot."

"That I remember. After that. The election. What happened in the election?"

Redfield holds up a finger.

"Hold on. I got something for you."

Redfield exits the room. He's quickly back, holding a laptop computer. He tries to hand it to me. I struggle to reach for it, my muscles atrophied from disuse. He helps me out and gently sets it in my lap.

"Can you operate it?" he asks, opening the laptop.

With effort, I move my hand to the mouse pad.

"I think so."

"Scarlet has been collecting news articles for you. She seemed sure this would be your preferred way to catch up. She said storytellers are unreliable. Said you'd want the whole story."

I nod. As usual, she's right.

"It's really good to have you back," he says. His eyes are watering a bit.

"It's good to be back. Thank you," I say. I fight with the weakened muscles in my arm and coax them to extend a hand toward him.

He shakes my hand and we hold tight for an extra moment. I give him a nod of appreciation and he returns in kind.

"I'll leave you to it," he says. "I'm posted right outside the door."

Redfield strides out of the room and I turn my attention to the screen in front of me. On the main screen is an icon labeled *EVERYTHING YOU MISSED*.

I click on it and a long list of web links populate the screen. They are organized by date, the first being October 19th.

On that date, the news of my assassination was splayed across the airwaves. Numerous articles and broadcasts spread the word of my death. A video of the last speech I would ever give quickly dispersed far and wide. The world watched as I called out the silence of the masses. They watched as I was shot down for my troubles.

A thousand miles away, on the campaign trail in Detroit, a presidential hopeful took the stage. He gave a speech so impassioned it brings tears to my eyes. It did that to a lot of people. According to YouTube, the speech has been viewed 450 million times, spreading like a virus at home and over seas.

I remember Gary sitting across from me at the strip club. He read my speech and told me that the ending needed work. This was the ending he had in mind. There's nothing like a tragic ending to galvanize the people.

Seventeen hours after the first report of my death, I was resurrected. But I wasn't me anymore. In less than a day, I had been transformed into something entirely different. A symbol.

As I lied comatose in a hospital bed, I became so much more than I ever could've imagined. I entered people's hearts and their prayers. Candlelight vigils outside the hospital became commonplace. So did protests outside the Capitol Building. I became a living martyr to the cause of revolutionary peace. Posters and coffee mugs and T-shirts began to flood the market.

I click on a link that takes me to an Amazon product page. Before me is a T-shirt emblazoned with a high contrast artistic rendering of my face. For a laugh, I consider pushing the Buy Now button, but my hatred of mindless consumerism convinces me otherwise.

In the days after my resurrection, the story of Gary Trindall began to unwind. He had spent the last two years serving as a lobbyist for the NRA. In the weeks before his attempt on my life, several large payments found their way into his Bitcoin Wallet. The payments could not be traced back to anyone in particular. I feel certain he sent them to himself, eager to feed the minds of conspiracy theorists. He succeeded. I have to hand it to my muse, he does good work.

Countless theories populated the minds of the masses. There was much talk of a consortium of politicians and lobbyists and the CIA conspiring to remove me from this world. According to just about everyone, Gary Trindall was just a small part of something much bigger. It was the system itself that fired that bullet.

But I survived and the cause thrived. Donations to the Mediator Party increased exponentially. Mediator Party candidates skyrocketed in popularity.

Four days before the election, polling showed our presidential candidate had risen to 31%. On the final stretch, the race was essentially a three-way tie.

I give my eyes a rest from the computer screen. They take in one of the many paintings that hang on the walls. It's Penny's flower, the stem still struggling under the weight of its bloom. Without being told, I know it was Scarlet who decided to decorate this otherwise sterile space. She wanted me to wake to the things I find beautiful.

I imagine Scarlet putting together this historical document for me, painstakingly selecting the stories and the links. I imagine all her sleepless nights, sitting beside my bed, holding my hand, and talking to me. But never did I respond. Never did I squeeze her hand in return. And yet she kept going, building the story in the mere hope that someday I would read it.

I click on the next article. It was three days before the election. At 3:58am, four pickup trucks converged onto the home of a US Congressman. He was a Republican.

The trucks hopped the curb and drove straight up onto the lawn. A total of eleven men filed out of the four truck beds. Their movements were well practiced and coordinated. Each of them carrying sheets of pre-cut plywood, some large, some small.

Hooked to each of their utility belts was something that looked to be a power tool. That power tool was later identified as a powder-actuated concrete nailer. It uses a gun powder load to quickly and easily drive a nail through concrete… or in this case, stone.

The men, covered head to toe in fabric, surrounded the home in a matter of seconds. Each man knew their job and moved with precision. Windows were quickly broken. Home-made incendiary devices were tossed inside. Within seconds, each window and door was immediately covered by a piece of plywood perfectly sized to the occasion. All around the house, the sound of .22 caliber pops could be heard in rapid fire succession as nails were driven deep into the stone facade of the home.

As quickly as they arrived, the men hopped back into their trucks. They drove away a mere 108 seconds after their arrival.

All of this was seen and heard by a neighbor's surveillance camera. The men could be heard hooting and hollering as they drove away.

"Burn in hell Trumper!" someone said.

"Antifa forever!" one of them yelled.

The first signs of the fire burning inside would come 38 seconds after the last truck pulled away. Within two minutes, black smoke billowed from the crevices around each boarded window.

By the time the fire trucks arrived, smoke was rising from the roof.

Inside… A Republican Congressman burned alive. He was known throughout Washington as a reasonable man. A moderate.

He wasn't alone. His wife would also burn in the fire. As would his four year old little girl, his six year old son, and his nine year old daughter.

The five of them were found fused together into a charred heap.

The news of the event struck to the heart of Americans. It somehow hit deeper than the bombs and the bullets ever could. The entire nation seemed to be in shock.

That Sunday, two days before the election, was a day of mourning. That day, our presidential candidate sat in front of his computer and told the world of his plans for Monday morning. He posted the video to YouTube and invited the country to join him.

Monday morning he woke up, put on a simple shirt and jeans, and walked out of his hotel. He walked for miles, never saying a word. The further he walked the larger the crowd around him grew.

Simultaneous 'Peace Walks' were held throughout the country. They were silent in nature. No words were said. No signs were held.

They were nothing more than a herd of humanity peacefully moving along the streets of every state Capital. In each state of the union, they converged on the Capitol and just stood there, staring at the building, thousands of people saying nothing so loudly.

They stood there until they were done, each person choosing for themselves how long they needed to stay. Slowly but surely, they dispersed, leaving the silence intact.

Over a million people participated in the Peace Walk of November 4th 2024.

Redfield opens the door and steps into the room.

"Hey Boss," he says. "Just checkin' on ya."

He takes a seat in the chair beside my bed.

"I'm good," I tell him, and I mean it.

"How far have you gotten?"

"I just read about the Peace Walks."

"Yeah," he says.

He rises from his seat and walks to the door. He closes it and returns to his seat.

"That fire was something else. Stroke of genius," he says. "I wasn't so sure about it, but clearly I was wrong."

"What are you talking about?"

He looks at me strangely, "What the hell do you think I'm talking about?"

"I don't know. You tell me," I say, but the look on his face tells me the truth of it. "That was us?"

"Of course it was. It was your idea."

"I never…"

"I know, you never got the chance to tell me your plan. Your girl told me."

"Scarlet?"

"No, the littler one."

"Astraea?"

"Yeah," he says, shaking his head. "That girl's something. She tracked me down. Told me you had a plan, but the guy with the rifle stopped you from ever telling it to me. But she told it to me. Told me every damn detail."

I nod. This is one plan I never dreamed up, but Redfield doesn't know that. I let him believe the lie he was told.

"She is something," I say.

"It was a hell of a plan," he tells me. "Can't believe it worked as well as it did."

"Me neither," I say.

"Only wish it would've worked just a little bit better," he says, holding his thumb and finger just millimeters apart.

"Why?" I ask, dying to skip to the end. "What happens next?"

Redfield shakes his head.

"I'm not even sure I know how to explain that shitshow. I don't wanna screw it up. You just keep reading."

He stands up.

"Astraea will be here in a bit. I'll send her in."

He moves toward the door.

"Hey," I say.

He turns back.

"Thanks," I tell him. "For everything."

He nods, "Back at ya."

Redfield walks out and closes the door behind him.

I return to my reading and bask in the glorious news.

We won election day!

Of the 129 campaigns we ran in Oklahoma, the Mediator Party won 58 of them outright. Another 23 were forced to go to a runoff. We won each and every one of them. In all, 81 members of the Mediator Party took office.

The shitshow that Redfield spoke of was the presidential race. By a wide margin, it would go into the books as the strongest voter turnout in the history of this country. When all the votes were tallied, our man won 44.6% of the popular vote. The Democrat pulled in 27.8%. The Republican came in third with 24.5%. The Libertarians managed 3 percent and threw a party.

To the people of this country, and the world in general, it was clear who won. But the Electoral College was another story. Faithless Electors became commonplace, but no matter how you counted it, nobody made it to 270.

Little known fact, when no one reaches 270 electoral votes, the decision falls to the House of Representatives. So after many days of squabbling, the Republican majority made their decision.

And so it was that the third place finisher became our next President.

The aftermath of that decision was written in the series of endless protests that soon followed. Cops died. Citizens died. Buildings burned. But nothing could stop the train that had already left the station. On a cold day in January of 2025, a new President was sworn into office.

He would later brag that it was the most heavily attended inauguration in history. And he was correct. Pay no mind to the fact that the vast majority of them were cursing at the top of their lungs.

The door opens and Astraea runs into the room. She throws herself onto me, our arms wrapping each other up in a long overdue embrace.

Pain courses through my feeble body, but I push it away and hold her with every ounce of me. She leaves her tears on my shoulder and I do the same for her.

It is minutes before we finally let go. She takes a seat and wipes her reddened eyes. She has finally managed to stop the flow.

"Hey Redfield!" I scratchily yell.

He pokes his head into the room.

"What's up?"

"Give us a little privacy."

He nods and shuts us in.

I look at Astraea sadly.

"I heard what you did."

She meekly looks down.

I ask, "Are you haunted?"

She looks up at me, her face contorting into something horrific. She bawls in a sudden outburst of uncontrollable agony. The dam has broken and she is drowning in the flood.

I open my arms and she returns to me. Scooting over is a struggle, but I manage. She pulls her body up onto the bed and she lays with me, sharing with me every bit of pain she's ever held. She is not alone in this endeavor. I can hardly breathe through the welling up of my battered soul.

Together, we wordlessly exorcise our demons. We hold tight to each other and expel the darkness from within.

We lie there exhausted for so long that it feels like the rest of the world has simply vanished. We are the last two people on earth and we know each other completely. We accept each other completely.

"You did good," I whisper.

I feel her head nod slowly, unsure.

"But I failed," she says.

"Don't say that. How can you say that?"

"After what I did… He didn't win."

"What you did changed the world. Can't you see that? Those Peace Walks don't happen without you."

"But he lost."

"We'll win the next time."

"But there won't be a next time. Didn't you hear? They asked him if he would run again. He said 'No'. He said it was too hard on his family. He was perfect."

"We'll find somebody else. Somebody just as perfect. Can't you see that we've laid the ground? Honestly, we didn't even want him to win. If he would've won, he would've had no support. He would have a Congress of Democrats and Republicans fighting him every step of the way. Nothing would get done and he would be looked at as an ineffective leader. A failed experiment. This way is better."

I speak softly to her, telling her of the future that is to be. Her breathing begins to soften and I feel her muscles relaxing.

"The people are angry. They've been betrayed. We are going to unleash our survey in every state of the union. And believe me, we'll have plenty of support. In two years, all those angry people are gonna give us exactly what we want. We'll take over the House and we'll take a third of the Senate while we're at it. Two years later, we'll take another third plus the Oval Office. And then, the real work can begin."

Astraea releases a happy little moan, accepting my vision of the future. She gives me a soft squeeze.

"I love you," she says.

"I love you."

We lay silent, quietly listening to each other breathe.

The door opens.

Scarlet rushes into the room. She throws her arms around both of us and the crying starts all over again.

Our little circle is complete.

We've all settled into our separate spaces, connected by something greater than touch. We talk and laugh and try to forget what it felt like when we thought we'd lost each other.

Eventually, the talk turns to 'what now?'. The nursing staff has sworn that nobody would talk to the press. The story of my recovery is ours to tell.

"I think we should hold a press conference out in front of the hospital," I tell them.

"Are you up for that?" Astraea asks.

"Throw me in a wheelchair. I'll get the job done."

"When?"

"Tonight. Primetime."

Scarlet looks at her phone.

"It's already 5:30."

"Better start making calls. It's gotta be now. Someone's gonna talk."

Astraea is saying something about the vigil site, which apparently still has activity every Sunday. I try to listen but my eyes get stuck on Scarlet. I almost can't bear it, the beauty I see. I should be out of tears by now and yet I've found a few more.

I say, "Why don't you guys find a place to start making calls. I need to get to writing."

"Good idea," Astraea says, rising from her seat.

Scarlet leans down to give me a soft peck on the lips. At least, that's what I expected. She lays into me with a passion that awakens every part of me. I am lost in her. I am so very alive.

"Gross," Astraea says.

Scarlet laughs and I do too.

She rises and turns away from me. Watching her go feels like a wound being torn open.

"Hey!" I say.

441

They both stop.

I look at Scarlet with a deep need. I hold my hand out to her and she returns to me.

"If I'm gonna write a speech, I need to clear my head. And I can't do that until you answer this question."

"Okay?"

I attempt to sit up, but my muscles aren't cooperating. They ache and burn.

Scarlet tries to assist, but I wave her off. I persevere and finally work my way into an upright position. It hurts, but it feels good to sit up straight, holding myself under my own power. I fold my legs in front of me and slowly manipulate my body to face Scarlet beside my bed.

I take her hand and look into her eyes.

I say, "I'd get on a knee if I could."

Out of the corner of my vision I see Astraea's eyes go wide.

"Oh my God, is this happening?" Astraea says.

Scarlet is speechless staring back at me in shock. Her eyes are beginning to water, her cheeks growing red.

"Scarlet..."

"Yes?" she says.

"How would you like to be the First Lady?"

Epilogue

A gorgeous smile bursts onto Scarlet's face. It is the most beautiful thing I've ever seen.

"Yes!" she says.

"Yes!" I say.

Scarlet throws herself into me, wrapping herself around me. The force of it nearly knocks me over. She whispers something into my ear, but the words seem far off... distant.

My attention has been stolen, drawn to the large canvas that resides on the wall behind my hospital bed. I hadn't known it was there, but from this new position, I can see it. It's been hovering over me all this time.

I remember Scarlet describing it as a black sun, peeking out from storm clouds...

But I know the truth of it.

Several shades of eye shadow meld seamlessly into one another with an artist's touch. The cloudy mix is broken by the curve of eye liner offset by bold flecks of mascara.

She is with me.

She is my broken place, and still she grows stronger.

Dear Reader,

You could call this novel a book of observations, a book of ideas, or even a book of warnings. It was meant to be all those things, but most importantly, it was meant to start a conversation.

We live in a country at war with itself. In an environment such as this, is it truly surprising that people, even rational beings, might find a way to justify acts of unspeakable horror? From tearing cities apart, to storming the Capitol, to chanting "From the river to the sea", are we really all that astonished? When a man loads up a gun and walks into a crowded building, he does so in a time of war. Whether he fights for a cause, or a group, or simply himself, his most deadly weapon is the hate he carries for the enemy. This is the world that we've fostered into existence.

We see the seeds of our destruction lecturing from their newsrooms, preaching from their podcasts, "teaching" from their classrooms, and sermonizing from their legislative pulpits. Angry and bitter and without an ounce of understanding, they help us to develop and produce and refine this thing we call hate. It trickles into our homes and our workplaces, infecting our friends and our loved-ones and even ourselves. The hate has become a part of us.

If we truly want peace, we must behave as such in our everyday lives. We must fight the hate. Not the hate of others, but our own. I am no friend of censorship, especially a censorship that is imposed by one side or the other. This peace cannot be compelled into being. It must be a choice, freely made. Choose peace. Everywhere we go and every place we look, we must choose it for ourselves.

Be assured, this is not a call to walk on eggshells or swallow opinions. It is simply a call to practice civility in the expression of those opinions. It is a call to seek peace as individuals. And eventually, together.

Now more than ever, it is imperative that we learn how to speak constructive words. And, just as importantly, how to listen. No more can we allow ourselves to shut off our brains when we hear certain words we don't like. We must find the strength to keep listening. It is up to each and every one of us to not only seek to be understood, but also seek to understand. These things don't happen through the expression of hate. They don't happen through yelling, interrupting, or belittling, or sarcasm, or sneers, or eye-rolls, or any other means of invalidating the arguments of your so-called enemy. They happen through open and honest discussion.

Though I have a severe distaste for social media, I have opened an account on X for just this purpose. @Mick_Carrion is my handle.

My Solemn Vow to You–

> In all conversations, from this point on, I will attempt to comprehend your views. And while I will not concede any points that I disagree with, I will require myself to consider them in full. I will listen just as much as I speak. I will seek common ground, endeavoring to hold discussions rather than debates. I will admit that outside of the confines of my head and my home, my opinion is no more important than your own. I will treat each conversation as if it could grow into a collaboration, enriching each of its participants and creating a less divided world.

If we could learn to simply talk to each other again… If we could somehow manage to accept our differences without labeling ourselves as good-intelligent-proper-people and our detractors as evil-stupid-defective-animals, maybe we could build something better. And maybe we could do it without turning ourselves into monsters.

There is much to discuss…

Made in the USA
Columbia, SC
04 June 2024